Acclaim for Gabrielle Goldsby's Fiction

"*Wall of Silence* is a cracking good read. I want to get that bit across right away." — *L-Word.com/literature*

"Of all the amazing tales…[in *Romance for Life*], the one that sums up this collection the best is Gabrielle Goldsby's Best of My Life. It's a letter from a woman to her partner who has breast cancer. It's moving and life-affirming, and only the hard-hearted will not shed a tear after reading it." —*Just About Write*

"The first person narration of the story is fresh and often sarcastically funny. 'She even slept like an innocent…like she hadn't a care in the world. I slept like a criminal, balled up into a fetal position with one hand under my pillow where my weapon was usually hidden' (p. 130). The novel is perfectly plotted and has a very real voice and consistently accurate tone, which is not always the case with lesbian mysteries." — *Midwest Book Review* (refers to first edition)

By the Author

Such a Pretty Face

WALL OF SILENCE

by
by
Gabrielle Goldsby

2007

WALL OF SILENCE

ISBN: 10-DIGIT 1-933110-90-2
13-DIGIT 978-1-933110-90-5

THIS TRADE PAPERBACK ORIGINAL IS PUBLISHED BY
BOLD STROKES BOOKS, INC.,
NEW YORK, USA

FIRST EDITION: 2003, REGAL CREST ENTERPRISES
SECOND EDITION: SEPTEMBER 2007, BOLD STROKES BOOKS, INC.

CREDITS
EDITORS: JENNIFER KNIGHT AND STACIA SEAMAN
PRODUCTION DESIGN: STACIA SEAMAN
COVER DESIGN BY SHERI (GRAPHICARTIST2020@HOTMAIL.COM)

Acknowledgments

This book would not have been conceived without the assistance of Mecheal, Diva, Raven, Day, and Barb. Thank you all for donating your valuable time during the earlier versions of this story.

I am eternally grateful to my editors, Jennifer Knight and Stacia Seaman. You two are the best, but you probably knew that already.

I am indebted to my brilliant cover artist Sheri, who listens to my disjointed ideas and still manages to produce something infinitely better.

Last but not least, I would like to express my gratitude to my publisher, Len Barot. Thank you for including me in your vision.

Dedication

For ME Walls, who loves these two main characters almost as much as I do.

CHAPTER ONE

E ver wonder if, before you die, there's an early warning sign? Sort of a "smoke all you want, drink tons of alcohol, fuck up a storm, because it doesn't matter anymore" free pass to hell?

Well, let me be the first to say, death is never that polite.

I'm not dead. At least, not anymore. But that's a long story and I'll never know exactly when I started to lose the life I'd been building. However, the day things changed forever began just like the rest. It was actually kind of pretty as days go in the City of Angels. My commemorative 1969 New York Mets alarm clock went off at six a.m. as usual. And as was my habit, I sent it sailing across the room. Sold as "childproof," it continued to tick after crashing against the wall and hitting the hardwood floor with a hollow clatter.

I rolled off my bed and stumbled to my sparsely decorated kitchen. A friend of mine, Stacy, says Starbucks is the devil's spawn. I, however, would gladly nosedive into the devil's ass for a decent mocha.

"Yeah, yeah, yeah," I grumbled as the phone started ringing its annoying little halfhearted bleat before I could brew my morning fix. I picked up as I spooned beans into the coffee grinder. "Everett."

I quit smoking cigarettes years ago, but I still have a morning cough and a huskiness that dissipates as slowly as the L.A. smog.

My caller said, "You better get your ass in gear. You're late again."

I pressed down on the grinder for a few seconds before answering. "I'll be there in a few."

My partner, Detective Joseph Smith, had married the boss's daughter, so he showed up on time for shifts. I had no such incentive.

Not waiting for him to launch into his familiar tirade, I dropped the phone back into its cradle. A slight movement caught my eye and I reached for my gun, which, since I sometimes sleep unarmed, was hanging in its holster on a chair across the room, one of only three pieces of furniture in my supposedly furnished studio apartment.

I slid to the floor and crawled on my hands and knees over to the corner where I had seen the flash of movement. Cursing up a storm and cackling with glee, I dove. "Gotcha, you little bastard!" I hated to lose, and this rodent had managed to elude me for the past two weeks.

The tiny white mouse simply stared at me with beady red eyes, as if *I* were the one that had been up at all hours of the night munching on *his* last box of Cracker Jacks.

"Don't look at me like that. I have every right to send you to mouse heaven."

I didn't have time to make good on this threat, so I located a shoebox I'd neglected to toss when I bought my last pair of Docs, and stuck my captive inside. This uninvited guest was not going to be munching on my shit at three in the morning anymore. As soon as I got the chance, I would find a field somewhere and let him go.

I quickly slipped on my baggy black cargo pants and a ribbed T-shirt, halfheartedly brushed my teeth, and put my long red hair into its customary ponytail. The mirror was always a mistake but I stared into the tired, hazel eyes of my reflection. I looked like a wreck. I hadn't been sleeping well; the dark circles were more pronounced than usual. I was one of the millions of people who suffer from nightmares, or so the police psychologists told me. I wouldn't know. I could never remember what they were about when I woke up the next morning. Whatever they were, I hadn't had a good night's sleep since joining the force.

Feeling much older than my twenty-nine years, I leaned closer to the Foster Everett staring back at me and whispered ominously, "That's because you see dead people."

❖

"If I wasn't in love with you, I would have to kick your ass," Smitty said as I walked into the office that we shared with six other detectives. My partner was one of those guys that other guys loved and girls ended up marrying: tall, dark, and vaguely handsome in that "nothing *ugly* about him" sort of way.

"Well, if I wasn't in love with your wife, I might have to kick *your* ass." I handed over the shoebox. "Don't look in there."

As curious as Smitty was, it would only be a few minutes before he had a look in the box. He hated mice, so it would serve him right for being nosy.

I made myself look busy, not difficult in a place where everybody is either coming or going, but nobody seems to really be getting anywhere in particular. That's about how the division is—a whole lot of chaos, all the time. The hustle and bustle soothed me. Hell, occasionally I was able to put my feet up on my desk and actually catch a few hours of shut-eye. I've been a part of that kind of life for as long as I can remember. My dad was a cop. My grandfather was a fireman, but his father was a cop, too. There's a long line of dumb-ass civil servants in my family.

"What the fuck?" Smitty stared at the box, his head angled.

I heard scratching sounds. "Don't look," I reminded him and fished a scrap of paper from my pocket. "I almost forgot, give this to Monica."

"You should try to come to the funerals sometime. They're really beautiful." Smitty folded the check and put it in his shirt pocket.

We both knew I wouldn't come. How could a child's funeral *ever* be beautiful?

Every year in Los Angeles County, hundreds of bodies were discarded like so much refuse. About two hundred were never identified. Most would be buried in mass graves in east L.A. Of those, ten to fifteen were children, and the numbers seem to rise every year.

Monica, Smitty's wife, raised money to provide decent burials for these Johnnie and Janie Does. She coerced, shamed, and threatened every cop and politician in the Los Angeles area to obtain donations. She and her father appeared on numerous television shows and got donations from as far away as China. Every couple of months, I wrote a check and told myself it was okay not to go to the funerals, and maybe if I did my job right I could keep a few children from ending up in Monica's Cemetery of the Unwanted.

How Smitty could voluntarily look at the young, untainted faces of dead children, children we had failed to protect, was beyond me. I picked up a piece of paper from my desk, pretending to study it. "The newspaper said over a hundred fifty people came last time."

"Yeah, it was a big one. We got a lot of donations. Monica's going to add a few more plots and maybe get some decent clothes for the ones that don't need closed caskets."

One of our colleagues paused at my desk. "Captain's looking for you."

Smitty seemed to find this funny. "Probably wants to discuss your tardiness again."

My stomach knotted. I looked around to make sure no one was listening. "I don't know why that woman got into law enforcement. And those tailored suits she wears. In this place?"

I refused to wear suits. They were just too damn confining. If I wore a suit, where would I keep my gun? Not to mention the illegal key picks, Swiss Army knife, the obligatory high-calorie snack, and the other nifty objects that I carry in the pockets of my pants. Smitty was right, though; the captain seemed to have a woody for me, and not in a good way. We were like two caged lions just waiting for the chance to piss on each other.

Smitty surveyed my pants and T-shirt. "Maybe you want to explain the appropriate dress code to her while you're in there."

"Very funny." I dropped my black bomber jacket over the back of my chair and headed for Captain Simmons's door. I hoped she wouldn't hear me knock, but of course she instantly barked, "Come in."

She didn't bother to look up as I closed the door behind me and waited a few feet from her desk. She continued reading some document while tapping her pen. Her arrogance was just one of many annoying things I hated about her. That and the fact that she was so good-looking it was easy to forget she dripped venom from every pore. I took the time to study her as she patently ignored me. She wore her long, dark hair pulled back in a severe bun. The body beneath the suit promised not to disappoint. She probably did aerobics or some other such shit.

"Everett, how come you're always the last one in every morning?" she asked as she continued to gaze down at the mound of papers in front of her.

As I sat down, I desisted from checking her out. I didn't want to be caught if she looked up suddenly. Besides, I wasn't interested in this witch. If I were, I would have gone home and used that damn dildo that Stacy had bought me as a gag. At least she *said* it was a gag. What it *was* was a waste of a perfectly good dildo. For reasons I preferred not to examine too closely, my libido had bailed on me around about the time I left my teens.

I spent my early twenties forcing myself into relationships I never found fulfilling. After a while, even the most understanding partner gets tired of one-sided sex, so I had to date women who were selfish enough to let me pleasure them without reciprocation. They weren't that hard to find, and I'd gotten used to women who were perfectly happy to let me take them where they wanted to go before they turned over and fell asleep. The last such fling—well, one-nighter really—was about two years ago.

I straightened, hoping to steal a look at the papers Captain Simmons had been so intent on finishing. I already had an idea what this was about, but I wasn't volunteering any information. "Well, Cap, you know I don't have a car."

"That's because you crashed the last two."

"Yeah, so I have to walk to work."

"You only live a few minutes from here," she said, still not bothering to glance up.

Bitch, I thought. "I was here pretty late working with Smitty on that snuff film case, so I kind of overslept."

"And what's the status? You two have been on that case for a month and from the look of things, you haven't made any headway."

"We should be bringing in some suspects in the next day or two. We just want to make sure the DA won't have a reason to let them go."

She nodded. The only person the captain hated more than me was the district attorney. I patted myself on the back for coming up with that on the spur of the moment.

"All right, just keep me posted. That's not why I brought you in here, anyway. I've had another complaint against you. This makes the third in as many months."

I sat quietly, not denying the allegations as she read them off. They were all true, and she'd probably missed a few gory details. She took a break from the infernal tapping and leaned back in her chair.

"Have you been seeing the psychologist?"

"Yeah, but I don't need a psychologist. I'm fine." I shifted in my seat and tried in vain to find some common ground with the woman. "You know how things are out there."

"You're going to lose your temper one time too many, Everett, and I won't be able to help you."

When had she ever helped me, anyway? "Look, jerks try to test me, probably because of my size and because I'm a woman. If I don't take them down a few pegs, they think they can run all over me."

"You kicked the last one in the balls so hard that he's still in the hospital. We'll be lucky if he doesn't file a lawsuit."

"It was self-preservation. He was coming at me. IA cleared me." The internal review had not only cleared me, but determined that if I hadn't disabled the offender, serious injury to me or my partner could have resulted. That finding had left the captain steaming for days.

I wondered about the new complaint. Was it the guy I shot in the toe?

The captain shuffled some papers. "This one reads like a nuisance lawsuit. I can't see anything sticking."

"That's good news."

"No thanks to you."

I grinned. This woman would never be on my side no matter what I did. "Is there anything else, Captain?"

"Yes, you can refrain from slamming my door on your way out."

"Yes, ma'am." I got to my feet and headed for the door, a triumphant grin already plastered across my face. That had been fairly painless as visits with the captain go.

"Oh, and Everett, get me something on who's distributing that trash on my streets by Friday or your ass is working parade duty."

"You got it, Captain." Her streets, huh? Yeah, right.

As I reached my desk I contemplated sending my trash can flying across the room. Throwing things always makes me feel better. But Smitty had the shoebox lid poised on the end of his pencil, so I settled back in my chair to enjoy the show. The shriek that erupted was worthy of the loud applause I received from the rest of the room when I retrieved the box.

"I told you not to look." I sneered in mock disgust at my 6'3" partner, who was cowering in the center of the room.

"God damn it, you know I hate those things. Why'd you give it to me?" Smitty glared at the shoebox as if a mouse attack was imminent.

I peeked inside to make sure the little guy wasn't traumatized. "Because I thought you were the one person I could trust. I'm going to let him go as soon as I find a good place."

"Make it a long way from here."

"No shit, Smitty."

From the glint in his eye, I could tell he was drawing his own conclusions about my attitude. "What did the boss want?"

"Let's just say I need some good news." I was still pissed off at the captain for threatening me with the rookie parade detail.

"Well, I just may have some." Smitty sat down at his desk with the self-satisfied air of a man with a good lead. Or at least something that looked like a good lead. As of the night before, we'd had nothing.

"Spill it," I said.

"While you were in there gossiping with Captain Simmons, I got you some coffee." He pointed to the cup on my desk. Smitty hadn't been my partner for three years without learning a thing or two about me. The most important was that bringing me coffee secured my undying love. Hey, what can I say? I'm a cheap date.

I sipped the vending machine concoction gratefully. "So, what's up?"

"I ran into Fuller. He and Jackson brought in Pistol Pete last night."

"Oh yeah, what for?"

"Same ol'. Flashing some rich chick."

Pistol Pete was so named because he loved to pull out his "six-shooter," as he called it, and fire off a few rounds at unsuspecting targets. Generally, though, he was harmless, and somewhat of a division mascot. I'd seen his six-shooter when he was showing it off through the bars of his jail cell. Personally, I thought it was more like a four-shooter, but who am I to judge?

"So, what, they put him in detox?"

"Yeah, he'd purchased himself several boxes of wine."

"Oh yeah? Where did the cash come from?" I feigned interest.

"He made a few bucks from a video store owner over on Hartford."

My antennae went up at the mention of videos, but I had to play Smitty's game. When he thought he had something good, he couldn't be rushed. He was also one of those people who had a story for everything and about everyone, and he would tell it over and over again if he could find someone willing to listen. I prompted, "So?" and started looking through the piles of paperwork on my desk as I waited for him to continue.

"Well, this guy paid Pete to move some boxes into his store. While the guy wasn't looking, Pete got nosy and took a look in the boxes."

"Let me guess, there were DVDs in there, right?" I asked sarcastically.

"Yeah, right, but the thing is, our friend Pete filched some so he could sell them for a few bucks. Only when he got back to his motel and took a look at them, there was some pretty wild stuff."

"Where are the DVDs?"

"Pete says he tossed them in the trash. He thought Jackson and Fuller were arresting him for the theft, not the flashing."

I put my empty cup down with a thud. "Well, shit, what are we waiting for? We need to search that trash, unless Jackson and Fuller already did."

"Those pussies? You have to be kidding me." Smitty was on his feet.

I snatched the keys out of his hand and raced out of the division. "I'm driving. You drive like an old lady!"

CHAPTER TWO

S mitty, of course, drove. I was still restricted from driving division vehicles for the next three months. Captain's orders. Pete's winter home turned out to be a seedy motel about eight blocks from the division. Most of the occupants made their living by waiting outside of the 7-Eleven on Guerra until some farmer came along to pick them up. They got paid next to nothing for backbreaking work, came home to a cramped room for a few hours of sleep, and started all over again the next day.

Despite the gaudy neon sign in the window promising that the office was open twenty-four hours, Smitty and I had to hold the buzzer down for ten minutes before an oily-looking guy wearing Bermuda shorts, a bowling shirt, and Vans shoes showed up to unlock the door.

Generally speaking, you need a warrant even to enter a rented room. However, the pock-faced man behind the counter was so intent on his handheld video game that he barely looked up when we flashed our badges at him. He handed us Pete's keycard without a word.

"Great security," Smitty said sarcastically as we walked across the parking lot to a depressing building with an "Out of Order" sign taped to the sole ice machine.

When we opened Pete's room we were immediately assaulted by the rank odor of cigarette smoke and that vague acrid odor left by cheap cleaning supplies. At least they tried to clean, I told myself as I stepped into the room. The idea of letting the stale, dirty air into my mouth almost caused a gag reflex. Never mind the fact that I had two weeks' worth of dirty clothes on my apartment floor at that very moment.

There is a huge difference between being messy and just plain nasty. "I'll check the bathroom, you check here." I snapped on a pair of gloves and Smitty did the same.

He was unusually quiet. Seemed I wasn't the only one reluctant to open my mouth in there. I was tempted to snicker at the "No Smoking" sign on the bathroom door as I entered. The place looked like a bar bathroom. Cigarette burns on every flat surface and permanent rust stains abounded. I checked behind the door, in the trash can, under the commode lid, under the sink, and in the shower stall before exiting the tight space as quickly as I could.

"Anything?" Smitty asked from his position on the floor.

"Nah, not yet."

Smitty lifted one of the comforters and peeked beneath one of the beds. "Think we got something."

I heard the crinkle of paper as Smitty dragged a brown bag from under the bed.

"Bingo," we said simultaneously.

I opened the bag and removed three DVDs, all of which were in unmarked cases. "Shall we take a look?" I slipped one of the recordings into the cheap-looking thirteen-inch TV/DVD combo this "upgraded room" sported.

We didn't have long to wait before we were bombarded. A thickset Caucasian male of about thirty-five was sexually assaulting a very young-looking Asian minor. Bile rose and threatened to escape my throat as the attack played out on the screen, up close and personal. The film quality was good enough that I could see droplets of sweat trapped in the grove of hair between the assailant's shoulder blades. At no point did the kid stop crying and at no point did the sick bastard assaulting him say a word. The movie was cut abruptly, and the assailant returned at a different angle, this time carrying a gun. There was a loud bang, and the DVD ended with a close-up on the victim, apparently dead.

We watched just enough of the other films to assure ourselves that they contained the same material, sexual abuse of a minor followed by a murder. Up until this point, my only thought had been to get the guy making these films; he was a murderer of the most horrible kind. Now I wondered what sort of people actually bought them.

"We've got the bastard! Let's get out of here before I get sick." Smitty picked up the DVDs and left the room.

I had to jog to catch up with him. "You all right?"

He started the engine and pulled out of the lot as if we could somehow escape what we had just seen. "Yeah. You?"

"No."

"Me either."

"How could anyone get pleasure from looking at that?" I looked out the window, blinking rapidly, trying to erase the images from my mind. The fear in that boy's eyes would haunt me forever.

"Don't try to rationalize it, Everett. These people are sick. You will never be able to understand it. All we can do is find them and put them away."

"Sometimes I wonder if it's worth it, you know? Our job is to make it so that law-abiding citizens can sleep comfortably at night, but what about our peace of mind?"

"You can't let that shit stay in your head. We have to do what needs to be done and then move on."

"But this is not just one guy we're talking about. It's not like if we get him off the street all this filth disappears. Thousands of pervs are downloading this stuff off the Internet every day."

"The Internet is the FBI's problem, not ours," Smitty said. "Our problem is getting the stuff off our streets and investigating the murders, if they are murders. No bodies so far. No crime scenes. The DVDs are the only evidence we've got."

We drove the rest of the way back to the division in relative silence. I was brooding and I figured Smitty was, too. We'd caught the case after several DVDs began circulating in the neighborhood. It had jumped from Vice to Homicide, then back again, as different detectives tried to figure out if they were seeing average, run-of-the-mill phony snuff films, or if the content depicted real crimes. If so, not only had children been molested and murdered, but the whole thing had been filmed and sold to numerous sickos. The MO was the same in each of the DVDs, the same visual backgrounds and the same twisted ending.

"Where are the bodies?" I wondered aloud. "Where are the missing persons reports?"

Everyone on this case had been through pictures of John and Jane Does, looking for any that could match the victims. The films could have been made anywhere. Eastern Europe was the source of a lot of the worst Internet porn these days. The DVDs could have originated there. Copies were easy to make. The best we could hope for was to arrest some middle man, one of a long chain of creeps making money from human misery.

"This is probably a dead-end case," I said. "No one over here takes a risk on making films like this when they can source them overseas and just distribute copies."

Smitty gave a gloomy nod. "At least we've got enough for a search warrant."

"Yup."

We'd be able to scare the video store owner. That was something.

❖

We pulled into the back parking lot of Reel Family Entertainment at around seven p.m. The overcast weather meant it was almost dark outside. There were hardly any other cars in the lot. This guy didn't seem to do much to keep up his legitimate front, so we were probably dealing with an amateur who had somehow avoided detection by law enforcement. Up until now, that is.

I told Smitty I would go in first. We'd brought one patrol unit along for backup. The uniforms would cover the rear of the building and help us carry out evidence if needed. Ignoring the smell of urine, I slid along the wall and peered inside the glass door. There was no one at the front counter.

I knocked, buzzed, and yelled, "LAPD. We have a search warrant."

We gave it the requisite ten seconds, knocked again, then I pulled out my trusty lock picks. Why risk injury by breaking the door down? It wouldn't be the first time we'd report executing a search warrant on an insecure premise. I checked out the alarm system. It was a cheap setup, with a wire running around the door. If the owner was on the premises somewhere and hadn't heard us knocking, I didn't want to alert him to our presence any sooner than necessary.

After I yanked the wires out, we entered the store, guns drawn. Shelves of G-rated DVDs filled every available wall space in the small front area. The counter was the only thing that separated the family-viewing section from the triple-X section, as denoted by the three red X's over the entryway. The adult area was garishly decorated in reds and pinks. A door at one end was screened by a purple bead curtain.

I trained my flashlight on the door and exchanged a look with Smitty. "Did you hear that?"

The sounds were extremely muffled, almost indistinguishable, like they were coming from a soundproofed room. Smitty parted the purple bead curtain and we both placed our ears to the door.

"Let's do it," he said and threw the door open.

My eyes reacted painfully to the glaring light. We advanced, sweeping the room.

"Clear." Even as I said the word, my mind belatedly processed what I was seeing but did not want to believe.

A heart-shaped bed was surrounded by all types of lighting and camera equipment. In the center was a small, half-naked child. His arms were shackled by chains so large that the mere weight of them could keep him in place. He'd been crying for a very long time; his sobs were hoarse and tired. My first reaction was to rush to him, but I didn't want to risk his life. The adult responsible for this had to be somewhere close.

Smitty cursed under his breath. He groped for a control box near the photograph lights and successfully killed them. Our breathing sounded loud. I wasn't the only one in a state of shock. We'd come here expecting to take a truckload of porn and make an arrest. In a best-case scenario, I'd imagined an offender who would cut a deal and name a few assholes higher up the food chain. Maybe we'd even involve the FBI in busting a porn ring, and get our names in the *LA Times*. The job had taught me to expect the unexpected, but I was having trouble getting up to speed.

I had to tune out the slow whining coming from the little boy. *Just a little bit longer, sweetheart. Let me get a bead on this sicko, and then I'm going to get you out of here.*

I had no sooner finished the thought than a rear door slammed and a blond Caucasian male wearing nothing but white boxer shorts and socks came crashing into the room via what I had thought was a carpeted wall panel.

"Didn't I tell you to shut up?"

He made a lunge for the child chained to the bed, but I tackled him, managing to land one solid blow to his chin before he collapsed to the floor, taking me with him. I heard the kid's dry scream before it was drowned out by Smitty's yell. I landed several more satisfying blows to the guy's chin and temple before Smitty dragged me off him.

Two uniforms burst through the beads, guns raised. The little boy screamed even more.

"We got him," I yelled. "Situation is under control. Can one of you secure the area and the other call Children's Services? And get a female officer in here."

I stood up just as Smitty yanked the now cuffed perp to his feet. "Smitty?"

"Yeah?" He growled his answer, as he often did when dealing with something or someone distasteful.

"Get it out of my face, please."

"You heard her." I waited until he had pushed the guy out of the room before I tried to approach the bed. The boy looked at me so fearfully that I stopped and held up my hands.

"See, nothing to hurt you here." I held out the chain that my badge hung on. "I'm a police detective. Do you know what that is?" The child continued to sob, but nodded.

"What's your name?"

He hesitated, but the sobs were waning and his posture had changed. He was more confident. "Jason."

I looked around for the keys that would open the handcuffs that bound his wrists. I spotted them on a dresser, along with a set of pliers, a vicious-looking knife, and ropes. The boy's blue eyes followed my every move as I grabbed the keys off the dresser and returned to the bed. "Would it be okay if I unlock those so that you can stand up?"

He nodded.

"Where are you from, Jason?"

"El-segun-doo." He hiccupped as he said it.

"El Segundo. Okay, that's real good."

I took my time asking him the key questions. His address. His mom's name and phone number. When his shaking and sobbing had stopped, I helped him off the bed. "Do you know where the rest of your clothes are, Jason?"

He shook his head and looked like he was about to cry again, so I wrapped a sheet around him. A female uniform entered the room from the rear door the perp had used earlier. She went pale and looked like she was about to burst into tears in sympathy.

"Hold it together," I told her, but I might as well have been talking to myself. "Is there a phone back there?"

"Yeah, I think so."

"Okay, call his mom while we wait for Children's Services. He knows the number."

She held out her hand and Jason took it after a tentative look at me. As he walked gingerly away, the sheet slid down. revealing a small back covered in bite marks.

Rage flooded through me like a future junkie's first dose of heroin. I fed on it because I needed an excuse for letting loose on this waste of oxygen. I stalked into the front of the video store where the perp was sitting on a stool with his face bathed in tears. Smitty stood with his back to the guy, a familiar stance, one I had seen him take on more than one occasion. It was a dare, an invitation for the slimeball to try something, anything, so Smitty could take him down. But people who attacked children were spineless bastards, and I knew that this one would not give either Smitty or me the satisfaction of blowing his brains out.

Hatred welled up within me as I stared at the guy in his pristine white boxer shorts and dress socks. The scent of his cologne was strangely heavy in the air, as if he had just paused to spritz some on while I was in the other room. Hugo Boss, I thought inanely. At that very moment he looked at me and uttered two words that broke the last vestiges of restraint that I had on my rage.

"I'm cold," he said.

And I was on him before his mouth had closed.

He never saw it coming. I landed four hard punches to his face, bloodying his nose and lips before Smitty had even turned around. Smitty rushed me and grabbed my forearms, but not before I had the perp's head in both of my hands. I slammed it into my knee.

"Everett, Everett, you got him, love, you got him." Smitty dragged me, struggling, into the back room.

I sobbed harshly, the rage still burning in my chest. I have never in my life wanted to hurt someone like I wanted to hurt this guy.

"Listen to me, we're going to make sure that he gets stuck *under* the jail. He'll get some of what he's been dishing out. He won't leave there alive, I'll make sure of it. You believe me, don't you?"

I nodded and without looking back, I stumbled out of the room. Jason was in the front seat of the patrol car and the female uniform was distracting him while they waited for Children's Services. She handed him her badge and put her hands up as if he was arresting her. A small smile passed across his face, only to fade as if it had never been there. She said something else to him, and the smile reappeared. She was good with kids. I wondered if she had her own. If she did, she must be sick with fear. I wondered what kind of life Jason from El Segundo was going to have now, thanks to that bastard inside. When was he kidnapped? Had he even been reported missing yet?

I clenched and unclenched my aching hands and then put them both under my armpits. Bile rose in my throat and I spat a couple of times. Finally I closed my eyes and leaned my head against the building. I was tired, so damn tired of seeing shit that made it impossible to think the best of people.

"Everett, I need to speak to you." Smitty stood a few feet away.

I didn't bother to turn around. I didn't need a lecture. I was sure I'd be getting one soon enough from the captain. "Can it wait?"

"No, we've got a problem."

"What do you mean? He didn't get away, did he, Smitty?" I was prepared to storm through the building to go drag his sick ass back.

Smitty grabbed my shoulders. He looked around the parking lot to make sure no one was within earshot of us. Beads of sweat glistened on his flushed forehead and cheeks like tears. Other than when we had to give chase on foot, I had never seen Smitty break a sweat over anything.

"Listen to me, damn it. He's dead."

"What are you saying?" I lowered my voice on reflex. "Smitty, what do you mean, he's dead? No, he can't be!" I tried to rush into the building, but Smitty stopped me.

"Would you just look at yourself? Your fists are bruised and you look shell-shocked."

I stared down at myself. Smitty was right. I looked like the loser in a barroom brawl. He turned us around so that anyone looking would only see his back.

"I want you to go home."

"What? I have to stay and give my statement," I said numbly.

"No." Smitty pulled me into the video store and out of view of the uniforms talking quietly near their car. "Go home and get cleaned up. I'll make some excuse about you not feeling good."

I didn't move. He shook me. I thought he was close to slapping my face.

"I can make this go away, but you have to listen to me. You're a good detective, and nobody cares about a child molester. He isn't worth spending the rest of your life in a jail cell. You were never here. Understood?"

I nodded dully as the ramifications of what I had done washed over me. My career…my life was over. The captain's words echoed in my head: *You're going to lose your temper one time too many, Everett, and I won't be able to help you.*

"Go home," Smitty repeated. "Don't call a cab. Just go home and let me handle this."

I started walking. My life was over and I'd had no warning whatsoever.

❖

I skirted the accusatory brilliance of the streetlights like a seasoned criminal. The long walk home was fine by me. I needed time to think. How could things have gone so wrong so fast? I realized there had been signs. The captain had identified them loud and clear. I was losing it by degrees. It was only a matter of time before I snapped. She knew it, but I had refused to see it.

When I got home I pulled off my bloody pants and T-shirt and thought about leaving them on the floor with the rest of my laundry, to be picked up sometime when I could be bothered. I'd always wondered why people who committed crimes didn't remove the evidence immediately. Now I had my answer. It was simply too damn hard. All I wanted to do was sleep, something I had never been successful at. But I was also a cop, and the bloody handprint on one of my shirtsleeves told me I needed to eliminate everything that connected me to the man I'd just killed.

I approached the bloody clothes as if I were approaching a meth house, with extreme caution. I picked up my T-shirt, purposely not looking at the glaring palm print. I had blood on my hands and I always would.

I shoved everything into a plastic grocery bag, along with my blood-spattered Doc Martens, and slipped out of my apartment. *Thank God I live in an old building that still has an incinerator.* Fire hazard that it was, it allowed me to get rid of the evidence. I made my way down to the basement, tossed the bag and all its contents into the incinerator, and watched as it ignited. I used a metal rod that had been left in the room to make sure that all of the stuff was incinerated beyond recognition. As the evidence of my guilt burned a hot orange, I thought how I would need to go out and buy the exact same boots tomorrow. I would have to be late to work and talk the same shit to the same people, like today had never happened. It would look suspicious if I suddenly changed my routine. Wouldn't it?

CHAPTER THREE

A lmost a month went by. I expected my life to undergo a drastic change in that time, but guess what? It didn't. Nothing happed. Nothing, nada, zilch. It was business as usual. Well, there was the fact that one Harrison Canniff, wanted on suspicion of murder, kidnap, and child molestation, was found floating in the water near the southern shore of Santa Monica beach. His body had been burned postmortem and he had floated for days before being spotted by lifeguards. They could smell him for miles.

Smitty had lovingly recounted all of this to me. When the body was removed from the water, a small ecosystem had already taken up residence. According to Canniff's driver's license, he had been 160 pounds, but by the time he was pulled out, he looked closer to 300. When a body floats for a certain amount of time, the fatty tissue starts to break down and the body can swell and bloat even though it may actually weigh less due to the chemical breakdown that it undergoes. The smell is even worse than your typical decomposing body. And I'm here to tell you there is nothing like the stomach-turning stench of a rotting corpse. Anyway, we closed the books on the case. The captain was happy, and the media and the public simply shrugged it off. No one feels bad about the death of a child molester, right? Nobody, that is, but me. I wasn't sleeping well. I explained this to Smitty when we stopped the car to pick up my third cup of coffee for the day.

"Well, shit, when have you ever?" Smitty asked as he eased us into traffic. We were headed into the division after following up dead-end leads on yet another cold case. "Hey, I was meaning to talk to you, though. You losing weight? You used to have some meat on your bones. Now you just look too skinny."

I tried to joke about the loss of my little beer belly but Smitty wasn't having it, so I simply shrugged and made up some half-assed excuse about going on a crash diet. I was so full of shit. A month earlier I was stuffing hot dogs down my throat and swigging beer with the rest of the guys down at Charlie's. And while my coworkers were complaining of stomach pains, I was already working my way through the baskets of peanuts on the bar.

Smitty made a right turn into an alley the patrol cops used to catch people making illegal right turns after six o'clock. He cut the engine and faced me. "You having problems with what happened?"

"Yeah. I just never thought it would go down like this. I never killed anyone, Smitty. I thought when I finally had to, it would be no problem. You know, my life or theirs. This wasn't that way."

I blinked furiously at the red brick wall. "Kimmy loves Stan" was crossed out with black spray paint, and the slogan "Stan is dead" replaced the earlier sentiment. I wondered how Kimmy was handling the loss. Probably better than me.

"Let this shit go." Smitty's voice was unusually gruff.

"I don't know if I can. I can't eat, I can't sleep. I can't do anything but see that guy's face as I whaled on him."

Smitty had a theory. He thought that when I kneed Canniff, I probably smashed the guy's nasal cartilage into his brain, killing him instantly. "You thinking about turning yourself in?" he asked tightly.

"Yeah." Before I could say another word, I was wrenched around so that I was facing him.

"Now you listen here, Everett. I know you're sorry. I know you hate that this happened, but damn it, there are other people involved. I've got a wife and a kid. Those rookies that corroborated the story have families, too. We can't afford to lose our jobs over some two-bit asshole who didn't deserve to live anyway."

I avoided his fierce stare. The hopelessness of my situation threatened to pull me under again. I couldn't even confess to my crime without taking people down with me. Smitty had gotten rid of the body, so that was aiding and abetting. The uniform cops had confirmed our story that Canniff was not at the scene when we arrived. They would be in trouble, too.

"Have you talked to your father yet?" Smitty asked.

"No, I haven't called him since it happened."

"He was on the force for thirty-six years. I think you should talk to him. He can probably give you some perspective."

Contrary to what Smitty might have believed, my father and I weren't exactly close. I respected the man for raising me when my mother left, but our relationship was always strained at best. He didn't seem to know what to do with me, and I was angry because he was never around. It didn't help matters that he'd married a woman only four years older than me when I was sixteen. I went through a wild, rebellious stage that basically didn't end until I got accepted into the police academy at twenty-one. Thankfully, Dad had cleaned up any mild scrapes I wasn't able to talk my way out of, so my record stayed clean.

I moved to Los Angeles and accepted a position with the LAPD because I didn't want to work in my father's shadow in New York. I thought Los Angeles was far enough away that my father's larger-than-life reputation wouldn't follow me there. I was wrong.

Shortly after I'd arrived in L.A., Dad decided to come visit me before he took his wife to Vegas for a vacation. We had arranged to meet at Charlie's because I didn't want him coming to my tiny studio and seeing that after six months, I still hadn't bothered to buy any furniture. I walked into the bar to find my dad surrounded by about seven guys from my division. He was obviously regaling them with story after story about what the dumbass crooks did in New York. It wasn't like New York had cornered the market on shit like that. *We see that every day*, I thought grumpily as I sat back and pretended not to listen. All of the guys, especially Smitty, were hanging on every word Dad spoke. I wondered why he'd never told those stories to me. Probably because he thought I wouldn't be interested. He was right.

"I can't tell my dad I killed some defenseless perp, even if he was a worm," I said.

Smitty let go of me and maneuvered us through downtown traffic. "When I became your partner, I promised your dad that I would look out for you. He cares about you and he knows how things are. Call him, okay?"

I said something noncommittal. I thought this emptiness in the pit of my stomach would stop feeling painful one day and all I had to do was cope until then.

"You saw that kid," Smitty persisted. "He would have killed him and sold the fucking movie, just like he did with the others. You know as well as I do that he has probably messed up more than just that one kid's life. The way I see it, you did the world a favor. That's how your dad will see it, too. Call him, that's all I ask. Tell him what you're thinking about doing and see what he says."

❖

"Just see what he says," I grumbled, holding my little roommate in my hand. "What do you think, Bud? You think I should call up old Dad and see what he says about this situation, hmm?"

I handed Bud a piece of cheese, which he held in his two front claws and, after turning it rather delicately, popped the whole thing into his mouth. Bud was turning into a chip off the old block. I had never gotten around to releasing him, and he had grown on me. I'd never had a pet before and I never intended on keeping Bud, but he gave me something to go home to. I put him in his little hamster-world-thingy so that he could roll around and crash into walls. He seemed to get a great kick out of it, and the noise kept me from concentrating on any one thing in particular. If it weren't for Bud, I wouldn't even have bothered going home. I would have probably just drowned myself in other people's squalid lives at work, and hoped I could forget my own.

I picked up the phone and dialed the number for my father's condo in New York. After his retirement, the stepmonster, as I called her, had persuaded him to sell the house I grew up in and buy a new high-rise condo. My stepmonster was a fairly accomplished author of those fat paperback romances you see in the grocery store with the gay-looking man and the busty woman bent in those awkward positions. I wonder if her fans cared that she was short and dowdy and married to a man twice her age.

The mean thought was enough to cheer me up, along with the fact that the phone had not been answered yet, so I was almost certain to get a reprieve. I was just about to hang up when Dad greeted me like he was happy I'd called.

We made a few meaningless remarks to each other, then he asked, "Foster, is there something you need to talk to me about?"

"What makes you say that?"

"Well, you never call to just shoot the breeze."

"There is something." A tear slipped from the corner of my eye, and I brushed it away. "I don't know where to start."

I expected my father to ask me, as he had for the last few years every time I called him, if I was pregnant. He refused to see the signs, even though I'd been hitting him over the head with them since I was about fifteen. I would never be interested in men. Nothing against them—Smitty was my best friend. They just aren't my thing, never have been.

Dad didn't make his normal comment, though. Instead, in a soft, commanding voice, he ordered me to start from the beginning. So I did, telling him all of it, starting from when Smitty got the lead from Jackson and Fuller, to today and my conversation with Smitty in the alley.

Several long seconds passed and then he said, "I think Smitty's right."

I expelled my breath, amazed that he hadn't lambasted me for going aggro on that guy. "You do?"

"What good will come of it if you tell the truth? It's not like the LAPD needs another lump, either."

"But Dad, the guy didn't even try to fight back. It was in cold blood."

"What's done is done. You saved that little boy's life, probably several others, too. That's what you should be thinking about."

"The point is that he had the right to—"

"A speedy trial the taxpayers foot the bill for, so we can watch the son of a bitch wearing a suit on Court TV, claiming he was molested as a child so he's not responsible for his crimes."

My dad's voice faded as I walked over to the window. I didn't have to listen to what he was saying, because I'd heard it all from Smitty. I stared down at the streets below. Brake lights flashed as the cars inched along in traffic like ants on a chalk line, all going somewhere and getting nowhere fast. I held the phone between my shoulder and neck as the drone of my father's voice continued in my ear. I assured him I wouldn't do anything without talking to him first. After I hung up, I wandered over to Bud's hamster house and watched him crash happily into one wall a few times before deciding on a different direction. *Going nowhere fast.*

❖

The House of Secrets was a neighborhood women's bar that went through stages of being seedy or trendy, depending on what time of year you went. I didn't keep alcohol in my house, as I was far too likely to anesthetize myself after seeing some of the things I saw on a daily basis. My father and every older cop I knew drank too much. I didn't want to be like them, so I regulated my alcohol intake. That regulation also included not going to Secrets as much as I would have liked.

I was surprised when a muscular brunette checked my ID at the front door. She was about six feet, looked my age, and was built like a brick shithouse, as my friend Marcus would say. She wore her hair in a braid as I did; however, that's where the resemblance ended. Where mine was always unruly and whispering around my forehead, hers was brushed back so tightly that it gave her an almost severe look. She glanced at my department ID and then stared hard at my driver's license before silently handing them back to me, her eyes already on the next customer. I found my usual dark corner at the edge of the bar and ordered a shot of tequila.

"Ouch, hard day, Foster?" Stacy, the owner and sometimes bartender slid the shot down.

I caught it and tossed it back in one continuous motion.

"Yeah, you could say that." My eyes watered and my chest burned from the drink. Tequila. Nasty shit, but it sure does the job fast. I ordered a beer to kill the taste, then followed this with another shot of tequila. As Stacy warily handed me the shot, I could tell she was thinking about refusing me, but I was of legal age and nowhere near drunk.

"So what's up with this place?" I tossed down the tequila, trying not to grimace and failing miserably. "It looks busier than usual."

"Yeah, the college crowd got hip to us. Lot of them graduate in a few weeks, though, so it'll probably be back to the regulars again. You should stop by more often."

Her eyes focused on my chest as I leaned over the bar and grabbed a bowl of peanuts. Stacy had been trying to get me into bed for at least two years. She and her partner Lisa had one of those open relationships that women sometimes have when they get bored with each other and are either too scared to be alone or too chickenshit to break it off.

"You know me, I try to stay away from the alcohol as much as possible."

"Yeah, so whatcha doin' here tonight?"

"Shit, I don't know. Thought I'd get my mind off some crap."

"Well, then, you've come to the right place. Let me know when you need something else." She moved off down the bar to help some chick in a leather vest and crisp new Levi's. I wondered how she could bear to sit down in those hard-assed pants.

Like every other seedy bar I had ever been to, Secrets had a line of mirrors that ran the length of the bar. Obscure brands of liquor lined the shelves in front of it, but there was enough space between and above the bottles to allow a person to check out the bar's patrons without looking like she was cruising. Stacy had just walked over and handed the big Amazon standing watch at the front door a bottled water, and was now standing with her hands on her hips, grinning for all she was worth. The bouncer was listening politely, but seemed as uncomfortable as I was with Stacy's blatant come-ons.

I snickered. Better her than me. I finished off the last of my beer and slammed the bottle down on the bar. I was already starting to get numb, which was good. It would be nice to get some sleep. Stacy returned and replaced my empty. More out of boredom than anything else, I kept watching the bouncer in the mirrors.

A group of women came staggering through the door. One of them, a drop-dead gorgeous blonde, held on to the big bouncer's arm as if she knew her. Her friends rolled their eyes and headed toward a table. I watched the scene play out, staring blatantly now. The bouncer towered over the blonde, who was probably my height if not an inch or two shorter. The chick seemed to be saying something pretty intense, because her eyes were half closed. The bouncer's face didn't register any emotion for a moment, then she said a few words and turned away. The blonde, looking severely miffed, stomped over to her friends and sat down in a huff.

"Whoops, shot ya down, didn't she?" I chuckled. "Damn, who is that anyway?" I was speaking to myself, but Stacy was walking by and overheard.

"Oh, you mean Riley? You sure have been away for a while. Things started getting rough in here with this younger crowd, so I called a security agency and asked for a female bouncer. They sent Riley down. She's finishing up her physical therapy degree over at the university, but she is working here for the last few months of the season to help me out."

"Big girl, isn't she?"

"Yup. She intimidates the heck out of most people. We never have any trouble when she's here."

"I should think not." I turned around and cradled my hands around my beer. "I wouldn't tangle with her."

"I don't know. I'd love to bed a big woman like that one."

My eyes were drawn to the mirror, and I was startled to catch the bouncer looking in my direction. My lips released the bottle with a pop as I swallowed the beer. Her eyes were so blue, I thought as she looked away.

"Too bad, though." Stacy wiped down the bar, her eyes still on the perfectly cut form of the bouncer.

"Too bad about what?" I realized Stacy was still talking and only just managed to keep from choking on another deep draught of beer.

"Too bad she's straight."

"Are you sure?" I stole another glance at the giantess at the doorway. She was looking right at me. "I mean, maybe she just isn't the obvious type."

Stacy grinned. She knew what I was talking about. We both eyed Chrissie, the part-time barkeep. It wasn't the dark labrys tattoos that adorned both of Chrissie's biceps, or the ragged haircut, or the tank top with baggy chinos that she wore pretty much every day; it was more the sparse goatee that Chrissie lovingly cultivated on her chin that sort of gave her away. Why she would go so out of her way to look like she did and still insist on being called Chrissie instead of just Chris was beyond me.

"Well, every so often Riley gets a call on her cell from some guy named Brad and she rushes off to talk to him in private. Tells him she loves him. Smiles when they're talking."

"Really?" I looked at her skeptically.

Riley stared down at some poor kid's driver's license, wordlessly handed the card back, and shook her head. The kid and her friends, embarrassed at being caught, walked out the door. The whole thing transpired without a word being uttered by either party.

"I would give my right tit to do her," Stacy said as we both were treated to a view of her tight ass and strong thighs when she bent to tie her shoelace. She straightened and stomped until her pants fell just right over her boots. I smiled, recognizing the gesture. I did the same thing daily.

"I don't know, Stacy. I prefer my women to be a bit more approachable. Oh, and let's not forget, gay."

I took a swig of my beer. Stacy had a good ten years on me. She should know that looks and a great body weren't everything. Her partner Lisa didn't have the body this woman did. Hell, most mortals didn't. But boy, was she sweet. Always ready with a smile and a kind word. I would love to have a woman like Lisa in my life. I glanced in the mirror again. Still, the bouncer was very attractive.

"So you're saying you wouldn't give her a try?"

"Who on earth would want to cuddle with a hardass?"

"Shit, I would."

I shook my head. I had been referring to myself when I made the hardass comment, but to explain would be inviting another come-on, so I joined Stacy in her little joke and hoped she would change the subject.

"So, when's the last time you got laid?" she asked.

Here we go again. "Don't you ever give up?"

"Nah, I'm not talking about me, though you could do worse. I'm just worried about you. You're so tied up in that job of yours that you don't even give off the vibe anymore."

"The vibe?"

"Yeah, you know." Stacy leaned in close. "The 'I'm a lesbian, come eat me' vibe."

"Ha, I see. Well, I'm glad I don't give off that vibe anymore. It could be dangerous."

"Hey, look." Stacy was staring at something behind me.

I didn't turn around immediately. I casually looked up into the mirrors instead. The bouncer had unclipped the cell phone from her belt and was answering it. She waved two women in while listening intently. I watched in shock as the deadpan features transformed right before my eyes.

"Shit!" I breathed.

"Told ya. Gorgeous, huh?"

"Damn, yeah, I guess she is." Gorgeous just wasn't the right word. She seemed so happy and alive that it was hard not to look at her. Vibrant perhaps was a better word, but it still didn't seem to cover her demeanor fully.

"Yeah, well, Brad is one lucky SOB," Stacy said as I stood unsteadily.

Having sufficiently dulled my senses, I said good-bye and steered myself toward the door, politely smiling at the welcoming eyes that greeted me on my way. *Trust me, girls, you really don't want me.* I passed the giantess without so much as a glance. I hadn't seen her say a word to anyone else who had left, or come, for that matter, so I didn't expect to get any different. But as the door closed, I heard, "Night."

"Good night," I replied, cursing myself for not wearing my bomber jacket. The thin shirt that I wore over my T-shirt did nothing to fend off the biting wind.

I cut through the dark parking lot to get to my apartment instead of staying on the well-lit sidewalks. Although downtown wasn't the safest area, there had never been any trouble at Secrets for as long as I'd been going there. The alcohol must have dulled my senses, because I barely had enough time to register the footsteps behind me before a powerful hand landed on my shoulder.

Instinctively I whipped around while reaching for my service issue. First thing they teach you is never stand close enough that you can get your gun knocked away. I stepped back and aimed carefully at my assailant's chest, which for whatever reason was swaying. I squinted in puzzlement.

The bouncer from Secrets had followed me outside. She was even taller than I thought. I only came to her chest, not that that was a bad place to be, but damn, she was a big woman. Her face had paled, and she looked like she was about to pass out. Her hands were still in the air. It took me a minute to realize that I still had the gun trained on her. I dropped my arm hastily.

"Sorry about that, but you should really be more careful about who you walk up behind. Oh shit." I grabbed her around her surprisingly small waist as she toppled forward. Her shoulder bumped into my nose, making me blink rapidly, and for a second we just stood that way. It was a strangely comforting embrace. I had the oddest impression of chocolate and a warm blanket.

"Here, sit down, okay?" She mutely allowed me to ease her down on the curb. "Put your head down, that might help."

"I don't like guns." The comment was muffled, but I could hear fear, anger, and embarrassment in her voice.

"I'm sorry. I'm a detective. It sort of comes with the job." For some reason, I was talking to this woman as if I was the one who had a good six inches and probably fifty pounds on her instead of the other way around. I touched her back. Smooth muscles undulated beneath my hand. "Do you think you can stand up?"

I helped her to her feet, and we stared at each other for a minute before we both looked away. I had been dating women since I was fifteen years old and fending off guys for about as long. I'd never felt so awkward around anyone before. And straight or not, she seemed to be feeling the same way. Suddenly I was mortified as I realized I was staring at her breasts.

"I should go," I told her nervously.

"I'm sorry for scaring you." Her voice still sounded faintly muffled, as if she had a cold. Probably from not wearing a jacket.

"I think that's my line. Do you need me for something?" I asked as I holstered my gun.

"No." Then, almost as an afterthought, she said, "You're not driving, are you?"

I frowned, then it dawned on me that she thought that I might be about to get behind the wheel after all the alcohol I'd had to drink. Stacy's worst fear was that someone would get loaded in her establishment and then go out and kill someone, and she would be culpable. She probably had this woman watching every customer. Disappointed, I said, "No, I only live a few blocks away. Thanks for the concern."

"Sure," she said again in that muffled voice of hers.

I shoved my hands in my pants pockets. "Okay, I should get going."

I started for home. I was tempted to look back because I was positive that she was still watching me from the parking lot. It should have made me uncomfortable, but it didn't. It made me feel like I wasn't alone, like someone actually gave a shit if I got home safely or not.

I stifled a chuckle. *Yup, my ass is drunker than I thought.*

CHAPTER FOUR

I picked the apartment complex I lived in because it was so quiet, thanks to its mostly elderly tenants, and because of its close proximity to the division. It took me less than five minutes to get to the local women's bookstore, the division, Secrets, Old Navy, or the grocery store. Anything other than that, I just did without. Normally, when I walked into the division it was bustling. This particular morning, it wasn't. With the exception of a few uniforms who were just coming off the graveyard shift, the place was almost empty. Glancing over at the captain's office, I noted the time: five thirty a.m. Shit. I honestly couldn't remember ever being at work this early.

I was standing at the coffee machine waiting for my cup to fill when I noticed a familiar-looking uniform standing behind me. "I'll only be a minute."

"Oh no. Take your time, Detective Everett."

Damn, I thought, *so this guy knows my name.* I guess I was supposed to know his. I never forget a face, but I'm not good with names. I gave the guy a fake smile and went back to staring at my coffee cup.

When I tried to leave, he came out with the words I'd come to dread during my three years in the division. "Detective, may I talk to you?"

I winced. Nearly every unmarried and not so unmarried man in the place had asked me out, and I thought by now they would have compared notes and decided I was frigid or something. I have a policy that I stick to, and that is, I don't date cops, especially not male ones.

Period. I only have room for one narcissistic asshole in my life, and that position is already filled by me.

As I waited for the uniform to speak, I noted the wedding band on his finger and thought, *I had better be wrong about the conversation we are about to have, mister, 'cause I don't take kindly to being asked out by married men, especially those not smart enough to remove their rings.*

"I just wanted to say thank you." He stretched out his hand and I shook it out of habit.

I could tell from the way he held himself that he was still wet behind the ears. Couldn't have been on the force very long for him to blush so easily. "You're welcome, Officer. Now can you refresh my memory as to what you're thanking me for?"

He stepped closer and spoke quietly. "For the package Detective Smith brought by the other day. I was able to get my wife something nice, and my kid some clothes, and pay off a few bills. It was a big help." He must have noticed my shock, because he shifted uncomfortably. "Smitty said that me and Grady shouldn't say anything to you, but I wanted to thank you for thinking of us. You and Smitty didn't have to take care of us, but we do appreciate it."

"You're welcome."

The rookie's mouth was still moving, but I wasn't listening. It was impossible for me to continue this conversation. Smitty had given this kid hush money to cover my ass. I didn't know what to feel. This was getting more complicated by the moment. Smitty had already committed several crimes to cover up something I had done. I tuned back in as the kid was finishing up his statement.

"We would have done the same thing if we had the chance, I want you to know that. And if you need anything else, I'm your guy."

I made the appropriate sounds, I guess, because the officer looked pleased as he walked away.

Why would Smitty pay this kid off and then tell him not to say anything to me about it? It didn't make sense. I walked back to my desk, put the coffee down, and stared out into space. I thought the nightmare was over, and after a few months, Harrison Canniff's death would become a cold case, which sickeningly enough was my and Smitty's territory. Once the case was given to us, it would be buried so deep no one would ever think to investigate. Smitty was right. He had taken care of it.

But meantime, Homicide still had an open case file. Sicko or no, this guy's murder had to be investigated. I doubted they would expend resources on it, though. I read through the file once more, to reassure myself that it was virtually inactive.

The homicide info was stark and no-nonsense. Harrison Canniff, age thirty-four, small business owner, died from blunt trauma wounds to the head and face. The autopsy report stated that Canniff was already dead when his body was doused with gasoline and set on fire. Nearly all the teeth in his mouth had been busted out, making it hard to do a dental ID. His wife identified him based on the vaguely discernable tattoo on his right shoulder, and a gold cap on one of his bicuspids. That creature had had a wife, someone who probably was missing him and in pain because of what I had done.

I sank back in my chair. I couldn't have kneed Canniff so hard his teeth were smashed, that much I was sure of. The bones of your nose are easily broken. I should know, mine have been broken twice while wrestling with some perp. But to break all the teeth out of someone's head, *that* takes a great deal of force and you'd notice teeth lying around. Smitty had dragged me away, but I was sure I would have seen that kind of damage.

The other possible explanation for Canniff's condition was that Smitty had worked the body over after I left. He said he had covered our asses before he dumped the body, namely burning it and making sure neither of us inadvertently left evidence on the body. But to beat the shit out of it? Certainly it had held up the identification process, but to what purpose? It seemed brutal and pointless. But then again, if Smitty was trying to make it look like a hit, maybe the extra damage was necessary.

It only took minutes for me to start blaming myself for what he was doing to protect me. I could never forgive myself if something went wrong and he was somehow screwed because of me. I hadn't felt like such a fuckup in years. I quickly exited the info on Canniff and stood up just as the captain walked in.

"Well, Detective Everett, I must say I'm pleasantly surprised to see you here so early. To what do I owe the pleasure?"

I was in no mood to deal with wisecracks about my tardiness. In fact, I wasn't in the mood to deal with the captain, period. I shrugged and tried to look as busy as possible in the hopes that she would go away. She didn't, of course.

"Detective, can I see you in my office for a minute?"

Shit, shit, shit, so much for a good day. I followed her and sat down in the rather uncomfortable chair across from her, feeling like a petulant child called to the principal's office.

"Is something wrong, Detective?"

"No, why do you ask?"

"I've noticed that you're not yourself lately."

I wanted to tell her that she didn't know what *myself* actually was, so how could she know when I wasn't it? I knew I was acting childish, but I hated feeling cornered and that's exactly how this woman made me feel.

"May I ask you something?" She folded her hands neatly on her desk. "Why is it that you and I don't talk? We're both women. You would think we would get along, but from the moment I came here, I sensed animosity from you."

Now what was this all about, I wondered as I stared at her in disbelief. It wasn't like she had ever shown any interest in whether or not I had any animosity toward her. I took in her suit and superbly coiffed hair. The woman was not a cop, she was a model. She was someone who would, and should, ride a desk her whole life.

"What do you mean, Captain?" I plastered a look of complete befuddlement on my face. "I always thought we got along great." Hot damn, this lying shit was starting to be too easy.

"Well, perhaps I've been getting the wrong signals. I just wanted you to know that if you ever need someone to talk to about work or anything, I'm always here."

"I'll keep that in mind, Captain. Thanks." I exited her office, resisting the urge to take a look behind me to make sure she hadn't transformed into something hideous.

Now, I am not an idiot. I know there wasn't an ounce of sincerity in that offer of friendship. The captain could normally give two shakes of a rat's ass if I fell off the face of the earth, as long as I did all my paperwork before I took the plunge. Suddenly she wanted to be my best friend?

I slumped down in my chair and racked my brain. Finally, I decided that I couldn't wait until Smitty came back next week. I needed to find out what the hell was going on. I decided to pay Smitty a visit at home.

❖

With Smitty out on vacation, the captain had broken down and allowed me to check out a car. I wasn't too happy about having to drive one of the big Crown Victorias, though. I would have much rather had something less…matronly. I hated not being able to see the ground when I drove, and Crown Vics handled like boats. Sighing, I pulled into Smitty's driveway and took an appreciative look around. My partner lived in a great neighborhood. Lots of nice, hardworking young couples that made sure that they kept their yards manicured and whatnot. It was a big difference from living downtown.

As I approached Monica's Ford minivan, the hair on my arms stood up as it always did. I vaguely wondered if she felt odd transporting infant bodies and her own young son in the same vehicle. I always imagined that the eyes of dead babies watched me from behind the Aerostar's tinted windows. I passed by the van swiftly, suppressing the urge to look back, and pushed Smitty's doorbell, admiring a welcome mat I hadn't noticed the last time I visited.

Monica opened the door and, with a squeal, launched herself at me. She hugged me so tightly I was hard-pressed to catch my breath. She then proceeded to plant a fat one on my lips, right there on the front porch—neighbors be damned. She had been greeting me like that since we first met. I had been somewhat reluctant to meet her when Smitty and I were first partnered, because she was the only daughter of Los Angeles Police Chief Herbert James. A singularly unmoving figure, he probably hadn't been out on the streets in at least twenty years. His ideas on law enforcement were outdated and ineffective.

Monica, however, was a smart, attractive woman who was exceedingly affectionate, at least where I was concerned. *Shit, all the good ones are taken.* I grinned as she started to fawn over me.

"My God, every time I see you, you just look so damn cute. Look at those pants, they are just falling off you. You look about sixteen years old. Is that a new earring? My God, how many do you have in your ear now?"

"Only three." I grinned. She pulled the silver chain out of my T-shirt and literally started straightening my clothes.

Her hands were heading toward my belt when I looked over her shoulder at Smitty. I begged him with my eyes to stop her before she unbuckled my pants and started trying to tuck my shirt in. He was grinning, and I could tell he was thinking about letting her continue. The big smart-ass. He was used to Monica's exuberant greetings. I think he liked to see how uncomfortable she made me. If he wanted to play, we could play. *Let her open my pants if she wants. My T-shirt isn't that long, and I haven't worn panties since I was in high school, buddy.*

I must have looked like I was starting to enjoy myself because he finally intervened. "Hey, hey, I'm standing here. You two cut it out." Monica stepped into his hug and they stood looking at me. They looked happy, but tired, or maybe just worried. Smitty wouldn't have told her anything. I was sure of that.

"Sorry for dropping by on your day off."

"Oh, please. You know you're always welcome." Monica pulled me by the hand into the kitchen and Smitty followed behind us. "So, what brings you here today, Foster?"

She plopped me down on a chair out back, where they'd obviously been sitting and relaxing before I came by. Snacks and glasses occupied the small table between the outdoor chairs.

Smitty sat down in the chair next to mine and handed me a glass of lemonade.

I knew what was coming but drank some and winced. I was never one to complain about sweets, but even I had my limits. "Smitty, you know you are supposed to put lemons in this, too, not just sugar."

"Hey, I put lemons in it. I like it sweet."

Monica was having iced tea and not the sugar water that we were drinking. I had promised myself to have her get my drink on future social occasions, but I always seemed to relent and accept whatever Smitty made.

"Hey, Monica, would you mind if I talk about work with Joe for a few minutes?" I always switched to "Joe" when I visited. Monica didn't like "Smitty." Someone should tell her the nickname was her husband's idea.

"Sure, I need to go check on the food anyway." Monica left us quickly. Like me, she had been raised in a law enforcement family. You learned when it was necessary to disappear.

As soon as she was out of sight, Smitty asked, "Did you talk to your dad yet?"

I ignored the anger that welled up in my chest at that question. "Yeah. He said pretty much the same thing you did."

He nodded and settled back in his chair, satisfied. I pretended to do the same but my mind was working a mile a minute. It was weird. I was always the one doing the questioning and talking to suspects. Smitty said I had the gift of gab, but I was speechless. I'm sure it was a temporary condition, but disconcerting nonetheless.

Eventually, I croaked out, "You gave those uniform cops money. The ones who were there that night."

I waited to see what his reaction would be, but he was watching Monica, who was flipping burgers over the grill. "I thought we weren't going to talk about this anymore. The whole idea was to clean it up, get all eyes off you, and then go on with our lives. As near as I can tell, you're home free. Why bring this up now?"

His voice was nonchalant, almost too much so. It could be the fact that I was having such a hard time with everything, but I was getting a feeling that there was more to this hush-money payment than Smitty was telling me.

"I know that, thanks to you, I'm not in jail right now, and I'm truly grateful. It's just…One of those cops came and thanked me for it. He seemed to think it came from me."

"They helped me with the body," Smitty said calmly. "They deserved it."

"Okay, but where did all this money come from, Smitty? You and Mon live on one salary. You have a mortgage."

"What are you trying to imply, Everett?"

Smitty was a wonderful guy, but I had seen him go off on a few people and had often thought I would never want to be on the receiving end of his anger.

"I'm not implying anything. I don't want you putting your family in hock for me. I would rather turn myself in."

Smitty tensed and leaned in close. "Listen to me. You are not going to turn yourself in. I did give Goldstein and Gable money, but it wasn't hush money, it was just for helping out. Both of them would have stood in line for the chance of taking that guy out themselves."

I so wanted to believe I wasn't screwing up anyone else's life but my own that I nodded eagerly.

"Look, I'm going to tell you this because I know you are bothered by the whole issue. But once I tell you, I don't want to hear about it anymore. I mean it, Foster, this could mean my ass this time. I'm not willing to risk my family because you've got a guilty conscience."

"I hear you, Smitty. Now tell me what's going on."

"The money comes from a friend."

"A friend?"

"Yeah. He was in law enforcement, too. He helps cops out when they are having trouble making ends meet or when something like this happens. Anyway, he created this special group with a few old cops. The fund was started a few years back when a bunch of cops got themselves into trouble and couldn't afford an adequate defense. When the press starts swaying the public, it is almost impossible for a good cop to survive trial by public opinion, so whenever possible, the coalition steps in. If we can, we try to stop it from ever becoming an issue—like in your case. In cases where we can't stop it from going to court, we provide anonymous donations for a legal defense. Only a select few people in the department know about it. The sole purpose is to help clean up situations that aren't exactly criminal. Like your situation. You aren't the first to take care of a scumbag, and you won't be the last."

"Hey, Foster, you want a hot dog or a burger?" Monica yelled from across the yard, giving me a chance to mull over what Smitty had just said.

"No thanks, I'm not hungry," I yelled back. She looked at me strangely for a moment, then returned to her grill.

"You should have taken the burger. Now she is going to think something is wrong when there really isn't."

"Tell her I had a stomachache."

"You have a cast-iron stomach. I'll think of something."

"Sorry, Smitty, you seem to be pulling me out of trouble a lot lately."

"Yup, that's my job. To pull people I care about out of trouble." He took a sip of his sugar water.

My mind reeled with what I had been told. Something in me rebelled against the very existence of such a fund. I didn't want to go to jail but I was disheartened that members of my field needed someone who would help us out when we broke the law. "I should get back to work."

"Yeah, I know," he said.

I could see that he regretted having explained so much, but I couldn't muster up enough energy to make him feel better. My world was tipping on its axis, and I was halfway hoping I would just fall the hell off.

Monica came out of the house holding their sleepy five-year-old son Eric in her arms. I patted his wispy blond curls and smiled as he hid his face against his mother's neck. Normally, I enjoyed the parting liplock from Monica; straight women are so funny. But this time, my mind was on what Smitty had told me. I followed him down a hall I thought of as "the shrine," because it was lined with pictures of Monica's deceased mother.

He opened the front door and said, "I know you don't like what you've heard, but I wanted you to know that this is taken care of. You can hold your head up."

I didn't know what to say. I felt trapped, not just by my own decision to walk away that day instead of coming clean, but also by the knowledge that strangers now had dirt on me. I could be blackmailed. I was vulnerable and now owed certain people a favor.

My uneasy silence obviously bothered Smitty. He launched into a small lecture about why I needed to forget any of this had ever happened. "A lot of people stepped up to the plate to make sure you didn't get the blame for this, but they are not going to take a fall for either you or me. If you don't play by the rules, they could take back their support and things could get real nasty."

I didn't like where this conversation was going. "That sounds like a threat."

"God damn it, Foster, get your head out of your ass long enough to hear what I'm saying. This is bigger than either of us."

All of a sudden I saw something in Smitty's eyes that I hadn't noticed before. I had been so caught up in my own guilt that I hadn't noticed that his face was almost two shades lighter than normal and a light sheen of sweat shone across his forehead. Detective Joseph Smith, my partner, was afraid of something. He had risked his livelihood for me. He didn't deserve to feel the way he did. I would simply have to find some way to get through this on my own.

"Shit, I'm sorry." I gave his shoulder a small shake, wanting to instill the confidence my tone seemed to lack. "This conversation never happened, okay? It's over. Chapter closed."

He took a deep shaky breath and nodded thankfully. This was not good. Smitty was no coward, and he certainly had not ever let me see that he was scared about anything. No, if he was afraid of something, it had to be pretty bad. We said good-bye and I left him standing in the entryway of his perfect house with his perfect wife and perfect child. I hoped he didn't feel as dirty as I did.

❖

"You're bullshitting us, right?" Chrissie and Stacy looked at each other with their mouths hanging open.

I had been telling stories, ranging from the perp who dressed up in his mother's clothes to avoid detection, to Jim at the Liberty Apartments who was tired of the low-flying helicopter making all that noise and decided he was going to take a shot at it with a rifle.

I threw back a free Buttery Nipple and grinned as the heat hit my chest. "I'm telling you the truth. That's the thing about criminals. Stupidity knows no bounds."

"Son of a bitch." Chrissie walked off, shaking her head.

We had been shooting the breeze for over an hour. Both of them were keeping me company as I drank to the point that I no longer heard that annoying self-doubt in the back of my head.

"Hey, don't you ever get scared out there?" Stacy asked. "I mean, I listen to my radio all the time, and some of the shit I hear is scary."

Stacy was what is commonly called a "police scanner ho." Some people were addicted to the Internet; Stacy's thing was the police scanner. She listened to the police frequency on the radio, day in and day out, and even went so far as to call in and correct people when they used incorrect call numbers. Didn't endear her to the folks in Dispatch.

"You can't be a good cop and be scared," I replied. "You would be a dead cop."

"But what if your partner isn't around and you have to deal with one of those big guys by yourself?"

"Spoken like a truly modern woman, Stacy." I saluted her with my empty shot glass. "I'm not scared of anyone. The bigger they are, the harder you gotta hit them." I knew I sounded like an asshole, but I was drunk and therefore suffering from a Napoleon complex.

"How about her? You're not scared of her?" Stacy pointed with her chin and folded her arms over her big boobs.

I blinked at them for a moment, then spun around in my chair to see who she was talking about. The quiet bouncer. As was her habit, she sat at the front door checking IDs and charging a cover after eight o'clock. She always waved me in, even though I had my money ready whenever I walked through the door.

"Her? You want me to hit her?" I gestured with my thumb and asked a bit too loudly. A few of the regulars sitting at the tables nearest us overheard my question and began to blatantly eavesdrop.

"Woman, are you sick? She would knock you silly, I don't care how tough you are. No, how about something a little more interesting, Ms. Bold and Beautiful."

"Sure, whatcha got?" I leaned my elbows drunkenly on the bar ignoring the water that seeped through my shirt and wet my elbows.

"Okay, I dare you to go over there and kiss her," Stacy said. "I don't mean a peck on the cheek, either. I mean a long, hot kiss on the lips. And it had better last for at least five seconds or no deal."

"I wouldn't do that," Chrissie chimed in helpfully. "Man, she isn't even gay, and she may try to kill you."

"Oh, and that's another thing. Hand over the gun." Stacy held out her hand and wiggled her fingers. "No pulling it on her when she goes to tear your head off."

"No way. I'm not handing over my gun to no civilian."

"What's the matter, shorty? You afraid of the big bad Amazon?" Stacy teased.

I ripped the holster off my belt and slammed it down on the bar. "Don't get any fingerprints or juices on it."

Most of the people in the club had no idea what was going on until I started the "I'm going to get me some" walk toward the front door. I don't know how it got started, but the girls began chanting something.

Riley's hair was brushed back into its usual tidy braid, and she was neatly dressed in pressed jeans and a meticulously ironed T-shirt. Who irons creases into their T-shirts, anyway? She seemed to be reading some type of magazine when I walked up. I wondered why she hadn't noticed the chanting going on around us. Maybe she was pointedly ignoring it, or so accustomed to the noise level she blocked it out automatically. I stepped in front of her. She was either truly into her magazine or I was of no interest whatever, because she didn't even look up. I tapped her lightly on her shoulder. She jumped, lowered her magazine, and regarded me quizzically.

"Hi," I said with as sexy a smile as I could muster, as drunk as I was.

"Hi," she answered. "What do you—"

Before she could finish whatever it was she was going to say, I stepped between her open legs, grabbed her behind the neck, and covered her mouth with mine. Her lips quivered a little as I gently opened mine to gain access. I held her shoulder with my other hand and stepped in closer until my hips were pressing tightly between her thighs. *So sweet*, I thought as I continued to kiss the softest lips I had ever felt. That kiss was everything I had ever hoped for. It was warm and comforting, as well as erotic and sensuously shy.

My hands, of their own accord, ran down her toned arms to the hands I hadn't realized were holding my hips. I let go of her wrists and reached for her face. I felt like I was lost and found all at once. Like I was suffocating, but breathing for the first time. *She's trembling,* was the last thought I had as the sweet lips abruptly rejected mine and I was pushed away. She was staring, stony-faced, at something behind me. The chanting had reached deafening proportions. Everyone was clapping and hollering.

I faced the room acutely aware of Riley's presence behind me.

Stacy swirled her towel around her head. "You win! My God, woman, you've got balls. All drinks for Foster are on the house."

The grin on her face started to fade and the noise level dropped abruptly. From the dawning trepidation on everyone's faces, I knew the scary bouncer was not amused and prepared myself for the major ass-kicking I was about to receive and no doubt deserved.

Ready to duck, I turned around and was shocked to find not anger but pain in Riley's blue eyes. She dropped her magazine, got down off her stool, and walked out of the club. The door slammed back against the wall before it slowly began to close. The room was almost completely silent. The women who had witnessed my attempt to win Stupidest Bitch of the Year seemed about as stunned as I was.

"Aw shit, Riley." Stacy dropped the towel and hurried toward me.

Brushing her hand from my shoulder, I rushed after Riley. She was already halfway across the parking lot. Her long strides ate up ground fast.

"Riley, please stop," I called. "I can explain everything." I couldn't really, but I was going to do everything in my power to try. I felt like such an ass. Hell, I *was* an ass.

She kept walking and did not look back.

Never drink five shots and go running after someone. I would be happy if I caught up to her without puking my guts out. I finally got within reach of her and pawed at her shoulder. She whipped around, her fist balled.

I jumped back and held up my hands. "I'm sorry, okay? I didn't mean anything by it."

Her face crumpled before my eyes, and then she seemed to get a grip on herself. "What did I ever do to you?" Her voice was even deeper than the last time I had heard it.

God, I hoped she wasn't going to cry. I already felt like a first-class asshole. "Nothing. It was dumb. Please come back to the club with me."

She just stared at me angrily, her jaw working. "No."

I grabbed her arm. I don't know what I was thinking when I decided to play with this woman, but based on the solid muscle beneath my fingers, I knew she could rip my head off with her bare hands. As guilty as I was feeling, I probably wouldn't put up much of a fight either.

"Listen, I'm so sorry for what I just did. I didn't think about how it might make you feel. I drank too much. I know that's no excuse, but I didn't mean to hurt…" I paused, worried about making her mad. Phrasing my apology more carefully, I said, "I didn't mean to embarrass you like that. It was a stupid dare, one I normally wouldn't have taken, but I—"

"Had been drinking," she finished for me.

Her deep voice so close to my ear, and the bluntness of the statement, caused me to start. "Yes."

"I've been watching you," she said.

I motioned for her to sit down on the curb with me, which, surprisingly enough, she did. A semi pulled up in front of a warehouse across from us and honked. Huge doors slid up, making a noise like the crashing of thunder. Men spilled from inside the building, yelling to each other over the sound of the semi's engine. I pretended to watch as they began to unload the truck. The noise they made would have been deafening if we had been any closer. I hoped Riley would wait until it quieted down before we continued to talk. I needed a chance to gather my scattered thoughts.

"You've been drinking a lot lately." The statement was made with little inflection. She didn't even bother to raise her voice over the din caused by the semi. She didn't have to; we were sitting so close that I heard every word.

I leaned my head forward on my knees, trying to break the tension I felt. "I know I have."

"What's wrong?" Her penetrating blue eyes scoured my face. "What are you trying to forget?"

I swear I think my heart stopped in that moment. It's not like I even knew her at all, but she could sense that something wasn't right with me. I wanted badly to be able to tell her everything. I wanted to tell someone. I hadn't heard from my dad since I'd phoned him about my problem. It hurt that he hadn't called to check up on me. Smitty had made it crystal clear that the subject was closed. I was feeling so alone I'd resorted to the numbing relief of alcohol, a choice I'd sworn I would never make.

"It's just some stuff I have to get through."

For a brief, crazy moment, I thought she might kiss me. She stared deeply into my eyes and her fingertips grazed my cheek. Generally speaking, I don't like people touching me. Okay, I have hurt people for less. But she was different. I enjoyed how I was feeling right then, and I was amazed to realize that I wouldn't be opposed to another kiss. "Did you think that was funny back there?" she asked.

The question should have left me speechless, but it didn't. I answered truthfully, "I wasn't thinking." I was disconcerted at the way she was staring at me, but I continued to look her steadily in the eyes. "I thought you might be pissed, or think I was crazy, but I never thought you would be hurt. Please believe me."

She dragged a stick along a crack in the ground, disturbing several ant beds in the process. "I understand. Thank you for apologizing."

"Will you come back inside, then?"

"No, I don't think so. Next Sunday was going to be my last day anyway. I'll come in early tomorrow and talk to Stacy. I don't want to go back."

I began to think that feeling subhuman was going to become a permanent thing. I felt the need to disengage from the penetrating blue eyes. I felt like she would see all my faults and find me lacking. "Is it because of what I've done?"

"Partly."

"There's nothing I can do to convince you of how sorry I am?"

"I believe that you're sorry. It's just…" She continued to dig in the ground, the muscle of her bicep flexing rhythmically as she twisted and turned the stick as if she planned to make it fit into the thin crack. "I hate to be laughed at."

"I don't think anyone is going to laugh at you again." I waited until our eyes met and then I stated firmly, "If they do, I'll shoot them all."

I couldn't help but smile at her expression. She wasn't sure if I was kidding. When she grinned suddenly, I caught my breath. I had only seen that carefree delight on her face when she was on the phone to her boyfriend. *Boy, Riley, you're a real heartbreaker, aren't you?*

Her body shook silently. I'd never really seen anyone laugh without sound; I thought it was wonderful. I stood up and tentatively offered my hand. She took it and we walked back toward the club.

"Detective Everett?" She was staring again. Obviously she had no idea how disconcerting that was.

"Call me Foster." I reminded myself that she was straight and probably thought I was a bitch.

"I don't like guns."

I looked up at her sharply. A joke? Shit, that was a peace offering in my book. "No worries, I can just arrest everyone, a lot less noise."

She did that cute silent laugh of hers and shook her head before opening the door for me. Stacy had turned up the music after we left. The bass was so loud that it forced my heart to adjust to its beat. At least, I hoped the bass was responsible. I couldn't afford to think a straight woman could move my pulse rate. I had enough problems. I glared at each and every person in the club as we walked in, letting them know that any wisecracks would mean tangling with me.

"See," I told Riley. "No one laughed."

She smiled. "No, I guess they didn't."

"I need to pick up my gun from Stacy and settle my bill. Want anything?"

She asked for water and took up her usual post at the door.

Stacy couldn't wait to apologize when I made it to the bar. Generously, I said, "I should have known better."

"Well shit, Foster, everyone knows something's going on with you. You've been coming in here almost every night and closing the place down."

I frowned at that. I wasn't sure I liked the idea of *everyone* knowing there was something wrong with me. Never mind the fact that Riley knew. I thought that was sort of sweet, but everyone else could just stay out of my business.

"I shouldn't have egged you on in the state you were in. I should apologize to Riley, too."

"Give her a minute, Stacy. She was really upset. I think she just wants to forget about it and have things get back to normal." I threw some money down on the bar and told her that Riley's water was free.

I picked up the bottle, said good night, and made my escape.

At the door, I bent down and picked up the magazine she'd dropped earlier. *The Incredible Hulk Meets the Fantastic Four.* Startled that she had been engrossed by a comic book, I said, "Pretty heavy reading for a college graduate." *Damn. Real smooth, Foster. You're just batting a thousand today.*

I exchanged an embarrassed smile with her, apologized again, and left her with the water, the comic, and a polite "Good night."

As the door to Secrets swung shut, I heard her reply, "Night, Foster."

CHAPTER FIVE

Premonition. That's what they call it, right? Like everyone I know, I've had premonitions before, but they were nothing like this. Foreboding pressed down on my chest like a tangible weight, creating a thickness that couldn't be cleared away with a cough or a swallow. I jumped from deep sleep to complete wakefulness for no apparent reason. I only had time to blink twice before I felt the worst kind of dread imaginable.

I lay in my bed wide-awake, waiting for *something*. The braying of my phone almost sent me into cardiac arrest. I glanced at my clock. Four in the morning is rarely a good time to receive a call. I leaned over and felt around on the floor. Almost regretfully, I found the phone under the smoky pants and shirt I'd worn to the club recently.

I sat straight up in bed, my heart pounding. The voice at the other end was indistinct. All I could hear was whimpering. I checked the caller ID. "Monica, is that you?"

"It's Joe. He…" She never finished her sentence.

"Monica, tell me what's wrong." Deep down I already knew. I knew, with a certainty I could never hope to explain, that my partner was gone. "Hang on. I'll be right there."

Dully, I placed the phone on its cradle and got out of bed. Somehow I had always imagined that I would be the one calling her, not the other way around. Tears streamed down my face as I pulled on some clothes. I grabbed my gun and my badge out of habit, and numbly walked out the door.

Maybe she's just panicking, I thought. *Smitty must have run into*

*an old friend and got to telling his stories. I'll get there and he'll be on
Monica's case for calling me in the first place.*

One of the benefits of living downtown was that I didn't need to
wait long for a cab. I sank into the backseat and pressed my right foot
to the floor, trying to make the idiot driver go faster. I only stopped
clenching my fists into the shiny leather seats when my fingers began
to ache. My mind had been telling me for days now that something was
wrong.

Smitty was back to his normal, happy-go-lucky self, our troubles
relegated to the past. But beneath that cheerful exterior, he seemed
to have something on his mind. I didn't want to get into any more
discussion about the hush money or Harrison Canniff. We were on
another cold case, following up leads on a child kidnapping. A guy
called Michael Stratford, out on parole, was a source of possible info.
Both Smitty and I were pretty certain we were dealing with a homicide
rather than a kidnapping. Victims usually don't show up breathing a
year after they vanish.

Stratford hadn't shown up for a meeting with his parole officer
on the last day of his parole. Not a remarkable occurrence, but he had
seemed to be doing well. He had a new job, a new girlfriend, and a new
baby on the way. Most telling was the fact that his own parole officer
seemed surprised at his disappearance. By nature, parole officers were
as cynical as they come. The usual possibilities were the only ones I
could think of: either he knew he was going to pop positive on his drug
test, or he was dead.

I didn't think Smitty was losing any sleep over our missing witness,
and I didn't ask what was on his mind. I wished I had. I just figured
he and Monica were having marital problems. As close as Smitty and
I were, we weren't that close. He didn't tell me about his marriage,
and I didn't tell him about the countless women, or lack thereof, I had
bedded. Our unspoken rule about personal boundaries worked just fine
for me.

I didn't bother knocking when I reached Smitty and Monica's
house. I turned the knob slowly, fighting down an irrational urge to grab
my gun. Apprehension burned a path down my esophagus like molten
lava, but I forced myself into the brightly lit room.

Monica held a crumpled tissue up to her nose as she stared fixedly
at a mug sitting on the coffee table. Chief of Police Herbert James paced

back and forth with a cell phone to his ear. The skin on his face looked blotchy, as if someone had attempted to drain all the color from him but hadn't done a thorough job. His lips were tight, though his voice was actually so low that I could only hear the tail end of his conversation.

"I don't give a damn what you have to do. Keep this out of the paper, do you understand? This is my career we're talking about!" He snapped the cell phone closed and tossed it to one of three plainclothes officers standing around looking like they would rather be anywhere other than Detective Joseph Smith's living room.

Monica buried her face in the chief's shirt. "Daddy, what are we going to do? You don't think he—"

"Shh, sweetheart, we can't guess that right now."

Until I'd arrived in Smitty's home, I had held on to the hope that he was fine and there was some misunderstanding or reasonable explanation for his absence. Maybe he'd followed a hot lead or was doing something under the radar.

I flashed my badge to anyone who cared to look, and Monica immediately let go of her father and jumped into my arms. I avoided Chief James's stony gaze. Now was not the time to start an argument with the man, but how could he be so worried about his career when his daughter was obviously in so much pain?

"Oh, my God, I can't believe this is happening," Monica sobbed.

She felt unsteady on her feet so I led her to a couch. As soon as she was settled comfortably, I stalked over to the chief and demanded, "What's going on?"

Chief James, looking every bit of his fifty-five years, rubbed roughly at his eyes. "Joseph drove his car off a cliff. I don't know why he did it. He left a note. Monica found it on the kitchen table."

"Smitty had no reason to kill himself, none whatsoever." My partner would have told me if things were *that* bad. *Wouldn't he?* "Where's the note?"

The chief handed over a slip of paper sealed in a plastic bag. Smitty had written fewer than ten words: "I'm sorry, I can't do this anymore."

"Were there any other cars in the vicinity?" I asked desperately. "Any witnesses?"

"Not that we know of, *Detective*."

One of the uniforms wasn't looking too happy about my questioning the chief, but at that moment I didn't give a shit who or what he was, I just wanted answers. I was about to ask another question when Monica called my name, so I stifled the urge to grill everyone in the place and focused on her.

I didn't leave the house until noon the following day. In that time I hadn't learned any more information than I'd walked in the door with. All I knew for certain was that my partner was dead, an apparent suicide.

As I trudged up to my apartment, I felt inexplicably angry. *How could he just take his life like that? Leave the woman he loved. Leave me, his partner, his friends. What had gotten so bad in his life that he decided to check out?* I had to wonder if I'd had something to do with it. Had he regretted the decision to help me? Did he still fear that I was going to turn myself in and bring us all down? Even if he did, was that a reason to *kill* himself?

I took a hot shower, dressed slowly, and dragged myself into the office. It was the second-hardest thing I'd ever had to do.

❖

"It's necessary to put you on a desk job for a few weeks, Everett."

I looked into the captain's cold blue eyes, searching for sorrow. I saw nothing, not even pity. I had seen eyes the same shade of blue before, though I couldn't remember where. But those eyes were different. Warm, somehow inviting. Either this woman was great at hiding her feelings, or she was one cold-hearted bitch.

"Wait, I must have missed something, because I thought I heard you say you were putting me on a desk?"

"It's standard procedure."

"Captain, I'm a detective. You're demoting me?"

"No, I'm putting you on a desk until we can find you a suitable new partner. And so that you can grieve for Smitty. I can only repeat how very sorry I am. We all are. His loss is a huge blow to us all." The words flowed from her mouth as if she rehearsed the speech daily, but I saw nothing in her eyes that made them ring true.

Anger threatened to send me over the edge, but I clenched my jaw and was able to contain myself. "What do you mean a *suitable* new partner? You mean one of those stiff-assed college grads you've got

walking around here? The ones that throw out the red carpet every time
you sashay through the door? No, thank you, I'll work alone."

"I wasn't *asking* you if you wanted a partner, Everett. I'm telling
you. You can't work alone. Look how much trouble you get into even
with a responsible partner."

That statement hit hard. *She's right. If Smitty hadn't helped me
when he did, I would be in jail right now. And maybe Smitty would be
alive.* My gut clenched. I felt the overwhelming urge to cry. I got to my
feet instead.

"I know how you feel, Everett."

I looked down at the cold woman in front of me. "How could you
know, Captain? Have you ever lost a partner? Have you ever even had
one?"

The thinning of her lips told me I had gone too far. What was she
going to do? Fire me? Shit, did I even want this job anymore?

"Report to Records. They're expecting you," she said grimly.

I walked out of her office without another word. I suppressed the
urge to slam the door, closing it quietly behind me instead. My hand
still on the doorknob, I gazed in shock at Smitty's desk. Two young
suits were going through his stuff. Both wore suits that had to be new
and way too expensive for a cop's salary. One, a chunky blond, had
his flabby ass propped against my desk. His forehead was too large,
a misfortune underscored by a severe haircut, and his skin could only
be described as an even pink color. Normally I would have felt some
kinship, as I suffer from fair skin myself, but I wanted to beat the guy
around the head already. His partner wore his brown hair in a slicked-
back ponytail that looked like it would start to fry if you added heat. I
sneered as I noticed the glint of clear polish on his nails.

"I wonder how these people even made it to these positions. Look
at this shit, man. Did this guy ever clean up?"

Flabby Ass poked a pile of papers on my desk. "This one isn't
much better. A dyke, from what I heard. So she probably made detective
by screwing anyone that asked. At least her loser partner went for the
big fish and married the chief's daughter."

I don't know if I yelled, screamed, or what, but I was on Ponytail in
seconds. I landed at least six blows before his colleague finally dragged
me off. I elbowed Flabby Ass in the stomach, and as he doubled over
I kicked him in the shin and emptied the contents of the nearest trash
can on him. Even winded, he howled in pain or outrage. I've always

been one to keep doing what works, so I kicked him hard in the shin again. I don't believe in fighting fair, never have. I do what I need to do to win.

"Everett."

I froze as the captain's angry voice screamed out my name.

"Get your ass in here right now."

I gave my two punching bags a glower. "I promise I'm not finished with either of you. Stay—away—from Smitty's shit!"

I watched them both pale, and then the chronically pink one seemed to get some balls from somewhere. "I'm going to press charges against your crazy ass. We've got a whole division that saw you attack me without provocation."

The look on his face was so triumphant that I wanted—no, needed to fuck with this guy. "Hmm, is that right?" I poked my head into the captain's office and smiled beatifically. "Be right there, Captain. Just need to tell someone something." I closed the door against her enraged yell before turning back to the two suits.

"Anybody in here see me attack this guy without provocation?" I asked.

When the puzzled shrugs and denials got tedious, the two jerks got flustered and mumbled something about the captain.

I said, "Yeah, by all means, feel free to press those charges and ask her to help you file them. I just hope you never need backup."

"Hey, is that a threat?" Ponytail asked angrily.

"What's your problem? Your partner here slap you upside the head with his dick stick too many times? That was no threat, that was a promise." With that, I walked into the captain's office to receive what I hoped would be no more then a stern lecture.

"I'm putting you on a medical leave of absence," she said, furiously scribbling on a sheet of paper. "I don't know why you're on this self-destructive tear, but I'm not about to let you bring this department down with you." She pushed the paper in front of me. "Don't come back without a clearance from the psychologist."

I grabbed the paper and shoved it into my back pocket. And without so much as a by-your-leave, I walked away.

"Everett!" she ordered coldly. "Leave your gun."

I stopped walking. "You want my gun?"

"You'll get it back when you're cleared for duty again."

I ripped my gun out of the nylon holster, emptied the clip, stormed across the room, and set both on her desk with a thump. "I suppose you want my badge, too, right?" I slammed that down as well and stalked toward the door that separated her from the real police officers.

"I mean it this time, Everett!" I heard her shout behind me.

I raised my hand in a regal half-wave and growled, "Whatever." As I exited the building, I checked my watch. 2:06. *Good. Perfect time to have a cocktail...or ten.*

❖

I slid off my bar stool and waved drunkenly to Stacy, or at least the blur I thought was Stacy. She'd tried to cut me off several times during the evening, but I kept reminding her that I was an adult and I wasn't driving. She was well within her rights to refuse me service, but she had no doubt heard about Smitty on that damned police scanner of hers and was probably trying to cut me some slack.

I avoided making eye contact with Riley as I approached the exit. She hadn't been there when I came in earlier, as Stacy didn't start accepting covers until the evening. I felt ashamed that I'd sat there all night silently getting plastered, but shame was not enough to stop me from drinking. I could feel Riley's stare the whole time, just like I felt it now, but I refused to look at her. I hoped she didn't think that a shared kiss and a few friendly words made us best buds, 'cause it didn't. I didn't want any friends. Actually, I didn't even want any acquaintances. Riley probably would have made a good friend. She seemed to be a sensitive and caring individual. But I wasn't used to dealing with people who gave a shit about others just because. It was in her best interests if she stayed away from me.

She didn't utter a word as I stumbled out into the night. Perversely, I was disappointed. Maybe I was wrong about her. Maybe she wasn't as caring as I'd thought. The chilly air hit my face, and I become annoyingly sober. Tucking my hands in my pockets, I emitted a soft curse. As usual, I was not wearing a coat, and as usual, I would be freezing my ass off.

I had just made the decision to jog the block or two home when I was grabbed from behind and pushed into a small alley between two buildings. I didn't have time to struggle, let alone scream, before several blows to my ribs doubled me over and dropped me to all fours. The act of breathing sent pain ripping through my body. Gingerly I reached for my gun, only to recall with stunning clarity handing my weapon over to the captain with nary a whimper. I always knew she would be the death of me.

"Listen up, bitch," my attacker growled before he landed a kick to my stomach that lifted me up off the ground and left me curled in a fetal position on my side. "We've got a message for you. Keep your big mouth shut. You got that?"

"Man, she got it. Let's go."

"Shut up. I know what I'm doing."

This was the first clue I had that there were two attackers, not just one. It would be harder to get away. When I'd felt the first blow to my stomach, it had instantly occurred to me that the two suits I'd jumped on were getting their revenge. They would rough me up a bit, but leave me alive and regretting the embarrassment I had caused them. But the voices of these two were all wrong. They were young, streetwise, and frighteningly unfamiliar.

"You see that, man?" the deeper voice gloated. "That's what you do to dogs when they're a problem. Kick them in the stomach, and they get the point."

Yanked up and pushed back against the wall, I waited for fists to rain down on me again. But they never came. I heard punches and groans but no one laid a hand on me. I slid slowly down the nasty-ass wall and waited with my forehead in my hand for either salvation or another ass-kicking.

When the staccato of running footsteps penetrated my fuzzy mind, I tried to speak, but I could only cough a few times.

"Foster, are you okay?"

I recognized that muffled voice instantly. "Riley?"

"Yeah, come on, let's get out of here."

She helped me stand, and I began to take a deep breath before I thought better of it.

"Who were they?" she asked.

"No idea. Probably muggers."

"Probably." Her voice sounded more clipped than usual.

"Shit!" I wheezed, running my hands over my pants pockets. "I can't find my keys. They were in my hand when I left the club, but now I don't know where they are."

Shockingly, I felt tears well up in my eyes. I was suspended from my job, Smitty was dead, and someone had just kicked the shit out of me.

"It's okay." Riley wrapped her arms around me.

Like a small child, I buried my nose in her shirt and inhaled her fresh, clean scent. No perfume, no special scented soaps, just cleanness that seemed to emanate from her very pores. And beneath all that, the faintest scent of chocolate, or maybe it was just a memory of happier times.

"We'll never be able to find those damn keys without a flashlight."

"I'll drive you to the hospital," Riley said.

I shook my head emphatically. Someone had just sent me a message, and until I knew what it meant, I needed to stay away from paperwork and mandatory reporting. "No. I just need to lie down."

"I can take you to my place." She seemed embarrassed. "It isn't much, but it's quiet. Maybe you can get some sleep."

"What about Stacy?"

"I'll call her after we get to my place."

As Riley helped me to her truck, I wondered how she had been there to save my ass. Had she seen my attackers follow me? It suddenly occurred to me that I was about to allow a woman I didn't really know to take me to some undisclosed destination in the middle of the night. Nobody knew where I was. Apprehension curled in my stomach like a cobra waiting to strike. My ribs ached and I had a splitting headache. I would not be able to fight if I had to. Riley helped me into the vehicle and slammed the door with a sturdy thunk. I've always enjoyed the smell and sound of older vehicles, don't ask me why. Some people like the smell of gasoline or rubbing alcohol; I like old vehicles.

I peered dazedly through the windshield as we drove. Eventually a dark building loomed in front of me with no visible lights on inside. I didn't see any other vehicles in the area. My door opened with a loud creak that amplified my fears. The dome light came on with a flicker that barely illuminated the cab. My heart beat an extra thrum of relief as I looked into Riley's honest blue eyes. This woman was trying to help me, someone she barely knew, for no reason other than that she was a nice person. I could see no animosity or dishonesty in her face. And frankly, right now I had no choice. I needed to trust her. I was too tired and hurt to do anything else.

"Let me help you." She took my arm and I eased from the vehicle, wincing as my ribs protested the movement.

I could barely see her. Pain was making it hard for me to concentrate. I wheezed as I put one foot in front of the other. I vaguely wondered whether I should be alarmed at the amount of broken glass that I seemed to be treading on. Where was she taking me? I had no idea how long we'd been driving, so I wasn't even sure if we were still within the city limits.

Although I was unsure of my footing, Riley was obviously used to trekking in the darkness. She moved with assurance for a few more steps and then stopped. I heard her stick a key in a lock and open a door. She flipped a switch and then stepped into the building, holding the heavy door open for me. The light from inside beckoned. I was not in any shape to argue, so I simply walked in, the theme from *Phantom of the Opera* playing eerily in my head.

"Riley, what is this place?"

"An old movie theater. This is where I live."

"An old movie theater," I repeated, holding my side and wondering if I was the stupidest moron on Earth to let her bring me here. For all I knew, she could be a serial killer.

"This way." She led me down a hall, flipping lights as she went.

Sweat rolled down my spine from the effort of walking while I was in so much pain. "Why do you live in a movie theater?" I asked. For some reason, I was trying to avoid walking through the door she was patiently holding open.

"Because I have no money and it's free." The statement was made without any self-pity or embarrassment.

"Oh." *Okay, Everett, you're going to have to trust her.* I mentally gave myself a shove and, with a final look at her, I walked through the door.

Though the lighting was dim, I could still see the vestiges of what had probably been a fine movie house in its day. High-backed burgundy seats close to a hundred in number littered the floors in varying stages of disrepair. The chairs themselves were a dark oak, and even underneath the film of dust, I could tell that they would look beautiful when cleaned up.

"I never knew this place existed."

"Beautiful, isn't it?" Her voice had a dreamy quality. I used that moment to study her face. Though her features were prominent, they weren't at all hard. I wondered why I had thought she looked mean or unapproachable when I first met her. Right now she looked...well, young, innocent, even naïve.

"Yes, it's wonderful," I said.

"Restoration starts as soon as the permits are issued." Riley looked into my eyes at that moment and seemed to get embarrassed. "I'm sorry. You're tired. Let's get to my apartment."

She didn't wait for me to respond before she started toward the opposite end of the theater. When she reached the stage, I watched in amazement as she slid a door back and reached in. She appeared to feel around for a minute before, with a click, she flipped a light switch. "Careful, the stairs are narrow."

I followed her, expecting to see a dive, a place that was suitable to crash in when one was without better living arrangements. "Holy shit," I breathed as we reached the bottom step. This was no dive. Someone had put a lot of time into making this space into a home.

The apartment, though not huge by any means, was actually bigger than my studio. It had a nautical feel. The hardwood floors were painted a dark blue, as were the walls and shelving. Only the ceiling was white. Though there were no windows in the place, there were actual portholes from a ship on both sides of the room. In one corner, on a raised platform, Riley's sleeping area was furnished with a double bed, a nightstand, and a cart that held a small TV and DVD player. A miniature kitchen area, complete with a sink, microwave, and stove, was to the right. Two doors were to my left, one of which I hoped led to the restroom.

"Wow, this place is really something." Pain shot up from my side and robbed me of my breath. "Aw shit," I moaned.

Riley caught me as I toppled forward. "I've got you."

And she did have me. She lifted me easily, carried me over to the bed, and laid me down. "I need to look at your side. Could have broken ribs." Her strangely clipped speech pattern seemed more pronounced. Perhaps it got that way when she was worried.

"No, these are just bruised. Hurts, though." I fought the urge to cough. I knew any sudden movement would mean a shitload of pain. This had been quite a day. I gazed up at the ceiling. "They're clouds. You painted clouds on the ceiling."

The luminous forms were outlined in a light blue, so delicate that at first glance it looked like a plain white ceiling. The effect was relaxing, like sleeping under the open sky. My eyelids fluttered a few times as I fought the urge to just close them and allow myself to sleep.

The bed dipped as Riley sat down next to me. She showed me a bottle. "Painkillers."

"Good idea. Thank you." I allowed her to feed me two white pills and obediently drank the cold water she offered. The annoying itch at the back of my throat abated for the time being. "Why did you paint the sky on your ceiling?" I asked her.

Her answer should have been sad, but it wasn't. She spoke with a straightforward honesty I wasn't used to. "Because for most of my life, it was the only pretty thing I saw."

CHAPTER SIX

"Foster, I'm back."
I jerked awake and looked up to see a naked Riley gazing down at me. Okay, so she wasn't exactly naked, but she might as well have been. She had on a cropped tank top that left nothing to the imagination and a pair of gray cotton shorts that hugged every curve on her body. If I hadn't been in so much pain, I'm sure I would have been salivating. Riley did have a gorgeously sculpted body. She obviously put in a lot of work for it to look as it did.

I eased upright and reached under my shirt to find tape wrapped neatly around my ribs. When had she done that?

"I was afraid you'd hurt yourself in your sleep," she explained. "I got you as comfortable as I could."

She had taken my bra and shoes and socks off, and unbuttoned my pants. I flushed. My habit of not wearing underwear had finally caught up with me. Hopefully she hadn't gotten a glimpse of my "world" while she was trying to get me comfortable.

She backed away and turned on the light in the kitchen. "You hungry? I went to the store."

"No, not really." The thought of eating made me queasy. I watched her hands as she quickly diced tomatoes. Her face was hard to read, but I knew I'd sounded ungrateful, so I tried to make amends. "Look, what I really wanted to say was, thank you." She didn't bother looking up at me, so I cleared my throat. "I mean it, Riley. Thank you for being there for me, okay?"

Finally the efficient hands paused, and she glanced up. I could see the smile in her eyes and concluded I was back in her good graces.

I decided to try to push my luck a bit. "Hey, do you think I could go with you when you go to work tomorrow? I want to check out the alley before it gets too dark."

"Why?"

"Those guys weren't really trying to mug me. They said something about not hurting me, and I should keep my mouth shut. It was odd."

She wasn't making eye contact with me. "I picked up your things. They're over there."

I figured she didn't want to talk about the incident. People got like that about frightening events. I instantly forgot about her behavior, though, as I zoomed in on Bud's orange two-story condo, complete with the long tube that he loved to storm through, and fresh food for him to munch on. "Oh, wow, how did you do this? Did you break in or something?"

"I went back to the alleyway and found your keys. I'm sorry I had to go through your stuff while you weren't there," she said. "I couldn't find underwear. I would have bought you some new ones, but the stores aren't open this time of night."

I grinned. *She is so cute.* She must have looked away when she unzipped my jeans, 'cause I hadn't had undies in my house since the last time I brought someone home from Secrets two years ago.

"Hey, you think I could take a shower?"

"You should rest."

"I need to go to the bathroom," I told her sharply. "And I want to get clean."

I wasn't being the best patient in the world, and I could tell by the look in her eye that she didn't appreciate being snapped at. What was I doing? In the few days that I'd known Riley, I had embarrassed her by kissing her in front of a dozen women, nearly gotten her killed, and snapped at her. And I'd only remembered to say thank you after.

She approached the bed, "Do you need help? I mean with the bandages?"

"Yeah, I probably will." I turned my back to her and carefully pulled my T-shirt over my head, holding it in front of me to cover my breasts. I waited expectantly for her to undo the bandages. After several seconds, I turned and looked at her over my left shoulder to find her glaring angrily at my back. "What?"

"Should have gotten there sooner," she growled. "They must've hit you a few times before I made it."

"I'm just glad you got there, period." I replayed the attack in my mind. "Riley, why *were* you there?"

She fumbled with the bandages, her knuckles grazing my back. I heard her go into her dresser drawer and remove what I assumed would be the scissors. It occurred to me briefly that I had turned my back on a woman I didn't really know.

"Stacy said that you normally don't drink that much," she said. "We were worried."

I waited patiently while she cut through the bandages.

"I follow you most nights. I usually watch you until you get to your apartment," she said.

"You do?" I frowned at the wall, shocked by her admission. That she had followed me without my knowledge was like a dash of cold water. I'd been so wrapped up with my problems, I'd failed to keep my guard up and it had almost cost me dearly.

She made a gesture with her finger for me to turn around again. I did, still clutching the T-shirt to my chest in some false sense of modesty.

"Why?" I asked. "I'm a detective, remember? I can take care of myself."

She looked at me like I had her in the sights of a deer rifle. "I wasn't going to. Stacy knew. She thought you might need help."

I smiled at her, wanting to ease her embarrassment. "Aw, shit. Look, Riley, I'm sorry about everything."

"You didn't ask for this," she said shortly.

"I know, but I am sorry for putting you through so much trouble. And I wanted to say thank you for helping me and letting me sleep here and, you know, taking care of me," I finished lamely.

"You're welcome. We'll put new bandages on after you shower."

I nodded and started the painful process of getting to my feet. Every move I made resulted in a dull aching pain that shot from one side of my body to the other. She gently wrapped her arms around my waist instead of taking my hands as I thought she would, and then slowly raised me to my feet. Even with her help, I still had to bite the inside of my cheek to keep from screaming.

"Okay?"

"Yes," I said breathlessly. Why was I trying to put up a front? I hurt so much I wanted to whine.

"Can you make it to the bathroom alone?"

I nodded while thinking, *Lady, I will hold it rather than let you see me sitting on the toilet.*

❖

I walked into the bathroom, turned on the shower, and stepped under the soothing spray. I had no idea how grimy I felt until I actually started getting clean. I washed my hair with some of Riley's shampoo, idly wondering what her hair looked like when it wasn't in a braid. I closed my eyes and my mind began to wander. I imagined being in this confined space with Riley, my hands gliding over firm, water-slicked skin. The sensation in my loins was not an unfamiliar one. I wasn't exactly a virgin, but I was never one to become aroused at the drop of a hat. In fact, it had been a long time since anyone had garnered a passing spark from me. But there was something about Riley, something so different that it aroused my curiosity, physically and mentally.

God, don't do it, Everett. Do not start thinking about Riley that way. She's off-limits. Hell, she'll probably be leaving soon—going to go and marry that boyfriend of hers, who probably looks like Mr. Charles Atlas himself. They'll have 1.2 children and a white picket fence, with a dog named Lassie or Skip or some corny-ass shit like that.

Surprisingly enough, none of that sounded bad—well, all except for the Mr. Atlas part. I leaned a flushed cheek against the tiled wall. I was behaving like an adolescent. Perhaps it was because she saved my life. Normally I wouldn't be worried about an attraction to a woman. I was a lesbian, after all. But Riley was straight, and could probably kill me with one look.

I stuck my head under the spray and rinsed the shampoo from my hair. I froze, my hand on the shower nozzle, as I realized where my thoughts had taken me. I was a self-proclaimed loner. I had never dated the same woman for more than six months. I was by no means a womanizer. I had never felt comfortable enough to share my life with anyone. It was almost an annoyance when a relationship went past the sex stage and progressed to the "let's talk about our future together" stage. That's usually when I started feeling trapped. So why would I suddenly think that settling down didn't sound so bad? *I must be getting old.*

Riley was waiting with a change of clothes when I came out of the bathroom. "I need a shower, too. That alley was filthy."

"All right." I plastered a fake smile on my face.

"Take it easy," she said, gesturing toward my ribs. "I'll bandage those when I'm clean."

As soon as she'd closed the bathroom door, I felt lonely so I went over to Bud's pet condo. Riley had already fed him. Bud shot through his tunnel and hooked a right. I grinned at his explosion of activity and took it to mean he was happy to see me. I looked around the room, awestruck at Riley's carpentry skills. She'd said something about doing most of the renovations to this apartment herself. I would have to ask her where she learned to do all this.

Most detectives are inherently nosy people, and I was curious about Riley. The only information I had was from Stacy. I knew Riley was a bouncer, originally from northern California, that she was straight, and that she'd just graduated from college. Oh yeah, and she lived in an abandoned movie theater.

I removed Bud from his condo and placed him on my shoulder. "You shit on me, and you're going to be sitting in the oven next to the chicken, you got that, mister?"

My mouse-escape alibi in hand, I started to explore. I figured I would hear Riley shut off the shower and have time to get back to the kitchen so I wouldn't be caught snooping. But if I was, I would blame Bud for escaping.

I pushed open the door and peered into the next room. It was extremely small with no windows. There was a large blue mat on the floor with a black padded bench and several round weights stacked neatly in piles. From what Riley had said, she didn't have much money, so it stood to reason that she didn't have a gym membership. Shit, she could have mine if she was gonna be staying here.

I was about to leave the room when the detective in me decided to look behind the door. Two pictures were taped to the painted wood. I leaned forward to read the names. Lou Ferrigno and Cory Everson. Both pictures looked pretty old, so my guess was that she had had them for a few years.

I had never heard of Everson, but Lou Ferrigno had played the Incredible Hulk on television back in the seventies. My father and I would watch that all the time when I was a kid and he was trying to make up for missing out on some aspect of my life. Remembering Riley's Incredible Hulk comic, I figured she must have a thing for the big guys. I shook my head in disappointment.

I left the room, making sure to leave the door as I had found it, and listened briefly as I passed the bathroom. Riley took long showers like I did. I pulled Bud off my shoulder, where he had been still for a little too long for my taste, and held him in my hand as I entered another small room.

This one was more interesting. A laptop and printer sat on a battered and scarred wooden desk. *Interesting. Riley has no money, yet she has a laptop and a printer.* On either side of the desk, boxes were piled high around the walls. After assuring myself that the shower was still running, I made a beeline for one of the boxes and lifted the lid. My God, the woman had hundreds and hundreds of comic books. I opened a few more boxes. Each held at least a hundred comic books, every one enclosed in a plastic bag with white cardboard. Riley was becoming more interesting by the moment.

With a twinge of guilt, I closed the boxes and sat down in front of the computer. The woman had saved my ass and brought me back to her place to nurse me back to health. Was it right of me to go through her shit, just to appease my curiosity?

"Definitely," I whispered. I only wished I'd looked in her medicine cabinet while I was in the bathroom.

I hit the power button on the side of her computer and hissed in disgust as a "request for password" window appeared. "Damn it, Riley, you live alone. Why would you need a password on your computer?" Of course, the fact that I was now trying to snoop through her stuff did occur to me, but that was different.

I halfheartedly tried Lou Ferrigno, The Hulk, and Cory Everson, to no avail. It occurred to me that I didn't know Riley's last name, or I could try that, too. Keeping one ear trained on the bathroom, I dug around in desk drawers, hoping to find a piece of mail that would tell me Riley's last name. I pulled out an unopened cell phone bill. I wasn't surprised that it was addressed to a PO box in town.

"Riley Medeiros, huh? Very nice, it suits you." I always talk to myself. It comes from being an only child. I put the phone bill back and was just about to close the drawer when I spotted a picture sitting on top of a stack of mail. "Son of a bitch."

I set Bud down on the desk and pulled the drawer all the way out. I would have recognized that picture anywhere. It was the one of me taken my first day on the force. I looked young and slightly dazed, but exceedingly happy. How did Riley get my picture? I didn't even have this one myself, aside from on my police ID, and I'd given that to the captain when I turned in my gun and badge. This picture was not the same size as the one on my badge. It was bigger. How did Riley get it and why did she have it?

It dawned on me then that I could be in danger. Riley might have some agenda in bringing me here and gaining my trust. She had a good fifty pounds on me, and with my injuries and her height, she would be able to handle me quite easily. I scooped Bud up, not bothering to turn off the laptop or close the drawers, or sweep off the little deposits he'd left on the desk.

It took me several painful minutes to get out of the theater and into the only vehicle in the parking lot, using keys on the chain I'd swiped from the kitchen counter. By now, Riley was probably out of the shower and aware that I'd gone through her stuff. I almost sobbed in relief when one of the keys turned in the ignition and the engine sputtered to life.

I turned on the headlights and gasped as the door to the theater flung open.

Riley came running out. "Foster?"

I threw the car into reverse and, in a spray of smoke, backed up the road. To my great shock, Riley managed to stay just in front of my headlights.

"Foster, let me explain," she yelled.

The smell of burning rubber alerted me to the fact that I had left the emergency brake on. I disengaged it with a lurch that sent me careening up the path and away from her. When I had put a significant distance between us, I whipped the car around and got my bearings. The movie theater was in an old part of Century City, where few people went because there wasn't much of a business district there anymore. In the sparse traffic, I made it to the Secrets parking lot in twenty minutes.

I didn't relish the walk home with my unbandaged ribs, but I didn't want to give her any reason to contact me again so I had to leave the car behind. Once I was safely locked in my apartment, I reached under my bed, pulled out my strongbox, and unlocked it. My father had given me a Glock 9 millimeter right before I joined the force. I had never really had a need to use it, though I preferred this gun to my service weapon. Riley, if that was even her real name, would have a surprise waiting if she ever tried to mess with Foster Everett again.

Chapter Seven

The day of Smitty's funeral dawned clear and bright, belying the fact that it was truly one of the worst days of my life. Sleep had evaded me the night before. I think I was half fearing, half hoping that I would hear from Riley. I didn't.

I made my way to the cemetery as if in a fog. Monica rushed to me and enveloped me in her arms. This time, however, instead of the sweet kiss or the playful teasing about my clothes, she clung to me, her hands balled into fists and pressing into my back. I closed my eyes and tried to stem the flow of tears that was coming down my face.

Bougainvillea graced the lattice at each end of the path we walked to Smitty's final place of rest. The lovely blooms perfumed the air and I gripped Monica's hand in one of mine and held on to a white rose with the other. I didn't listen to any of the words that were said by Smitty's friends and family. I couldn't. Pain wrenched at my heart as I realized so little of him had been removed from the molten heap of his car that Smitty's remains would not even fill half of the coffin.

When it came time, I dropped the rose into the hole that served as a receptacle for the sorrows of the living. I wished Smitty good-bye, made the mandatory small talk with Chief James, then held Monica and kissed her cheek. "If you need me, you know where I am."

With a final look at Smitty's gravesite, I walked slowly away, my ribs protesting every calming breath I took. I would not return. There was nothing of my partner here, just remnants of a body. I would hold him close to my heart and in my memory. I climbed into the backseat of a cab and looked out the window. As we drove, I waited for the beautiful, sunny day to thaw my overcast heart with its spiteful warmth.

❖

"Well, Everett, I see you put one over on the shrink again."

"I don't know what you mean, Captain."

I could tell that she wanted to say more, but in deference to the fact that I had just lost my partner, she forced herself to let it go. I watched with interest as a small vein pounded in her temple. To think that I'd once grudgingly conceded that she might be attractive. There was nothing vaguely attractive about this woman. Even the clothes she wore seemed contrived to make people think she was powerful.

She pushed a sheet of paper toward me, a malicious glint in her eye. "Your new assignment."

I told myself not to flip, but when I saw the department head listed, I almost lost control. In general, civilians staffed the Records Department for our division. Occasionally, if someone on the force got hurt or, for whatever reason, could not perform on the street, they were allowed to work in departments like Records. In other words, it's a boring-ass desk job.

I asked coolly, "What is this, Captain?"

"The psychologist felt that in your emotional state it isn't a good idea for you to not be at work. But he can't make me reinstate you in your normal capacity."

"I'm a detective, not a goddamn file clerk!" Okay, my voice was raised a little, but I still felt I was in control.

"You're a loose cannon, is what you are. You think anyone wants to partner with you? They know they'd not only have to watch their own back, but yours, too. Poor Smitty—"

"*Poor Smitty* killed himself, lady."

I stopped myself from continuing because my anger wasn't really directed at her, it was directed at Smitty. I felt betrayed that he'd left me here to handle this shit on my own. His suicide made me realize I didn't know him at all. It's one thing to lose your partner in the line of duty. It's another if he takes his own life. It's almost like you failed in some way. Like you didn't have his back when you should have.

Over the week since Smitty's funeral, I'd racked my brain for a reason. I looked at his dire decision from every direction, and I still couldn't see why he would do such a thing. Every time we talked, he was the strong one and I was the one who couldn't handle the heat. Even if he was afraid I would come clean, he had to know I would never implicate him. What could be so bad that he would give up on his life and family?

I had gone back to the psychologist because it was either that or waste away in my apartment. I told him what he wanted to hear so that I could get back to work. By the time I left his office, the psychologist was chastising the captain for having removed me from the "only stable thing in her life right now." It was a short-lived high.

The captain started tapping her pen on a yellow legal pad. "You're of no use to me right now, Detective. I can't put you back on the streets, not in the state you're in, and that's final."

Anger fought to be let loose on this pompous, self-confident bitch, but I controlled myself and sighed. "For how long?"

"For as long as it takes you to get control of yourself."

"Come on. You need to give me something better than that."

"You have a follow-up appointment with the doctor in a month. If he clears you to return to your usual duties, we can talk then." She leaned back in her chair and waited. I could tell she expected me to fly off the deep end, and indeed, I almost did.

"Okay, Captain. Thank you for your time."

I stood up. The look of shock on her face was almost enough to make my demotion, however temporary, seem worth it. Who was I kidding? I was furious. All I wanted to do was quit this damn job and move to the deep backwoods for twenty years. But I would not give her the satisfaction of scaring me off, not yet anyway. I walked out of her office, deliberately avoiding the eyes of the traitors who had buttered me up with their concern just moments before but who had not wanted to partner with me. Cops are a superstitious bunch, detectives even more so. The fact that Smitty had killed himself left a stigma on me worse than the stink from a corpse.

❖

The Records Department was located in the basement. For all that it didn't have any windows to the outside, it was actually a rather cheerful place, thanks to the head of the department—Marcus Vansant. As I walked up to the bulletproof glass, I frowned. Why would anyone want to shoot up a records room? The need for security, definitely, but bulletproof glass was just plain overkill. I would have to ask Marcus about that.

"Hey, is Marcus here?" I asked the woman sitting at the desk, popping gum.

"No." A bright, fake smile spread across her face, which disappeared as she returned to her computer. *In other words, go away, annoying bitch,* I thought.

Her smart-ass response pissed me off so I asked, "Do I have a 'fuck with me' sign plastered on my face or something?"

"Hey, Maaaarcus?" she yelled, without looking up from her computer screen.

Aside from the constant working of her jaw, she was attractive. Her short hair had a slight tinge of pink to it. Made me think of some of the girls from my neighborhood back when I was a kid in New York. Many of them would get a similar effect with raspberry Kool-Aid. I wanted to do it, but my father forbade me. He said I would look like a homegirl.

Heavyset Marcus emerged from somewhere and walked up to the window. His attractive brown face lit up as he realized who was standing on the other side of the bulletproof glass. "Oh my gawd, Foster, where you been, girl? I haven't seen you since the drag show over at Stacy's."

Marcus and I went way back. I didn't get to talk to him much, but I really liked him. Partly because he was the only openly gay person in the building, and partly because he was just a personable kind of guy. Marcus was also a drag queen. He wore these six-inch heels that made me wince just thinking about them. They probably accounted for his ability to walk like he was balancing a book on top of his head.

"Hey, Marcus." Maybe this wouldn't be so bad after all. "Captain told me I had to come down here and work with you for a while until I can get myself 'emotionally together.'"

"Well, shit." Marcus pursed his lips and looked me up and down. "Maybe you should have your own office, then, 'cause you're going to be here for a while."

The henna-haired chick at the computer cackled, and they high-fived while I just glowered. "All right, you two, that's just wonderful. Make fun of the traumatized white chick over here."

For the first time in a long time, I felt some of the pressure around my heart lift. I had to crack a smile. Marcus could always get one out of me, no matter how hard I tried to be mad.

He unlocked the door to the file room. "I was sorry to hear about

Smitty. You going to be okay?" He touched my shoulder, and I had to blink several times to keep the tears from brimming over. Damn, I was turning into the biggest wuss.

"Marcus, I didn't come here to cuddle. Show me what I'm supposed to be doing here, so I can get on with it." I hoped he wouldn't take offense, but I needed to get some semblance of order in my life. Hard work was the only thing that would keep me from feeling sorry for myself.

"You got it, woman. Follow me." He led me around large shelves overflowing with files from cases that had been worked on in the last ten years. As we walked, he explained some basics I would need to know. The files were color-coded according to the year they were opened.

Marcus pulled out a file and opened it. "See this? It's a log we keep whenever a new piece of evidence or info is added to the file. You folks are not supposed to return the file unless it has all its parts. Nor are you supposed to add anything without having me or Chandra code it. But it happens all the time. That's why every year we have to go through this gigantic process of making sure each file is fully intact."

"What if it isn't?" I really didn't care, to be perfectly honest, but Marcus was my friend, and the least I could do was pretend to find his work interesting.

"Well, then, that's where the fun begins. Technically, we can't send files out to storage unless they are complete. Your desk is over here." He pointed to a desk piled high with case files.

My job would be checking files that were not intact and trying to find the slob detective who had the missing material.

"All you have to do is scan in the barcode and you'll see the name of the last person to check out the file. That's the cop who probably has the missing documentation."

"What if they don't know what they did with it?"

Marcus shrugged. "The file gathers dust for a while. Occasionally we find things in the wrong case file, but most of the time we just note the log and send it off to storage incomplete."

I knew from my cold case work that once a trail went cold, cases were seldom picked back up again unless we received new information or a confession. On those occasions files were pulled out of storage. Thank God criminals were dumbasses and often couldn't keep their mouths shut. That's where Smitty and I came in, I thought sadly.

Marcus went on to blind me with science about how each piece of information was bar-coded based on category, such as "crime scene photo," "informant info," and so on. A white gunlike apparatus read the barcode on the folder and the file name popped up on the computer.

Marcus loved his work, and the pleasure on his face as we talked made me wonder about my own happiness. I could never be this happy running a records room for the rest of my life. But did I really want to be a detective for the rest of my life, either?

In my first three weeks as a Records lackey, I had two psychiatric evaluations that came to nothing, but my ribs weren't hurting so much anymore. I avoided any and all contact with the detectives from my division. I also didn't answer my home phone, which had developed the annoying habit of ringing off the hook. Much to my delight and or chagrin, depending on the time of day, I had also not heard from Riley, and thoughts of her intruded at the oddest moments. I did my best to ignore them.

I could have contacted her, of course. I could have asked her what she was doing with my photograph and how the "coincidence" of her following me around really came about, but instead I let time drift by. By this point, if her story was remotely true, she would be back in northern California and on her way to a career in physical therapy of some sorts. I told myself that even if there was an innocent explanation for the photograph and stalking behavior, Riley was a straight woman. What would be the point in getting in touch with her?

Marcus said I was one of the best workers that they'd had down there in years. The reason being I liked the slow, mind-numbing work. I didn't have to think or feel or use anything other than common sense. I was in the midst of doing just such a task when I came across something that made me pause.

"Hey, Marcus, look at this."

Several of the documents that should have been in the file were missing, and from the looks of it, whoever had taken them hadn't even bothered to remove them properly. There were still ragged pieces of paper in the seam of the folder where they had ripped the pages out.

Marcus had no doubt seen it all before. "Someone was in a hurry, and whoever it was is going to hear from me." He picked up the electronic gun and scanned the barcode.

I scrolled down my screen and clicked on the last date that the file had been checked out. In blocky red letters, the name of the guilty party appeared. I couldn't stop the gasp from escaping my throat. "Detective

Joseph Smith" flashed accusatorily before Marcus clicked out of the window and snapped me out of my stupor.

"You okay?" he asked.

"Yeah, I'm cool." This had been my automatic answer to most questions since Smitty's death. But you know what? I wasn't cool. I felt like I was in a fog and couldn't find my way out. Things had been happening to me that I had no control over. I felt powerless to stop whatever was going on, so I just sat back and let life wash over me.

I grabbed my keys and told Marcus I was going to get my lunch. With the way I was feeling, I wasn't sure I would even be back. Is this what it was like to have an emotional breakdown? I took the elevator up, making sure not to meet anyone's eyes directly. It was a relief to finally reach the exit, and I walked out into the damp air gratefully.

Rain had left the ground wet and smoke gray, and the sky wore a matching cast. Dreary though it was, being outside made me feel less lonely. I shoved my hands in my pockets and walked, head bowed, as thoughts of the last three weeks weighed me down. All of them kept leading back to two things that just didn't add up.

Smitty just didn't seem like the type who would ever commit suicide. Cops didn't do things like drive their cars off the sides of cliffs. That was the kind of thing that some drama queen would do. I would like to say that I'd never given this subject much thought, but everyone in my grim line of work has at some point. I would venture a guess that most cops would eat their own bullet rather than drive a car off a cliff. What if you survived and were maimed, or some such shit?

I stopped abruptly. White fog billowed out in front of me as I stood there frozen on the sidewalk. *Maybe it was an accident. Maybe something happened to the brakes, or Smitty fell asleep.*

Call it instinct, call it wishful thinking, but I knew with a certainty I couldn't explain that there was more to this "suicide" than a man deciding to kill himself because he hated his job or his marriage was rocky. The fact that Smitty had left a suicide note had closed my mind to alternatives. I was still baffled by his few words, but I wasn't satisfied with the obvious conclusions. If there was another explanation for his death, I wanted to uncover it.

I ran back to the office as fast as I could, thrilled when I found no one in the file room. I logged in and pulled up Smitty's accident report. Thanks to Marcus, each page held the file number of the original evidence pictures. The investigation seemed textbook. For whatever reason, it looked like Smitty had simply driven off the cliff. I printed out the documents, thumbing through the file Smitty had damaged while I waited.

Why would he tear out the pages? The case involved some porn ring masquerading as a cult. According to the ledger on the front of the folder, the missing pages had to do with the witness information. I tried to pull up the file on the computer, but was surprised to get an "access denied." The case was over four years old, but it should still have been in the database. I clicked on another window, pulled up Smitty's investigation code, and clicked on the file number to check the status. A blinking red "file not available" message told me I'd just reached a dead end. Not only had someone tampered with the paper file, it looked like they'd removed the computer record completely. I went over to the long wall of shelves and found the place where the rest of the porn case files *should* have been, but weren't.

Puzzled, I racked my brain for the next course of action. I didn't feel like traipsing upstairs and going through Smitty's desk, at least not until the area was clear, which meant I had to wait until the early morning hours. There had to be something I could do in the meantime.

I was vaguely aware of Chandra laughing at something from beyond the walls of files that screened me. I had been nothing but nice to her since I joined the Records team, even offering to take her to lunch a few times, but she still treated me like a pariah. Risking her wrath by interrupting one of her many personal conversations, I rolled my chair around the shelves and beckoned her with my finger. She resisted for a while, but my presence was a disruption to her personal life, so she finally pulled her headset off and flounced toward me with a lot of exasperated sighing. The woman even walked insolently. Her hips swayed from side to side in her long wraparound skirt, and the tight bodysuit left nothing to the imagination.

"And don't be checking me out, either." She glowered down at me sternly. "You ain't my type."

My pleasant thoughts screeched to a halt. "What makes you think you're *my* type?" I asked.

"You trying to say I'm not?"

Her question was probably one that I myself would have asked in a similar situation, but coming from Chandra it was just, well, shocking. She actually made me forget what I was going to say. "Yes. I mean no."

"Uh-huh." She popped her gum and leaned over my shoulder to look at my screen. "I mean, don't get me wrong, you're cute and all, but I'm married now. You're about two years too late. So, what are you trying to do here?"

I blinked at the screen. Straight woman were soo…I don't know what they were, but I needed to stay away from them. "Is there any way I can pull up all the cases that a certain detective has looked at in the last year? Marcus showed me how to find out who checked out a certain file, but he didn't show me how to do anything else."

"What do you need to see that for?"

"Aw, come on, Chandra, help me out here."

She folded her arms. The cute thing wasn't working for me today, so I made up what I hoped was a plausible excuse.

"Look, I just want to make sure that those idiots upstairs aren't screwing around with me and Smitty's cases, okay?"

"If you get me in trouble for this, I'm going to have that ass, *comprende*?"

Mind you, I didn't like her tone of voice, but I was trying to accomplish something. "Okay, I got it. Now will you show me, please?"

I watched carefully as she navigated the database through pull-down menus and eventually typed in "Foster Everett." *So she does know my name*, I thought smugly.

Every case I had ever requested popped up on the computer screen. "Wow, that's awesome, Chandra, thanks!"

"Mm-hmm." She was still unimpressed with me. Her hips were already sashaying back to her desk as I offered suitably flattering praise and thanks. "Just remember what I said. If you plan on messing up something, you didn't learn that from me."

My hands shook slightly as I returned to the menu and keyed in "Joseph Smith." A long list of entries appeared. About a week before he died, Smitty had requested several files that were no longer on the premises. It looked like his request had been frozen because he'd died before they could be transferred from storage. The odd thing was that even though he was my partner, I didn't recognize the cases he was looking into. They weren't ours.

Out of curiosity, I entered my code into the criminal records database and typed in "Riley Medeiros." The only thing that came up was an address in Oakland, California, and a code ARS, which meant she'd had a record as a minor and this had been sealed. There was also a reference to a Children's Services record dating back some twelve years. It was no longer listed in the database. I typed in my name and the division address. I could have Riley Medeiros's files in my hands in about three weeks. All I had to do was push send.

Impatient with myself, I clicked out of the screen instead and looked at my watch. It was after six and I hadn't eaten. Today was Thursday, chili day at Secrets, and normally I was the first in line when the small kitchen opened. But I hadn't been to the club since I'd dropped Riley's car off that night. I was still reluctant to go back. I knew Stacy wouldn't leave me alone until I told her everything.

I stood up and stretched the cramping muscles of my back, logged off the computer, and shut off my lamp.

As was her habit, Chandra had gone home for the evening without so much as a good-bye. I guess the bonding session wasn't as meaningful as I thought.

❖

The Records division doors automatically locked behind me as I walked toward the elevator. As usual, the hairs on the back of my neck stood up and I could not resist looking behind me. For some reason this hallway always creeped me out. It was a relief when I was finally in the relative safety of the enclosed elevator.

I picked up a burrito on my way home and made sure to check behind me as I turned the two corners that would lead me to my apartment. I had been cautious since the attack. If I didn't know better, maybe I could have convinced myself that I was the target of a gay-bashing, but my attackers were looking specifically for me, and were told by someone not to harm me too badly.

I entered my building with a sense of relief and pulled my keys out of my pocket. The plan was that I would let Bud take a quick spin around the studio while I ate my dinner/lunch, and then both of us were going to turn in early and hopefully get some sleep.

What is it they say about best-laid plans?

CHAPTER EIGHT

I'd actually been in a deep sleep for once when a sound at my window had me reaching instantly under my pillow for my Glock. I sat up in bed, my heart pounding loudly. I had almost convinced myself that it was my imagination when I heard it again and slid my feet to the floor. Someone was trying to raise my window. The sound I had heard was the squeaking of fingertips on glass. Someone had climbed up my fire escape and was trying to get into my apartment.

In a half crouch, I moved toward the curtained window, adrenaline pumping. I forced myself to relax as I waited for my would-be intruder to show his hand.

Tap, tap, tap. What the fuck? The person attempting to break into my apartment had the audacity to knock, like perhaps I would open the window and tell them to have at it. I was about to make my move when I saw a hand reach in the gap below the window. Stepping away from the now billowing curtain, I readied myself for a gun battle as a dark form gained entry so quickly I almost gasped aloud.

"Don't even breath, asshole," I said in a voice that could have been misconstrued as calm. I stuck my 9 millimeter between the intruder's shoulder blades, ready to fire in an instant.

"Foster?" The gruff familiar voice was deep, but definitely female.

"Riley?" I almost lowered my gun in shock before I remembered she had entered my home uninvited. "Stay right there. Don't you move."

I pushed her to her knees and backed away to flip on the light. Riley could easily have passed for your stereotypical house-breaker in tight black jeans, a knit cap that obscured all but her ponytail, a black leather coat, and a black T-shirt.

I circled her, gun poised. "How dare you come here."

"Foster, listen to me. We don't have time—"

"Time for what? You want to finish off whatever you were trying to do when you took me back to that damn broken-down theater?"

Her face tightened and her delivery was jumpy. Nerves, no doubt. "I never lied to you. This is all a mistake. I was waiting until you calmed down, then I was going to explain everything."

"Explain, huh? You broke in through my window to explain something to me?"

She started to get up. "We don't have time for this. Please trust me."

"Get down," I said coldly. It was all I could do not to jump on this woman. The fact that I was a law enforcement officer and the fact that I wasn't one to rush into a fight I might very well lose kept me from doing just that. "Put your hands behind your head and lie down on the floor."

Her face paled as the realization that I was not kidding hit home. "No. Please don't. You're making a mistake." Riley was doing a really good job of looking anxious. "We have to get out of here."

"Why?"

"Please just come. We can talk in the car."

"You know, if this is about that kiss, you should really lighten up. It wasn't all that great anyway," I told her snidely.

A look of hurt passed over her face before she hid it. "If I lie down, will you listen?" she pleaded calmly, as if she was the one dealing with a nutcase and not me.

"Yeah, I'll listen if you lie down."

I had no intention of listening to whatever lies she wanted to tell me. Once she had sprawled her long frame on the floor, I took a set of handcuffs from my dresser, dropped them on the floor, and kicked them toward my captive. "Put them on."

"You don't have to do this," she said softly.

"Yes, I do. I don't trust you."

"You're wasting time," she complained, reaching for the cuffs. "We need to get out of here. You have no idea—" Her statement was interrupted by the sound of pounding on my front door.

"Police. Open up, Everett."

I stared toward the door. "Foster, don't answer that," she whispered fiercely.

I trained my gun on her again. "Don't move, damn it. I didn't call them, but they have good timing. You can tell your story to whoever books your big ass down at division. I don't have time for it."

As I started backing toward the door, she froze, staring at the gun. "Don't open the door."

I peeked through the peephole and recognized the two nimrods I had beaten up. They'd since taken over my and Smitty's cases and made a point of engaging me in spurious dialogue over every misspelled word in a report. "Great!" I grumbled as I unfastened the security chain and opened the door. "What are you guys doing here?"

Ponytail, also known as Dan McClowski, pushed past me and into my apartment, followed closely by his flabby-assed, chronically pink partner, Alvin Wilson. I was about to demand that they get out of my apartment forthwith when out of the corner of my eye, I noted that the room was empty where Riley Medeiros had been only moments before. The white curtain billowed out at that moment and the loud siren of a car alarm sounded through the broken window.

"Son of a bitch!" I yelled. I had barely taken one step, however, before I found myself flying forward. My gun clattered across the room as I hit the floor with a crash.

"Oh, how the mighty have fallen," someone said from behind me, and I was yanked up by my hair and shirt to look into beady gray eyes. "Now you weren't going to just run out on me, were you?"

I was too shocked to struggle. First a woman I barely knew had broken into my apartment, and now in the span of about five minutes, two detectives I had assaulted a few weeks ago had just ambushed me, obviously not on official business.

"I'm going to have both of your badges," I warned.

"Oh you are, are you?" Ponytail sneered. "Well, let's see. Who do you think they're going to believe, a murderer who was trying to save her own life, or the two upstanding detectives who volunteered to bring her in?"

"What the hell are you talking about?" I managed to say, even though guilt clawed at my throat, desperate to emerge by way of a confession. "I'm not a murderer."

"That's not what we heard." Ponytail tightened his grip on my shirt. "Does the name Harrison Canniff mean anything to you?"

I guess he and Flabby Ass both heard the breath wheeze from between my gritted teeth. They exchanged a smug look.

"Give it up, Everett," Flabby Ass said. "We've got one of your fingerprints *on the inside* of the plastic bag that was wrapped around the dead guy's face. Now that just seems strange to me."

"Bag, what plastic bag?" This had to be a joke or some ploy to get me to admit guilt. There had been no bag, I was sure of it.

"It's called evidence." Ponytail pulled his gun, and for the first time in my career, I knew what it felt like to be on the receiving end of a cop's weapon. I didn't like it. I didn't like it one bit.

"Is this because I hurt your little male pride? Is that what this is about?"

"Haven't you been listening, bitch? You're wanted for questioning in the murder and mutilation of one Harrison Canniff. And you know what? We might want to know your whereabouts when your partner suddenly ran his car off the highway. You've got a lot to hide. What happened, were you trying to keep him quiet?"

"You know, man, you may have a point there," Flabby Ass chimed in. He took a hanky from his coat pocket and used it to pick up my gun. "Hey, I bet this has all the prints we need. And lookie here, it's loaded, too."

"Look, cut the macho bullshit and take me to the captain so I can get this mess straightened out," I demanded. I was scared, but I was also angry. The fact that they brought up Canniff horrified me, but the fact that they were trying to frame me for something was even scarier. Never mind the fact that I actually did it.

"Man, stop stalling and let's get this over with," Flabby-ass Alvin Wilson said. "I told my wife I'd be home in a half hour."

They both grinned at me and in that instant I realized that I was in serious danger. I only knew one way to fight. Dirty.

Blood spurted from Ponytail's mouth when the top of my head slammed into his chin. I followed up with what I hoped would be a debilitating strike to the larynx. I swung around to go after Wilson, but I was hit from behind.

As I dropped to the floor, Ponytail yelled at his partner, "How are we going to explain a bruise on her head? No other damage. That was the instruction. Jesus."

A part of me wanted to just lie there and let them kill me. Hell, I was dead anyway. I had been since the day I'd killed that Canniff guy. I just wanted it all to end. I closed my eyes and waited for the loud report, pain, or peaceful oblivion. Instead, I heard a shout and a loud thud. I opened my eyes to see Riley, her face contorted with rage, standing with her foot on the back of Wilson's neck. Ponytail was lying on his stomach, his arm trapped under his body at an awkward angle.

"Don't kill him," I said weakly. Not because I cared about the sniveling idiot on the floor, but because Riley didn't deserve to feel like I did.

She took her foot off his neck and, with a single kick to his temple, knocked him out cold. When she knelt next to me, I was so confused I didn't know whether to hug her or try to run away. Since I was in no condition to run, I chose to pull her to me fiercely. "I'm so tired of getting my ass kicked," I said to keep from crying.

"I'm sorry," she mumbled into my hair. Her much larger body trembled as I held her.

"For what?" I asked, knowing in my heart that she had nothing to do with this whole affair, and that somehow I'd failed to see that.

Finally she seemed to gain control of her body, and with some effort got to her feet. I struggled to mine unassisted. She stared down at the unconscious detective. A dark spot clouded his temple where she had booted him.

I touched her arm. "What made you come back?"

"Come back?" Her voice sounded disoriented and fuzzy.

"Yeah, after the way I treated you."

"I never left. I was hiding on the side of the bed."

"You were hiding? Why didn't you help me sooner? Damn it, I could have been killed!" In my anger, I had lost sight of the fact that I had accused her of being one of the bad guys only moments before. "You know, you sure do have a knack for showing up right when I need you," I said under my breath.

She didn't reply, so I tapped her on her shoulder. "You're not going to respond?"

"To what?"

"Damn it, are you deaf or something? I asked you how you manage to be around whenever I'm getting attacked."

A fierce frown blossomed on her brow. "I'm just trying to help you." She started for the front door and looked back at me as if to see what my decision was going to be. "Coming?"

I looked down at the two men on the floor of my apartment, then back into her tempestuous blue eyes. I had made my living on gut instinct, and it had seldom led me astray. If I had to make a choice about whether to trust the two on the floor or the woman who had put them there, I didn't even have to connect with my instincts. It was a no-brainer.

"Okay, let me get dressed," I told her numbly.

"No. We have to go *now*." She propelled me toward the door. "They've probably called for backup."

"Wait! Bud!" I didn't care what she said, Bud was coming with me. I ran back into the apartment and spotted his orange contraption partially hidden under a pile of my dirty clothes. I scooped him and the clothes up and we ran out of my apartment, leaving the door open and the two detectives lying in the middle of the floor.

I was screwed, I thought, as we jumped into Riley's old Land Cruiser. A dead suspect. My fingerprints on evidence. Resisting arrest. Assaulting cops. How much worse could it get?

❖

I closed my eyes and rolled over between Riley's jersey sheets, inhaling her scent. It seemed so familiar already. She really was something else. I was only sorry that I hadn't noticed her when I could have made something out of our connection. Even a good friendship wouldn't be so bad, although maybe Riley only thought she was straight because she didn't know any better. It was too late to think about the possibilities now. As of the present moment, I had no misconceptions about my future. My life, as I knew it, was over, and Riley had so much ahead of her. That is, if she didn't have anything to do with whoever was after me.

I ran through the explanations I'd heard as we drove to the theater. Stacy had sent her to my place after hearing something about a 6AD on North Third at my apartment. She thought a 6AD was the code for picking up a felon. This detail made my stomach churn. A 6F was a simple felony code. A 6AD told officers approaching the scene that they would more than likely draw fire. The sons of bitches were setting me up.

Then there was the photo. Riley claimed she found it in the alley with my keys the night I was attacked and had been so preoccupied with nursing me and getting my stuff that she didn't get around to telling me.

This seemed possible. There was only one problem with the story. I didn't drop that photo in the alley, which meant someone else had it, presumably one of my attackers. How did a couple of street thugs come by a picture of me? That picture in particular?

I wondered why Riley wasn't back in northern California. We hadn't got that far in our Q&A. The question preyed on me for another hour or so as I tried to get enough sleep to clear my head so I could leave her place. Riley didn't deserve the trouble I was in for. No one did. I was a wanted person. On the run, like the countless men and women I had hunted over the past eight years.

I stared into the darkness and became gradually aware of a noise I could not ignore. Paranoia immediately had me wondering all over again what Riley's agenda was. For a few minutes I lay wide-awake, allowing myself to zero in on the sound. Heavy breathing? I got out of bed and found the LAPD T-shirt that was bundled with the clothing I'd grabbed in the escape from my apartment. It was long enough to give me some cover. I didn't want to show Riley my meager goods if I was caught wandering around. I crept through the living area to the spare room she'd chosen rather than share a bed with me. The labored breathing grew louder as I reached the partially closed door. Jumpy and ready to fight again if I had to, I peeked in.

Riley sat on a weight bench in a pair of form-fitting gray cotton shorts and matching half-top. She had her eyes closed and a rather impressive-looking weight poised above, and slightly behind her back. A bruise shadowed the flesh above her eye. As she steadily raised then lowered the weight, every muscle in her body tensed and released. Steady breaths hissed from her tightly clenched jaw. Her stomach muscles clenched each time she raised the barbell above her head. A stream of sweat trickled down her temple to her neck, then to her chest, only to disappear tantalizingly between her breasts.

I shook myself from my trance and backed away before I was caught and had to explain myself. Talk about horrible timing. I'd always assumed that my sex drive was nil-to-none. Most of the sexual encounters I *did* have—there hadn't been many—were not initiated by me. *Girlfriends* was a magazine I scanned, but I never really had one to call my own, and that was just fine by me.

Never in my life, even in my rambunctious teens, had I experienced a flash of pure lust like the one that struck me while I watched Riley Medeiros sweat.

I'd killed someone. I was wanted for questioning by the LAPD, also my employer. The two jackasses assigned to my case were trying to frame me for a murder I *did* commit. I was beyond stressed, but my libido had suddenly decided this was the time for full-blown reactivation, and to top it all off, the comeback was for a straight woman.

Tears threatened, but I pushed them away. It wouldn't do any good to cry. I would just have to deal with this logically. My first thought was to call my father, but I was sure the men hunting me would expect that. As was his habit, Dad would try to help me clean up the mess I had gotten myself into. No, no matter what, I couldn't get him involved, not this time. This was not stealing a bag of chips, or a pair of earrings for a high school sweetheart. This was murder, and not even the great Clive Everett could get me out of this one.

I'd already decided I had to leave here as soon as possible. I didn't want Riley in any more trouble than she already was. I hoped the jokers at my apartment wouldn't identify her and trace her to Secrets, but I wasn't counting on it. Loneliness crept in as I contemplated my options. I'd often wondered about the life of a criminal on the run: always afraid that someone might recognize you; never being able to contact loved ones or friends, or create new ones, for that matter. My head hurt and I retreated to the kitchen, lamely imagining I could find comfort in a glass of milk or something.

I had to stop myself from gasping out loud as I opened the refrigerator and stared at the disaster area inside. My God, where was the six-pack of Coke? The gallon of water seemed to laugh at me from its haughty position on the top shelf. I would have accepted Diet Coke, even, but just plain water? Unless she had some Kool-Aid, I was in big trouble. And where was the whole milk I craved? I looked disdainfully at the bottle of nonfat milk. The water shared its shelf with a blender containing some noxious-looking substance. Her deli tray was equally disturbing. She didn't even have any Kraft singles or dry salami, for goodness sakes.

I opened the pristine white drawer at the bottom of her refrigerator marked "vegetables" and gasped at the greenery spilling out of it. I cautiously inspected the drawer and found a bunch of carrots, ears of corn, a cucumber, a zucchini, a squash, and an eggplant. *An eggplant? Who in their right mind buys a purple...anything to put into their mouth? What do you do with an eggplant, anyway?* And what was with all the phallic-looking veggies? There was no evidence of ranch dressing to dip all this rabbit food into. The fruit drawer was another discouraging experience. I kept Fruit Wrinkles candy and yogurt in mine. Riley had cantaloupe, strawberries, blackberries, and apples. I should say three types of apples, to be precise. Don't most people just get the red ones? I always thought the green ones weren't ripe yet. Smacking my lips in disgust, I gave up on the fridge and opened the freezer in quest of ice cream.

Two large Ziploc bags of chicken breasts occupied center stage. No sausage, no TV dinners, no ground beef, and no ice cream. Like everything else about Riley, her food choices were inexplicable.

Disheartened, I closed the refrigerator door and started toward the sleeping area when I heard her voice. I froze in the middle of the dark, nautical living space. Riley's door was wide open and she had her back to me, talking on the phone. She had taken off her shoes and was clad only in her workout shorts and top. I was able to admire her back and shoulders for a few moments, unnoticed. I was so involved with my ardent perusal that I almost missed her next words.

"I'm not sure how long I'll be, but I'll call you, okay?"

I was right. I was putting her out by being there. Someone was expecting her. I tried to ignore the heaviness in my chest, but failed. I told myself that it was just pure and simple fear of loneliness, nothing as complicated as jealousy. To feel that way now would be just plain ludicrous.

"Yeeess, Brad, I won't forget them." I could tell by her tone that Brad was someone that she cared for a great deal. "I love you. Bye."

I thought about backing into the bathroom but decided to let her think I had only just got out of bed. I waited for a moment for her to sense that I was standing behind her, but she didn't. Undoubtedly she had been so engrossed in her conversation with *Brad* that she hadn't heard me at all. I almost laughed at myself, situation notwithstanding. I wouldn't know what to do with Riley Medeiros even if I had her. That's right, folks, I can talk the talk, but I can't walk the walk, and I'll be the first to admit it.

I cleared my throat and, receiving no response, said, "Hi," a bit too loudly.

She jumped, as most people would when complete idiots stand behind them yelling "Hi." Turning sharply around, she said, "Oh, I didn't hear you."

"Sorry." I took a few steps into the light from her doorway.

She continued to stare at me for a moment, as if she wanted to say something else but thought better of it. I wondered briefly if she was going offer up who was on the other end of that loving phone call I had just overheard. *Snap out of it, Everett. Stop acting like you have a license to stick your nose in her business.* Feeling foolish, I looked around the small room and noted a pair of black nylon basketball shorts, a T-shirt that said "Body by Me," and a pair of orange flip-flops. All were laid neatly on the bed.

"Are these for me?" I asked.

"Yeah." She set her glass of water down and approached me, a worried frown on her face. "I thought I would wash some of the clothes you brought. They were sort of dirty."

I nodded, embarrassed and grateful at the same time.

"You okay?"

"Yeah…considering." I tried to smile.

"I thought you'd be asleep. Did I wake you?"

"No, I had stuff on my mind." I didn't mention that it was pretty strange to get up and find her working out in the middle of the night. "I just wanted to come and thank you for helping me." *My God, am I really talking?* Words were spilling out of my mouth without my consent. "I want to repay you if I can, but I need to get myself out of trouble first."

She said solemnly, "It was my pleasure."

You know what? People say that all the time—"my pleasure." But I've never once thought that anyone really meant it. In this case, I believed her. For whatever reason, Riley Medeiros wanted to help me. I backed away from her. She flicked on a light and followed me to the sleeping platform like we were just friends chatting.

"I'm going to shower now. Will you be here when I come back out?" she asked cautiously.

I guessed she'd read my mind and thought I was going to run off without saying good-bye. *I should do us both the favor*, I thought cynically. But what I said was, "Yeah, I'll be here."

She smiled. "Try to get some sleep. You're safe here."

My knees hit the back of the bed, and I all but slumped down in exhaustion brought on by relief. It is a trying thing to be alone in the world. And now, thanks to Riley, I didn't feel so alone. It was too bad that I couldn't accept whatever she was offering.

CHAPTER NINE

I had decisions to make. I wanted to talk to Marcus and find out what was going on, but phoning the division was not an option unless I used a disposable cell or a public phone. Stacy might have his home number, but that would be risky, too.

"Do you have the phone number for Secrets?" I asked Riley.

She dialed for me and handed the receiver over.

Stacy sounded worried. After we'd said our hellos, she said in a low, hurried voice, "Look, I won't ask you what's going on, but I just want to tell you that I talked to Marcus about fifteen minutes ago. He said they ransacked your desk in the file room. They took your computer and pretty much anything and everything you've had your hands on in the last few days. Apparently, whatever they are accusing you of, they're keeping it hush-hush."

"Have they traced me to Secrets?" I asked fearfully, worried about being on the phone in case they were listening in. A call from Riley's place to her employer would mean nothing, but if my voice was on tape, she would be an accessory.

"No, not yet. And if they do, they won't get shit out of me or anyone else in this place."

"Stacy, what about Riley? Did Marcus say that they knew about Riley?"

"Nah. The story he heard was that the cops who went to go pick you up at your apartment last night were jumped from behind by a couple of armed men in ski masks."

I grinned. "Score one for the large male ego. Listen, I'm not sure where I'll be, but I'll try to call you at the bar to see if you've heard anything else, all right?"

"Yeah, okay. Foster, you and Riley take care of yourselves, okay? You've got people here who care about you."

My heart warmed at her words, so much so that I didn't think to correct her assumption that I would be with Riley much longer. I said, "Thanks for sending Riley out for me."

Stacy chuckled. "I didn't exactly send her, hon. I told her what I'd heard, and she was out the door before I had finished my sentence." I looked over at the large woman who was tapping at Bud's condo with the tip of her nail and making little clicking noises.

"Oh, well, I still want to thank you." I said good-bye and returned the phone to its cradle.

"I'm going to miss her," Riley said.

Much to my chagrin, I was already starting to have a negative impact on her life. "Don't worry, I'll be out of your hair here pretty soon and you can go back to the club. I don't think those two idiots will put two and two together."

"No, it's too risky. I don't want to bring any trouble to Secrets. Besides, I only stayed there as long as I did because I wanted to talk to you."

"To me? What for?"

"I needed to explain about the picture and the other stuff. I wanted you to know that I wasn't involved with whoever was out to hurt you."

It was on the tip of my tongue to question her motives, but I stopped myself. What's that saying about a gift horse? Currently, Riley was my gift horse, my tether to reality, as it were. I didn't want to piss her off until I could stand on my own two feet. And that wasn't possible when wearing neon orange flip-flops, or shorts and a shirt—both of which were three sizes too big. If I'd had my wallet, I could have easily grabbed some money out of my savings account; I had enough to get me through a few months. But as things stood, I was penniless.

"Riley, I need to run a few errands. May I borrow your car?"

"You can't go out there in broad daylight. Every cop in the area is probably out looking for you. They would pick you up in an hour, tops."

"Stacy said they were keeping it hush-hush, and they won't be looking for your vehicle. I'll wear a ball cap."

She wasn't happy, but she tossed her keys to me. "Do you really want to take the risk?"

"I don't have any choice." As soon as I'd done what I needed to do, I would exit her life for good. The thought made me want to stay put, slumped in my chair, hoping I would wake up soon and find this was all a nightmare.

She nodded gravely. "Be careful out there. You think you're going to be warm enough?"

I looked down at my bare legs and feet. "Thanks for the flip-flops, by the way. I'm surprised they fit." Okay, I know I really shouldn't snoop, but I couldn't help it. I wear a size 6 1/2 shoe, and just from looking at Riley's foot I would have guessed she wore a size 8 1/2, if not larger.

"I know, wasn't it a fluke that I had those? Somehow they got put in my bag at the grocery store, and I kept forgetting to take them back."

"Well, I'm glad you didn't throw them away. It would be a hassle having to go shopping for shoes right now."

She looked at me curiously. "I would give them to charity before I'd throw them out."

Of course she would give them to charity. I found a smile for her. "Thanks for the car. I'll see you soon."

She walked to the door with me. "I think I should come. What if something happens?"

"Then you can't be there. I don't want you involved."

"I'm already involved." Her blue eyes were bright with an emotion I couldn't read. "At least tell me where you're going, so I know where to start looking if you don't come home."

Home. I told her an East Side address and said, "Don't even think about following me. I'll be back in a few hours."

She had a stubborn look on her face, and I thought of how formidable a woman she was. She seemed to wear her ferocity like a cloak she only put on when she deemed it necessary. Deep down I sensed it wasn't a guise she enjoyed wearing, and given half the chance, she would toss it off and become the caring person I was getting to know.

"I'll be waiting," she said.

I didn't linger. I knew if she kept staring like she could not bear to see me close the door, I would weaken and take her along with me. I didn't need to add another irresponsible decision to the long list. It was time to start thinking like the smart detective I was supposed to be and get ahead of the game.

"It takes a lot to freak me out," Riley insisted as I started to close the door behind me.

Indeed, she had simply rolled with the punches through this whole ordeal. I think I was more hysterical than she was, but then again, I was the one who was wanted for murder.

"I know," I told her. "You've been great."

She started to say something else, but I closed the door. A strange thought crossed my mind as I strode rapidly away: If I somehow got out of this, and if I was ever lucky enough to spend more time with Riley Medeiros, I would never shut a door in her face again.

❖

Pollard's Billiards was a local hangout for every street thug in East L.A. Lighting up in public establishments had been banned in California since '98, but Pollard's smoky atmosphere remained unchanged. The place had seen any number of crimes; however, no case had ever been successfully prosecuted against the owners or any of its denizens. Eventually the police just turned a blind eye to the goings-on as long as nothing got too messy. This was a mutually beneficial arrangement. The cops didn't look dumb for trying to pursue convictions and failing, and the patrons of Pollard's basically had a safe haven.

I pulled into a parking spot in the back of the billiard hall and exited the vehicle, automatically glancing around for any sign of trouble. I hadn't even taken two steps into Pollard's when some wannabe homeboy was in my face. Homeboy seemed to sense what I was and that I was in no mood for a problem, and figured he would do well to back away before he was mauled to death.

"Where's Big Sherm?" I slammed my teeth down over my tongue as soon as the words left my mouth. In my own stupidity and eagerness, I had just given any fool in the place looking to make a name for himself a way to get it, and fast. Kill whoever was looking for the Big S, and you no doubt would be riding sky-high off the gratitude.

My question was initially greeted with the loud crack of a cue ball knocking into the black eight ball. No one said a word as the guy who hit the shot scratched on the last ball and forfeited the whole game.

"You got a lot of nerve coming up in here, girl." Homeboy and one of his friends seemed to have gotten themselves some nerve all of a sudden. Probably delusions of grandeur, or some such shit. The friend, who stood about two feet taller than me, actually cracked his knuckles like in some bad mafia movie, while Homeboy, who was apparently too chickenshit to fight fist to fist against girls, was smart enough to pick up a pool stick.

I rolled my eyes and braced myself for a fight. I thought about kicking off my orange flip-flops, but the idea of stepping on the nasty floor in this place was incredibly unappealing. I had barely begun to tense for action when Homeboy's hefty friend loomed closer, waiting for me to look menaced and run away.

"You want to piss Big Sherm off?" I dared them with the brazen calm of someone who knew something they didn't know. "Go right ahead."

They were uneasy. The big guy cast a glance toward a door to the rear of the pool area.

Translating this, I asked pleasantly, "In the back, is he?"

I didn't wait for an answer or for them to ask their boss if he wanted a visitor. I walked on by like I had business to do. They didn't stop me. The element of surprise had them temporarily out of their zone. I would probably get the shit kicked out of me later, but for now I marched through the place with the reckless audacity of someone with nothing to lose.

The "Big" in Big Sherm's name derived from the fact that he was well over three hundred pounds. His real name was Dexter Wilmington. I figured the Sherm part was some drug-related nickname, but I never cared enough to ask. The back room looked as if it was used for illegal casino games. It wasn't so much the smell of stale smoke and old liquor that convinced me, but rather the huge roulette wheel embedded in the far end of the table.

Every time I saw Sherm, he had a new hairstyle. The rather unattractive ponytail he'd sported for a while was gone and his hair was now short and brushed to the point that it waved like ripples in a stream. He'd trimmed his sideburns so they connected with his beard. I thought the effect was quite intimidating, much more so than a bushy, chemically processed ponytail.

"Hey, Sherm."

"Shh, hold on, let me see this here." Sherm stared mesmerized at the nine-inch TV on the poker table as if it was a window. On the screen two women went at each other in a blatant rip-off of *Dynasty*. "So are the days of our lives" blared a moment later.

"Whew, that was a good one." Sherm sat back in his chair, staring at the TV with wistful adoration.

"Sherm, it's Foster Everett. Remember me?"

He tore his eyes from the television and turned to me as he picked up a cheap blue Bic pen and wobbled it side to side between his fingers. I swallowed the bile in my throat and refused to let my top lip rise. "I know who you are, Foster Everett!" He broke out in a fit of coughing. I tried to keep the look of disgust from my face as he spat into a tissue and placed it in his shirt pocket.

"I need your help with something," I said coolly.

"Why should I help you? Not like you ever did shit for me."

I hated to do this, but he did owe me and I needed all the help I could get. "You know that's not quite true. Don't make me discuss the situation with other people, 'cause you know I will."

He glowered at me and pulled the little blue top from his pen, cupping it in his hand. "What do you want?"

The pen dropped to the table, already forgotten. I hoped I would luck out and escape without witnessing the disgusting exhibition to come. "I need a gun. Make that two guns."

Before I met Sherm, I used to chew on the end of my pens when I was thinking. Not anymore. He had a fondness for sticking things in his ear. Namely pen caps. He would scrape it around like most people use Q-Tips. That, however, was not the most disgusting aspect of his habit, and he went through the entire ritual as he contemplated my request. As he plucked the cap from his ear, the tip of his little pink tongue appeared between his lips. He lapped at the tip of the pen cap once, twice, three times before it disappeared into his mouth. His eyes closed and his foot began to tap on the floor in unconscious pleasure. This disgusting display went on for what was probably only about fifteen seconds but felt close to a millennium.

Finally, the decision was made and he yelled, "Clovis, bring me my case!"

A boy of about fourteen came running into the room in seconds with a large brown case and a key. He handed the key to Sherm and disappeared.

Sherm put the pen top on the table, opened the case, and folded the sides down revealing an assortment of handguns, all expertly cleaned and displayed, probably thanks to Clovis.

I made my selections, two chrome 9 mm semiautomatics similar to the one I'd left back at my apartment, plus two fifteen-round clips for each and the nylon rear double-belt holsters that went along with them. I held the Glock 19s out in front of me, easing them both one way and then the other, as I checked both dust covers for cracks. The 17 I'd used in the past was larger and heavier; these felt just right.

"They're new. No cracks." Sherm sounded as if I had insulted him by inspecting the guns. "I don't want to see you again, Everett."

"Don't worry. The feeling is mutual." I was getting bold because I had my two new best friends and enough rounds to blast my way out of the building if I had to, but I knew better than to push it.

He didn't respond, and I left the smoky poolroom unmolested. Sherm probably thought we were now even. When I was working the streets, I'd picked him up for indecent exposure. He was having sex in the backseat of his car. Normally, who would give a shit? But Sherm knew how many of his boys would do his dirty work if they found out his partner was a man.

I had never said a word. I figured one day the information would come in handy.

❖

"Foster?"

"Yeah?"

"How good are you at setting bones?"

"I don't know, why?" For the first time since I'd gotten back from Big Sherm's I noticed a few beads of perspiration on the side of Riley's face.

"I think I broke my hand when I hit one of those detectives."

"Son of a bitch!" I was angry. So angry, in fact, that I went through the entire process of wrapping Riley's hand without saying a word. Occasionally, I would look down at her, but Riley was staring trancelike at the floor. So I continued with my ministrations in a fuming silence. How could I have missed the signs that she had an injury like this? What had she been thinking lifting weights with a hand that had to be incredibly painful? I finished securing the Ace bandage and stepped away.

Mumbling thanks, she stood up and walked into the kitchen.

I was afraid to open my mouth for fear a Tourette's-like stream of obscenities would come flowing out. I took a deep breath and exhaled slowly. I couldn't remember ever having been this angry outside of work. It didn't feel good. My temper was what had gotten me into this trouble in the first place.

"You're mad, huh?" She stood there like a child waiting to be scolded.

I opened my mouth to tell her that hiding her injury until now was the stupidest thing she could have done, but something stopped me. Body language can tell you a lot about a person. Riley expected to be yelled at. Her shoulders were slumped, and she wouldn't look at me. Why she would give a shit if I was mad at her was beyond me.

"Yes, I'm mad." I was proud of myself. I actually didn't sound mad at all, I sounded serious, but not like a raging lunatic, which was my usual reaction.

Riley poured herself some water and leaned back against the refrigerator. Her eyes sought mine tentatively. All of the anger left me as I looked at her, I mean really looked at her. It's not that I hadn't noticed her before, mind you. Certainly I'd admired her body in a totally detached sort of way. No one I'd ever known put so much effort into their body, and hers was amazing. But there was something about her I'd missed in my previous perusals.

Her T-shirt rode up and out of her unbelted jeans. The waistband was too big. She had probably bought the jeans because they fit her comfortably everywhere else, but her waist was too small to fill them. I stared at her sculpted stomach for a moment before following a path down her body and then back up again. I don't know why I had the impression of her being big, because she really wasn't. I had seen larger women down at Muscle Beach. There was something about the way Riley held herself, along with the muscles, that gave the appearance of menace. Right now, however, she looked like she was afraid she was going to be put on restriction.

"I'm sorry," she said softly.

My heart beat painfully in my chest. *I want to hold her so badly* floated through my brain and I took a step toward her before I could stop myself. I froze inches away from her. "It's okay, Riley. I just wish you hadn't gotten hurt."

She inspected her bandaged hand. "It'll be fine."

"You need to go to the hospital."

"No, I don't think so. It feels better already."

"Let's go," I told her sternly. "You need to have that looked at, and I don't have time to stand here arguing with you."

She didn't move. "Foster? Will you leave?"

I knew what she was asking me. A thought flashed through my head so foreign that I had to push it away before I could even give it a name. No, there was no way I could let Riley get hurt. I cared about her. As a friend. I didn't want to see her get into any trouble, and the longer I stayed here the more likely that was.

"Yes, I'm leaving pretty soon," I answered truthfully.

She nodded. "I was surprised you came back."

"You thought I'd steal your car?"

She was silent, and I suddenly felt like the world's biggest asshole. After all she'd done for me, she was even willing to let me drive away in her car, believing I had already decided I wasn't coming back. Sure, I needed to get out of town, but I could do it with some class. Panic welled up in my chest. Exactly how was I going to leave and where was I supposed to go? Back to New York City? To Dad? How predictable.

I could not allow myself to succumb to panic. If I did, I would start making mistakes. I needed to think rationally. I took a deep breath and began a mental inventory of my needs. Money would be my first priority. I couldn't ask Riley, I had already asked for too much. I supposed I could talk to Monica. She adored me, maybe she would help me for Smitty's sake. Or then again, maybe she would decide I'd done something terrible that involved her husband and was somehow to blame for his death. No, I would have to call Stacy and ask to borrow a few bucks and the spare car I knew she had. Perhaps she could meet me somewhere.

I relaxed a little now that I had a plan. I would hit an ATM on my way out of town, then double back and take another route in another direction. If I got going pretty soon I could be halfway to Canada by tonight. If Canada was where I wanted to go. Right now, I couldn't think about a destination.

Refocusing on Riley, I said, "I'm taking you to the hospital, or I'm leaving right now and you can pick up your car from Stacy. Which is it to be?"

"I don't like hospitals," she said with a faraway expression. "The last time I was in one, someone I care about very much was badly hurt. I hate thinking about it."

I had assumed that as a therapist she would probably have to work in a hospital, so her comment surprised me. Without thinking, I said, "I'll go in with you."

She shook her head. "What if someone sees you?"

"I already have a cap and sunglasses. Give me one of your largest shirts, too. That should throw people off enough so that we can get your hand x-rayed."

She went to the drawer beneath the bed and opened it with her good hand.

"Nothing too girly," I said gently, trying to break the tension, but she was so focused on her task that she didn't seem to hear me.

"How about this?" She held up a plain gray hooded sweatshirt. "You could put the hat over it and no one would even know you were a female."

I grinned at her sudden burst of enthusiasm. Any self-respecting cop would take a second look at a person wearing a hood under a cap and sunglasses. Soberly, I said, "It worked for the Unabomber."

She laughed. Not the usually silent shaking but a soft, delicious sound I wished I could hear every day for the rest of my life, even if it only happened across a table with us eating a meal as friends. I told myself to make the most of it. After today, the likelihood of seeing Riley again, as a friend or anything else, was next to none.

❖

The small, round Wonder Woman clock on Riley's dashboard made me smile. As a ten-year-old I had lusted after a similar one that came out of a friend's Cracker Jacks box. I wondered how Riley's childhood compared to mine. I wished I had time to ask her. I glanced toward the hospital entrance and almost asphyxiated on the spot as the flashing lights of a passing squad car caught my eye.

"Shit." I rested my moist forehead on my hands for a minute to catch my breath. "I need to get out of this town."

A loud honk from a hospital shuttle bus shattered my nerves and I pulled out of my parking spot and drove to a drugstore I didn't normally patronize. I had planned to send Riley to make the necessary purchases, but I had the urge to move. Staying in the same place for too long made me nervous. The clerk barely even looked at me as she rang up my hair dye. I also purchased a smaller pair of sunglasses, a few toiletries, and a cheap gym bag.

I got back to the hospital just in time to see Riley exit with her arm encased in a bright pink florescent cast up to her elbow. I swung close and pushed open the passenger door like we were making a getaway. She got in without saying a word.

"You okay?" I asked.

"Yeah," she bit out.

I kept my voice gentle. "What's wrong?"

"Can you just drive, please?"

I was hurt by Riley's snippy responses. *Well, screw you, too, Riley Medeiros. Who told you to hit that guy in the head anyway?* Anyone else and I would have spoken my thoughts and told them where to get off, but I found myself curbing my tongue. "Sure, I'll have you home in a jiff."

"I'm sorry I snapped at you," she said after a few minutes.

"No worries." I waited to see if she would offer an explanation.

"Did you see the cast?"

"Yeah, so it's broken, huh?"

"No. Couple of dislocated knuckles." There was a pregnant pause, then she continued, "I meant, did you see the color?"

I glanced at her quickly and then back at the road. "Yeah, rather loud. Why didn't they just give you a white one?"

"I think they thought it would be funny."

"What makes you say that?" I asked, wondering why she was making something out of it.

"I saw how the nurses were looking at me when I came in. And I saw what they said to each other when the doctor told them to get the stuff for my cast. People are so stupid when they think no one can hear them, but I—" She broke off. I had the impression she was irritated at herself. She seemed to think for a minute before she continued. "I can read lips…a little."

The admission seemed awkward for her, so I didn't comment on what a useful skill that must be. I'd often wished I could read lips myself. "What did they say?"

Riley sighed and looked out of her window. "It's not important. Let's get out of here."

"Suits me," I told her, all the time thinking if my ass weren't in so much trouble, I would go back to the hospital and hurt somebody for whatever they had said or done that made Riley look sad and defeated.

When we got back to the theater, Riley took a couple of painkillers and set the glass down on the kitchen counter with a thud. "I think I'll take a nap." She headed toward the weight room.

I hurried after her and said, "Riley, sleep in your own bed. I'll be leaving soon anyway."

She took an odd little step sideways and I had to reach out a hand to steady her. Instantly, the almost forgotten night of the kiss flooded back to me. The way she'd held me had made me feel, well, special. The way her mouth had quivered tentatively beneath mine was one of the most erotic things I had ever felt. The alter ego had to pipe up and dash these thoughts before I got carried away. *Of course she was tentative, you idiot. She's straight, and some lesbo had just come up and latched onto her lips like a damn suckerfish.*

"I thought you wanted to get some rest before you leave."

"If I do I'll sleep on those mats."

"No, you won't. I wipe them down after each workout, but still, I sweat a lot."

I had an instant image of sweat rolling down Riley's body and onto those mats. I clamped down on my lecherous thoughts. My God, I was turning into a horndog. Well, maybe that was a good thing. When they finally caught my ass, prison wouldn't be so bad. No problem finding a quickie in there, especially after they found out I used to be a cop.

"Go lie down," I said. "I'll get you some more water."

"I've got it. I'm going to have to take care of myself after you leave anyway, right?" she said cynically.

I have to admit I was a bit shocked. Riley had never been anything but sweet with me. I had assumed that was just her personality. "Look, I can stick around here a bit longer if you need me."

"No, I'll be fine. You should go."

I tried to ignore the pain in my chest as she said those words. I thought for sure we were at least friends, but perhaps I was more trouble than I was worth. Thanks to me, she had gotten into fights and possible trouble with the law, and I hadn't even given her the benefit of knowing the truth. I stared at her distant blue eyes and waited for the pain in my chest to disappear so I could make believe what I felt was heartburn. Instead it embedded itself more forcefully the longer my gaze with Riley remained unbroken. Finally, I had to turn away.

"Your jeans are lying over my computer chair."

"Thank you." I couldn't believe she was kicking me out. *Why not, you fool? What are you to her?*

"There's money in that drawer next to the bed. Take it all."

"I can't take your money, Riley."

"I want you to have it."

"But you'll need it to get home."

"I don't want to risk driving back to northern California until this hand heals a little. I'm sure I can get back on with Stacy for a few weeks. I'll save some more."

I didn't reply, because there wasn't much more I could say.

"Will you still be here when I wake up?" she asked quietly.

I didn't know what she wanted me to say, what the right answer to that question was. So I shook my head. "No."

Her blue eyes searched my face for a moment, and then she nodded and walked away. Making it clear there was nothing else to be said, she didn't go to her bed but shut herself in the weight room. I gathered my now clean clothes and stuffed what I wouldn't be wearing into my cheap nylon bag. I folded the shorts up and placed them on her bed. The guns and gun belt I strapped on, and pulled Riley's sweatshirt over them. I had the vague sense that I should be feeling something, anything other than the cold that cascaded over me when I thought of leaving this place, leaving her. *Well, I guess I better get over that, huh? She all but showed me the door.*

I went over to Bud's condo and looked at him sadly for a minute. Riley had put a toilet paper roll inside, and Bud was peering at me suspiciously from inside of it. I told him good-bye and opened the drawer that held the money she'd offered. I took two quarters so I could call Stacy, but I wouldn't take any more. I just couldn't bring myself to do that.

So many thoughts ran through my head that I couldn't make sense of them. Why had her attitude changed so drastically? Had I said something wrong? I let myself out and sat down in one of the ancient theater chairs in the semidarkness. I pretended that there weren't tears trailing down my face and that I didn't feel so drained. Maybe she was just tired of all the drama that went along with being my friend.

"My friend?" I murmured to myself.

She *was* my friend and she was hurting, and I had left her alone. Why? Because I'd never been good at being there for anyone. I never even knew Smitty was having problems. I should have seen that, and I hadn't. Jarred, I left my bag sitting on the burgundy-carpeted floor and made my way back down to Riley's place. I found her standing just inside the door with her back to me, staring into Bud's cage. I touched her shoulder.

Without turning around, she said, "You forgot Bud."

"No, I didn't. I thought you might be able to take better care of him than I could."

"I'm sorry." She cradled her plaster cast to her body, and I wondered if her hand was hurting.

I gently squeezed both her shoulders. "What for, Riley?"

She finally turned around. She looked incredibly sad. "For being so rude to you."

"You weren't rude."

"I thought you had left."

"I did. Well, I got as far as the front row of the theater, but then I got lonely."

"Came back for Bud?"

"No." Fuck it. What did I have to lose by telling the truth? "I came back for you."

CHAPTER TEN

I finally got Riley into bed. Not quite, but I got to sit beside her while she lay down. While she was trying to relax, I kept her wide-awake by telling her about the murder and how I had ruined my life. It was hard, but I answered every question honestly. I wanted her to know what she was getting herself into.

"What about that bag with your prints?" She frowned. "I don't see where that fits in."

Neither did I, but there wasn't much I could do about it. "It's not like I can go walking up to the captain and say, 'Hey, I did kill that guy, but I didn't touch any plastic bag.'" I tried to sound lighthearted, but deep down I was still waiting for Riley to tell me to get out of her life.

"The little boy you saved. Will he be okay?" she asked after a brief pause.

"I don't know, Riley. His mother is probably going to need to get them both help."

"What about you? Did you talk to someone?"

I opened my mouth to tell her that I had seen worse, and that "talking to someone" didn't change the simple fact that I dealt with sick creeps most days of my life. I wanted to say that the whole nasty affair had rolled off my back like water. But innocence is a powerful thing, and when I looked down into Riley's blue eyes I couldn't lie to her. "I'm talking to *you*, aren't I? That counts, doesn't it?"

She studied my face for a moment, then said somberly, "Yes."

"You should get some sleep."

"I don't really want to."

I smiled at her. She looked like a stubborn child who had just been told it was her bedtime. I only wished I had told her a fairy tale and not something that could cause her nightmares.

"You're not going to leave, are you?" she asked.

"No. No, I'm not going to leave. I'll be here when you wake up."

Riley even slept like an innocent—on her back, mouth slightly open and body splayed out like she hadn't a care in the world. I usually slept like a criminal, balled into a fetal position with one hand under my pillow where my gun was often hidden. She deserved better than I could give her.

Deep in the recesses of my mind, something told me that I should go. That if I really cared for Riley, I would go so she could be safe. I watched her smooth, even breathing for what seemed like forever. Under my gaze, her white T-shirt slowly rode up over the exquisitely sculpted, tanned muscles of her tummy. I felt excruciatingly sad. Sad because I knew, with a certainty I could not explain, that Riley Medeiros would be hurt when I finally did leave. I stared at that tummy, and I felt an overpowering urge to protect her. I bent a little lower over her, half expecting her to awaken, but she didn't, she continued to breathe evenly. Carefully, I reached down and drew her T-shirt back down over her stomach. I resisted the urge to kiss her forehead.

Unsettled, I left her on the bed and sat down at her kitchen table. I moved my chair around a little and stretched out my legs. It made me strangely content sitting there, watching over her while she slept.

❖

At some point, I must have rested my head on my arms and fallen asleep. I was rudely jerked awake by an unfamiliar sound. Out of habit, my hand went to the back of my waist where I wore my guns as I looked around frantically for trouble. I ignored the residual pain of my ribs as my fingers wrapped around the handle of my gun. The sound was repeated, and I realized that someone was tapping at the door. I could hear my name being called softly. The voice was unmistakable.

"Marcus?" Horrified, I checked that he was alone and let him in. "What are you doing here? Are you crazy?"

"Stacy told me where you were. We have to talk." Before I could object further, he said, "I've been doing some research since those two cretins absconded with one of my computers and trashed my filing system while they searched your desk."

"Aw, Marcus, damn." I could understand why he came by instead of phoning me. Marcus knew how paper trails worked. A phone call between us would create a record that could later put him in the frame for obstruction of justice or accessory. But I wasn't happy that he was taking risks on my behalf. "You can't be snooping around in shit, okay? I don't want them pinning any of my mess on you."

"They don't know we're friends. Besides, I'm the only one with the file maintenance codes for the databases. I can erase my tracks."

I was starting to get a migraine. Marcus wanted to play Hardy Boy, which would probably get us all in a lot more trouble than any of us was prepared for. "I appreciate what you're doing," I said. "I really do. But there are some things you don't understand."

"Which is why I've been getting to the facts," he said patiently. "It's the weirdest thing, but they are keeping everything really hush-hush. I mean, no one knows what's going on. The official version is you went ballistic over Smitty's death and the captain made you take some time off."

I frowned. A cop gone bad is usually the *only* topic of conversation, especially if that cop is someone you work with every day.

"So, anyway, I checked the arrest warrant for you. And get this, it's issued by a Judge O'Malley the day *after* they tried to pick you up."

O'Malley? Why did that name sound familiar? It took me a minute to remember that Judge O'Malley had issued the warrant to arrest Canniff. He was also a friend of the captain's. She was probably sitting in her office salivating like Pavlov's dog at the prospect of nailing my ass.

"I can't believe those two trolls didn't even bother to get the arrest warrant *before* they came to pick me up."

It wasn't the first time LAPD detectives rushed to pick up a suspect without a warrant, but I was surprised they would do that with me. Any cop being arrested would insist on seeing a warrant. Unless…

"Shit. They never intended to take me into custody." How my thoughts got from point A to point B is beyond me. But it did occur to me that one of them had mentioned that he wanted to get home in a hurry. Bringing me in and booking me properly would probably have meant hours of paperwork, and it was already late when they came to my door.

Marcus seemed to have reached this conclusion already. I could tell he was enjoying himself, taking a turn at detective. It made me sad because his enthusiasm reminded me of Smitty's. He'd loved when a case suddenly got interesting.

"That bag that was supposedly wrapped around Canniff's head when they pulled him up. I can't find anything about a bag in the coroner's report."

"Oh my God," I breathed. "His wife couldn't identify him. They had to base the ID on a tattoo. His face was annihilated by the water and whatever was nibbling on him down there." Realization washed over me with the relief of a high colonic. "Smitty didn't beat Canniff's teeth out in order to protect me. So where did the plastic bag come from?"

"Don't know."

"Marcus, can you get a copy of that coroner's report over to Stacy? I'll get it from her somehow."

I was supposed to be a detective, and it hadn't occurred to me that something wasn't right. There was no reason Smitty would have wrapped this Canniff's head in a bag. If anything, it would have made decomposition take longer. Even if he had, my fingerprints shouldn't have been anywhere on it. I hadn't touched anything. I already knew someone was trying to frame me for a murder I *did* commit. The question was, why? Why go through the trouble?

Unless they didn't know I actually did it. I was shocked out of my thoughts by Marcus's next words.

"Oh, one other thing. They know about the files you ordered."

"God damn it!"

"Yeah, but don't worry. When they come in, I'll photocopy them for you."

I thanked him and told him to be careful. As I watched his large graceful frame vanish up the narrow staircase, I felt light-headed with relief and shock. I had been so overwrought with despair and so afraid of going to jail that I hadn't been reacting like a detective. I was too close to the situation, too afraid of being picked up. Knowing someone was trying to frame me using fake evidence, and I could prove it, I felt better. They had nothing on me or they wouldn't be doing this.

I crossed the room and gently touched Riley's shoulder, amazed she hadn't stirred while Marcus and I were talking. "I need to get going,"

I said, sorry to wake her and talk instantly about leaving. "I have to get out of town. I'm too close to things here. I'm not thinking straight."

She nodded sleepily, as if she had known this was coming. "Do you have any idea where you'll go?"

"No, not yet. It will be somewhere quiet, though. I'm tired and I'm scared and there's some shit that's just not making sense to me right now." I gave her the short version of what Marcus had told me.

"You can take my car."

"No, I can't. If I'm spotted in it and they trace it, then your name will pop up. Like I said before, you don't want to be involved in this." She didn't say anything for a minute and I racked my brain. "I can tell this is too much for you. It would be for anyone. I should go now."

Damn. See, I flunked this part: deep thoughts and conversations and other shit that makes your heart break. What I wanted to do was hug her and tell her I would be back soon, as if I was just going to the store or something. I almost stumbled as remembered pain hit me with the force of a battering ram. That was how my mother left us. She gave me a hug and my father a kiss on the top of the head and went to the store for OJ or something stupid like that. I remember what she wore like it was yesterday—a yellow dress, with white stockings and white shoes. I remember thinking that it wasn't Sunday, so why was she all dressed up? After she had been gone for three hours, we even made jokes that she must have had to fly to Florida to pick up the orange juice. I think we knew even then. We got a phone call twenty-four gut-wrenching hours later, saying she was in love and would never be back.

I couldn't do that to Riley. I wouldn't. I felt something for her. I wouldn't call it love, but I did want more time to spend with her. Maybe this was one of my punishments. At this particular time in my life, I would find someone who made my chest hurt when she was sad, and I would have to walk away without ever knowing what that meant. I mentally shook myself. Maybe one day I would have time to admit my feelings for her, but not today.

"Foster, wait!" She had that "I have an idea" look on her face. "You could come with me."

"Come with you?" I couldn't help the leap of hope that crashed the walls of my rib cage.

"Yeah, I know a place where you can rest and maybe figure out what you want to do. It's secluded and quiet. No one would bother you."

In the seconds it probably took me to answer her, hundreds of reasons why I should refuse her offer poured through my head, and only two reasons why I should accept: I didn't want to leave her, and I didn't want to be alone. I was ashamed. All of my life I had been telling people that I didn't need anyone. Going out of my way to push people away, even holding my own father at arm's length, for fear I would become tied down. But the real truth of the matter was I didn't want them to leave me. Being *left* alone and being alone because you *choose* to be alone are two different things.

I leaned against the side of the bed and waited. Maybe I wanted a sign or something, but I didn't get it. All I got was utter quiet. Even Bud had ceased his normal hundred-miles-an-hour evening run.

"Where would we go?" I asked.

Wary hopefulness flashed in her eyes. "I was planning on a vacation before I start work. There's a cabin on the Mendocino coast I go to. It's very beautiful, and quiet. There are only about four hundred people in the whole town. You can think, or hide, or whatever, but you'll be safe."

"How long were you going to stay?"

"I don't start my new job until September. I was going to go do some fishing, maybe read a little." She shrugged. "Just relax. I had so many courses this last semester that I think I wore myself out."

She did look sort of tired. A few months off would do her some good, and maybe a nice secluded place to hide would do me some good, too.

"Okay," I said. "Let's get out of here."

The silence was so loud that I wondered if she already regretted the offer. She got off the bed and before I could think of the right way to let her off the hook, I was swept up into a hug. I mean a real hug, the kind you want when you're feeling awful and need to be shown that you're loved.

"God, sweetheart, you give the best hugs." I stepped away from her quickly and knew she wasn't the only one who looked like she'd just swallowed a rather large ice cube. "I said that out loud, didn't I?"

And I sounded so damn aroused when I said it, even a straight woman would notice. No more of those hugs, I thought, I might do something crazy like beg her for a repeat of that first kiss we'd shared.

We both smiled nervously. Riley plucked at the edge of her pink cast like she was about ready to pull the damn thing completely off. *So this is sexual tension, huh?* Not only did the timing suck, but it was the single most uncomfortable feeling in the world.

❖

It didn't take long to get Riley's meager belongings loaded into the back of her Land Cruiser. She left everything for the owner of the theater except her clothes, computer, boxes of comics, and weights.

"Wow, this guy must be a real good friend. You're basically handing him a fully furnished, newly remodeled apartment," I told her. I was really being nosy. I wanted to know how close she was to this "friend."

Riley shrugged. "Well, that's how it is."

The fact that she was a good friend came as no surprise. The way she was going out of her way for me told me what kind of person she was. But I think I wanted to believe that maybe I was different. I said, "I have something to show you."

I had decided to take the time to make myself a better disguise than Riley's cap and sunglasses. I would probably continue to wear the sunglasses, but the cap just made me look suspicious and I didn't want to call any more attention to myself than I already had.

As I removed the cap, the irrational thought, *I hope she likes it,* floated through my mind.

Riley's eyes went straight to my hair and she blushed beet red. I wondered why she was the one blushing. I was the one having to stand still while she stared at me like that. "You don't like it?" I drew my hand through my hair. "I should have let you help."

"No, I mean, yes, I like it. It suits you." Riley lifted her plaster-encased hand. She stopped just short of touching my hair, and I forced myself not to sigh in disappointment.

"How does it feel?"

"Different. I've had long hair all my life. I never really thought of cutting it but…" I rubbed my hand along the back of my neck. "I don't know. I guess I sort of like it. It feels nice not to have so much back there. I sort of like the blond color, too. Or do you think it's too much? I'm sort of pale."

Riley started picking at the space between her cast and her thumb joint. I wondered if those assholes at the hospital had put it on too tightly. "I think you look really good."

"Thanks." What else was there to say?

"If you get the trash bag we can go, all right?" She scooped up Bud and, without a second glance, walked out of the place that had been her home for months.

I know she would have left there eventually, but I couldn't help feeling that I was taking advantage of her. I took one final look into the trash bag. The long, red hair I'd always intended to get cut and styled, but never did, now lay in a pile of garbage. The short, newly dyed blond tresses seemed to want to stand out on my head in every direction. I frowned at myself in the bathroom mirror as I checked for anything left behind. I felt weird. Different. The fear was still there, lurking just out of reach, but now there was that childlike excitement that came with road trips and new adventures.

I walked out of the apartment and shut the door. I didn't look back, either.

CHAPTER ELEVEN

Riley's resting place, as she called it, was in a town called Albion, located a few miles outside of Mendocino. We arrived at three in the morning in the middle of an electrical storm. She had thought it would be better if we took Highway 1 all the way. The route was scenic and we were less likely to encounter any police. Instead we took 101, after I convinced her the trip would be safer and faster. What I didn't tell her was that on my way to start a new life, I couldn't bear to pass the section of road where Smitty had ended his; it was too anticlimactic, too clichéd, and too damned painful.

I leaned forward and tried to see through the sheeting water and the black wiper blades that appeared and then disappeared. Riley had told me to make a right turn. I couldn't see the road, let alone a driveway.

"Turn or you're going to miss it," she reiterated.

I whipped the wheel around and veered blindly into an obscure side road. Our headlights illuminated a sign that warned, "Private. Keep out." I shivered, already missing the end of a warm Southern California summer. Sitting in the dark car, squinting through the sleeting rain on the windshield at the unfriendly sign made it hard to believe this place had ever been warm.

"Now let's hope the key is where Dani said it would be," Riley said as I jerked to a halt.

I assumed "Dani" was the friend she'd mentioned a few times when we got stranded in crawling traffic on my idea of the smart route to take. They knew each other as kids. They had stayed close. I rejoiced to know that their bonding included Riley playing the role of model for a comic book series Dani authored.

Riley ran out into the rain, groped around in some bushes, then jogged back in front of the headlights and wrestled the gate open.

I drove carefully through and waited for her to close it. She jumped into the car and the dome light briefly illuminated her face. She was grinning happily, not at all perturbed with the fact that she was drenched. Something heavy welled up in my throat and sat there as if to say: If you don't say it, I will.

Riley guided me along a fairly smooth dirt road to a gravel path and I cut the engine as we reached a low-slung building that was almost completely obscured by trees. The sound of the engine cooling and the rain hitting the windshield made our location seem even more solitary. I opened my door and waited for her to come around to the front of the truck. I could barely see as she led me around the building and to a door.

"Watch your step." A warm hand briefly touched the middle of my back.

Chills shot through my body. I carefully stepped up onto a deck and waited as she fumbled with the key. I could hear the ocean, and to my right, the low hum of some type of generator. Riley finally got the door open and we both stumbled into a dark interior. If possible, it was even colder inside than out.

Riley found the light switch and I had my first view of the cabin. The Ritz it was not, but this was far from the shanty I'd been expecting. Hardwood floors throughout, and double doors that led out to a deck I could just make out as I squinted through the dark window. A built-in couch was located in front of the double doors, and to the left was a nice-sized fireplace. The kitchen was functional, with a small table that seated two, a sink, and a dishwasher.

"It's not much." She seemed embarrassed.

"Are you kidding? This is great."

I was rewarded with a large grin. "I helped build it. Dani's the one who got me into doing house renovation stuff."

Dani again. Man, I wished I knew what was up with Riley and this *Dani*. Whoever she was, I didn't think I liked her much. And this was her cabin, a fact Riley had only clarified when we were two hundred miles out of L.A. "You sure your friend isn't going to mind us using her place?"

"I called her, remember? She isn't going to need it anytime soon."

"Well, you guys did a great job fixing it up. You want to show me the rest?"

"Sure." Riley embarked on an enthusiastic tour.

The bathroom was decent and even featured a shower with three spigots, perfect for environmentally conscious friends who wanted to share. I wondered if she and Dani had tested that feature out. A small window that opened into the shower was the only ventilation. Riley explained that Dani had put in glass blocks instead of just a regular wall for light.

"But couldn't someone see you? If they were out on the deck, I mean?"

"Nope, we checked. Couldn't see a thing."

Aggravated by her response, I said bitchily, "Boy, you guys sure do have a lot of steps in this place." We were heading down into what was obviously the bedroom. Though sparsely furnished, it did have two end tables and two chairs with a bureau and an electric heater. The king-sized bed was the main feature of the room. It stood nearly four and a half feet off the floor.

"Damn! That's a big bed."

Riley chuckled. "You should see Dani trying to climb into the thing. She's shorter than you are."

Okay, that's it! "Hey, Riley, is Dani married?"

"Dani? Noooo." She got this far-off look on her face for a minute. I stood there not knowing whether to question her further or let it go. I couldn't help but think that this place was built as a love nest. I wondered if it was Dani and Riley's love nest. That huge bed was made for lovers. The thought of that hurt more than the idea of Riley being straight.

Riley mistook the reason for my shiver of misery. "You're cold. I'll start the fireplaces." She indicated a drawer. "Why don't you get changed and I'll get a fire going. You'll find some spare clothes in there. Help yourself."

My damp clothing clung to every part of my skin. As soon as she'd left the room, I removed everything and pulled on warm sweats and dry socks. I really needed a shower, but I was too cold to think of staying undressed for the minutes it would require. I took a step out of the bedroom door, intending to join Riley, and hovered, transfixed by the sight of her in front of the fireplace with her back to me.

Arousal flooded me as I watched her lift her arms and slide a dry T-shirt over her head. From the sensuous play of muscles in her shoulders to the arch of her back and the narrow waist I wanted to hold, she was beautiful. I wanted to say something, but words seemed like a feeble disguise for my thoughts.

She must have sensed me standing there because she turned abruptly and smiled. "You look comfy."

I glanced down at the gray Army sweatshirt that was drowning me and the sweats that fit better, but were still slightly too big. "Yeah, they are pretty warm. Are they Dani's?"

She nodded. "Oh, I brought Bud in." She pointed to a corner of the room where the orange pet condo sat. "I didn't bother with the bags. We can get them when it's light."

I wanted to know about our sleeping arrangements, but broaching the subject felt awkward. I wasn't usually so feeble. Riley seemed to sense my discomfort. "What's wrong, Foster? Don't you like it here?"

"What? No, it's not that. This place is wonderful!" I could see that she didn't believe me, so I decided that I would come clean with her, at least partially. "I guess I thought that since this was your place with Dani, that you might want her here with you instead, and resent that I'm here. Oh, hell, I don't know what I mean."

I slumped down on a comfortable if not eye-pleasing couch and stared blindly out the darkened double glass doors. The cushions moved as Riley sat down next to me, with her hands clasped in front of her and her head slightly bowed.

"Dani and I have never stayed here together, other than when we were working. Not even one night. I've never stayed here with anyone."

I felt like a heel. Riley didn't deserve my petty jealousies, and she certainly didn't need to explain herself to me. The fact that she was doing exactly that got me thinking. She hadn't given me the kind of strange look a straight woman might have after hearing a weird comment about her and a female friend. When I really thought about it, she'd never seemed straight to me. I had based my assumption on Stacy's guesswork and the simple fact that she'd overheard Riley talking to a guy called "Brad." Like talking to a man was any indication. Maybe it had just been easier for me to believe Riley wasn't a lesbian. I didn't have to do anything about attraction to a woman if she was straight.

Heat started at my forehead and flooded down my face and neck. Now, I do not blush. Fair skin or no, blushing is for kids and people who haven't seen crack babies crawling over their mother's dead corpses, and pimps who have beat the shit out of pregnant hookers. I knew I was keeping her waiting for a sensible reply. The best I could offer was a garbled apology.

"I'm sorry, Riley. I guess I'm just feeling like I'm taking so much from you and not giving anything in return."

"I wouldn't have offered if I didn't want you here," Riley said. "Besides, I'd like to get to know you better."

I wanted to scream, *And I'd like to kiss you senseless and then I want to explore every part of your body naked.* I couldn't say any of those things because even if Riley was gay, available, and God forbid, faintly interested, what kind of relationship could I offer her? No, it would be better for both of us if she kept thinking of me as just a friend.

So I smiled at her and said, "I'd like that, too. You've been a good friend to me even though we hardly know each other." In that moment, I almost wished I could be captured by the LAPD and instantly deprived of that tantalizing boxful of "what ifs," because dreaming about the possibilities hurt.

Riley yawned. "You can sleep in the bed, I'll sleep out here, okay?"

"Sure." We said good night and I left Riley on that couch. The rain had stopped, and I could hear the faint sound of the wood popping in the fireplace in the front room. I got into bed, cut the lamp, and shivered under the thick down comforter. Even though Riley was only four or five steps away, I still felt uneasy. The glass doors opposite the bed were pitch black, the world outside a creepy void. I was a city kid, born and raised; all of this quiet was unnerving to me. I took a deep breath and told my overactive imagination it was time to sleep. Through the door to the living room, I could make out the top of Riley's head and her knees in the dim light cast by the fire.

I lay very still for a few more minutes, listening to my own breathing and hoping to succumb to physical exhaustion. Riley was still awake. I could tell from the restless stirring and the soft thud of cushions landing on the floor that she was having as much trouble sleeping as I was, if for different reasons. That couch. What was I thinking accepting her offer of the bed?

Guiltily, I slid my feet to the floor and padded into the other room.

"Foster? What's wrong?"

The rose-petal softness of her voice temporarily robbed me of breath. "Would you like to sleep in there with me?"

When she didn't answer immediately, I realized I should have offered to swap places. I had meant to do that, but somehow I'd told her what I wanted by mistake. "Are you sure?"

I tried to sound offhand. "That bed is huge."

She unfolded herself from the cramped couch and checked the fireplace. It was almost as if she was delaying coming into the bedroom until I had settled down. I got back into bed and forced my breathing to stay even as I felt the covers lift and settle.

She snuggled down. "It's a lot warmer in here. I was freezing."

I scowled into the darkness. Once again Riley had put my own comfort before hers. I had never been around such a selfless person in my life. I didn't like it. Riley's self-sacrificing tendencies made me feel like even more of an asshole. "Why didn't you say something?"

"I wanted you to get some sleep. I didn't think you'd be comfortable with me in here."

I didn't bother to reply, because she was probably right. If she had suggested that we share a bed, I probably would have told her to take it and slept on the couch in the freezing living room. I nestled further under the blankets. Even though it was a lot warmer in this room than the front, it was still cold as hell. I moved closer to Riley, but was careful not to touch her. The slow rush of her breathing evened out, and I could tell that she was nearing a peaceful sleep.

My mind began to wander toward questions both thrilling and frightening. Questions like, what would it feel like to make love to Riley? Where did she like and dislike being touched? What would she taste like? If I'd been alone, the final thought would have made me cry out. I had let her in. I shivered from cold and an ache that appeared from nowhere and suffused my body. Riley murmured in her sleep and turned over. I caught my breath as her arm encircled my waist. I tried to move away, but she pulled me closer.

We lay that way for hours as the fire in the front room died down and the biting cold began to skulk back in. Being wrapped in her arms, taking in her scent with every breath, was the most excruciating, yet wonderful thing I had ever felt. As I drifted toward sleep, I must have stirred against her because she gave me another hug that sent warmth seeping through my body. The last thing I remember thinking was, *God, she is so damn sweet.*

❖

I lifted my hips. Close, I was so close.

"Foster?"

"No," I breathed. "Please don't talk. I'm so close."

"I understand. I just need you to open your eyes."

"No, I don't want to. Then you'll go away, and I'm so close. I don't remember ever being this close." There was a firm stroke to my clitoris and I groaned loudly.

"Does that feel good?" a husky voice asked.

"Yes, please don't stop."

"Then open your eyes for me, Foster. Open your eyes."

I complied because I didn't want her to stop. I wanted the strokes to continue until I found relief.

Aroused blue eyes floated above me.

"Riley?" Fear snatched me away from the pleasure she was giving with her rhythmic, steady strokes. "Riley, I can't. You don't understand. I won't—"

"Yes, you will," she said softly. And then she was entering me.

"Oh, God," I breathed, rocking my hips back and forth.

Usually by this time, unless I was alone, my body would have betrayed me. No matter how gentle the partner, I would become uncomfortable, sometimes downright sore. But this…this was different. The pulsing between my legs felt so good I wanted to draw her deeper inside.

I tightened my legs around her hand and closed my fingers around her arms. Her legs were bare and over mine. We were molten.

"Open your legs for me. Open them now," she begged, and I did. In my ear, she murmured, "That's right, don't think, just trust me. For me, you will." And she began to move with more force. Each stroke was excruciatingly slow. When the tremors began, I fought down the urge to scream. It had been so long since I'd had an orgasm that the intensity scared me. Riley continued to thrust into me. The pleasure was almost too much.

"Riley, please stop. I can't…" I felt like I was drowning, and she still continued to move inside me, not pausing to let me think or breathe. "No more. Please, I can't take any more."

❖

"Foster…Foster, wake up."

The warm hand on my stomach and the pulling in my crotch were the first things that I became aware of.

I opened my eyes to see Riley looming over me. The morning sun illuminated the fact that she was standing beside the bed fully clothed and not a hair out of place. "Are you okay?" Her concern was genuine, but there was no inflection that a night of lovemaking would bring.

I tried to answer, but only a sob came out as I felt the tail end of my orgasm die away. Spent, mortified, I lay trapped beneath Riley's concerned gaze.

"You were calling my name," she said.

"Oh, God…" was all I got out as I slid off the bed and moved quickly away from her. *She knows. She knows I was dreaming about her.* My feet hit the freezing-cold floor, and I stood still as the shocking cruelty of our situation hit me all at once. She was the only tie I had to the real world. Hell, the only person I trusted. And now I was having dreams in which she made love…no, had sex with me.

I ran into the bathroom, shutting the door behind me. In lieu of a lock, the door had a small skeleton key. I turned it and backed away. I sat down on the shower ledge with my hands over my head and eyes closed, and started to rock. My God, if she knew I was fantasizing about her, what then? I didn't want her to put two and two together and come up with *Foster is a perv.* One-way attractions were a disaster for both parties. She would get all self-conscious. Everything would be ruined.

"Foster? If I scared you just now—?"

"I'm just going to take a shower," I called out, trying to make my voice sound as normal as possible.

"It was just a nightmare." She tapped on the door. "Foster, open up. Please. I would never do anything to hurt you."

I couldn't help it, I sobbed. I don't know if it was from relief or pain. She didn't know what I was dreaming about. She thought I was afraid of her. I slowly got to my feet and unlocked the door. She was standing in the doorway, both arms stretched within the frame, her head bowed as if she had been resting it on the door. "Don't cry," she said softly. "It's just a nightmare, okay?"

She looked so sad that I ran into her arms. "Okay," I whispered into her T-shirt.

I didn't explain that I was crying because it *was* just a dream. What good would it do to embarrass her? She was my friend. She cared about me. That's all that mattered.

CHAPTER TWELVE

I know you will never tell me that you need me, and that's okay. I know what you did, and what's happened to you, so you don't need to hide from me. I am going to fall in love with you and you don't have any say in it. Yell at me if you need to, but I'm not going anywhere."

Her voice faded as I clawed my way out of a deep sleep. "Riley?" I gasped.

Burrowed beneath the warm down comforter like a hibernating bear, I peeked toward her side of the bed. Her head had left an impression in the pillow. I stretched out a hand. The sheets were still warm, but she was gone. I must have been dreaming again. I could have sworn she was talking to me, saying the sweetest things. The alarm clock claimed it was already past ten. *Who gets up before ten if they don't have to?* Slowly my body began to relax. *I am going to fall in love with you.*

I had to fight down a small curl of arousal that threatened to turn into something dangerous. My God, I'd had an orgasm in my sleep while Riley was watching. Then I'd fled into the bathroom like a fourteen-year-old schoolboy with his first boner. My skin was hot with humiliation. At least Riley believed I had been in the throes of a nightmare, or I would have been too embarrassed to look her in the eye. As it was, I didn't think I would be in any hurry to face her. I'm not the shyest person in the world, but you just don't have a wet dream while someone watches and then converse like nothing happened. At least *I* couldn't.

I lay rigid for a moment, rehearsing a nonchalant greeting and a comment about the slightly improved weather. The smell of fresh coffee drifted in and tantalized my nose. Riley was not playing fair. I pushed the covers aside, only to be treated to one of the finest views I had ever seen. Though the glass doors were tinted, it was still possible to see the ocean through them. I craned, detecting a movement just to the right of the door. As a long, muscular leg became visible, I leaned so far out of the bed, I would have fallen if I hadn't grabbed hold of the bedpost. Riley was on a bench, leaning back against the cabin, sipping from a mug. She appeared to be staring out at the ocean. She was dressed in running shoes, a sweatshirt, and shorts that displayed an expanse of thigh. I made myself look away. She must have gone out to the car and retrieved some of our things. I got down off the bed and, sure enough, when I walked into the living room, I found our bags sitting neatly against the wall. Riley had already taken out a sweatshirt and pants and set them next to my flip-flops.

I slipped the pants on, as well as the overly large sweatshirt. Like Dani's, it too engulfed me. But unlike Dani's, the sleeves were also too long. I pushed them up my forearms and found a mirror. "Oh yeah, real cute."

After I'd poured myself a mug of coffee, I joined Riley on the deck. "Aren't you cold?"

"No, not really." She stared out at the water. "I love it here."

I gazed out at the choppy ocean. Fog made visibility bad, but I could still see for miles. To the right of us were a few dark rock outcroppings. The water crashed against these rhythmically before cascading back down into the ocean, leaving a white froth that dissipated like the foam on mocha.

"It is very beautiful," I said. "I hope the weather gets better soon so it won't be so foggy."

"Hmm."

I thought it was a grunt of agreement, but I couldn't be sure. She seemed preoccupied, watching a small boat out on the rough water. She lifted a long telescope that was leaning against the bench.

"This was Dani's when she was a kid. She leaves it here because this is the best place for star watching at night."

I was really jealous of this Dani chick. Riley seemed to talk about her an awful lot. She set the telescope up and peered into it, then gestured for me to come stand in front of her. Adjusting the eyepiece, she said, "Look."

It took me a minute to find what I was supposed to be looking at. "Oh my God, is he going to dive in that water?" I asked breathlessly as I saw two men in the fishing boat, one wearing a wet suit. "It must be freezing out there."

Riley leaned from behind me to look into the telescope. "More than likely, they're putting out lobster traps."

I shivered a little as the warmth of her body and the chill in the air caused my nipples to become painfully hard. My mind started to wander back to my dream and how much I would enjoy touching her without pretense.

"I meant what I said." The words were very soft in my ear. "I would never hurt you."

I froze. "I know you wouldn't."

"The nightmare…"

"It wasn't a nightmare." I lifted my eye from the telescope. "It didn't have anything to do with you."

"But you called my name."

"Riley. Let's not talk about it. I just want to enjoy this. I don't want to think about things."

"I understand."

Apparently I had convinced her that I was having bad dreams about stuff in L.A., not imagining her screwing the hell out of me. *Welcome to an all-new low, Foster Everett.* I thanked her and tried not to look as grateful as I felt. I leapt on the first safe topic I could think of. "So, tell me about your friend Dani. You're pretty close, huh?"

"She's my best friend." I could tell by the sound of her voice that she was uncomfortable. "When I first moved here with my brother and mother, I met her at school. She was the first person who took any interest in me. Usually I was shy, but I saw her drawing a picture of the Incredible Hulk." She paused, smiling to herself with faint irony. "I used to have this thing for Lou Ferrigno."

"Used to?" I chuckled nervously. "I thought I saw his picture on the back of a door at the theater."

"He was sort of a role model."

"Is that why you started lifting weights?"

"One of the reasons." Her mouth was tightly pursed and a muscle flexed rhythmically in her jaw.

"Hey." I put my hand on her shoulder. "I wasn't trying to pry."

In an absent voice, she said. "It's okay." She seemed to have something on her mind. "Do you want to take a walk? This is a private road. There isn't anyone else on it."

"Sure." I followed her off the deck.

Large logs edged the dirt path for a few hundred feet, then we seemed to be in the deep woods. The only link between us and the outside world was the road we were on and the barely visible telephone poles.

We walked in silence for a while, then I remarked, "So you moved here with your mother and brother."

"Yes. My father…"

She made an odd noise and I thought she'd stumbled on a root or something. But then I realized the words were to blame. I sensed a sadness in her so deep that I wanted to hold her close to me. Two things were clear to me before she spoke again: Riley loved her father, and he was no longer living.

"My father died when I was nine," she said gruffly, and resumed her walk at a faster pace.

I used to think that I knew what it felt like to lose a parent. The deep resentment I felt for my mother burned in the back of my mind constantly. Anger can be a powerful force, even more powerful than love. Mine had helped me through a lot of emotionally tough times. But the utter sadness I could feel emanating from Riley was nothing like the feelings I had for my mother. Riley had known the love of a parent, not just someone who had put on her Sunday best and left with a cross-country trucker, like my mother had.

"I'm sorry," I told her.

"Me, too."

"What happened?"

"Dad was a pilot in the Air Force. His plane went down because of a faulty part. After he died, I stopped talking for a while."

Did she mean she stopped completely, sort of stopped, or what? The idea that someone would willingly not speak left me completely befuddled. I wanted to question her further, but instead I decided to employ a little-used strategy of mine, the "shut the fuck up and listen" strategy.

She kicked a pinecone off the path. In a voice that sounded like it hadn't been used in years, she said, "I was very skinny. I guess with that and the not speaking much, kids thought I was weird."

"Kids can be cruel," I said, though I sensed Riley had endured more than the usual bullying.

"They would play at who could make me cry out by hitting me." Riley glanced at me. "I never did."

I felt my fingers curl into my palms. I felt sure that if I were to look, I would see little crescent creases in them. "What about your mother? Didn't she stop them?"

"She was too busy to care. Things got better when I started to grow. By the time I was in the eighth grade, I was already taller than anyone else in my school, including most of the teachers. Most of them were scared of me by then, though there was always someone who believed the bigger they are, the harder they fall."

I turned away, blinking. I had expressed the same opinion many times myself, but I had never hurt anyone without provocation. The vision of a blond man in white boxer shorts flashed in my memory. A tear rolled down my cheek. "I'm sorry."

"You don't have to be sorry. It was a long time ago. I'm glad that my life turned out the way it did."

I was tempted to let the subject go, but Riley seemed willing to talk and I wanted to know everything about her that she was willing to share. "So is that why you got angry when everyone was laughing in the club that night?"

Her eyes focused briefly on my lips, and I wondered what she was thinking. "Yes. I guess I still don't like to be laughed at." She fidgeted with the florescent pink cast on her wrist.

"Tell me what happened with that? Please."

She hesitated; I thought she was going to refuse before she said, "I saw them talking. One of them said that no man would want me, and that it was probably for the best because I could never get one looking like I do."

"What else did they say?" I was amazed that my voice didn't sound as angry as I felt.

"They thought it would be funny to give me the pink cast because I'm not…feminine." Almost to belie her words, she reached up and delicately brushed back a piece of hair that had blown across her face.

For some reason, this struck me as incredibly feminine. In fact, as strong as Riley was, there was nothing at all masculine about her. I, upon occasion, could be damn manly when I wanted to be. But Riley? No, I didn't think of her as anything but a woman. I was angry that two strangers who were supposedly there to help her had made her feel bad about herself.

"Riley, I know it's hard when people say hurtful things like that. But trust me, you are definitely feminine. You would have no trouble getting a man, if you wanted one, that is. Or anyone else." Shit, so much for my verbal prowess.

"You don't think so?"

When I saw her smile, I almost forgave the fact that she was making me squirm. "I think you could have mostly anyone you want."

"Oh." There was a moment of silence that I would've called awkward, but she might have considered companionable. "Hey, Foster, I want to show you something."

She pulled me off the path and down a small slope that led to another less defined trail. It was only wide enough for us to walk single file, and I took advantage of the opportunity to study her body. Nice ass, nice calves, nice legs, great back, shoulders, and arms, nice everything. I personally was hanging on to what little definition I still had. Thanks to genetics and a rapid metabolism, I had never had to worry about what others thought of me. But Riley, well…she made me very self-conscious.

"Look."

She pointed and I inhaled as a fine spray of salty water hit me. The path we'd walked down led us to the beach. Unlike the few Southern California beaches I'd visited, there wasn't much by way of sand here, and the small gray rocks that led right up to the water would make walking barefoot near impossible.

"See those rocks?" Riley pointed with her cast toward several dark boulders that skirted the beach. "I used to fish from up there. You should see it when the water hits the rocks. It makes this huge rainbow." My grin seemed to bother her, but I was only reacting to her enthusiasm. "Well, I think it's pretty anyway," she said, a little less exuberantly.

"It's beautiful." I was touched that she'd shared this place with me. "If you like, we can get some rods and fish one day."

"I'd like that."

"Riley, I…" I stopped myself because I had no idea what I was going to say. This woman seemed to bring out the worst in me.

I pretended to be distracted as a wave crashed against the rocks. When I turned toward her again, her eyes were already focused on my mouth. She was standing so close I had to tilt my head to look up at her. I closed my eyes and waited for her to kiss me.

"Foster?"

Oh shit. I backed away from her, light-headed with mortification. She hadn't been about to kiss me at all. The surprise on her face told me all I needed to know. As quickly as I could, I retreated up the path, ignoring the urge to steal a backward glance. I was certain she would still be wearing that look of utter confusion she'd had when I had first opened my eyes.

I thought I heard her call out to me once, but I didn't bother to turn around. She knew where I would be; after all, I had nowhere else to go. She probably thought I was making a pass at her or something. Which I was, I guess.

I walked faster as I spotted the cabin's peaked roof. A complete idiot, that's what I was. Why would anyone want to get involved with me now? I didn't have anything to offer but a sob story and a mediocre attempt at sex. No, not mediocre. I would have...*Oh, shut up*, I yelled internally.

I stomped onto the sun-faded burgundy deck and walked around to the double doors leading to the bedroom. Turning the knob, I was disappointed to find it locked. God damn it, why was Riley so damn security-conscious? Who in the hell would break into a cabin in the middle of nowhere? I crossed to the railing Riley and Dani must have put up for safety reasons, and glared out at the ocean. I let the salty air coax one tear from my eye before I scrubbed it away. Feeling sorry for myself was not something I wanted to start again. I had done enough of that after the Canniff incident. It had been a long road back to halfway living, and it wasn't going to get any easier if I let myself get caught up in hopeless feelings for a woman who obviously didn't return them.

"Foster?"

"Look, Riley, I'm—" I never finished my sentence. I was pulled into the same warm, comforting embrace that I remembered from last night. Her lips covered mine and gently pressed until, with a sigh, I parted my lips. She tentatively explored my mouth, as I wondered at the taste of chocolate and mint. The kiss deepened. It sure felt like she knew what she was doing. *Okay, Foster, you can rule out the straight factor for sure.* This woman had to have been kissing women for years, and if she didn't stop kissing me, I was going to pass out.

Finally, the pressure lightened and she eased her lips from mine. I opened my mouth and a loud gasp escaped. I had forgotten to breathe. I felt the warmth of her fingertips against my chin. My heart started that traitorous pounding again as her eyes locked on my lips.

Someone cleared their throat. I pulled away from Riley and reached for the guns I *should* have been wearing but wasn't. I had let myself be lulled into a false sense of safety by her assurance that no one was around. We were being watched by a small, well-built woman leaning against the side of the cabin. Her eyes were hidden behind black sunglasses, her muscular stomach visible under the skimpy T-shirt she wore even on this chilly day. She and Riley must have had the same source of constant heat running through their bodies.

She would be considered pretty in most people's books, if she seemed more approachable. The motorcycle helmet she carried tucked underneath her arm was as black as the rest of the clothing she wore. The wind plucked at her fair hair. She removed her sunglasses, and I could see that her eyes were blue. She looked faintly amused at having caught us in an awkward position. I glanced at Riley to check her response, just in time to see utter delight spread across her face.

"Dani!" She bounded up on to the deck to sweep the smaller woman into her arms.

Dani, I thought darkly. Things were just starting to get interesting, and who should show up but the infamous Dani, who never stayed here with Riley and who supposedly had no plans to use the place while we needed it. Someone up there had it in for me.

CHAPTER THIRTEEN

"What are you doing here, Dani?"
"I wanted to see you, squirt. I haven't seen you in forever."

"I know. The last year kicked my butt. I had to double up on some classes so I wouldn't have to stay another semester."

I was starting to feel slightly ignored when Riley remembered I was standing there and said, "Dani, there's someone I want you to meet."

I could see that Dani was not as enthused as Riley was about the introductions. *The feeling is mutual, sister.* Still, I held out my hand and waited for her to shake it. For some reason I expected her to give me a death grip, but she didn't. Her hand was dry and firm.

"Dani, this is Foster. Foster, Dani, my best friend."

"Nice to meet you," I said politely. What I really wanted to do was grill her on exactly how far she and Riley had taken their friendship. I probably wasn't the only one who had played doctor with my friends as a child. The idea of Riley doing that with this blond dynamo made me feel betrayed.

"N…nice to m…meet you, too."

I blinked in surprise. Was she cold or something? Her voice was about as deep as Riley's, if not deeper. Although I was partial to Riley's particular huskiness, I could see where Dani's could be considered attractive, too. Sensing some expectation on Riley's part, I racked my brain for a sociable remark. I refrained from asking her how long Dani would be staying.

"Everything okay, Dani?" Riley asked.

"F…fine."

There it was again. This woman was either incredibly nervous, or she had a stutter. Not that it mattered, but it was odd that Riley hadn't mentioned it. Of course, it wasn't like I'd given her a chance to talk about her friends or family. Everything was all about my troubles and me. I felt guilty that I had never even asked about Dani, or about the mother and brother she'd mentioned in passing.

I was drawn from my reverie when Riley handed me a set of keys and said, "Please give us a few minutes, if you don't mind, Foster."

"No problem." I mumbled something polite to Dani and excused myself. As I closed the doors to the cabin behind me, the wind carried Riley's voice.

"I know something's wrong," I heard her say.

Almost as if to make sure I wouldn't overhear anything else, a low engine began to hum. It had been so dark when Riley and I had arrived at the cabin that I hadn't been able to ascertain the origin of the humming noise then. I'd assumed it was a generator or something. Now I realized it was a Jacuzzi. Small tufts of steam seeped up through its brown, weathered cover. Dani had probably turned it on. Had she expected to catch Riley here alone? I peered out to see if I could get a glimpse of the two of them, but they must have moved toward the front of the cabin because they were no longer within view.

With a sigh, I backed away from the glass doors. Feeling the need to keep busy, I made the bed, then folded my sleeping things and set them on the bureau next to Riley's neatly folded clothing. I noted the small neoprene pouch she used as a wallet sitting on the table by her side of the bed. I had seen her pull money out of it when we had stopped to get snacks and gas. It wouldn't do for Riley to find me going through her wallet, so instead I treated myself to a thorough inspection of the drawers. I was disappointed. There was barely anything in them. Most people go to cabins to rest. Well, here's a news flash: this shit is boring. I grew up in the city. The peace and quiet of this place was scaring me. Sure, it was beautiful, but once you've seen everything, you've seen it.

Disenchanted, I moved on to the wall unit, which housed an all-in-one thirteen-inch TV/DVD set-up similar to the one in Pistol Pete's motel room. I wondered if I had been formally charged yet, and if they were still looking for me. *God, Marcus, I hope like hell you're not still digging, 'cause if they catch you, you're screwed, my friend.* I ran a hand around the top shelf, seeking a remote to turn on the TV. All I found was a picture that looked as though it had been taken a few years earlier. In it was a younger, smiling Dani, a brunette holding a baby, and a man in a pair of coveralls. I wondered idly if this was a family portrait, but decided it wasn't. The couple didn't look like they were quite old enough to be Dani's parents, although she did resemble the man.

I put the picture back and continued my search. My fingers ran through several dust bunnies before they finally closed on the remote. Shaking the dust away, I found myself thinking about the endless supply of rubber gloves Smitty and I used to keep in our trunk. I missed my partner. The fierce onslaught of guilt made me feel queasy; I'd run away when I should have been searching for the truth about his death and everything else that had happened since the day I let my temper rule me one time too many. Harrison Canniff's death was on me, and so was anything else driven by my choice to avoid responsibility. How much longer could I keep running away?

I powered the TV on with the remote. I never watched television. The number of shows featuring law enforcement issues was depressing. Who found that kind of thing entertaining, anyway? All I ever wanted to do was escape from it when I got home. Knowing the kind of crap people did to each other made it hard for me to sleep at night. Dealing with those situations was probably the main reason I never really enjoyed my job.

When I was a uniformed cop, I had seen my partner get knocked on the head when he was trying to cuff an abusive husband. The thing is, the wife had called 911 because he'd been kicking her ass for the better part of the day. When we arrived, she already looked like Riverdance had done a performance on her face. I don't know what she thought we were going to do, but once we had him handcuffed, he started crying, and I guess her protective instincts kicked in. Ignoring the screaming, grubby child that had probably been sitting in his high chair for God knows how long, she started whaling on my partner. I finally had to punch her in the face and handcuff her to get her to stop. On the way in, her husband pleaded his case by pointing out that the only way I could get her to listen to *me* was to punch her in the face. We took them both down to division and booked them for domestic abuse. She also got charged with assaulting an officer. We were called back to that household two more times before I was promoted to detective.

I stared at the TV, trying to move my train of thought away from my own private reel of cop dramas. For some reason, another case leapt to mind. Just before Smitty died, we'd been chasing up this guy, Michael Stratford, who supposedly had information about a child kidnapping. The case was pretty cold after a year, and we couldn't track Stratford down. As a last resort, we'd decided to go see if he was laying low at his ex-girlfriend's dilapidated house.

Alicia Alexander was a skinny white woman with scraggly bleached-blond hair who greeted us at the door with a sheet wrapped around her apparently naked body. She wasn't happy to see us at first, but when we showed her our badges, she wrenched the door wide open and said, "Come on in."

Somewhere in the background, a baby was wailing, but she didn't seem to think anything of it, so I tried not to worry either. I skirted broken toys and a beer bottle as we entered a squalid living room.

"Move, Fee Fee," Alicia yelled, and a little girl of about four with almond skin and dark curls immediately hopped off the couch with her doll in tow, eyeing us as if we were devils incarnate before settling on the floor to play. "It's about time y'all got here. Shit, I called yesterday on that punk-ass motherfucker."

I winced and looked down at the child who was still happily playing with her doll, seemingly not bothered in the least by the language. "Ma'am, who are you talking about? Michael?"

"What you talking about Michael for? If I see him I'm going to bust his ass. He late again with my child support. I heard he got hisself saved by the Lord, and now he too good to come around here."

I heard Smitty's impatient grunt. We were both frustrated with our lack of progress. After the kidnapping a year earlier, we'd expected to find the missing boy dead or alive within the week. But there was nothing. Like so many other missing kids, he'd simply vanished. An informant had told us Stratford knew something about the kid. He was the only lead we had.

"Do you know where he is?" Smitty asked. "We can give him a reminder about that child support."

"He got some new girlfriend that's a secretary in one of them law firms downtown. I got the name somewhere. He done forgot about his firstborn, ain't that right, Fee Fee? It's just me and you, baby. Come give Momma a kiss."

I watched, vaguely disgusted, as mother and daughter shared a moment obviously orchestrated for me and Smitty. After Alicia found the name of the new girlfriend's employer, Smitty was about to thank her for her time, but I stopped him, curious about something she'd said.

"If it's not Michael, who did you call us about?"

"That punk-ass mo-ther-fuck-er, Popeye Jenkins, stole some shit from me. That's what I called y'all slow asses for." She grabbed Fee Fee's arm. "Now go give PJ his pacifier. I can't even hear myself think up in here."

Fee Fee scampered off, and in seconds the howling in the back room ceased. I found myself feeling really sorry for both Alicia's kids.

"Popeye Jenkins." I had busted him at least five times when I was a patrol cop. He was about twelve at the time. The charges ranged from petty theft and drug possession to auto theft. Sometime after I was promoted, I heard that he'd started to rise pretty high in the drug-dealing ranks. He then committed the ultimate sin for any businessman, legal or illegal—he started enjoying his product too much.

"What did he steal?"

The scraggly blonde surveyed me and Smitty suspiciously. "Like I told the woman at the 911, I ain't saying what he took."

"What do you mean, you can't say? How are we supposed to get it back for you if we don't know what it is?" Smitty's annoyance was showing.

She thought about it for a moment, and I could have sworn I saw a lightbulb go on above her head. "Come on, I got something." She marched us down a hallway strewn with broken toys and children's clothes. "Look here," she said, pointing triumphantly. "Look what that fucker did to my toilet. How about that? I want to press charges about that. Bet he will give me my shit back then, won't he?"

"Ma'am, are you saying Paul Jenkins...Popeye...broke your toilet?"

"You damn right that's what I'm saying." She was so angry that she forgot to hold up her sheet, and her scrawny ass was hanging out.

Maybe Smitty couldn't see where this was going, but I sure as hell could, and it was damn funny. I was hard-pressed not to laugh that this half-naked woman was trying to convince us to arrest a known junkie for breaking her toilet. Sometimes this job was insane.

Chagrined, Alicia said, "We have to go to the neighbor's house to pee till I can pay to get someone out here to fix it. Shit, I don't get my next check till the fifteenth."

"So let me get this straight. Jenkins was standing on your toilet, doing what?"

I tried to bump into Smitty to get him to shut up. It wasn't our job to investigate her complaint. We could send some uniforms over later. Smitty ignored me. I could tell his curiosity was piqued, so I decided to shut up and let him go for it. I slipped my hand as casually as possible into my pocket and pushed the record button. The small tape recorder that I used instead of lugging around a notepad was about to pay off. Smitty would be buying me coffee for a month if he didn't want this e-mailed to every detective he ever worked with.

"I guess he was trying to get out this here window," Alicia said.

"Now why would he do that?" Smitty probed.

I knew why, but I wanted to see her try to wiggle out of answering the question. I had so few pleasures in my job, I had to take amusement where I could find it. *Aw shit, she's losing more of the sheet.*

"Well, see, he was sneaking out the window with the shit that he stole from me."

"Uh-huh." Smitty adopted a kindly tone. "Popeye's going to say that the toilet thing was an accident. We really can't hold him for that unless he was trying to do it on purpose. And if you won't tell us what he stole, we can't arrest him for that either."

"You want to know what he stole?" She was worked up now, her left breast exposed. I hoped she wouldn't decide just to be done with the sheet and toss it aside. Now mind you, I'm not opposed to looking at naked young ladies, but I draw the line at crackheads.

"He stole my god-damn pipe." She had a talent for dragging out her curse words; "god-damn" and "mo-th-er-fuck-er" just sound so much better with every syllable pronounced.

I giggled my ass off under the guise of a cough. Hell, I needed to go have a seat on one of the ripped chairs on the sagging front porch before I was forced to go ask to use the neighbors' toilet. Smitty nudged me for help, but I was too busy staring at the floor, trying not to howl. *You're on your own, buddy,* I thought.

How was I supposed to know that we would never investigate another cold case? That I would never play another practical joke on him. That nothing would be the same again.

❖

I gave up trying to find a TV channel I could stand to watch. Riley had been outside with the mysterious Dani for nearly twenty minutes. What the hell were they talking about? I was pretty sure Riley wouldn't tell her friend I was a fugitive, but I couldn't help feeling nervous. I peered covertly out the double doors. They were on the bench and Riley was holding her "best friend" tightly.

I shouldn't have felt hurt or betrayed, but I did. Riley and I had shared a kiss, that's all. She was a nice woman who was willing to help me until I got my shit together, that's all. I put my head in my hands and swallowed down my disappointment. I didn't feel up to unpacking, so I climbed up on the ridiculously tall bed and leaned back against the pillows. *You should see Dani climb into this thing.* I should have known there was something more there. *How could I? She's never told me anything about herself.*

"Why did Dani come out?" I asked. I'd been asleep for a couple of hours when the sound of a motorcycle revving woke me up, and a few minutes later Riley came back inside.

"She needed to talk to me."

"I thought you two never spend time up here together."

"We don't. This place is so that we can be alone and think, not socialize."

"Okay, so that's my point. Why would she come up here knowing you're here?"

A frown creased her forehead. I could tell she didn't see where I was going with my questioning, which made two of us. "She came up here because she wanted to make sure I was okay. And for the record, this is her place and she can come here anytime she wants."

Her emotionless voice reminded me of the tone she used when talking to strangers, if she bothered to speak to them at all. I felt a certain amount of regret at hearing it used with me. Riley threw a white bank envelope on the bed. She obviously wanted me to look inside, so I opened it. Crisp twenty and fifty dollar bills all faced in the same direction, all brand spanking new, and all with the huge presidential faces that were meant to make them counterfeit-proof. To me, the design only succeeded in making American money even more ugly than it already was.

"Shit, Riley, there has to be over five thousand dollars here."

"Five thousand five hundred." She slid a bill into her back pocket. "I came to take you shopping, but you were asleep."

"So your *friend* just gives you an envelope full of cash and leaves?" I was angry, and it wasn't over the money. It was because of the kiss, because of the fact that Riley Medeiros had kissed me and then as soon as her best friend came on the scene, it was as if it had never happened.

It occurred to me then that Riley might have kissed me because she thought I wanted her to. I flashed on myself a few years back, leaning in to reluctantly kiss women I had been seeing before bidding them good night. As their doors closed my hand would, of its own accord, go up and wipe my mouth, as if I had been given the cooties. It had only happened a few times. I had quickly forgotten those unwanted kisses, but now…The thought that Riley would do that to me hurt like hell. Suddenly, I just wanted her out of my face.

"So, you have your friends give you money all the time?" I asked her bitingly. I expected anger, maybe a fuck you or two, but not the look of pure rage that crossed her face.

"I have never taken one cent from Dani. Never!"

"Then why the hell would you start now?" I yelled back at her, hating myself for starting the fight, yet unable to stop myself from adding tinder to the burning flame.

Riley snatched her pouch from the bureau. "You want to know why I took her money?" Her voice was so deep now that I could hardly understand what she was saying. She stopped in front of the bed and emptied the contents of the pouch onto my lap. I looked down as her driver's license, a student ID, and a social security card along with ten dollars, a few dimes, and a penny with a nasty-looking green patina landed in my lap. "I have ten *fucking* dollars, Foster!"

I jumped as she said the word "fucking." *My* mouth was created in the gutter, but I had never heard Riley say so much as "damn" since I'd known her.

"That's all I have to my name, and I bet it's *ten more* dollars than you have."

She was right, but I just glared at her, unwilling to give in and unwilling to admit my jealousy. That's the problem when you get in an argument with someone and realize you are totally in the wrong and should probably stop right there and apologize, but instead you keep going because you don't know how to say you're sorry. What I really wanted to do was beg Riley to tell me why she was holding Dani like that so soon after kissing me, and with me only a few feet away. But what I said was, "Why in the fuck did you kiss me, anyway?"

The question was meant to hurt, but when I saw the pain in her eyes I felt ashamed of myself. It was quickly hidden, or should I say covered, by anger. The side of her mouth quivered and a look of disgust crossed her face.

"Why did you want me to?" she bit out before snatching her pouch and its contents from my lap and stalking off toward the deck.

She didn't bother to close the double doors, but went to the edge of the deck and gripped the rail, staring out at the ocean. A gust of wind blew past her, filling her shirt with brisk air. She wrapped an arm around herself, a shield from the cold. I wanted to comfort her and explain that it was all my fault because I was jealous. But in order to do that, I would have to own up to the growing feelings I had for her. I wasn't ready for that. Why *had* I wanted her to kiss me?

I clawed my fingers through my short, unfamiliar hair. I was a mess, and I was taking it out on Riley. I wanted something that I had never had. For me, a faithful lover was like a myth, something lesbians wished for and claimed they had, but never really did. I had seen Stacy and her girlfriend as they practically cooed at each other in front of people; and then as soon as she was alone, Stacy would make a pass at someone else. I'd known women who acted as if they were joined at the hip with their partners because they were too afraid to take a step alone. Swearing fidelity, when every last one of them secretly wanted more than they were ever willing to share with the other. I'd never wanted that. I would have been happy alone…until her. I really wanted to talk to her, but I was afraid I would do something stupid, like tell her the truth.

I got down off the bed and paced around the room, both angry and ashamed. Since when had I become so callous? Testy maybe, but not outright cruel. I had really hurt Riley. Maybe hurt her pride. And I, of all people, knew how awful that felt.

Taking a deep breath, I marched out onto the deck ready to humble myself. I was just in time to hear her truck wheels spin in the rough gravel driveway as she left me to enjoy my latest screwup alone. I knew she'd be back. The envelope full of cash was still on the bed and she hadn't come into the room to get her stuff. I plopped down on the edge of the deck and gazed out at the Pacific Ocean. It really was a beautiful place. I didn't even remember if I'd thanked her properly for bringing me here. The dull ache that had been building up in my chest was now too strong for me to deny. Why had I said those things to her? Why couldn't I just shut the fuck up and be happy that Dani was gone and I was still here? Why had she kissed me? Was it because she felt something for me, or was it because she thought I wanted her to?

Folding my arms in front of my chest, I leaned forward as I had as a child when I didn't want to go inside to get a coat. Hell, I didn't *have* a coat. Like Riley said, I didn't have shit and she didn't have much more. If the situation were reversed, I would have done what I had to do to take care of Riley…or would I? Would I have helped a stranger the way she had helped me? I finally understood about the money she'd accepted from Dani. Of course she would not have taken money if it were just her; Stacy said Riley had had two jobs and had put herself through school. But she had me, she was trying to take care of me. Her selflessness made me hurt more. I had never been one to go out of my way. I wouldn't borrow a dime for anyone except myself. I was more the norm; Riley seemed to live by a different code.

"God damn it, Riley. Why can't you be like everybody else?" I said out loud.

My question was carried away by the increasingly gusty winds. I supposed I should go inside, but the chill air seemed to be clearing the past few weeks' fog from my mind. I sat for a while longer, until my teeth started chattering and I heard the Cruiser crunch onto the gravel next to the cabin once more. I refrained from rushing to her, telling myself to give her some space. I heard her step up on the deck, heard the crinkle of a paper bag, and felt her gaze. She sat down next to me, and neither of us spoke as the wind billowed around us like ghosts playing with our hair.

Her voice sounded gruff. "I'm sorry. I don't want to fight anymore," she said, and I felt something tap me on my enfolded hands. I looked down at the red and yellow package of a dual Slim Jim. "It's for you," she said.

I thought it was the sweetest thing she could have ever done, and I felt like a big wussy. I didn't even think Riley knew what a Slim Jim was. "You don't need to be sorry. You didn't do anything wrong. It was all my fault."

She didn't respond, so, like a child given a lollipop so she would stop crying, I began the difficult task of opening the Slim Jim with my teeth. I wasn't really hungry, but tearing at it gave me something to do while I waited for her to speak. Or maybe she was waiting for me. I bit into the spicy treat and chewed vigorously.

"Why *did* you want me to kiss you?" she asked.

"Huh?" The "huh" was reaction more than anything. I had heard what she said.

"Down at the beach, you wanted me to kiss you. Why?"

"I don't know. It seemed like it was the right thing to do at the time," I said lamely. Seeing the look of disappointment that she wasn't successful in hiding, I recanted. "I just wanted you to kiss me. I didn't really think about it much. It's just...how I felt."

"Did you like the kiss at the club?" she asked.

I frowned. Why did she sound so damn unsure? Hell, if we hadn't had an audience, I would have probably been on my knees with my ass in the air, like a cat in heat. "I loved the kiss at the club." Suddenly *I* was the one feeling insecure. "Did you?"

"Yes, very much."

I swallowed the piece of meat I had been holding in my jaw. It occurred to me that I was making myself very unkissable by chomping on the Slim Jim. In fact, I hoped for a change in wind direction because I was sure Riley was being treated to my halitosis at that very moment. "Good, I did, too."

If she was feeling anything like I was, she was wishing for a piece of lined paper with a few boxes that said: I like you. Do you like me? Check "yes" or "no."

She moved a little closer. "I thought you weren't interested in cuddling women with hard asses."

I choked on my beef jerky. "Where did you hear that?"

"You said it at Secrets one night, Foster."

"I did not." Under her disbelieving stare, I was forced to explain. "I did, but that's not what I meant. I can't believe Stacy told you."

"She didn't. I saw you say it."

"You saw?" I had a flashback of talking to Stacy while I watched Riley in the mirror. I remembered Riley's special skill and groaned. "You read my lips?"

She nodded and stared broodingly out to sea for a moment before facing me.

As the ocean air blew past us, moaning loudly as it passed through the rocky area, her eyes met mine frantically. Her eyes locked on my lips, and I opened my mouth to apologize when questions that should have occurred to me before hit me with the force of a sledgehammer.

Riley's deep uninflected voice, her habit of staring at my lips, her ability to read lips, and even her hero worship of Lou Ferrigno. I had seen him on TV once, talking about his bodybuilding and his hearing impairment. Although Riley's speech pattern was not as distinctive as his, there was definitely something there. I loved her voice. I'd had no reason to wonder at its origins.

A sob left my throat before I could stop it, and I struggled to calm myself down. Riley started to shake her head, as if denying the question that I had yet to ask. She reached out, and I grabbed both of her biceps to stop her. The muscles beneath my hands tensed as if she was preparing for a blow.

"Foster, calm down. Please, don't cry," I heard her say, as if from far off, but I shook my head.

I reached up and grabbed her face in my hands. I wanted to know, and I wasn't going to let her get away without telling me. She tried to pull away from me, but I held her face firmly as I repeated her name. The wind had teased her hair from its neat braid, and she looked scared and rumpled. The tears were running unchecked down my cheeks. Finally, I asked, "Riley...can you hear me?"

She nodded, but I knew there was more to it than she was telling me. Had she been hiding this from me? She had no reason to. I cared about her. I would never…"*Are you deaf or something?*" I heard it as if I was saying it aloud again. The pain in her eyes was almost tangible, and I had caused it. I silently begged her for forgiveness, even though I would never forgive myself.

Her body started to shake, and I wrapped her in my arms as best I could as she cried soundlessly. *They would hit me until I made a sound. I never did.*

I cried harder, my face buried in her T-shirt. Unlike her, I cried with great wrenching sobs. "I'm so sorry, baby. I didn't know," I whispered, because my throat was too tight to speak any louder; and then I cried harder, because I didn't know if she could hear me.

CHAPTER FOURTEEN

I am not a touchy person, but at that moment, I felt the need to be as close to her as I could possibly get. I clung to her as I have never clung to anyone in my life, and she seemed to need that as well. Occasionally, one of us would tear up and the other would wipe the drops away.

Finally, with a sigh that rocked her whole body, Riley said, "I don't want you to think I'm ashamed, Foster. I'm not. I'm hard of hearing. I've always been this way."

"I just wish I had known."

"Why? Would it have changed anything?"

"No." I looked at her steadily. "Riley, when I was talking to Stacy, I was referring to myself as a hardass, not to you. I let her believe that I meant you because I didn't want her hitting on me. I was too tired to deal with her that night."

"I'm sorry I didn't tell you about my hearing. There just never seemed to be a good time to bring it up."

I put my hand back on her thigh. "May I ask you something?"

"Sure."

"Why don't you wear a hearing aid?" I didn't want her to think I was prying.

"I used to, but," she put her hand up to her left ear and smiled as if to reassure me, "there's nothing here. I have one hundred percent hearing loss in this ear. I had to wear the aid in my right. It amplified sound, but I didn't like it. I couldn't tell where sounds were coming from, and it made me feel disoriented. I stopped wearing it a few years back, and I feel I do a lot better without it."

"You talk on the phone. How does that work?"

"The phone is easy. I can press it against my right ear or turn up the volume." She shrugged instead of saying *no problem*. "It's when there is a lot of background noise and you don't look right at me that I have problems."

"Has it—always been this way for you?"

"Pretty much. I lost my hearing when I was two years old. My parents didn't realize until it was too late. It's hard to tell with an infant. Now they know more about these things, but back then it was fairly common not to take a child to the doctor for a simple fever. I got better and it was a while before anyone realized I had permanent damage to my hearing."

Riley looked out at the water, and I absently noted that the sun was going down, leaving its distorted imprint glistening on the ocean like a fun-house mirror. "That must have been really difficult when you were growing up."

"I had a hard time articulating. My father would tell me that I needed to practice, but once he died, there was no one I wanted to talk to. So I stopped talking as much. It was easier that way. People, kids mostly, used to tease me about how I spoke."

"What changed things?" I asked as I placed my hand over hers to stop her from picking at her cast. I was fairly sure that, at some point, she would just pull it off, whether her hand had healed or not.

"Dani," she said simply, and a smile appeared on her face.

I smiled back, even though a small part of me wished it could have been me who had helped her. I'm sorry, but jealousy doesn't just die—at least, not in my case—but it does sort of grow up. And though I still felt jealous that the mention of Dani could bring a smile, a small part of me was grateful. The fact that I cared for Riley so much that I was grateful when a rival was kind to her scared me more than I cared to admit.

"When I moved to Marin County, they decided to put me in a speech therapy class designed for kids who were hearing impaired or had speech impediments. That's how I met Dani. They sort of lumped us all together in this one class. Her hearing is normal, but she had speech problems."

"I noticed that she stutters."

"She has pretty good control now. She only stutters when she's nervous."

I ran my finger up Riley's arm and back down again. *My God,*

I'm touching her like I have every right to and she doesn't seem to mind. Which is probably a good thing, because I don't think I could stop anyway. "Didn't you say she's in the Army? What did she have to be nervous about?"

"Not anymore." Riley shifted and looked down at me. "She was sort of nervous about meeting you after she saw us together."

Not expecting that answer, I blinked. "Oh."

"And I had already told her that I'd finally met someone special I'd love to bring here with me someday."

I couldn't help it, my mouth fell open. I clamped it closed. This honesty shit was not really my thing. I wasn't sure if I was supposed to admit to her that her words thrilled me, or if I was supposed to play coy. The whole idea of me playing coy almost made me grin. I stopped myself, of course. With our track record, Riley would more than likely think I was laughing at her, and we would be back to square one.

"When did you tell her that?" I asked, in order to give myself time to think.

"After you stormed away from the movie theater. I knew you needed some time, so I stayed away, but I asked Dani if I could use the cabin because..."

"Because?"

"I'd planned to take a few months off before I started working. I knew you were stressed out, so I thought you might be willing to come up here with me, if you could get some vacation."

"You mean even then you were going to ask me to come here?" I dragged my hand through my hair. It was still a shock to me to have so little of it up there, but I have to admit I much preferred the shorter haircut and its easy maintenance. "I thought the only reason you brought me here was because I was in trouble."

I stopped talking as I noticed her staring at my lips. A thrill went down my chest and straight to my crotch.

"No," she said.

"I thought you might have wanted to be here alone, or with Dani."

"Dani's like a sister to me. I'm about the only lesbian around here she *hasn't* slept with."

Oh my God! Riley used the L-word. "Riley, did you just call yourself a lesbian?"

She smiled at me bemusedly. I think she was starting to question my sanity. "Yeah, I did."

"Are you really?"

A full-fledged smile spread across her face. "Well, sure, Foster. Do straight women go around hitting on you often?"

I contemplated telling her that they did, but decided not to. Besides, the question made me think of Monica, which made me sad. I wished I could somehow get word to her, but there was absolutely no way I would risk that. Chief James would no doubt be waiting for me to make contact with Smitty's widow. Belatedly, what Riley had said finally sank in. She'd been hitting on me? At no point during our acquaintance could I remember her hitting on me, or on anybody else, for that matter.

"I think you might need to work on your technique."

"Well, I sort of wanted to ask you out, but it just seemed like you were having a bad time of it and then when you, well you know, the drinking…"

"But why would you be interested in *me*?" I started picking at her cast before she covered my hand and stopped me.

"I just knew from the moment I saw you, I just knew you needed me. I felt it here." She touched the place over her heart.

Her words flooded me with so much fear and uncertainty that I seriously considered jumping up and running away. But only for a brief moment. Riley looked down at our hands. They were so different. Mine was much paler than hers, and smaller. Her fingers closed around mine, and I had to lean forward to hear her.

"I was attracted to you before you got in trouble. I really respected you for apologizing to me that night. You had enough on your plate without dealing with me."

I nodded and looked away from her. *My God, it wasn't a dream!* Her softly spoken words flowed over me like a warm caress. She was going to make me cry again. "I thought it was a dream." I chuckled nervously. "I guess I'm a little…"

"Scared?"

"Yeah," I admitted with a tight smile.

"Me, too. But I meant what I said last night. I'm not going anywhere."

"Riley, you have to know…" I shrugged helplessly. "I'm in serious trouble."

"I know. I just want you to give us a chance."

"I can't pretend that my life isn't screwed. I can't do that to you."

"Why can't you?" she asked softly. "I'll take you however I can get you."

I swallowed the lump in my throat. "Riley, I can't stay with you for long, you know that. I can't take the chance that they'll find us together."

"Then can I ask you something?"

"Anything. I owe you that much."

"You don't owe me anything, Foster. I just want your friendship. If you can't be with me I understand. But if you weren't in trouble, would you still want to see me?"

"In a heartbeat." Though something in me had to question if I would have taken her kindness for what it was, a genuine wish to help me. Would I have come here if she had asked me when I wasn't on the run? No, probably not. It was an earth-shattering discovery that caused me to catch my breath. The knowledge that I could have missed spending time with Riley was almost too painful to even consider.

She held out her uninjured hand and I took it gratefully and allowed her to pull me up. I stepped up on the higher part of the deck and turned to face her. The elevation brought me in line with her lips, which parted, and she moistened them once before biting down on the lower, as if to keep it from trembling. It worked, but not before I saw the sign of her nervousness.

"Sort of disconcerting, isn't it?" I said.

"Yeah." Her voice was soft and had a breathy quality to it that made me smile.

"You do that to me a lot."

"I do not," she denied with a straight face.

I pulled her up on the deck. "You totally stare at my lips when I'm talking to you. Like you want to *devour* them or something."

A tremor went through her body and I knew she was laughing at me. We walked hand in hand toward the cabin. I followed her into the small kitchen where she had left six or seven bags on the counter and table.

"Are you hungry?" she asked, reaching into one of the bags.

"You get frozen dinners? I could go for three or four of those."

I checked out the kitchen and noticed that there was no microwave. Shit, I was going to have to wait forty-five minutes to an hour before I could eat. I stuck my hand into one of the bags and started rooting around, looking for something edible in Riley's idea of food. The weird thing was, I was wanted for murder, had no money to speak of, was in hiding, had even gone out of my way to disguise myself, and all that aside, I was happier than I had been in years.

❖

I stared blindly at the watercolor that hung above the sink. *Going to bed with Riley.* I closed my eyes. The thought of actually sleeping with her hadn't even occurred to me. It had been hard enough sleeping next to her when I didn't think she had any feelings for me, but now... The word "torture" came to mind.

I will admit to killing time on dishwashing and showering because I wanted Riley to be asleep when I got out of the bathroom. It was nearing midnight and I was exhausted, so I figured she must be even more tired than me. I finally had nothing else to do, so I crept into the bedroom half expecting to find her asleep. The bed was turned back, music played on the stereo, and for once the sky shone clear and black through the glass double doors. I walked around the bed to look out, and nearly shrieked when Riley stood up from her position hunkered down in front of the stereo.

"Damn, you scared the shit out of me."

"Sorry." Her voice was so much softer than mine that it made my outburst seem even louder. "Would you dance with me, Foster?"

"Dance with you?" I repeated.

She walked toward me and, not waiting for my answer, folded her arms around me and pulled me close. I was still a little in shock, so I just stood there for a minute before I began to relax into her embrace. She even moved well. Not that what we were doing was all that complicated, but I could tell that if she wanted to, Riley could probably hold her own on the dance floor. I pressed my face into her shirt and inhaled. I don't know when I had gotten into the habit of smelling her, but I was fast becoming addicted. Intensely aware of her hand moving up and down my back, I groaned and melted into her. I don't know how I felt it, the sensations were almost intangible—a slight pressure in my back, a small bend of her knees—but a bloom of hot arousal flared in my crotch as our height difference became an asset rather than a hindrance.

"Foster, I want to kiss you. Just a kiss and a dance, that's all. We don't have to do anything else."

It sounded simple enough, until I looked into the pools of compelling blue that told me that this was anything but simple. One kiss wouldn't be enough for either of us. I knew it, and so did she. I almost laughed at the fact that I was supposed to be the reasonable one here.

"Relax," she said.

Her breath, or was it her lips, brushed mine. We were barely moving now. Her lips trailed lightly over my cheek as we swayed to the music. I felt fingers run up and down my sides. I inhaled sharply as she finally gave up all pretense and her hands went under my shirt. I felt heat roll off my face as she caressed my back. I buried myself against her so I didn't have to pretend that I was unaffected.

"It can't be wrong, Foster," she said in my ear, and I shook my head, my fingers going up to her ribs.

I could feel her every breath, her every move. We were both spiraling out of control, but I was still surprised when she finally gripped my ass and pulled me tightly into her hips. Breathing hard, I rested my head on her shoulder before I looked into her eyes. She used my confusion against me then, and warm, soft lips were soon urging mine apart. My heart began to pound in concert with my crotch. I was shocked to realize that the right amount of pressure from Riley could possibly make me come.

I tore my lips away from hers as realization slammed down hard. Riley's arms trembled with the effort of holding me up. Her breathing came in heavy gasps, and I knew it wasn't from the effort of holding me. Both of us were about two seconds from saying to hell with it. Well, I think Riley was already past that point.

"We can't," I said.

"Why can't we?" Her voice sounded as desperate as mine.

"Because it will be too hard…when I leave."

"It's going to be hard anyway, for me," she said.

"For me, too." I put my hand on her ribs just below her breast, needing to know what her heartbeat felt like. I moved my hand up to her neck, my thumb grazing the hollow of her throat. I felt her pulse racing. I shuddered.

Riley had not released her grip on my ass, and the pressure, along with what had to be the longest fucking love song on Earth, was starting to make me think that perhaps she was right. Maybe us being together was something we shouldn't fight against.

"You know I want to make love to you," she said.

I could feel her heart beating so hard that I stroked her back in an honest effort to calm her down. That lasted for about two seconds before my brain spiraled downward again with the thought of how good she felt beneath my hands. I thought, *Maybe she's right. Maybe it won't make things worse. Maybe I can make love to her and not feel guilty.*

"Foster, I want to make love to you."

She wants to make love to me. I began to push away from her. *I can't let her.*

"Shh," Riley breathed, her lips against my temple as I pushed weakly against her unmoving shoulders. "It's okay. I'm going to let you go. Can you stand on your own?"

"Yes," I said desperately. I wanted—no, *had* to make her let me go. Panic flooded through me. Even as I reached desperately for some distance between us so I could think, my fingers refused to release her shirt.

Riley eased me away from her body, but continued holding my hips. "I'm sorry, Foster. I didn't know I was upsetting you."

I shook my head, avoiding her eyes. I couldn't seem to catch my breath. "You didn't. It's not you. God, I'm sorry." I struggled to catch my breath. "I just panicked."

Her smile was gentle. "You have nothing to be sorry for. I didn't mean to scare you."

"You didn't. I scared myself."

"Will this," she squeezed lightly at my hips, "change things between us?"

"Well, I don't think either of us can deny that there's sexual tension between us." I tried to laugh, but even I had to admit that sounded pathetic.

Riley's eyes went up as the love song finally ended. "Were you trying to deny it, Foster? Because I always knew you wanted me."

A tentative smile played at the edges of her mouth, and I recognized her attempt to lighten the mood.

I decided to play along. "Puhleeze! You are not all that irresistible," I lied.

"Uh-huh, whatever. That's because I didn't show you my real moves."

"Oh, those weren't your 'real moves,' then?"

"Nah, those weren't my real moves. You'd have to pay to see those. And you would have to promise to control yourself, as I won't be held responsible."

"Ah, I see. So now you're so good that I'm going to start throwing myself at you?"

Riley shrugged. I couldn't turn down her challenge. "Hadn't you better start dancing? You're a long way from making me lose all control."

She grinned, and in that moment I knew. I knew without a doubt that I should back down from this game. If not then, perhaps I should have when she started to sway her hips and her good hand went to the front of her shirt, pressing in so that I could see the small indentations of her nipples against the cotton.

"Uh, this is a fast song," I reminded her nervously. And she quickened her hips and began to lip-sync.

"Thanks," I said dryly.

Riley closed her eyes, which was a good thing, because I mouthed "Oh shit" as her hands disappeared under her shirt and lifted, revealing her tummy and the bottoms of her breasts. *And exactly when did her pajama bottoms drop so low on her hips?*

She was still mouthing the lyrics to the song, her eyes open now but droopy. She looked at me like I could have her if I wanted her. I licked my lips and to my shock, she did the same. This was not playing fair. I watched her hand go up to her breasts and graze them before moving away. I blinked, forcing my lids to drag across eyeballs exposed to the heat of the moment entirely too long.

"Uh, Riley?" That smile that I used to think was so innocent turned seductive. I think I went catatonic as she turned around and lifted her shirt so I could see her ass. *Oh my God, she's going to open her shirt.* The moment the song ended, Riley ripped her shirt apart, sending buttons flying across the hardwood floors and my heart skittering right behind them.

"Oh sweet baby Jesus," I said and blinked in disbelief at what *should* have been naked, bobbing boobies. Instead, I was looking at a tank top—a thin but perfectly modest tank top. I had seen more skin after she'd worked out.

"You are a cruel, *cruel* woman," I said, and flopped back on the bed. There was nothing but silence, and I opened my eyes to see Riley nearly doubled over and shaking, holding on to one of the bedposts for support.

"The look on your face!" she said.

I yanked the covers over my head. *She can laugh at me all she wants, but I don't have to watch.* She really had gotten me good. Beneath the blankets, I stifled a laugh. I bet I looked hungry when she ripped that shirt open.

I heard a click as Riley turned my lamp off, and I pushed the blankets down around my shoulders and stared into the dim light cast by the living-room fire. Crisp, faintly salty air drifted through the cabin. Riley got into bed and immediately cuddled into my back, her palm resting on my stomach. I wondered if I should really be feeling this happy.

"You mad?"

I could still hear the smile in her voice, and it made me feel good that I had put it there. She really didn't smile enough. "Nah."

"Are *we* okay?"

"Better than okay," I said with a contented smile.

I squirmed a little as memories of the dream surfaced, making me uncomfortable to be lying so close to her. Behind my lids, the clear vision of Riley thrusting into me made me grit my teeth. I felt a numbing sensation in my crotch as I became acutely aware of her body pressed into my backside. I tried to breathe soundlessly so she wouldn't know I was still awake.

"Riley," I whispered, listening to her soft, even breathing.

She was asleep. *And what did I call her for, anyway?* My face burned as I realized that for all my good intentions, if Riley had been a little more insistent on making love, I would have probably given in. I was long past denying my attraction. As if she had somehow sensed my surrender, she shifted in her sleep and pulled me tightly back against her body. I stared into the dimly lit living room for an eternity before succumbing to sleep. In my dreams I didn't have to tell her no.

CHAPTER FIFTEEN

It had been so dark and rainy when we first drove to Albion that I hadn't noticed much about our location. Some of the homes were exactly what I expected, small and quaint, but many of them were what I would consider to be large and stately. The area was probably a retirement destination for wealthy San Franciscans. Who else could afford to live in such a rural area and own such large houses? It wasn't as if there were any high-rise office spaces that would support a white-collar workforce. The only people who even looked like they worked were the fishermen, and they for damn sure weren't living in big, fancy homes.

Riley had been quiet during the short drive into town. She didn't think this trip to the public library was a good idea. I thought my dyed hair, hat, and sunglasses were a good enough disguise. It's not like we were going to see wanted posters of me stapled up around the town. Besides, as much as I was enjoying the cabin, I did need to get out every so often. It had been several days since Riley first told me she was hard of hearing, and since I'd turned into a touchy-feely beast that couldn't seem to keep its hands to itself. I don't mean sexually, either; there was just this need to make sure that she was still there. She always was. We ate together, slept together—but not in the biblical sense—and walked together. It was the most at peace I'd ever felt.

"Here it is." She pulled up to a pristine white building and we both stared out the car windows, checking the surroundings for police. The library looked like it might have been an old schoolhouse or church at some point. A small picket fence skirted its perimeter, and it had a large steeple at the top, minus the bell.

I got out of the car and walked into the building ahead of Riley. At first, I felt self-conscious in my sunglasses and orange flip-flops, but the library showed few signs of life. The idea of being cornered didn't sit well with me, so I scanned the room for the fire exit, my retreat route if I needed to make a quick escape. My nerves jangled as we explored the stacks of magazines and the newspapers that hung on sticks, each section separately suspended by a system of string dividers.

We started with the Marin County papers and worked our way through to the San Francisco and even the Oakland papers, looking for anything that mentioned me, Smitty, or even Harrison Canniff. I studied Riley occasionally during the next hour or two, enjoying the fact that I could stare at her openly. She looked so sweet sitting there poring over the papers, a frown creasing her otherwise smooth forehead, and her hair loose for a change. I wanted to tell her that I liked when she wore it down, but I felt inexplicably shy. I've never been one to pass out compliments freely, and I was afraid of veering too far from my normal path.

Keeping Riley at arm's length is for the good of us both, I told myself. For the past few days, arm's length had included talking—mostly I talked and she listened—kissing, dancing closely, and spooning at night. I put my foot down when Riley suggested we get in the Jacuzzi. It sounds harmless but neither of us had bathing suits, a fact that didn't seem to bother Riley half as much as it troubled me.

"I think I've found something," Riley looked up so fast that I was unable to hide the fact that I had been staring and thinking about how much I wanted to kiss her. Her lips quirked into a smile as she whispered, "Concentrate."

She pushed a paper in front of me, and my heart slammed against my rib cage. It stood to reason that we would eventually find something. In fact, it was starting to look really odd that nothing appeared to have reached the news media.

Los Angeles, California

LAPD detective Foster Everett is sought for questioning in connection with the suspicious death of Harrison Canniff, a Los Angeles County resident and small business owner suspected of making and distributing illegal DVDs. Everett's partner, Detective Joseph Smith, died in an apparently unrelated car accident on Highway

1. The coroner's report is inconclusive as to whether alcohol was involved.
> See related stories:
> LAPD Detective's Death "Suspicious"
> The Forgotten Children

"Son of a bitch. Smitty never..." I stopped myself then. I had been about to blow up because they were implying that Smitty drank, which he never did while driving. I heard the squeak of chair rollers on hardwood floor and turned to see the librarian coming around her desk and toward us. She was a small woman, probably in her late fifties, wearing tight jeans that looked like they were better suited to a sixteen-year-old, Sperry topsiders, a thick pink sweatshirt with a cat on the front, and a large pink barrette on either side of her pixie-cut, mouse brown hair. Though we were the only people in the library, she still wore a disapproving librarian frown on her face.

"Is there something I can help you with?" she asked, peering over the rim of her glasses.

"No. But thank you," I said and we both fell silent until she returned to her desk.

"Is that the only entry you've found?"

Riley nodded. "I checked two weeks in either direction."

I frowned. "That's weird."

Usually the papers were full of shit like this. Murder or not, this was news. A cop suspected of killing a perpetrator was front-page stuff, and it would take people a lot more powerful than the LAPD to hush up a big story like that.

"Let's check the related stories," I said.

"They probably have those articles over there on the computer," Riley said, already on her way over to the computers. Her fingers moved nimbly across the keyboard, and within seconds of me leaning over her shoulder, the small article was up and on the screen.

The Forgotten Children of the City of Angels
by Staff Reporter Lana Morgan-Archer

Los Angeles County Coroner's Office
"I've done this too many times," she says as she covers the 12-inch form. She holds a clothespin in her

mouth while another volunteer hands her dried flowers to place into the tiny makeshift body bag. Citing a near-fatal accident with her own son as her motivation, she has made it her life's work to champion those less fortunate. She shakes her head as if it is almost too much to bear, but continues because she knows if she doesn't, no one else will. She named her Ann.

"Ann was my mother's name," she explains, teary-eyed, as she lifts the body onto the borrowed gurney. "Someone let this baby die, threw her away. She never had a chance at dignity. I thought Ann was a dignified name."

She watches the volunteer disappear with the gurney. Ann will be loaded into a van and chauffeured to her final place of rest.

You see, Ann has been adopted by Monica Smith, daughter of Police Chief Herbert James and wife of LAPD detective Joseph Smith. Ann, who was discarded by her birth mother and perhaps unwanted by her birth father, will now be laid to rest in a graveyard filled with adoptive brothers and sisters of every race imaginable. Ironically, over 185 strangers will show up and mourn Ann's passing.

Ann, who will be buried with her umbilical cord still attached, will never celebrate her first birthday.

There have been 23 others, and there is room in the donated plot for 6 more.

It will be full before year's end.

"I remember hearing about this," Riley said softly.

I sucked in a breath "Yeah, Monica used to hit me up all the time for donations. I never went to any of the funerals but I heard they were really...nice."

"How sad," Riley said.

I nodded. "Yeah. I always feel like it's my fault somehow. Like if I had done my job better, the babies would be safe."

"Something's broken in our society," Riley said sadly. "I don't think you or any other cop bears the responsibility for this kind of thing. All of us are responsible for protecting them. Not just you."

"It's more than that. It's as if all Monica thinks about is those dead babies. How can someone base their life on something so sad?" I hesitated. I'd never realized how much Monica's obsession freaked me out, until now. "I used to walk around her van, I mean *wide* around her van, because I knew she carried the babies in it. But it didn't seem to bother her at all. She puts their son in there to go to daycare and doesn't even blink."

I thought Riley might be shocked by what I was saying. I was sort of shocked myself. But she just placed her hand on mine for a few seconds. I could tell she was conflicted about what to say to me, so she said nothing. We avoided each other's eyes because there were no easy answers. And then, as moments often do, that one passed and we scanned the rest of the database for related stories.

The piece about Smitty's death was just a few inches long and said nothing I didn't already know. The wording struck me as careful, but that wasn't so unusual. When cops killed themselves, the LAPD tried to be tactful in any public statements. After searching a few minutes longer and finding nothing new, I stood up and stretched. From the way my back cracked, I wondered if I had aged ten years from the stress of my situation.

"Nothing to photocopy?" the librarian asked as we started toward the front doors. She was inspecting Riley like an organism under a microscope.

Riley's face wore the same bland, unemotional expression I'd seen at the club, and I realized the look hadn't been there in a while. I didn't appreciate someone making her feel like she had to hide behind it.

"We found what we were looking for," I said, hoping to discourage further conversation.

"Visiting from Los Angeles?" she asked, eyeing my flip-flops.

I didn't like the way she was looking at us, like we didn't belong and she was imprinting our images in a mental file she would be able to call up on the witness stand. How could she have guessed we weren't from San Francisco? It was much closer. I supposed my look could put me in the "Hollywood flake" category.

With a vague shrug, Riley said, "You know what it's like 'round here, everyone comes from somewhere else."

We escaped before the woman could take our photographs.

"See why I didn't want you to come to town?" Riley said. "People notice you."

I thought it was *her* they noticed. But I kept my opinion to myself. Making Riley feel self-conscious was a dumb move if I wanted to kiss her. And I did.

I was so deep in thought that we were damn near in the store before I happened to look up and catch the Doc Martens sign on the window. I immediately perked up. The bum look I'd been wearing hadn't done much for my spirits. Riley seemed comforted that my face wasn't spread all over the newspapers and argued heatedly that the clothes were so I wouldn't look so damn out of place, and based on the librarian's reaction, I had to agree with her there. So I allowed her to buy me three pairs of jeans, some socks, a few white shirts, and a brand-new pair of boots.

By the time we left the store, I was laden with shopping bags and a whole lot of guilt for allowing Riley to spend Dani's money on me. After I got settled in my seat, I flipped the sun visor down and checked my hair in the mirror. I would need to dye it biweekly to keep it blond. The prospect filled me with gloom. I had never been one for serious hair maintenance. Riley got into the car. "Ready to go home?"

A thrill shot through me as she said "home." I disguised the fact that I was touched by her question with a casual, "Yup."

"What are you thinking?" she asked as we passed over the small bridge and prepared to make a right turn onto the private road that led to the cabin.

"I don't know, I guess I'm still wondering why there was so little in the newspapers. Nothing makes sense. This thing has been hushed up. Maybe it was Smitty's father-in-law." Was Chief James embarrassed about the idea of a suicide in the family and just trying to protect Monica? I supposed it was possible. But why come after me?

Riley stopped the car and dealt with the gate. "You have to stop second-guessing everything," she said when she was back in her seat. "What's done is done and you can't change it. You have a chance to live a new life, and maybe this time you'll be happier."

I didn't look at her because her voice was entirely too soft and I was already feeling odd about my admissions. "I don't think so. Every time I'm happy, it's like I feel guilty about it because Smitty isn't here and that creep Canniff will never feel happy again. Whatever his crimes, I had no right to take his life, and I keep waiting for my luck to catch up with me."

Riley could talk about "moving on" but that wasn't an option. My life was on hold until I could clear my name. I stared out at the cabin, knowing I could not hide indefinitely. I had a choice to make: I could run and spend the rest of my life looking over my shoulder. Or I could go back to L.A. and find out what was really going on and why.

Changing the subject, I asked, "Are you happy, Riley?"

She was quiet for a minute. "I don't remember ever being more happy."

"Good." I got out of the car and stared out at the view. It was going to be chilly tonight. I could already see fog rolling in.

We stood there for a while, side by side, just looking out to sea. I relished the quiet moments I spent with her. Riley, unlike most people, had learned the art of silence. Even though I professed a wish for silence, like most people, I felt the need to verbalize. Riley didn't. She just enjoyed the moment, soaked it in like a sponge. "This has been the perfect day," I breathed.

"Would you like to watch the sun go down with me, Foster?"

I slid an arm around her waist, unwilling and unable to keep myself from touching her. The day had lulled me into a comfort zone I vaguely recognized as dangerous, but I stayed there all the same. "I would love to."

"We could sit in the Jacuzzi."

"How did I know that was coming?"

She smiled. "Probably because I have been trying to get you in there for days."

"We still don't have bathing suits."

She shrugged, and we pulled the cover off the Jacuzzi before heading into the house to undress—me in the bathroom, Riley in the bedroom. When I came out in a pair of Dani's shorts and a T-shirt, Riley was already in the Jacuzzi, eyes closed. A smile played across her features, and she ran a finger slowly back and forth along the edge of the tub as if she was tracing something in her mind.

I placed one foot in the water, hoping to get in before she opened her eyes. She sensed my presence, though, and gave me a welcoming smile as I stepped into the hot, oscillating water. My flesh goose bumped, not the usual response to warm water.

"I was just thinking," she said.

"About what?"

"About you."

I had no idea what to say to that, so I moved closer and leaned in for what I thought would be a sweet kiss. I was unprepared for the passion. So much so that I turned away from her.

"No," she said against my temple. "Stay. You want me, you want this. I can tell."

I wanted to tell her that it was a mistake, but I didn't because she was right. I wanted to feel her mouth on mine, her chest moving against me as she breathed. And most of all, I wanted to feel her body responding beneath my hands.

I straddled her hips, and she placed her hands around my back to give me support. Her eyes latched on to my lips and she met me halfway for a kiss that left us both breathless. Achingly aroused, I drew away, quickly pulling in air tinged with salt and chlorine.

"We missed the sunset," Riley said.

"I didn't," I said softly. And even though my face was hidden in her shoulder, I could feel that she was smiling.

The Jacuzzi's motor kicked in and the water swirled around us. Even the warmth from the steam was not enough to keep my nipples from rising in the chilly night air. Riley held my butt with one hand, pressing me intimately against the hard muscles of her stomach. To stabilize myself, I put my hands on both her biceps. Her skin radiated heat like a small furnace. The round muscles in her arms flexed and then hardened beneath my palm.

For some reason, I could not breathe in enough air through my nose when kissing her. I needed to think. There was a reason why I shouldn't do this, wasn't there? The kisses continued until I had to break away from her sweet prison. I slumped into her and closed my eyes. With one arm around my back, she held me so close that our billowing T-shirts were crushed between our bodies.

If I had to put my finger on the moment when I lost all control of the situation, it would have to be this one. As aroused as I was, as much as I wanted Riley Medeiros, it wasn't until I felt the rapid beating of her heart that I gave up the last vestiges of denial.

"We should get out of here, I'm getting all pruny," she said, and I could tell she was as reluctant as I was to stop kissing.

She stood, and her wet T-shirt clung to the muscled contours of her body like a see-through second skin. I stood up as well, hoping she would admire me in the same way I'd just admired her. She did.

"It's as cold as a witch's tit out here," I said, basically ruining the moment, but I was too damned cold to care. Even Riley, the living torch, was shivering violently. I threw all pretense of trying to look cute out the window as I ran into the cabin, my arms crossed in front of my chest.

"Get in the shower," Riley said as I dripped and shivered in the living room. "I'll put more wood in the fire." She spoke with her back turned, something she rarely did. I don't know if it was because of her hearing deficit or personal etiquette, but when talking to Riley, you got her full attention.

I didn't argue. I did a kind of frigid hop over the cold hardwood floors and rushed to get the faucets running. I was halfway hoping that Riley would be delayed building the fire, but when the water was warm enough to thaw us out, I heard her behind me and quickly stepped under the showerhead. She joined me and we rinsed the chlorine from our clothed bodies in silence, avoiding touching each other in the confined space. Riley kept her right hand on the wall so as not to get the cast wet.

With her head under the water and her eyes closed, she looked younger than her twenty-six years. Her one-handed rinsing had a tense, desperate quality. I wanted to help but all I could do was stare. The agitated movements ceased and she opened her eyes, gazing directly into mine. Something passed over her face that was akin to fear, then arousal, and then the kind of wariness people have when they don't know if they can trust someone.

A psychologist could probably tell you a lot about me based on the fact that seeing the emotions on Riley's face sent me into overload. My dream, the heavy kissing, even my situation, all converged in an explosive mixture. The electricity crackling just below the surface exploded full force. The feeling was so foreign I was drunk with its power.

"Come here, Riley." I was used to giving orders. "Put your hand up on the wall so your cast won't get wet."

Her reaction was automatic. She did as she was told, and the pink cast flashed obscenely in the corner of my eye. I stepped closer. Her agitation showed in the pulse beating at her throat.

I placed my hand on the back of her neck and kissed her firmly. Her lips quivered under mine, fanning my ardor like fresh air ignites a flame. I slid my free hand beneath her shirt and backed her against the wall, exploring the soft skin of her stomach. Riley inhaled and I felt a brief stiffening that could have been her last-ditch effort to get things back under control. I ignored her faint uncertainty. Fingers spread wide, I trailed up her muscled abdomen until I reached the soft skin of her breast. She flinched as I ran my thumb over the nipple of her right breast.

"Do you want me to stop?" I asked.

She shook her head, her lips forming the word "no." I pulled her soaked T-shirt over her head, leaving her upper body exposed to my hungry eyes. My breath caught as I got my first look at the muscles I'd only recently touched for the first time. Riley brought up her free hand to cover herself, but I stopped her with a gentle hand on her wrist.

"No...please, I want to look at you."

Her hand fell, but a quick glance at her face told me she was almost sick with apprehension. Why, I didn't know. I had never seen anyone as beautiful as Riley Medeiros. Each muscle, each curve, was perfect. I stepped closer as I gently cupped her breasts in both hands and closed my mouth over one of her nipples.

In a small flurry of movement, Riley placed her hand against me, trying to push me away. I increased the pressure on her nipple and wiggled my hands beneath the elastic of her shorts. Gripping her ass, I pulled her into me and kissed her with renewed hunger.

She jumped as my hands glided over her breasts. Her skin felt silky beneath my fingers. She leaned back against the wall and her eyes closed as I touched her under the pretense of helping her wash. I gently coaxed water from the shower over her firm breasts and down her tapered stomach. Except for a soft inhalation, she didn't move.

Hooking the waistband of her shorts, I squatted and slid them down her legs. From my position, I could see the rapid rise and fall of her stomach. Droplets disappeared into the dark thatch of hair and joined a stream of water that poured from her. I leaned in to kiss her, detecting the unmistakable scent of her arousal over the chlorine and the smell of soap. It was so faint, so light, that I almost thought I was imagining it. I kissed her gently, the water from the shower dousing my hair fully before I rose.

Riley's lips were parted, and her eyes were closed. Her legs were spread just wide enough for me to stand between, and I placed my lips on the pulse at her neck and sucked gently.

"Foster, I can't stand up," she moaned weakly.

"Yes, you can, sweetheart. Just lean back," I whispered, not bothering to move my lips from her neck. The whole time I kissed her, my eager hands continue to rove her body. When my fingers stroked her stomach, she jumped slightly, and I paused. I had never felt such a frantic need to pleasure someone, but I waited, preparing myself not to be disappointed if she wanted me to stop.

Her muscles felt like skin stretched across steel. She murmured something I took for encouragement and shifted my caresses to the water-slicked smoothness of her sex. She did jump again, but this time arched her back, inviting one of my fingers to slip between the lips of her sex. Her clitoris was full with her need, and the mere fact that she was so aroused sent my own arousal up a notch. I was surprised to feel the insistent heat between my own legs as I continued to stroke, and kiss, and prepare Riley for my entrance.

I should have taken more time with her, but I couldn't. I had never felt rushed in lovemaking before, a fact that had gotten me called more names than I can mention. The lack of anything other than a vague sense of arousal had always given me a fairly steady hand. But with Riley, my hands shook and blood rushed in my ears. I couldn't wait any longer. I sought and found her opening, pressing my thumb into her clitoris. I closed my eyes and prayed that I wasn't hurting her as my finger slid into her tight opening. A slow shiver moved through her body, and I paused to let her get used to me. The water that sloshed down on my back had ceased to be a pleasure and now felt like one more thing that was keeping me away from Riley. Her hips were slowly relaxing, and I began to move my finger in and out of her. I wanted to enter her with one more finger but feared it would be too much, so I contented myself with pressing closer to her and putting firm pressure on her clitoris with my thumb.

Her hips began to take on a confidence as I withdrew my finger almost fully and slowly eased it back in. I took her nipple into my mouth, and she moaned and shifted her stance so her legs were farther apart. I tugged gently on her nipple and pressed firmly against her mound. I felt her muscles tighten around my finger once, and then begin to spasm. I didn't hear her make a sound, but I looked up just in time to see a grimace cross her face. She gritted her teeth, head thrown back. A corded muscle stood out in her neck as she met her orgasm with a determination that aroused me no end. The grimace and the way her muscles tensed told me how powerful her release really was. The hands that held me close were incredibly gentle, and not once did she say a word.

I slowly and reluctantly withdrew from her and hugged her, resting my head on her shoulder. Finally, I leaned over to cut off the water. I could feel her staring at me, waiting for something that would tell her that it was okay, that we were okay.

"Riley, I don't know what to say." I stepped out of the shower, feeling exposed. I had been resisting making love with her all this time. I didn't understand fully why I had given in. Hell, I hadn't just given in, I had gone after her like I was in heat or something.

Riley followed me out of the shower, holding on to her soggy-looking cast. "It's okay. I won't expect more from you," she said flatly.

Wrapping a towel around her body, she left the bathroom. Was she angry with me? Stunned, I watched her walk away. I felt certain I had pleased her: I had felt her body orgasm; the evidence of it was still on my hand. *I thought she wanted...*

I found her standing in front of the window, staring out into blackness. Ignoring my initial urge to just turn away and leave her be, I touched her lightly on the shoulder. "I thought you wanted this, Riley. I'm sorry if I upset you, if I moved too fast. I didn't mean to."

The shoulder beneath my hand began to shake, and I jerked my hand away as if scalded. Fear swept through me. I hadn't imagined it, had I? Surely she hadn't asked me to stop.

She turned to me then, in tears. "I did want you."

"Then why are you crying? Did I do something wrong?"

"No, I guess I just realized."

Sorrow strangled my breathing. Riley had finally clued in to what I'd known all along: our relationship had no real future. How could she ever be with someone like me? For as long as I was with her, she was at risk, too. I knew this, and had resisted my attraction for her because of it. "I realized how much I love you," she said.

The words could have been spoken in another language. She watched me for a moment before turning away, embarrassed. "You don't have to say anything. I already know how you feel."

"No, you don't understand. No one has ever said that to me." I laid my head on her back. "I'm not going anywhere. At least, not if I can help it."

I must have stumbled into the right words, because her body relaxed.

"I'll give you all the space you need, but I can't change how I feel," she said.

"I don't want you to. Can we just…can you hold me? I want to be close to you."

We dried off quickly and climbed onto the bed, and she wrapped her arms around me. Even though she was supposed to be comforting me, I felt the need to ease her discomfort as well. "Everything's going to be okay, I promise."

A salty tear trickled down the soft skin of her breast, mingling with my kisses. And as one part of my brain rebelled against my promising that, the other part stood fast. I had no choice but to make good on my promise, because I loved her, too. I just didn't know how to say so yet.

I wanted her to hold me. I needed to be as close to her as I could. I kissed her hard, my mouth giving no quarter and asking for none. Silently I was begging her to take me. It seemed like her hands were everywhere I needed them to be, until I felt so much heat in my center that the mere weight of her pressing into me wasn't enough.

I wrenched my mouth away from hers. "Riley, please. Inside me. Now."

She complied instantly, thrusting inside me so hard that I almost cried out. Her mouth closed over mine as salty tears trailed down her cheeks. I held her tighter as she continued to push into me, my passion systematically rising as I moved with her, holding her tighter than I'd ever held anyone in my life. Her breathing increased every time I lifted to meet her. I felt the wild beating of her heart and knew she had to struggle, as I did, to keep at least some sense of control.

The light film of moisture beneath my hand told me how much that control was costing her. And there was, as always, her scent. That endearing, sexy scent I was trying to burn into my memory…just in case. I moved with her because this was one more moment we could share together, one more thing I could think about when I was alone. Deep down, I hoped she would do the same.

When my body tensed, my eyes opened wide from the shock of it; and for one clear moment I saw stars and made a wish before my eyelids had to close. Muscles that I had forgotten I owned began to tighten rhythmically around her fingers.

"Yes," she said, her lips still on mine as she eased her impassioned attack on my senses. My body continued to grip her fingers until her thrusts slowed to a stop. She kissed me long after the ripples of pleasure had dissipated. Tears rolled down her cheeks and pooled with those on mine. Eventually, they coalesced at our lips, where they were sealed between us like a promise.

❖

My fingers dug into the bathroom sink as I stared at myself in the mirror. The circles under my eyes were almost nonexistent, and I seemed to have grown into my haircut because I honestly couldn't remember it looking any other way. I pushed my hair back a little and noticed that my usually pale skin seemed to have a glow to it. I might have actually tanned instead of burned for once. My eyes even looked darker. Probably because of my new hair color, but I still looked…well, different. That gaunt, haunted look that I had somehow accumulated over the years seemed to have faded. I looked loved. Happy? Maybe that was it. I was happy. Damn. I realized, with sadness, that I was right all along. She made me happy. And now? Well, now it was going to be time for me to make my own way.

Straightening, I strode back into the bedroom. Riley's eyes were closed, allowing me to study her unobserved. I felt like I needed to imprint her permanently on my brain synapses. I stared at the dark hair that looked even darker against the white of the pillowcase, then worked my way down.

"You took your cast off. Was it because it got wet?"

Her eyes flicked open. "I was going to take it off anyway." She looked sad, almost as if she was in need of a hug.

I got into bed and she moved away from me. I was so surprised that I'm sure that she saw the pain in my eyes.

She was willing to throw caution to the wind, but I was the one keeping her at arm's length to keep from hurting her. From the sound of her voice I had already done the thing I had been trying to avoid. Even though she said she understood, I don't think she did. I'm not so sure I even understood anymore.

"Riley, maybe we should talk."

Disappointment and pain flew across her features and then were gone so fast I almost thought I had imagined the expression. "I'll understand if you want to go."

She spoke more quickly than usual, and I had a hard time understanding her. I closed my eyes. Her voice, I was going to miss her voice so much.

"Let's go outside for a minute." She gathered a comforter in her arms.

I followed her out the double doors and she wrapped us tightly together. We hunkered down on the deck and gazed up at the clear night sky. Thousands of stars glimmered light-years away. I felt small and inconsequential but, for once, not alone. A deep contentment rippled through me. I hugged Riley and kissed her cheek. I had to speak, but the moment was so perfect that the words refused to come

It was Riley who spoke first. "It's time for you to leave, isn't it?"

CHAPTER SIXTEEN

I awoke before the sun came up the next morning. The house was completely still, as if it had taken a front-row seat for the play in which I ruin my life. Riley's breathing was soft and even. I slowly removed my arm from around her and made my way into the bathroom. I was already planning how I was going to get back to Los Angeles and what I was going to do when I got there. I needed to take care of this, but if I could, I would get back to Riley and make it up to her.

I walked out of the bathroom fully clothed and approached the bed where she still slept. I propped the note I had painstakingly written in the bathroom against the lamp on her nightstand, so that she would see it when she first woke up. Her face was completely shrouded in darkness, and although I longed to kiss her good-bye, I couldn't risk waking her.

Feeling like a thief as well as a murderer, I took half the cash from the envelope. I explained in the letter that I would get the money back to her as soon as I could. I also confessed to loving her with all my heart. And I did. I wanted to be with her, that's why I was doing this. And if she would have me, I would try my best to come back. Leaving her was going to be the hardest part of the journey, but I knew it was for the best. I had contemplated taking Riley's car, at least as far as the interstate, but decided against it. I would have hated to have to explain that I had not only taken her money, but also her car.

I lifted Riley's cell phone from the nightstand and crept out of the bedroom. As I let myself out onto the deck, I scrolled through the contacts until I found Stacy's home number. I felt bad calling her so

early, but I needed to find a place to stay when I got back in town, and if anyone could organize discreet accommodation for me, she could.

"Stacy?"

"Foster? My God, is that you?" Her voice was croaky from waking up too soon, but there was something else, a tightness that unsettled me.

"What's wrong? Have you been crying?"

"It is you, isn't it?"

"Yeah, it's me. What's up, Stace?"

"Is—Riley with you?" Her voice sounded hesitant and unsure, totally unlike the Stacy that I knew. I wasn't being silly. Something *was* wrong.

"Yeah, she is." I sat down on the edge of the deck, my heart pounding fast and hard in my ears.

"Maybe I should talk to her."

"Why? I'm the one who phoned you. Damn it, Stacy, tell me what's wrong."

"It's Marcus. Someone killed him."

I was sure I'd heard wrong. Marcus wasn't dead. He couldn't be. "Killed him?"

"I'm sorry. I know. After Smitty...I just thought you would want to know."

"How? What happened?"

"I don't know. The police are classifying it as a hate crime."

I pressed my fist into my forehead. *A hate crime.*

"Listen to me," Stacy said urgently. "I wanted to speak to Riley first because I know you'll want to come back. You shouldn't, Foster. They are still looking for you. You need to stay away."

"I know," I said dully.

It all came flooding back: Marcus's excitement over snooping through the records, my telling him to leave it alone. What if he hadn't? What if he'd been murdered because he was sticking his nose into something no one wanted him to see?

"Stacy, I...I should go." I ended the call before she could reply.

Dazed, I walked around the side of the deck to get one last look at Riley's sleeping face. I put my hand on the windowpane. *Marcus, my friend...Marcus was dead.* I had lost two friends. Two people who had tried to help me in the last year were dead, more than likely because of me. Riley was right, it was time for me to leave.

❖

The traffic on the way to the main road was as stagnant as the frigid air around me. Hitchhiking is not something that I would recommend, but the 9 mm's gave me some sense of safety and I was reluctant to spend the cash I had taken if I didn't have to. I was determined to send it back to her, even if she wouldn't have me back. I waited there for what seemed like nearly an hour as several truckers passed me by without so much as a flash of their brake lights. I shivered. I had taken one of Riley's shirts, but I was still freezing.

My plan was to get to Mendocino and catch a bus back to L.A. I hoped Riley wouldn't follow. I had told her in my note that I needed to attend to problems of my own making. It would only stress me out if she was there, too. I stuck my thumb out but dropped it as the SUV rolled by without so much as a brake light. Then I saw a blue Land Cruiser. Riley's Land Cruiser.

She pulled to a stop not ten feet away from me. I shielded my eyes against the glare of her headlights. *She came after me.* My heart did an excited flip-flop as her door swung open and she stepped out. She hadn't bothered to cut the car engine or shut her door. The look on her face was enough to send my heart right back to its resting place. *She looks like she's going to kill me.* I stood my ground, shivering as she stalked toward me. She stopped inches in front of me, her ice blue eyes burning me with the force of her anger. But then her face crumpled. I reached up to hug her, but she stepped back.

"Don't."

"Riley, I'm sorry."

"Don't you dare! After what…How could you just leave?"

"I had to, damn it! People who tried to help me are dying, and I'm afraid. I explained it in the note."

The stricken look on her face silenced me. Did you know that you can actually hear a heart breaking? It's not a shattering sound or a hard crack, like you would think. It's a weak pounding, a steady loss of energy, and a loss of hope—like air escaping from an inner tube. And it hurts. It hurts like hell. Especially when you're the one who caused it.

I shook my head in frustration because all I really wanted to do was go back home with her and forget everything. I reached for her again, and even though she let me hug her this time, her body was stiff and unyielding. She stood silently as I tried to speak over the pain. "I'm so sorry. I never meant to hurt you, Riley, but I have to do this."

"I'm sorry about Marcus."

"So am I."

"What are you going to do?"

"Find out who killed him, see if it's somehow connected."

She gently pushed me back so that I was no longer able to hide from her hurt. "Then I'm going with you."

Her tone left no room for discussion. "Promise me one thing," I said. "If anything happens to me, don't try to help. Just leave. Come back here, or go home. Okay?"

She nodded and walked back to the car. I hesitated only a second before following. I didn't believe her for a moment.

❖

The ride back to L.A. was a tense one. Losing two friends in less than two months was more than coincidence. Smitty, a suicide? Marcus, a hate crime? And I had been framed with some phony evidence.

My mind swung back and forth between denial and paranoia. I tried to convince myself that Smitty's death had nothing to do with me or the Harrison Canniff debacle, that he had been having family problems, but it just didn't feel right. My reaction to the whole thing had been atypical so far. I hadn't asked questions. I hadn't even followed up on my request for Canniff's autopsy report. I didn't want to see it. To look at it would be to face up to my own guilt.

Marcus was the one who'd been digging around. He'd suspected something and now he was dead. How convenient. For someone. But who? I thought about the "serious people" Smitty had mentioned, the people who would get angry if I didn't play the game by their rules. They had covered my ass. Had Marcus known who they were?

I looked over at Riley's pensive features. "You okay?"

She didn't answer, just nodded and continued to watch the road. I put my hand on her thigh and frowned when I felt the tension there. She wasn't okay, and in truth, neither was I.

"Riley, I want you to know I'm not on a death mission here. I'm not trying to get caught. I just need to do this. Something in my gut tells me this isn't right."

"I know you can't let it go, Foster." She glanced at me, then back at the road. "They were your friends."

"Right," I said, relieved that she understood.

"Then why can't you understand that I can't let you do this alone? I love you."

"Riley—you can't say you love me."

"I can. Because I do," she said with a determination that left no room for argument.

Her words, though wonderful, elicited a menagerie of feelings ranging from guilt, unworthiness, and joy to utter and unadulterated fear.

Something Riley saw in my face made her smile. "You look like you're ready to run again."

I didn't know what to say. Who was I kidding? I knew exactly what I should say. But how could I complicate things more by telling her the truth? If I loved her, I mean really loved her, would I allow her to be here with me, in danger? I should have done something, stopped things before things got so far out of hand. The last thing I wanted to do was hurt Riley.

"Don't worry Foster. I don't expect you to tell me you love me, too. I just wanted you to understand why I couldn't just let you go alone."

A muscle worked in her cheek as I stared at her. "I do understand, Riley. I'm just scared. I don't want you to get hurt."

"Then you'll have to trust that I can take care of myself." Her voice was quiet but determined.

"Riley." I squeezed her thigh to get her attention, but aside from a flicker of her lashes there was no response. "I'm trained for this kind of thing. I know how to handle this."

She looked at me then. "What if you're right?"

"What do you mean?"

"What if this does have something to do with you? What if these people caused Smitty's death? Smitty was trained for this, too, wasn't he?"

"If someone killed Smitty, then they could have killed Marcus. He must have found something." Somehow I would have to gain access to the records office and find out what Marcus had discovered. I hadn't answered her but the question hung heavily between us.

"Do you think those two detectives were planning to kill you that night?" Riley asked.

"Maybe. I'm just glad you were there to prevent whatever they had planned."

I could hear Captain Simmons now. *"Shot while resisting arrest. A tragedy. I knew her temper would land her in trouble one day. She wouldn't accept the professional help she needed."*

I glanced over at Riley, hoping to see some softening of her expression, but she was as determined as I'd ever seen her. Whatever happened, she wasn't going anywhere. She loved me. How could I expect anything less?

❖

Our arrival in L.A. was about as uneventful as one could hope for. The night air was cool and crisp. Riley's friend had left the marquee on above the theater, probably in order to keep people from parking in the parking lot and doing illegal things. Riley cut the motor on the truck. Before I could say a word, she was out the door and had disappeared into the darkness. I frowned. It was perfectly understandable that she would be stressed, but her uncommunicative behavior was starting to get on my nerves. I hadn't asked her to come with me, and as far as I was concerned, my job would be easier if didn't have to worry about her.

I followed her into the theater, puzzled by her mood. My failure to follow through with a Hollywood "I love you" moment weighed on me. But I couldn't just gush the way some people did five minutes after they met. I did have feelings for Riley—in fact, I loved her. But I wasn't free to explore my feelings right now. Until I could offer Riley what any woman in love deserved—a partner not in jail—I wasn't going there.

"I never thought I would see this place again," she said as we entered her neat little apartment.

"Me, either." My anger and frustration faded as she dropped our bags and leaned back against the kitchen counter with a weary sigh. Riley was putting herself in danger for me. Of course she was worried. I would be, too, if the shoe were on the other foot.

"I'm sorry for putting you through this," I said gently. "I know it's not an ideal…beginning."

I went over and drew her to me. For a brief instant she was rigid in my arms, then she melted into me. "I just don't want it to end," she said.

I nodded, wondering what I had done to deserve her in my life. "I know. I don't either. And when this is all over, we'll start fresh, like two normal people."

"Where will you begin?" I could tell she was making an effort to keep her voice light.

"I need to find out exactly how Marcus died. Stacy just told me they were classifying it as a hate crime. Then I want to find out what he was up to." Hopefully he wasn't still digging around in the stuff connected to me. "Either way, Marcus is dead, and someone is going to pay."

She stepped away from me and pretended to look for something in my bag. I reached past her and pulled out a cloth I'd used to clean the guns. Sitting on the bed, I removed the clip from one gun and began to clean it.

She said, "I missed my brother Brad's birthday."

Brad is her brother? Of course he's your brother, you idiot. "Did you call him?"

"Yes, but it's not the same. I was supposed to be there."

I caught on. Here was the reason for her brooding and monosyllabic replies for most of the ten hours we'd been driving. From the little Riley had told me, hey were a close-knit family, the kind I used to dream of belonging to when I was up in my room alone reading Trixie Belden mysteries and dreaming of being a detective. That was way before I became disillusioned with the world. There was a certain amount of sweetness in ignorance.

Relieved that I wasn't in the hot seat, I said, "You could take some of the money and hop a flight. You'd be there in a few hours."

"You're trying to get rid of me."

I smiled at the trace of laughter in her tone. "Maybe. I mean, if you're here I'll only want to make love with you, and that's going to be a distraction."

Riley lifted her eyes from my mouth. We stared at each other. She stopped whatever she was doing with our folded clothing and said, "I think you should get undressed."

I insisted on a shower before bed, much to Riley's chagrin. By the time we headed to her narrow bed, we were both yawning. I thought for sure Riley would be asleep as soon as her head hit the pillow. I was wrong.

My hips rose off the bed and were suddenly held down by two strong hands. Riley's tongue was tormenting me. Every time I tried to quicken my pace, she would stop me or slow down. I wanted to tell her to stop teasing, but I couldn't seem to verbalize anything other than a whimper or a moan. She sucked my tormented bundle of nerves between her lips and began working her tongue across the tip, sending me into convulsions. Her hands gripped my buttocks and held me firmly in place. My stomach muscles clenched and I gripped the bedding so hard I could hear the sheets coming loose at the corners. I sobbed her name and couldn't seem to make myself shut up. She gentled her tongue as my orgasm slowed.

I blinked up at the dim outline of the clouds on her ceiling and vaguely wondered if I was too old to start an active sex life. My heart felt like it was about to burst from my chest at any moment. My hand went to the dark head that now lay on my hip. It was a long while before I was capable of speaking.

"You're going to kill me one day, baby." I let my fingers sink into her thick hair with a final deep sigh.

She grinned. "Not unless I can go with you."

"Oh, yeah? You want to go together, huh? Well, we'll see about that."

I pulled her up the bed, probably because she was allowing me to. If someone would have told me that I would make love all night after driving all the way from Albion to Los Angeles, I would have reminded them that crack kills. But I just couldn't seem to get enough of her.

We wrestled playfully for a moment until I pinned her hands above her head and began placing little kisses up her neck and along her jawline and finally around her right ear. I heard her gasp as I eased my leg between her thighs and began to move teasingly against her.

"You are so wet, Riley."

Her response a shiver. She turned her head. The braid she usually wore had long since come undone, leaving the delicate curve of her right ear exposed to my lips as I moved against her. I kissed her ear again and felt her inhale sharply. I looked down to make sure she was okay, and noticed that she was biting her bottom lip. I kissed her ear again, and she had the same reaction. Frowning, I slowed my movements.

"Do you like that, baby?" I whispered.

She inhaled again, her breathing so ragged it scared me a little. Riley didn't make much noise when we made love; I'd noticed that the first time we were together.

"Sweetheart, is it okay?" I whispered again, and the hands that were always gently on my waist helping me to move against her suddenly tightened and small chill bumps rose on the skin just below her collarbone. She was more than okay. She really liked this. I cupped her head with my hands and put my lips to the curve of her ear.

"Riley, I can feel how much you want me." I continued to whisper, "I love how wet you are. How you smell. How you grit your teeth when you're close. How you watch me when I have an orgasm. Does that turn you on, baby? Knowing how much I want you?" A small noise escaped from her throat but other than that, she continued to move in rhythm with me. "I love touching you," I whispered, my eyes closing as her breathing became even raspier. "I love feeling how strong and hard you are underneath such soft skin."

She moaned, and my body delighted at the sound. I could tell she was losing control. What was thrilling was that I was barely moving against her now. My thigh firmly pressed into her center, I whispered hotly into her right ear, "But you know what I love most of all?" She answered with a swallow and shake of her head. "I love how you look when you come."

I let my lips graze her ear, and her grip on my hips tightened. A deep groan escaped her normally silent lips, and I held on to her as her hips began to move violently. I slowed my movements in gradual increments, letting her dictate when she wanted me to stop. Finally her hips sank weakly onto the bed. I remained pressed firmly against her, so I knew she was still experiencing small convulsions.

She looked too vulnerable to be allowed out of my eyesight. "Wow," I mouthed, making her blush, which turned me on even more. "You okay?"

"Yes," she said her eyes pasted someplace to the right of my shoulder. I moved my head until she was forced to look me in the eye. The time for shyness had passed a long time ago for us.

"You should have told me you liked being talked to."

"I didn't know."

"So nobody else has ever talked while...?"

"No."

"Oh." I smiled down at her, and she got the cutest look on her face. *I think I need to perfect my technique a little.*

"Again? I thought you were tired from the drive?"

"I didn't drive. You did." I cupped both sides of her face and moved my thigh closer, smiling as I felt her clench against me.

I slowly and gently turned her head and lowered my own until my lips were grazing the delicate ridge of her right ear. "Can you hear me, sweetheart?" I whispered. She gasped and nodded. "I'm in love with you, Riley Medeiros."

She gasped and she moved as if she was going to turn away, but I had to finish before I chickened out. "I'm going to love you with everything I have because I know it will never be good enough. Do you hear me?"

Her "yes" was mangled by tears and moans of pleasure, but I heard her.

CHAPTER SEVENTEEN

We'd been parked across the street from Pollard's Billiards for ten minutes and no one had gone in or come out. Granted, it was twelve in the afternoon, but I had always found this place open no matter what time of day it was.

"You sure you don't want me to go in alone?" Riley asked nervously as we stared at the deserted-looking bar.

"No, Big Sherm won't talk to you. He doesn't know you."

"What if he goes to the police?" she asked worriedly. "They would know you're in L.A."

"Trust me, there's no love lost between Sherm and the police."

"From what you told me, he's not crazy about you, either."

"Okay, I'm going to go around the back and see what's happening. Do you want to wait here?"

"No." Riley looked for the entire world like she was ready for a fight.

We got out of the car and crossed the road. I'd traded in my blue jeans for black cargo pants and a black T-shirt. I still wore the sunglasses, just in case someone might recognize me looking blonde and sexually satisfied.

I tried the front door out of habit. As I'd expected, it was locked, though I was positive there were people just inside, probably watching us on a monitor. We went around the back and I hammered on the back door with my fist. I probably put a little more into it than I needed to, but hell, I was more than a little frustrated with my life right now.

"Who the fuck is it?" a bodiless voice yelled from the other side.

"None of your *fucking* business," I yelled. "I'm here to see Big Sherm."

A square plate near the top of the door slid back and angry brown eyes shifted from me to Riley. They seemed to linger on Riley for a moment, no doubt reading her as muscle I'd brought along for respect. The little window slammed shut, and I was about to hammer on it again when I heard a metal bar being removed and several locks being turned. The door was swung open by none other than Homeboy.

He hitched his thumb in an obscure direction behind him. "Sherm's in the back."

I pushed past him, leaving Riley to follow. I fought down the insane urge to stop right there and ask her if she still loved me. I mean, she couldn't just change her mind, could she? I know I couldn't. My chest literally felt like someone had stuffed dirty rags into it by way of my throat, making sure to scrape every surface as they passed. Instead I made a beeline for the room I had seen Sherm in the last time we were there, and found him sitting in the exact same place.

"Hey, Sherm." I prepared to field insults in order to get my information.

He turned the TV off in the middle of what looked like one huge catfight. "I was wondering when you would show up."

"I'm sorry, Sherm. I know how much he meant to you."

He didn't move for a moment, then a large fat tear rolled down his face. "I shoulda made up with him, you know?"

I noticed that Sherm's usually superbly coiffed hair was not brushed into its typical neat waves, and the thin line that connected his beard to his sideburns was in dire need of trimming. Even his manicured nails were looking…well, overlooked.

"I just figured he was wrong and I was right. I thought if I waited long enough, he would come apologize, you know."

"Yeah, I know." If there was one thing I did know about, it was how pride could make you do things that you regretted later. Or make you not say the things that you should. I was thankful I'd finally told Riley I loved her. If I got my head blown off now, at least she would not have to wonder where to sit at the funeral. Family and partners always sat in the front row.

I glanced sideways at Riley to see how she was taking all this. Her eyes were riveted on the big man as if she were watching something she couldn't comprehend. I knew how she felt. I didn't like Big Sherm, never had. Aside from some pretty disgusting personal habits, he was also a drug-dealing gang leader. I was shocked when I found out—by catching them in the act, so to speak—that he and Marcus were an item. I'd been so sure that he was no good and would end up hurting Marcus. I had been partially right. Marcus and Sherm had split up within a year. I never got the full story, but apparently it was because Marcus felt that Sherm would always be ashamed of who he was. I'd never known two more different people.

"What happened to him, Sherm?" I gently lured him away from whatever memories he was plugged into.

"He was killed coming home from the drag show. I told him. I told him not to wear that shit in public, you know? Some punk with a hard-on for trouble sees it as an invitation. He must have had a flat or something, 'cause they found him in his car. He was beaten and..." Sherm choked up. "They beat him so bad that his casket was kept closed at the funeral."

I felt myself sway, and Riley's hand moved to my hip to steady me. I didn't want to think about what his final moments had been like.

"Random hate crime. That's what they're saying. Someone saw him standing there and decided to fuck him up. I don't know, Foster. I just don't know. I checked. I had my boys on every corner out there. Made it sound like he owed me money or something. No one knows who did him."

"Do you know if he was involved in anything, maybe something he shouldn't have been?"

Sherm looked up then. I didn't see any joy or any sorrow, just complete emptiness. "I haven't talked to Marcus since we stopped seeing each other. But you know him, he was as straight as they come. He was always trying to get me to give up the game."

I nodded. I didn't feel like explaining to Sherm what I meant by Marcus being into something. I didn't want him asking me questions I wasn't prepared to answer. "I'm going to try to find out who did this."

"I heard you were off the force."

I stiffened. So word *had* gotten out. "I am. What does that have to do with anything?"

He looked at me appraisingly. "Why are you here, Foster? That friend of yours...Stacy...could have told you what happened to Marcus. She probably knows more than I do. The police won't tell me shit." Sherm glared at me as if I were withholding information.

I was tempted to console him, but I knew as well as anyone why Sherm had not bothered to go to the police. Not because he was afraid of any backlash from them, but because he was afraid of anyone finding out about his sexuality. That was something *he* would have to live with. I had my own demons to fight.

"Yeah, she could have, but I need your help."

His brown eyes immediately shut down. There was no evidence of the man who had lost his ex-lover. "Why should I help you? Not like we were ever friends."

"No, but I'm going to find out who killed Marcus. I figure you want their balls on a plate about as much as I do."

He sneered. "How you gonna do that? You're not even a cop anymore."

"I don't need to be a cop to find out who did this. Now, you going to help me or what?"

"What do you want?"

"I need a car with legit tags that can't be traced, and some equipment. More weapons, some lock picks, a penlight, and a police ID. Oh, and a tiny tape recorder. Quality shit, Sherm, not that costume shit." I remembered the money that I had taken from Riley and added, "A couple grand would help, too."

He didn't laugh or turn me down flat. "When you need it?"

"Yesterday."

"Come back later."

We were halfway through the door when Sherm called out, "Everett?"

"Yeah?"

"You should go see his gravesite. They laid him out real nice. He would have been proud."

❖

Back in the car, Riley cupped my face in her hands and kissed me sweetly. "I love you."

A small tendril of arousal caused my nipples to harden. *Oh boy, this is going to take some getting used to.* "I love you, too," I said, and although I was as shocked to hear myself say it as I was the first time around, it still felt right and good.

If I had any doubts about my lapse in control in admitting the truth before, her smile was enough to convince me I'd done the right thing. It was far simpler to make sure she stayed out of harm's way than to keep denying my feelings.

We drove to Secrets and Stacy opened the door quickly, almost as if she had been waiting for us.

"Are you two nuts? Get in here!" She slammed the door behind us before grabbing us both in a bear hug. "Why in the hell did you come back?"

I tried to speak, but had to stop because I was trapped between Riley's body and hers.

"Sorry, baby." Riley stepped back with a rakish grin on her face.

Stacy gave us a look. *Baby, huh?* "You just here to give me a show or what?"

Riley and I exchanged a lingering look.

"Sorry, Stace," I said.

"No, you're not. Come back to the office. There's no one here but me. Chrissie won't be in for a while. This is inventory day."

We adjourned to the small, cramped office she only used when doing paperwork and other things requiring concentration. I contemplated perching on Riley's lap, but thought better of it and instead sat on a corner of Stacy's desk.

"We went to talk to Big Sherm."

The vague look of disgust faded from her face as she realized, as I had, that Big Sherm was probably hurting as much as we were over Marcus's murder. "How is he taking it?"

"Not so good. Stacy, what happened the last time you saw Marcus?"

Stacy sighed. "Marcus was in the Miss Secrets contest, like he always is. It was a packed house, so I didn't get a chance to do much more than wave at him from across the room. I did see his show, though. You know how the girls hoot and holler for him."

I nodded. Everyone loved Marcus, and we all secretly did what we could to sway the vote, even though there was a panel of judges that determined the winner.

"Anyway, he won. The last time I saw him was when he got crowned," she said regretfully.

"You didn't notice when he left?"

"No. Chrissie told the two cops who questioned us that he left a little after one."

"Did they say where they found his car?"

"Yes, right off the freeway over on Barham. The keys were still in the ignition, and he had the trophy for the contest plus the check for two hundred fifty dollars still in his bag. That's how they tracked him here to Secrets."

And why they figured it was a hate crime. "Nothing was stolen," I said, more to myself than to Stacy, but she nodded as if that odd fact had occurred to her as well.

"Did he ever say anything to you about something he might have been working on or looking into?"

"You mean something to do with you?"

"I don't know. I told him to leave it alone, but Marcus was stubborn when he got on the scent of something."

"As far as I know, he stopped. He didn't say anything to me about it."

Something else occurred to me. "Do you remember which two cops questioned you? I want to make sure they are putting the best they can on Marcus's case and not just pushing it under the rug."

Stacy opened her desk drawer and pulled out a small white card. "One of them gave me his name, just in case we remembered anything else."

It could just be coincidence, I told myself as the name "Alvin Wilson" stared me in the face. But I couldn't help wondering why two detectives assigned to the Cold Case division were investigating a hate crime.

"Mind if I keep this?"

"Sure, go ahead. Anything wrong?"

"No. Not at all." I handed the card to Riley, even though I was sure it meant nothing to her. She didn't ask any questions, just put it in her shirt pocket.

I couldn't think of anything else to ask Stacy, so I told her we would be in touch. "Stacy, do me a favor and let me know if those two cops come back around, okay? I want to know what they're up to."

"Sure, I'll give you a call." She hugged each of us. "Be careful, you two. I don't need anyone else to visit at the cemetery."

❖

"I'm going to break into Marcus's house. If he was hiding some information it's probably there somewhere."

Riley flipped our steaks. "How are you going to do that?"

"Sherm's going to give me lock picks."

"That's illegal," she said evenly.

"Highly, which is why you need to stay here."

I put a piece of tomato in my mouth. Riley's dressing gave it a tart but pleasant taste. I chewed it appreciatively. My appetite had been lousy ever since I heard about Marcus, but tonight I felt like I was doing something at last, so I was hungry.

"What if the police are watching his house?" Riley placed our steaks on the table.

"I don't see why they would be. If they really believe it's a random hate crime, why watch his house? And if they think he was up to something…Well, he's not anymore."

"I'm coming with you," she said in that no-nonsense voice of hers.

Shit…shit…shit! I dug morosely into my salad. "No, that's not a good idea."

Riley got up to get me more water. "I can be the lookout while you pick open the lock."

I don't know when it happened, but the tide had turned in our relationship and I was not the one calling the shots. I chomped down on a big-ass piece of cucumber and wondered sullenly if I had ever *really* been calling the shots.

Riley sat back down in her chair and, almost as if she'd heard my thoughts, gave me a large grin that I couldn't help but return. The words "pussy whipped" came to mind. I decided to eat my steak. When in doubt, do something you're good at.

❖

This time when I pounded on the door to the bar, we were admitted immediately. Both Riley and I were dressed in black and probably looked ridiculous, but I wasn't so much worried about that. My conscience was starting to give me trouble. I didn't mind breaking the law myself, but the idea that I was going to drag Riley down with me, well, it didn't sit right.

Sherm was sitting in the same room that I assumed served as his office when there wasn't any illegal gambling going on. The minute we walked through the door, he tossed me the keys to the car I had requested. "It's the midnight blue Blazer in the back parking lot." He snapped open several cases and turned them toward us. "Here are your tools. This shit was hard to come by."

"Sorry." I turned the tiny tape recorder over in my hand before shoving it, along with the case that held my new lock pick set, into my pocket.

He pointed to Riley with his chin. "You want the big one to have a gun?"

"No, and her name is not…the Big One."

Riley gripped my hand under the table. I felt like knocking the shit out of Sherm for talking about Riley as if she wasn't sitting in front of him.

He shrugged. "Look, I don't have time for polite conversation. Can we get on with this? I got things to do."

I made myself calm down. I did need Sherm, probably a lot more then he needed me. I picked up a box of ammunition and a .38 caliber Smith and Wesson that had already been shoved into an ankle holster. I still had the two Glock 19s that Sherm had given me before I left L.A., so I took two more clips for those as well. "What about the money?"

Sherm slammed a white envelope on the table and sent it sliding over to me. I resisted the urge to count the stack of money and instead handed it to Riley.

"How do I know you're going to get me my stuff back?"

"Who the *fuck* are you kidding? You didn't pay for any of these stolen goods. As for the money, that's nothing to you, so don't get started with me."

He knew as well as I did, whether I found the guys that murdered Marcus or not, he wasn't getting one red cent of his money back. I held my breath and waited to see if Sherm would blow his stack. Normally I wouldn't give a shit; I was determined to go after Marcus's killer with or without his help. I just figured it would be a lot easier if he supplied the necessary hardware.

"Later, Sherm. I got things to do, too." I rose and followed Riley to the door.

"When am I gonna hear from you?" Sherm called after us.

"In a few days, unless I find something before then."

Sherm pushed a card across the table. I walked over and scooped it up, glancing at it quickly before pocketing it. There was a phone number on the card—no name, no title, just the number.

"That's my cell," he said. "Not too many people have that." I put it in my pocket and turned to leave. "How do I reach you?" he asked.

I looked back at him in surprise. *Does he think I'm stupid?* "You don't."

I was tempted to grab Riley's hand as we walked back to the parking lot, but I figured it would just fuck up my tough-girl reputation, so I didn't.

"He loved Marcus." Riley said. It wasn't a question, it was a statement.

"Why do you say that?" I had come to the same conclusion, but I was curious how she had, after only meeting Sherm once.

"Because when you love someone, you let go of lots of things."

"Like?"

"Like pride…safety."

Pride, I understood. Sherm was holding his tongue with me because he loved Marcus, and he wanted his killers found and punished. But safety? I didn't think Big Sherm was in any danger. "One of these days, I'm going to have to ask how they met, sort of an odd couple."

"Any more odd than the two of us?" Riley asked.

"I don't know. You're not secretly pleasuring yourself with pen caps in the ear, are you?" I bumped against her so she would know I was kidding.

Riley grinned. "What do we do now?"

"We get over to Marcus's place."

She shoved her hands into her front pockets and slowed her pace. "Tonight?"

"Yeah, we have to. They may have already reached Marcus's family. It's possible that they could start clearing out his stuff soon."

We walked toward the blue Blazer. I could smell the new-car scent from four paces away. The tires probably had a bottle of ArmorAll on each one, and the paint job was pristine. I opened the door and hit the button so that Riley could jump in, too. I whistled.

"Damn, this is nice." I squished back into the leather.

Riley was looking around the truck as if something was going to reach out and grab her. "This isn't stolen, is it?"

I could tell she was worried, and something in me wanted to lie to assuage her fears, but I couldn't. So I went for a little vagueness and hoped she would leave it at that. "Riley, I told him I wanted a car that had legit tags. I'm sure it's okay."

That seemed to appease her. I didn't tell her that a man like Sherm probably had a few people down at the DMV on his payroll. I hadn't exactly lied. If we should ever get pulled over, this car would come back clean, but as for if it was stolen? Was Riley really that naïve?

❖

I knew I had the right place before I even pulled the mail from the mailbox. Still, I thought it prudent to check before breaking into someone's home. As I removed the crumpled mail from its tight confines, the mailbox lid banged loudly, making my heart speed up. I paused, waiting for a light to go on inside the house or at a nearby neighbor's. When there was no flurry of activity, I absently waved Riley over, certain her eyes would be on me.

A cursory glance gave me no helpful phone bills or anything else that might give clues to what Marcus had been up to the last few weeks. I pulled out the case holding the lock picks. The set had a small penlight, which I held in my mouth to illuminate the doorknob as I worked. As an afterthought I went ahead and rang the doorbell, just in case.

The place was empty, but we still entered quietly, using the tiny flashlight to find our way. Marcus had a two-bedroom, one of which he'd turned into a home office. I figured the office was as good a place as any to start. He'd taken his time in decorating the split-level townhouse. The carpet was a light tan color that bordered on white, and all of the walls were painted a similar color. From the glance that I got of his living room I could see that it was also in a light color pattern. Marcus liked to entertain. In fact, he had, on several occasions, invited me to his dinner parties. But fearing I would be out of place, I had always cited a prior engagement. I sort of regretted that now; I would give anything to have spent more time with him. Being in his home made his death more real than seeing his gravesite ever could.

Marcus's office was different from the rest of the house. In fact, if I hadn't known better, I would say someone else had decorated it. The furniture was extremely masculine: dark oaks and leather, with what I hoped were faux animal skins on the wall. His desk was huge and strewn with papers. *So much for orderliness*. I walked over to the blinds, taking a cursory look out the window before closing all of the slats with a sweep of my hand. I drew the heavy brown drapes together, then turned on a lamp and clicked off my penlight. I wished I could have convinced Riley to wait in the car.

"How about you check those bookcases over there?" I told her. I didn't expect her to find anything, but I wanted to give her something to do while I went through Marcus's stuff.

It was very uncharacteristic of Marcus to leave his office desk with papers on top when he left work for the day, and I couldn't imagine him being any different at home. I glanced back at the bookcase that Riley was painstakingly checking for clues, and noted that not one book looked out of place.

"Are those books in alphabetical order?" I asked.

"Yes."

I could tell she was perplexed by my question. I didn't want to scare her, but this didn't make sense to me. "Marcus organized everything. It just seems odd to me that his desk at home would be so messy," I said casually. Either he had been in a hurry, or someone else had gotten there before us. I would bet money on the latter.

I sat down in his chair and started going through the documents. It looked like someone had just dumped his files out and started combing through them. After fifteen minutes of sorting bills and mortgage documentation, I came up with nothing and checked through the drawers. Marcus was fanatical about keeping all of his bills, everything from grocery store receipts to his electricity and water bills for the last two years. But other than that oddity, I found nothing.

"We should check the rest of the house," I said, looking around the room again in case I'd missed something. I had this feeling that if we were going to find anything, it would have been in here. I was just about to go around the desk, when I noticed a balled-up piece of paper near the empty trash can. I opened it and stared at the little stick-figure doodles that ran along the margin.

"You find something?"

"Nah, just some doodles. I just remembered Marcus used to doodle all the time. Sort of makes me sad thinking about it."

"I'm sorry, baby," Riley said quietly, and I smiled despite myself. I loved it when she called me baby. Made me feel...well, like I belonged to someone.

"Come on, let's go check out the bedroom." I wadded up the paper and banked it off the rim of the trash can, prepared to follow Riley to the bedroom, when I had a flash, sort of a vision of Marcus sitting at his desk in the file room, doodling. Whenever he was in deep thought about something, he would doodle. He always kept a pad of paper near his desk just for that reason. I hadn't seen anything like that on the desk tonight, other than the balled-up piece that had missed the trash can.

I got down on my knees and peered under the desk. "Yes," I hissed as I retrieved a small pad.

Marcus had scribbled things like *pay bills*, *call Grandma*; and there were a few of his signature stick figures all over the margins of the paper. I thumbed through before I stopped on my own name drawn with heavy bold lines around it several times. Beneath it were Smitty's and a few other names of people I didn't know.

"Bingo," I said under my breath.

I tried to ignore the chill that had been stealing up my spine since the moment I saw my name written at the top of the list. There was my proof. Whatever was going on, whatever Marcus had been working on, I was involved. I showed Riley the list.

Foster Everett
Joseph Smith
Nathan Stein
Michael Albert
Eric Ann

She frowned as if she'd been offered a word puzzle. "Do these mean anything to you?"

"I'm bad with names." I tried to ignore the chill stealing up my spine. Whatever was going on, whatever Marcus had been working on, I was involved. The list was my proof. We found nothing else in the office, or in his bedroom, but I wasn't ruling anything out, so we started on the kitchen. Marcus's refrigerator was full, as if he'd just gone to the store. His cabinets were full of airtight containers, each labeled with a date and a name. A container marked FB was the largest in the cabinet, and it was marked over a month before. I sniffed the contents and decided against a taste test. There was something just too fucked up about raiding a dead man's cupboards, even if he had been a friend and probably wouldn't have been offended. The kitchen, as I expected, netted us nothing, so I turned off the light and Riley followed me toward the front door.

I was reaching for the doorknob when I heard it, a metallic banging noise. Someone had just removed the mail from Marcus's mailbox. Riley and I froze. The sound of jingling keys and someone fumbling with the doorknob finally jogged me out of my stupor.

The air left my lungs in a soft gust as I grabbed Riley's hand and pulled her into the living room. Luckily for us, Marcus's couch was facing the fireplace. I pushed Riley down on the floor and, heart thumping, pulled the .38 out of my ankle holster. I held my breath at the whisper of fabric and the tap-tap-tap of high heels on linoleum. A light went on in the kitchen, giving Riley and me just enough illumination that we could vaguely see each other.

"Yes he did, girl. I told her ass to dump him a long time ago. Hold on a minute. Here, FB…FB, come on now." Then we heard the sound of something being shaken; it sounded like a cereal box.

Shit. I remembered Marcus picking cat hair off his pant legs. "I think he has a cat," I mouthed to Riley.

A loud popping noise made us both jump as the refrigerator and a cabinet door were opened. The noise was repeated three more times rapidly, right after each other, like automatic weapons being fired from a distance. It took me a few seconds before I realized what I was hearing. "Son of a bitch!" I eased my head up and over the back of the couch, confident that the darkness would hide me as long as the person wasn't looking directly into the living room. I recognized her instantly, right down to the cell phone attached to her ear like a deformed twin.

"Girl, I don't know where this cat is." Chandra prefaced her words with three more machine-gun pops of her gum. "Last time I saw him, he had hard-ass dingleberries just a-swinging off his ass. I'm not lying. Looked like Swedish meatballs."

I sank back down on the floor and slapped my hand over my mouth to keep from laughing. Neither Riley nor I would be partaking of that particular entree for a very long time, you could bet your ass on that one.

Chandra chuckled. "Marcus named him Funky Butt for a reason." Her voice lowered a little as she said Marcus's name. "Oh yeah. So anyway, girl, she called me the other day, just a cryin' and carrying on. She said her and Keith broke up. So me being me, I'm like, 'Beverley, you know men need to be reminded about anniversaries.'" Chandra lowered her voice as if she were afraid of being overheard, but we could still hear her just fine. "She then proceeds to tell me that he *didn't* forget. No, girl, he didn't. *He* comes running into the house, hands her a gift, and runs into the bathroom." She paused and took a dramatically deep breath, "Girrrl, he got her a weed whacker." Chandra cackled loudly. "No, I'm not lyin'. But that's not even the kicker. He comes out the bathroom fanning hisself, right? Like he just ran a marathon or something. And he says…are you ready for this?"

I rolled my eyes, wishing I had an Oscar for best dramatic actress in my hand so I could hit Chandra over the head with it.

"That fool said he was *going* to stop and buy her roses, but he couldn't 'cause he had to shit."

Riley and I looked at each other, horrified. *That poor, poor bastard*, I thought.

"Girl, I'm not lyin' to you. That's what she told me he said. Hold on a minute."

I heard a beep as she hit a button on her cell phone. "Hell-o? Yeah, Terence, I'll be home in a minute." The beep told me that Chandra pushed *end* in lieu of a good-bye to Terence.

"Girl, let me let you go so I can get this man his dinner before I have to hurt him. All right now, bye-bye." Chandra's heels skittered across the linoleum, and a moment later, the door shut behind her.

"Who was that?" Riley whispered.

"Her name's Chandra. She worked with Marcus. I guess she came in to feed the cat. She always did that when he was on vacation." I paused as the beginnings of a plan started to take form in my head. "I have an idea. Come on."

❖

I sat at the table staring down at Marcus's pad of paper as Riley moved around behind me. She handed me bottled water, which I accepted gratefully, my eyes not leaving the pad. It could be nothing, but I couldn't see Marcus writing my name and Smitty's—who he hardly even knew—along with these other people's, unless we were all somehow connected.

"They're all neat," Riley commented. "It's like he wrote the names first and then doodled all around them."

"Yeah, I noticed that, too. But I don't recognize any of them, other than Smitty's and mine. I can't help thinking that I'm missing something."

"It could be just a list, for a party or something."

"Could be, but Marcus didn't know Smitty that well. I doubt he would have invited him to one of his parties. I could probably ask Stacy if any of these names look familiar. She knows more of Marcus's friends than I do. They go way back."

"So what's your idea?"

I hesitated. "I think Chandra might be able to help."

"Can you trust her?"

I thought about that for a minute. Chandra and I had never exactly been friends. I wasn't sure why, but she'd always seemed to avoid me like the plague when I worked down in Records. But Marcus and she were really close, and I was hoping that she would want to find out who'd killed him as much as I did.

I rearranged the toys in Bud's mouse playhouse to avoid those penetrating blue eyes. "I think so. She was a good friend of Marcus's."

"So you're going to ask her what he was working on?"

"Yes, and I thought she might be able to run the names on the list." The Records Department had access to the same databases that I had when I worked a case. "It's very possible that whoever these people are, they may come up in the system."

"She works with cops, Foster. What if she…"

I pressed the side of my face into her back. To my surprise, she turned around and hugged me.

"Chandra won't turn me in, okay? Please trust me. I know her. She will want to get the bastards that killed Marcus as much as I do." I felt Riley sigh and realized just how tense she had been as her muscles relaxed beneath my hands. "It's late. Why don't we get some sleep?"

She willingly allowed me to lead her to the bed, neither of us having the energy to be apart long enough to shower in the cramped bathroom. I lay awake long after her breathing had evened out.

I had told Riley that I was positive Chandra wouldn't turn me in. It was more than just a *little* fib. I wasn't at all sure Chandra *wouldn't* turn me in. I was banking all my trust in her friendship with Marcus. I hoped that I was right, because if I wasn't…

CHAPTER EIGHTEEN

C handra?"
        "What the fuck?" She turned around, swinging a big-ass purse.

I reached for my gun with one hand and held the other out to calm her. "No, wait. It's me, Foster."

She swung the purse again, this time barely missing my head. "Are you trying to scare the shit out of me?"

"No. I just want to talk to you for a minute, okay?" I lowered my gun. "Calm down, please."

"*You* calm down. Some crazy shit has been happening." She glared at me. "And you know what? I just bet you're the cause of most of it."

That comment hit a bit too close to home. Annoyed, I said, "I'm here to find out what happened to Marcus."

"I don't know what happened, okay? If I did, I probably wouldn't tell you anyway. The police say it was a hate crime, and maybe that's all it was." She stormed into the kitchen and started slamming cabinet doors.

I looked toward the living room, where Riley would be listening. It would be easy to just go over there, tell her "That's it," and drive back to the cabin tonight. But I couldn't do that, not until I was sure.

I reluctantly followed her into the kitchen. "Shit, Chandra, will you just listen, please? Can you at least tell me what Marcus was working on?"

She took down the large container marked FB and set it on the counter. "Look, all I know is things got weird after you left. Marcus started looking at some files, and then some guys came in and took your computer. Thing is, everybody knows they're after you for something, but nobody knows what it is. Marcus said he was going to find out. Then he turns up dead." Her eyes bored into mine, and I felt the sickening nausea of guilt as it settled in my stomach.

"He was trying to help you, and it got him killed. So pardon me if I ask you to stay the fuck away from me, 'cause if I wanted a death sentence, I would go suck on a crack pipe. Least I would feel good before I committed suicide."

"Damn it, I told…" The hairs on the back of my neck stood up. Marcus *was* still looking into the case; it was even possible that he had been killed because of me. I stood there, breathing harshly as pain settled in the base of my throat. It was almost too quiet. I wanted, no *needed*, out of Marcus's house.

"I don't want no part of what you're selling, so why don't you just leave. Seems to me you've already got enough people hurt." Her voice held a note of compassion in it, almost as if she knew I was hurting but couldn't do anything to help me. Hell, I didn't know what to do to help me. I needed to see Riley.

"Chandra, please…I just need…" I stopped and swallowed. I couldn't seem to think clearly. Had I given Marcus a death sentence? Should I have been more firm when I told him to stop looking into things?

"Foster?" Riley's voice interrupted my spiraling thoughts.

"Aw shit, what the hell?" Chandra jumped as Riley suddenly appeared from behind the couch. "How many people you got in here?"

"You were supposed to stay out of sight," I said with absolutely no conviction. I felt like my energy had been drained.

Riley didn't bother answering me; she just grabbed my hand and looked at Chandra with a scowl that nearly joined her two dark eyebrows together. I don't think I had ever seen Riley so angry with anyone before, and I was really glad it wasn't directed at me. "Let's go. You don't need her help."

I allowed her to pull me toward the door, feeling as if I was in a nightmare that wouldn't end. First Smitty and now Marcus.

"Wait!" Chandra took a couple of steps, click clack. "*Just*…tell me what you want, okay? I'll tell you if I can help you or not."

A meow rose from near my feet and a longhaired white and orange cat, about the size of a small dog, stood next to me. I moved out of the way, and it walked daintily into the kitchen with the elegance of a queen. Well, the whole thing *would* have been regal, if not for the large dingleberries hanging off its ass.

"We found some names. Smitty's and mine, along with a few others that I don't recognize. I was wondering if you could run them to see what comes up."

I pulled the neatly printed list out of my pocket and handed it to her.

She looked down at it for a moment. "Okay, I'll see what I can do." As I grinned, she added, "I *said,* I would see. I ain't making no promises, so don't get all happy and shit."

I nodded. "All right, that's cool."

"Can I speak to you alone for a minute?" Chandra looked nervously at Riley.

Before I could reply, Riley walked away toward the living room. Frowning, I watched her go. *Is she angry with me now? I didn't even do anything.*

In the kitchen, Chandra set a bowl of water on the floor for FB. She peeked around the door and then whispered to me, "Where the hell did you find her?"

"She's my friend, I didn't *find* her anywhere," I said evenly. Chandra was free to insult me to her heart's content, but that freedom *did not* extend to Riley.

Chandra waved me off. "I don't know what you're into, and frankly, I don't give a shit. Once I get you this info, I want you out of my hair for good, okay?"

"Sure, I understand. Thank you very much for helping me. I appreciate it." She glowered at me harder. "What?" *Damn, there is no pleasing this woman.*

"You're being too nice," she said.

"What are you talking about?"

"Oh my God." She pointed toward the living room, and I tried to pretend like I didn't know what she was talking about. I couldn't help the silly-ass grin that spread across my face. As inappropriate as it was, I was proud when the look of admiration crossed her face. "That's some nice-looking woman you got. I didn't know you had it in you."

I think I should have felt insulted, but I just shrugged. "Hey, I'm not going to hang here while you fantasize about my girlfriend. I'll give you Riley's cell number, and you can call us if you find anything."

Chandra wrote the number down and finished feeding the cat. After she'd gone, I found Riley and said, "Let's go."

"Sorry about losing it back there," she said.

I grinned. "That's how you lose it? Man, remind me to tell you a few stories." I gave her a peck on the lips before opening the door and peering outside. "You know, ever since I was about thirteen or fourteen I would blow up at the drop of a hat," I said as we crossed to the Blazer. "I just couldn't seem to control my anger."

"What changed?"

"It hasn't changed, really, but I think being a cop helped me redirect some of it." I bit my bottom lip. "I don't think I liked myself all that much, you know, when I was lashing out, but I didn't know if I could stop doing it."

"You were a lot calmer than I was back there." A small smile threatened to take over her somber expression.

"I was, wasn't I?" I grinned at her, and started the motor. It wasn't so bad having her along, I thought as I steered us toward the freeway. She was right, I was more relaxed.

❖

Chandra called me back in an hour. "So far, I only had time to do a query on Nathan Stein."

"Oh yeah? What did you find?" I found a pen and notepad and sat down on one of the chairs in Riley's small kitchen. I heard her shuffling papers.

"Arrested four years ago for child endangerment and abuse. It was dismissed, though. His sheet dates way back…Well, shit, he probably had juvenile records, too."

"Four years, huh? Nothing after that?"

"Nope. Nothing."

"Hey, wait. You got an address on this guy?"

Chandra read off the last known address for Stein, as well as the phone number. "I'm getting busy over here. Oh, and by the way, you forgot to sign off on the arrest report."

"Wait. What?"

"Says here that Smitty was the arresting officer, but neither of you signed off on the documentation."

"Nah, it wasn't me. I wasn't Smitty's partner back then."

"Well, Smitty checked it out a few days before he died. Damn it, who spilled coffee on this? I got to go."

"That was Chandra." I filled Riley in on Stein's crimes and the fact that we now had an address and phone number, at least the one from four years ago. "It's weird. She said the case belonged to Smitty, but our division didn't even open until about three years ago. I guess it's possible he could have been assigned something like this before we partnered up."

I frowned. It was sort of odd that as close as I considered myself to be to Smitty, I didn't know much about his previous partner or the cases they'd worked.

"It seems kind of strange," Riley agreed. "But maybe he got some new information and didn't get around to telling you."

"Well, Smitty checked the file out a few days before his death. The only reason he would do that is if he thought it was related to something in our existing caseload, maybe a similar MO. But he never mentioned it to me, and this guy's name doesn't ring a bell."

"Didn't you say you were bad with names?"

"Yeah," I had to concede. "But I usually remember the assholes that hurt children. I have nightmares…" I shook my head, trying to fathom why Smitty had decided to chase up a file for a go-nowhere case like Stein's. "Whoever was Smitty's partner at the time would probably know what significance this guy held, but I can't just walk up to him and ask. He would probably haul my ass in."

"Then what can we do?"

"Let's see if Mr. Nathan Stein is still at his old address."

❖

"Is this the right address?" Riley ducked her head to get a better look.

The home's mud-colored exterior was nothing like the other older homes in the area, and its impeccably manicured landscape, easing around the house, no doubt led to a swimming pool. *Probably shaped like a dollar sign,* I thought dryly. Nathan Stein lived in an enclave of verdant estates and palatial homes.

"Not where you would expect to find a child abuser living, huh?"

My generalization was based on the simple fact that poor people were arrested more often for physical assaults. And they got convicted. Rich people were better at avoiding consequences.

"His place sort of looks like the tract homes we passed to get here," Riley said.

"Yeah, it does." Although the place was much larger than the homes we'd passed on our way to Stein's suburb, it had some design similarities, as if whoever had built the tract homes had been given carte blanche to build this place. The residences on either side of Stein's looked at least ten years older than his.

I opened the door to the truck and got out. "You sure you want to come with me?" Before she finished nodding insistently, I added, "Let me do the talking." I joked to put her at ease. I always did the talking.

The imposing wood door was opened while I still held the large, rustic knocker in my hand. A woman of about thirty with brown hair and eyes stood there, her expression unreadable. First impression? Cold-hearted bitch. Long lashes closed slightly as she looked Riley and me up and down. A well-manicured hand went to a nonexistent hip that was encased in a bright orange, one-piece workout suit. She looked like all the women I hated rolled into one person, the type that walks around the grocery store in workout gear. You gotta figure that either they didn't really work out, or are walking around with dewy crotches and an odor waiting to happen.

"That's for decoration," she said tightly.

"Huh?" Yup, I'm the talker all right.

"The knocker. It's antique. It came off a monks' monastery in... Never mind." She shook her head as if she was wondering why she was explaining art to a couple of Philistines. "May I help you with something?"

"I sure hope so, ma'am." I gave her a polite smile and flashed her the fake badge and credentials that Sherm had gotten for us. She looked at the badge, and I slapped the cover shut before she could notice that not only was the picture not me, but the badge was for the Boulder Colorado Police and not LAPD. "May I ask your name, ma'am?"

"Caroline Stein," she bit out. Her thin lips stubbornly refused to move over the *o* in Caroline, so it came out Care-line.

"Would it be possible for us to come in and talk to you?"

She seemed to mull that over, but obviously couldn't think of any reason not to allow us into her home. She led us into a nicely decorated living room. Leather couch, neutral walls, and a distressed wood armoire. She sat down in a large chair across from us. A large wood ledge protruded from the adobe wall directly behind her, adorning an impressive fireplace. Several pictures lined the ledge. Most of them were of Caroline, but two caught my eye.

One was of a man with painfully short hair, almost military in nature. His stern brow was creased as if he was frowning into the sun, and his chin was dimpled almost as if to contradict the harshness of his expression. The other was a family portrait. The same man held a newborn at an angle so that a picture could be taken. His expression was no different from that in the other picture. Caroline Stein stood next to him. The smile on her face was strained, and there was just enough space between their bodies to verify what I had already guessed. Drama queen though she was, Caroline Stein did not look like a happy new mother in that picture. Her expression reminded me of so many other battered women I had seen that I was tempted to reach into my pocket for the card that I used to carry with me when I wore a uniform—the card with the names of the closest battered women's shelters.

I was almost relieved when I didn't recognize Nathan Stein at all. Up until that moment, I had half wondered if I *had* arrested him for something and forgotten his name.

I glanced around the home, taking in the curved walls and Berber carpet, all very expensive and very new. Through a patio door, a swimming pool glistened in the afternoon sun. Though not shaped like a dollar sign, it was large enough to be Olympic size.

"What can I do for you, Officer?" I could tell I would have to tell her my name, or she would get suspicious if she wasn't already.

"Jones," I said easily, as I reached out to shake her hand. She nodded and reached over to shake Riley's hand as well, so I quickly jumped right in. I didn't want her to ask Riley's name. One false officer named Jones was a lot easier to hide than two.

"Ma'am, we were wondering if we could talk to Nathan Stein." There it was again, that tight mouth. I wondered if she was going to ask for a warrant.

"Don't you people keep track of these things?" She blinked furiously. "My husband was reported missing last month. I would think the LAPD would know that, since I filed a missing persons report with them."

I could almost see the wheels turning in her head. If she called and checked our credentials, we were screwed, so I needed to move fast. I pulled the tiny recorder out of my pocket and said, "Ma'am, would you mind if we record this conversation?"

"What for?" she asked, her eyes shifting from me to Riley and back again. "If you're not here about Nathan's disappearance, then why are you here?"

"The recording is just a formality. I use it so that I don't have to worry about whether or not I misinterpreted something you say," I explained in a voice that probably sounded mechanical. As if the tape recorder could somehow interpret whether or not a person was lying better than my ear. I don't know why I even bothered. For all intents and purposes, I was no longer a cop. I had already broken so many laws, it seemed ridiculous to let a little thing like privacy become an issue.

"Fine, can we please get this over with? Frankly, I don't know any more than I've already told the other officers."

"Well, we have reason to believe that your husband may have information relevant to another case. So if you would answer a few routine questions—"

"Well, I would doubt that!" She said it as if she thought it would be highly unlikely that her husband would have anything to do with the likes of us. I finally figured out exactly why Mrs. Caroline Stein talked the way she did. A woman her age with braces? Not unheard of,, but *interesting*. I decided to get to the point of the visit before she needed to go floss or something.

"Mrs. Stein, how long have you and your husband been married?"

"Five years. What does that have to do with anything?"

"Are you aware that Mr. Stein was arrested for child abuse?"

She inhaled sharply, and any sign that she was distressed disappeared as if she had two personalities. "Officer Jones, my husband is a man of faith. He went out of his way to teach children right from wrong. The Bible says, 'spare the rod and spoil the child.'"

Now *my* mouth tightened. "Ma'am, your husband was arrested for child abuse, not a spanking."

"I understand that." Her lips drew back in a snarl that displayed the plastic stoppers on her teeth. "That girl lied because she was punished after not doing her chores. You know how children are. They get in trouble, and they tell lies about their parents because they are spiteful."

She shrugged as if that explanation settled everything. "She admitted that she'd lied, and the charges were dropped. It's just too bad that so many were hurt as a direct result of that child's deceit."

"So your husband makes his living as a minister?"

I could almost hear her nails digging into the palm of her hand. "He has many small business investments."

"Small, huh? So then, his main source of income would have to be ministering to his flock?" I raised my eyebrows innocently.

"My husband has yet to rebuild his congregation after the fallout from that incident," Caroline Stein said bitterly.

I looked around the house. "Really? Seems like you're doing okay."

Suddenly she was back in her grieving-widow mode. "Why are you bringing this up? My husband is missing, for God's sake. And as far as I know, you people haven't done anything but ask me questions about that damn abuse charge." Her sobbing grew almost hysterical, and I felt Riley shift next to me. "Why can't you just go find him? Why do you need to bring up this old charge?"

"Care? Are you crying, sweetheart?" A bare-chested man of about twenty-two hurried into the room, tucking a towel around his middle.

Instantly, the crying fit stopped and the stranger slid to a halt when he noticed Riley and me. His towel hung just low enough to leave no doubt that he was either wearing a very revealing swimsuit, or nothing at all. With his shock of curling blond hair, he reminded me of some child star, maybe it was Shirley Temple. Anyway, it was not an attractive characteristic on a young man.

"I'm Officer Jones. And you are?" I said quickly.

He received the evil eye from *Care* but good manners won out and he shook hands with both Riley and me. "Terry...Terry Powell."

I tried not to wince. His grip was soft, limp, and vaguely moist; exactly what I would think it would feel like to shake hands with a cadaver. His eyes flitted from mine to Caroline's, perhaps on a quest to figure out which was the lesser of two evils. He settled on me.

"I'm sorry, did we interrupt you?" I asked Caroline.

"No." The tears had dried up. She had no doubt guessed that they were wasted on me. "Terry is my personal trainer. He was just cleaning up before he headed out."

Terry's discomfort was tangible. I had my doubts that he was her personal trainer, and I also wondered if that was the extent of his duties for Caroline Stein. As there was no way for me to find that out, I decided to let her off the hook. I couldn't care less what she did; I was interested in her husband. I allowed her to lead us to the door.

"Your daughter must be taking your husband's disappearance pretty hard?"

"I don't have a daughter, Officer Jones." Something in Caroline's voice told me I had gotten a rise out of her.

"I'm sorry, I saw the picture on the mantel. I just assumed…" She opened the door, and Riley walked out of it. "Oh, one more thing. Do you happen to remember the names of the officers who arrested your husband?"

I didn't expect her to know the answer to the question; I really just wanted to fuck with her.

"Now why would I remember that? Can't you go look it up or something? This is ridiculous. You should be looking for him instead of harassing me." And with that, she slammed the door in my face.

"That guy Terry? I don't know if he is her personal trainer," Riley said as we strolled back to the Blazer.

"He looked pretty fit to me."

"Well, it's not that. It was his hands."

His hands. I shuddered as I remembered how his handshake had given me a chill. "Yeah, kind of grossed me out, too. Limp."

I absently rubbed her palm with my thumb as I tried to understand where she was going with this. I loved the feel of Riley's hands. They were large and strong; the calluses that she had built up from working out drove me crazy when she touched my skin. The contrast between her gentleness and the obvious strength in her hands…"Oh, you mean he didn't have calluses."

"Right." She grinned happily.

"But do all personal trainers weight train?"

"No, not necessarily. But do you remember shaking hands with her?"

I nodded. "Shit. She *did* have calluses."

"Yeah, she did. Just like mine."

"Nah, nothing like yours." I gave her hand a squeeze. "So you think if she weight trains, as her personal trainer he would too."

"It could mean nothing. He could be her aerobics instructor or something. He could also wear gloves. But I wear gloves, and I still get them. I just thought it was worth mentioning."

"Yeah, but usually when people say personal trainer, they mean just that. I didn't pick up on it. If I was working her hubby's disappearance, I would certainly be interested in why Powell is in the house, naked as the day he was born, only a month after Stein's disappearance. I'll talk to Chandra."

Riley seemed happy. "I knew it wasn't nothing."

"You're good at this," I tried not to sound surprised. I had expected her to cramp my style. But the opposite was true. She was an asset.

❖

Big Ol' Burger was known for...well, its big ol' burgers. Though they were known to have the best burgers in town, cops avoided the place because it was frequented by a lot of locals. There was nothing worse than trying to enjoy a burger and having someone ask you what you're going to do about that crack house next door.

I scanned the crowded restaurant, but I didn't see Chandra. It was already well after seven and I was beginning to get worried. I hoped she'd gotten the voicemail message I had Riley leave after my encounter with Caroline Stein. Riley had sounded very convincing pretending to be another one of Chandra's relationship-obsessed girlfriends.

At Big Ol' Burger, they give you a hamburger patty with a large bun, and you're allowed to pile all the condiments you want on top of your burger. It was one of the things that I loved about the place. I watched Riley add lettuce, tomato, and a pickle to her plate. Soon she would try curly fries. I was slowly but surely winning her over to my way of thinking. We sat down in a booth far away from the other patrons and with a clear view of the door, so we could keep an eye out for Chandra. I had never seen her in anything but her work clothes, so I almost didn't recognize her when she approached wearing jeans.

"Sorry I'm late." She set a file on the table and sat down next to me in the booth. "Fools sent me two people that don't do half the work in a day that you did in one hour."

I felt strangely pleased at the backhanded compliment. "Find anything?"

"No, nothing. Weird, though. I ran a cross-reference with the socials on the other three names."

"You can do that?" I perked up. "What did it bring up?"

"Nothing."

Riley placed a glass of water in front of me, which I drank without thought. "Hang on. You should have gotten something?"

"Exactly right, Einstein."

"Aliases? Those are all aliases?" I asked.

"Yeah, they would have to be. I guess it's possible that one of them wouldn't have a social security number, but all of them?"

"Hot damn, nice work," I crowed until I realized that the info left me absolutely nowhere. If the aliases hadn't come up when Chandra ran the check in the first place, then they weren't in the system. Where did Marcus get the names, then?

I wiped my hands on my napkin and opened the file. Chandra had used her initiative. His original arrest report was attached to a dark photocopy of a mug shot. The picture on the mantel was indeed that of Nathan Stein, and the mug shot also confirmed for me that I had never seen Nathan Stein before in my life. He'd been arrested four years ago for child abuse and was released because the girl in question recanted her statement. Smitty was listed as the arresting officer. He had signed the document, but whoever had been his partner hadn't. The signature on the file could have been a forgery, but it looked like my partner's handwriting. I was usually pretty careful about signing paperwork and Smitty had been, too.

To my great horror, Chandra giggled. She opened that smart-ass mouth of hers and giggled like a schoolgirl.

"What?" I asked.

She jumped a little because she had been staring at Riley, who had gone back to eating her burger. She reached for a fry and had the audacity to dip it twice into my ranch dressing before biting into it.

"Can you check to see if a missing persons was filed on Stein?"

"It's in the file." She and Riley were making eye contact.

"I talked to Marcus about a bunch of files Smitty had taken out," I said, wanting to send a signal that this wasn't a social event. "There were pages missing. Looked like someone had torn some stuff out. Can you get me those files, too?"

Chandra helped herself to another fry. "Okay."

Was she sick? She hadn't said one smart-ass thing to me the whole time we'd been sitting here. She suddenly pulled out a phone similar to Riley's and looked at the display.

"Shit, I got to get going. Do Riley and you need anything else?"

Do Riley and I need...What the hell is this "Do Riley and you need anything else" shit? Since when had she been so polite? She could remember Riley's name after meeting her once and yet she conveniently forgot mine.

I slid out of the booth and Chandra said good-bye, escaping with another one of my fries.

Riley pointed with her pinky at the documents. "Anything interesting?"

I sat down again and picked up my burger. "Yeah, Chandra has a little crush on you." I expected Riley to deny it, but she didn't.

I harrumphed and told myself that I wasn't jealous. "It's about like Caroline Stein said, as far as the child abuse charges are concerned. Stein was apparently the pastor of a religious group called the North Star Family. The kid was supposed to do some chore or something, and decided to play instead. Stein spanked her, and afterward she went to the police. According to her, some of the women and children in the group were forced to perform sexual acts with the male members of the group. The arrest was based on the kid's word and no other evidence was ever found, so after she recanted the case was dropped."

I rifled through the other papers Chandra had supplied, before picking up my burger again. "The missing persons report is pretty black and white. Stein never came home from work June third of this year. Caroline Stein reported him missing a few days later, and that's about all. They haven't found any evidence to suggest foul play." I flipped the top page out of curiosity more than anything else, and stared in disbelief. "Son of a bitch," I said, reading the names of the detectives assigned to the case. "Alvin Wilson and Daniel McClowski again."

"You're kidding."

I wiped mustard off my mouth. "I'm thinking those two detectives are popping up a little too often for my taste."

"Maybe it's a coincidence?"

"No," I said. "Twice is a coincidence. More than twice is a common denominator."

She stopped chewing. "What are you planning to do?"

"I don't know. I thought we could follow them, see what they're up to?"

"Is that wise?"

"No," I said honestly, "but do we have much choice?"

"I don't know. But it seems to me there must be something else we could do besides following the two cops who tried to drag you in."

"They won't know we're following them, Riley."

"I think you should come up with something else." Riley's frigid blue eyes melted as I smothered a protest. "I had a nightmare last night."

I had to lean closer to decipher what she was saying. "You did?" She hadn't told me that, but I remembered waking up during the night and hearing her in the other room, exercising. It had been in my head to get up and make sure she was okay, but I had fallen back to sleep. "What was it about?"

"You were hurt, shot."

"Oh, baby..." There was something to be said for not remembering your nightmares.

"Foster, I think we should go home."

I knew she meant back to the Bay Area, back to the cabin. Even though it wasn't really our home, I think we both thought of it that way because it was the first place that we gave in to our feelings for each other.

"Please, I want to spend time with you."

"Riley, I can't. We're making progress."

She nodded as if she had expected as much, and I sat waiting for her to say something else to try to convince me that we should leave. Her fear was starting to rub off on me. What if something happened to her? I could never forgive myself.

"Riley, I want you to go back and wait for me. I'll be back as soon as I can."

"No, I am not leaving you."

I bit the inside of my cheek hard to keep from grabbing her and hugging her. "Just give me a few more days, okay? If we can't figure this out by next week, we'll go home."

"You promise, Foster?"

"I promise, baby. I won't let this tear you up. I want to spend time with you, too. I feel like I owe this to Marcus, but not at your expense." I looked around the restaurant, my mind spinning. I had promised her that we would leave in less than a week if we didn't find anything. That did not leave me much time. *I'm sorry, Marcus, but I just found her; I'd like to keep her for a while.*

"Okay," I said, clearing my throat. "We'll talk to the Steins' neighbors before we deal with Wilson and McClowski. See if they can shed some light on the subject."

We got to our feet. Riley's dream weighed heavily on me. I didn't want to give up, but at the same time I wanted to make her happy, and I could tell that this was starting to get to her. She was afraid I would be careless. In the past I had been, but that was in the past. Now I felt like I had too much to lose. *Hell, maybe I should just take Riley home and let the LAPD handle it.* Even as I thought it, I knew I wasn't ready to let go. I owed myself something, too.

CHAPTER NINETEEN

The first house on the Steins' street was a Victorian with a gaudy cherub fountain in the front. Riley looked so nervous as we strode up the driveway that I racked my brain for an anecdote that would put her at ease.

"Can I help you with something?" A petite, elderly woman emerged from some shrubs.

"Ma'am. I'm a police officer with the LAPD and this is my partner. We wanted to talk to you about your neighbors, the Steins." I smoothly excluded our names from the introductions.

"My name is Zelda." She gave me a cursory look, then studied Riley with interest. "I don't know what I can tell you about the Steins, except that I ought to file a report on them for thievery."

"They stole something from you?"

"Damn right they stole something from me." Zelda gestured wildly with a pair of dangerous-looking pruning shears.

I put my arm in front of Riley, much like I did in the car whenever we came to a sudden stop. This time she didn't give me the usual exasperated look. We both eyed the old woman warily.

She gestured that Riley and I should follow her. "When they first moved in there, I took them over some cookies—a welcome to the neighborhood. And do you know, that woman took my platter, thanked me, and shut the door in my face? Didn't even have the manners to invite me in. I never saw that platter again, and it was a family heirloom."

"That's a great pity," I said.

Zelda whipped off her gardening gloves and stared at Riley like I didn't exist. "You look like you could use a drink, dear."

"Yes, ma'am," Riley said sweetly.

"Oh my, aren't you the cute one." Zelda beamed. "And so polite, too. That's what I like to hear from you young folks. Come with me." She led the way through a gate and around a pool that was equal in size to the Steins'. "Wait right there, I'm going to get you a nice glass of iced tea. Would you like some too, dear?"

"Yes. Thank you, ma'am," I said, just as sweetly, but all I got was a nod while Riley got another grin.

I narrowed my eyes as the woman walked into the house. "She's probably into bondage and sadomasochism and she's going to offer to buy you." I nodded my head because Riley was shaking hers. A smile started to spread across her face as I went on. "Just wait. She'll come out that sliding glass door holding a whip and wearing black lipstick, a rubber unitard, spiked heels, and a dildo the size of one of *your* biceps." I leaned in close and intoned, "And it's all going to be for you...*the cute one*."

Riley pulled a face. Her body shook.

"Oh, you just went on sale, baby. Fifty percent off, no coupon required." I couldn't hide the fact that I was having a hard time catching my breath. Zelda was right; Riley was indeed cute with that mischievous little smile of hers. Hell, I might have to borrow that rubber unitard my damn self.

I clicked on the minuscule tape recorder just as Zelda returned with our drinks. She sat down heavily and frowned. "Now what was I saying, dear? Oh, yes. Those two are a strange couple. I don't know much about them. They don't want to speak half the time. And this mess about him missing, I don't know what that's all about, but you can bet it's some scheme that he cooked up."

"Why do you say that, ma'am?"

"The eyes. You know, he has those shifty eyes that people have when they're up to no good. Mr. Dooley, the nice gentleman that lives next door to them. He says they *killed* his tree."

I made sure to look suitably outraged. "Why would Mr. Stein do that?"

"The tree was blocking his view. Mr. Dooley said that the tree was older than he was, and that it stayed as long as he lived. Mr. Stein said that he could arrange for him to go sooner than he expected, and he would too, if he didn't get rid of that damn tree."

"He *did not* threaten that nice Mr. Dooley?" Okay, I'll admit that I was pouring it on a bit thick here, but she was still talking and I wanted to keep it that way.

"No, I'm telling you the truth. About a month later, someone drove a copper nail into that old tree and killed it. Mr. Stein called the city, and they made Mr. Dooley cut it down." Zelda smacked her lips in disgust. "It was a beautiful old tree, too. Mr. Dooley's grandkids used to love to play in it. You can bet if those two had children they wouldn't have been so callous."

"I thought they had a baby."

"I vaguely remember someone saying that they had lost a baby to crib death or something. I never believed it, though. Mr. Stein is barely ever there, and that woman doesn't strike me as the motherly type. Lord knows why men like them so young. They don't know the first thing about raising a family. Of course, us women like them young, too, when we can track them down." She winked at me, and I opened my mouth to deny that I wanted any part of that statement. "Whew." She fanned herself and her eyes got glassy. "You should see that pool boy of hers, Terry."

"Terry is the pool boy?"

"Yes, well, that's what *she* calls him."

"So you don't believe that Mr. Stein is really missing, then?"

She waved me off. "Of course not. That man is a mean one. Either he's faking it, or someone has already done away with him. I wouldn't be surprised either way."

"Well, thank you for your time, ma'am. I appreciate it." As we prepared to leave, I had another thought. "Zelda, do you know where Mr. and Mrs. Stein lived before they moved here?"

"They said they were from New York, but neither of them look or sound like they are. If you ask me, they probably lived right here in California and won some money or something. They strike me as that type. Nouveau riche." She pronounced "riche" as if it were "reach."

I thanked her again and Riley praised the iced tea. We were walking toward the gate when Zelda yelled out, "Talk to Mr. Dooley. He can probably tell you more than I can. I can call him and tell him you're coming, if you want?"

"That would be great, Zelda. Thank you," I called back.

❖

I was starting to think the rich really did live better. Mr. Dooley welcomed Riley and me with as much hospitality as Zelda, and he, too, seated us on patio furniture around his pool. It sort of made me sad, because I don't think either of them got many visitors. Their outdoor furniture was almost identical, so I convinced myself that he and Zelda had gone shopping together to buy it. For some reason, it made me feel better that they had each other.

I bumped Riley with my shoulder to get her attention. Her eyes were already twinkling, as if she knew I was going to make some off-the-wall crack. I had to oblige her, of course. "If one more person gives me a glass of iced tea, I'm going to start pissing like a racehorse all over this nice furniture."

Her body trembled and she shook her head as if to say, "What am I going to do with you?" I let her know with a wicked smile just what I thought she should do with me. Her slight flush and sharp intake of breath told me she got the picture.

Mr. Dooley returned with the iced tea, and I took a few polite sips before clicking on the tape recorder and asking my questions. "Mr. Dooley, what can you tell us about your neighbors, the Steins?"

"They aren't worth the lot that house stands on." Mr. Dooley pushed back a long lock of gray hair with a quick, unconscious sweep of his wrinkled hands.

"Why do you say that?"

He launched into the story about the tree, and I tendered my condolences.

"Anything else odd you've seen over there?"

"Well, there was that big black fellow that came over late at night sometimes. I can't sleep, you see, and I would see them driving away in a big white delivery van. They wouldn't come back for a few days."

"Did the van say anything along the sides? Maybe the name of a business?"

"I don't know if I paid much attention."

"And the driver? Think you'd recognize him if you saw him again?"

"Maybe. My binoc…Well, my eyesight isn't as good as it used to be."

I nodded. As I'd suspected, Mr. Dooley was a watcher, one of those people who feel it's their civic duty to observe what's happening on their block. There were a few of them in my apartment complex. They'd never bothered me. I always felt safer knowing someone was watching.

I pulled out a blank card and wrote Riley's cell number down. "If you should see or remember anything else, would you give my partner or me a call?"

"Of course, Officer. Anything I can do to help."

❖

We had to wait nearly two hours for McClowski and Wilson. I had instructed Riley to park across from the station. I concealed myself in the back of the Blazer screened by the tinted windows. I pulled the cap down low on my head and donned the cheap sunglasses.

"I guess the captain isn't on their asses like she was on mine, or they would be out doing some work instead of sitting at their desks pushing papers." Just as the words left my mouth, the two detectives in question came out of the building and walked toward their car.

"Okay, here we go," I told Riley calmly. "Follow, but make sure you leave a few cars between us and them."

McClowski and Wilson halted at a brand-new doughnut shop near Ninth, emerged from their car, talked briefly, and walked off in opposite directions. McClowski handed a flyer to a kid on Rollerblades, who promptly crumpled it up and tossed it in the trash can after the detective turned the corner. I waited five seconds.

"I'm going to go get that," I said. I was already halfway out of the car when Riley dragged on my shirt.

"You promised no unnecessary risks, remember?" Riley jumped out of the car and scooped up the ball of paper. She handed it to me and closed the door behind her.

I stared down at the familiar mug shot. "What the hell?" I handed her the picture.

"You know this Pete 'Pistol' Armstrong?" Riley asked.

"Pistol Pete. Yeah, he's a homeless guy who sometimes hangs out around here. Other than the flashing thing, he's harmless." I stared in the direction McClowski had gone. "I wonder why they're looking for him."

He'd helped Smitty and me on a few occasions, so that could be it. These idiots didn't do their homework, though. Pete wouldn't be down this way for a few hours yet. He came for the food, and to flash the rich bitches that come out of Maverick's. It doesn't open until six on weeknights. I frowned when something else had occurred to me.

"Pete was the one who reported the snuff tapes that led us to Canniff's store."

"You think this is related?"

I thought about it for a minute. "I don't know, but one thing's for sure, we'd better find him before they do."

❖

Between talking to witnesses and tailing McClowski and Wilson, I think Riley had had all the excitement she could stand. She only put up a lukewarm protest when I asked her to stay in the car this time. I walked up to the check-in counter at the Motel 6, and the same clerk that had given Smitty and me the key to Pete's room was on duty. I gave a silent cheer. I felt sure that I would be able to get Pete's room number without hassle. That is, if I could tear the guy away from his video game for a few minutes. "Hi, I'm with the LAPD. I was wondering if you still have a Pete Armstrong staying here." As with the first time I had come here with Smitty, the pock-faced clerk didn't bother to look up from his video game. In fact, I thought he wasn't going to answer me at all.

"Twenty bucks," he said, still not looking up.

"Twenty bucks?" I repeated.

"Yeah, twenty bucks. I know you guys got that informant fund or whatever. I want twenty bucks for my information."

The fact that he didn't look up was extremely unsatisfying. I reached into my pocket, pulled out a twenty, balled it up, and tossed it at him. It struck him in the chest and settled between his small potbelly and the handheld video game. He picked up the twenty and put it in his shirt pocket. "I wish I would have thought of that earlier," he said with a small grin. "Pete checked out weeks ago."

"Are you sure about that? Maybe you should check the ledger."

"Positive." He groaned and gave the game a shake. "Just like I told those other cops. He ain't here."

"Did the other cops say what they wanted with him?"

"Which ones?"

I was about two seconds from grabbing that damn game and launching it across the room. "How many cops have been here?"

"A few. First there was a guy by himself, then a guy and a woman, and then two guys just the other day. But like I said, Pete was already gone before the first cop came by."

"Wait a minute. What first cop?"

Smitty and I should have been the first to come looking for Pete's tapes. I waited for the clerk to say something, but he'd already tuned me out. I leaned over and slammed my hand down hard on the counter to get his attention. "Hey!"

He did not look at all intimidated. In fact, he took one look at me and dismissed me as no threat. Big mistake. "Look, I already told you, I haven't seen Pete in weeks. As you can see, I'm pretty busy here. So unless you have a warrant…"

I hated people whose answer to everything was "Get a warrant." They didn't know what the hell they where talking about. Next thing he would be saying was…

"You know, my tax dollars pay your salary." Yes, smug words from a bottom feeder who probably hadn't filed a tax return in ten years. "So why don't you go out there and fight crime or something instead of coming in here and hassling me."

The self-satisfied smirk disappeared from the clerk's face as he went back to his video game. Something pounded in my temple. I squatted down in front of the counter. *You know what? I'm not a fucking cop anymore, and I'm trying to do the right thing here. And pretty much all I want to do is get back to the cabin with Riley and start apologizing in every position I know of. And this jackass is standing in the way of that.*

"Hey, what the hell are you doing down there?" The clerk got up from his chair.

I grinned. This was going to be fun. As his hands slapped the countertop, I was up with the .38 in my hand. "You know, I'm thinking we're having a *bit*," I grabbed his tie-dyed T-shirt and put the barrel of my gun up his right nostril, "of a misunderstanding."

I nodded, and just as I expected, he nodded with me, as if we were indeed just having a discussion.

"You seem to have mistaken me for someone who has the patience, or the desire, to waste time talking to you. Obviously you have the patience to sit around and pop pimples all day, so you probably don't understand how it is for someone *impatient* like me. So let me explain it in terms even you will understand. I mean, it's the least I can do, since the tax dollars from your Motel 6 job happen to pay my entire salary."

A film of perspiration formed tiny droplets on his face. "Hey, you don't have to break my balls," he whined.

I shook him into silence. "Now listen carefully. Either you stop *fucking* with me, or this office is going to look like a larger version of your bathroom mirror. Only your face is my pimple. Understand?" He nodded vigorously and I loosened my grip on his shirt. "All right, now that we understand each other, I'm going to ask some questions, and you're going to answer them nicely." I rested the gun on his lower lip.

"What first cop?"

"He said he was a cop and a friend of Pete's and he needed to get into Pete's room."

"When did this happen? Do you remember?"

"I can find out."

"Uh-huh. Don't make me come across the counter." I let go of his shirt, and he went straight to his desk and started rifling through papers. I took the opportunity to check to make sure Riley couldn't see me through a window. Reassured, I returned my attention to the clerk.

"Here it is. April sixteenth. I know the date because I closed up the office to get my new game over at the mall." He flipped open the magazine to a large ad proclaiming that Final Fantasy 9 would be at a store near me April sixteenth. "I told the guy to slip the key under the door when he was done. It was here when I got back."

If this guy was telling the truth, then someone had been in Pete's room *before* Smitty and I had gotten there. "Did you get the detective's name?"

"No, I didn't." The clerk didn't seem to care that he'd given out Pete's key without getting proper identification. If I ever got so bad off that I had to stay at one of those motels, I would make sure I put a chair up to the door.

"Do you remember what he looked like?"

"Kind of big. He was a black guy. Clean cut. That's all I know."

I nodded and held out my hand. He stared at me for a minute, then I raised my eyebrow and he reached in his pocket and slapped my balled-up twenty into the palm of my hand.

"Thank you," I said politely.

He hesitated. "You're welcome."

I put the little .38 back in its holster and walked out of the office without another word. I got in the car and smiled at Riley.

"How did it go?"

"Like I said, pretty uneventful. You were right to stay in the car." I patted her leg and pulled out of the parking lot feeling quite invigorated.

❖

"Someone else knew about the DVDs Pete took," I told Riley. "The clerk thinks a big African American cop searched that room just before me and Smitty."

"Well, he didn't find them," Riley said. "Or they wouldn't have been there when you arrived. Maybe he was looking for something else."

I had my doubts. Pistol Pete didn't have anything worth stealing. The DVDs were the only items of interest in that disgusting room. I wondered who had bothered to read the arrest report for Pete's flashing offense. His drunken statement about stealing the DVDs would normally have slid under the radar, but the two cops who'd brought him in had thought it was worth bringing to our attention. Everyone had heard about the snuff films Smitty and I were trying to trace. The information would have traveled up the food chain to the captain and anyone she told. Fuller and Jackson, the arresting officers, would also have mentioned it to their colleagues. There was no way Smitty and I were the first and only detectives to hear about it.

"We need to find Pete," I said. "And I have a pretty good idea where he is. I just hope Wilson and McClowski haven't heard about this place yet."

Pistol Pete was keeping house these days in an old Montgomery Ward store that had closed down a few years back. The city was still trying to determine the fate of the building and its mammoth parking lot. In the interim, its covered parking structure made it the perfect spot for the homeless to crash. If Pete wasn't earning enough from odd jobs to afford a motel room, that's where he would be.

Twenty minutes later, Riley and I exited the car and ducked into the parking structure. Several large cardboard appliance boxes littered the area, serving as makeshift beds. The familiar smell of stale beer, urine, and lost hopes hung heavy in the air.

"Watch your step, baby," I said as we moved cautiously through this city of forgotten and unwanted individuals. A hodgepodge of garbage covered the ground. Used condoms, needles, dirty tissues, candy wrappers, soiled clothing, food wrappers—the usual debris of the displaced.

"Why all the candy wrappers?" Riley asked.

"The junkies eat sweets when they're coming down off a high."

I spotted Pete's shaggy head peeking from beneath a dirty red plaid blanket. He didn't look like he'd had a bath in weeks.

"Pete, I need to ask you some questions." I waited two seconds because I was trying to appear polite in front of Riley and then yelled, "God damn it. Get your ass up!"

The look on his face would have been funny under normal circumstances. He shuffled upright, rubbing his eyes. "You scared me. I thought you were my wife."

"You married, Pete?"

"Oh yeah, worst move I ever made…that and trusting my business partner."

"Business partner?"

"Yup, I was an accountant. Owned my own business with my best friend Jerry. Only I didn't know he was screwing my wife and me at the same time. They took everything." He rose to his feet, tottering forward at one point, only to regain his equilibrium like the true pro that he was. "Who are you, anyway? I think I got my glasses around here. Hold on." He started high-stepping through a pile of dirty clothing.

"I'm with the police." I flashed my fake badge before he could find the means to read.

"Ah, there they are." He picked up his glasses, placed them on the bridge of his nose, and squinted. One lens was totally missing and a crack ran diagonally across the one still present. "Hey, now look, you can ask anyone, I been here all day," he blustered.

"I know, Pete, that's not why I'm here. Please lower your voice."

"Do I know you?"

"No, I'm sure you don't. Listen, a friend of mine, Smitty, told me that you helped him out with this case he was working on. He said you were minding your own business and found some DVDs. Remember?"

He frowned. "Oh, yeah, I remember. Those aren't for nice folk. You don't want to see nothing like that."

"You're right, I don't. But something happened to Smitty, and he didn't get the chance to tell me about all of the stuff on the DVDs. Did you look at them?"

Pete mumbled to himself and picked something from his scalp. "They were doing bad things to kids. I only looked at three of them. The tape didn't work in the machine."

"Are you saying there were three DVDs and a videotape?"

Pete swayed drunkenly for a minute. "Three DVDs and a video."

"Are you sure?"

"I can count."

I frowned. Pete claimed to be an accountant, and accountants were good with numbers. Even a drunk accountant would know the difference between three items and four. If there'd been a video with those DVDs, Smitty and I would have found it when we tossed Pete's room. "Do you still have that video?"

He squinted at me like I was stupid. "The cops took it. I was in jail."

"So when you went back to the motel after you were released, it was gone?"

"Three DVDs. One video. All gone. I wanted *The Green Mile,*" he lamented.

"Pete, do you remember talking to Smitty about the video?"

"I don't know any Smitty. I told the cops I don't want nothing, I don't know nothing. Just leave me alone. Hey, you sure are pretty. Want to see something?" He started to fumble with his pants, and I realized that our interview was officially over.

"No, that's okay. We don't want to see it."

Riley took a step backward.

"No?" He looked sadly at both of us. "Neither did my wife."

I gave him two twenty-dollar bills and told him to lay low because some people were looking for him. How much of that he understood, I couldn't say.

As we walked back to the car, Riley said, "I feel sorry for him."

"Me, too." My mind was elsewhere.

"No one uses VHS anymore," she noted in puzzlement. "Why just take the one tape?"

The hairs on my arms stood up. "And why leave the three DVDs? There's enough evidence on those to put someone in jail for a long time."

"So you think whoever took the video was specifically looking for it?"

"Yeah, that's exactly what I'm thinking. I'm also thinking that whatever is on that video has to be pretty bad."

"What could be worse than child pornography?"

"That's a good question, baby." I rubbed the back of my neck and closed my eyes. "A very good question."

❖

I called Chandra's cell phone from the Blazer.

"I got to make this fast," she said. "I found those files you asked for and I got a cross on one of your aliases. You never handled him because he was arrested in San Diego. Anyway, here's the thing. Michael Albert is an alias for Michael Stratford. They're the same person."

"How did you figure that out?" I knew I sounded impressed. "Because whatever you did is probably what Marcus did."

"I got to thinking," she said as if she'd just worked out a particularly difficult puzzle. "Albert sounds like a first name. So I switched them. You know, started running Albert Michael and then I started looking into files with Michael Albert as first and middle name. Stratford was the only one that popped up,"

"That's good work. Thank you," I said sincerely.

"You're welcome."

I worked through the list of names in my mind: Foster Everett, Joseph Smith, Nathan Stein, Michael Albert, Eric Ann. Michael Albert was Michael Stratford, the guy Smitty and I had been looking for. Where did he fit into this? Nothing was adding up.

"Hey, can you pull Stratford's records? I need everything you have on him."

"Sure, I can do that. You okay? You don't sound right."

"Yeah, I'm good." I wasn't, though. I felt like I was getting more questions than answers. "What about Eric Ann?"

"Dead ends so far," Chandra grumbled. "He's not in the system." After we said our good-byes, I leaned back against the seat.

Riley rested a hand on my thigh. "Any progress?"

"One of the names on the list is an alias. Michael Albert and Michael Stratford are the same person. Stratford's name came up in connection with a kidnapping case Smitty and I were working a few months back. Thing is, we could never find the guy to interview him."

"So you think he's involved?"

"Yes. The question is, how?"

Stratford could have made contact with the mother of his child by now, I thought, and if not, I could always get the details of his new girlfriend from Alicia Alexander again. Smitty and I never had the opportunity to follow that lead before events overtook us, and the information was among his papers. I groaned aloud at the prospect of another conversation about how Alicia's toilet got broken.

"Don't worry, you *will* figure this out," Riley said.

"But what if I don't?"

Riley's nightmare was starting to bug me. I swallowed bile that left a taste like a copper penny in the back of my throat. Anxiety hovered in the cab of the Blazer, silent, like a scavenger waiting patiently for a meal.

CHAPTER TWENTY

A licia Alexander?"
"Yeah?" She looked blankly at my badge, then at me. As I'd hoped, there was no spark of recognition.

"We're here about Michael Stratford."

She sighed and rolled her eyes. "For the last time. *I don't know* where Michael is. Y'all can keep sending more people over here if y'all want, but I'm going to keep telling you that I ain't seen him."

I was tempted to ask about the health of her toilet, but she hadn't recognized me and I was determined to keep it that way. I stifled a yawn. I hadn't finished my morning coffee before we set out. Riley seemed to be in a hurry to get our day started. She said she had a feeling we were closing in on something.

"Would you mind if we come in, ma'am?" Alicia reluctantly opened the door, and Riley and I stepped into her domestic chaos. I didn't see Fee Fee.

"So, what y'all want? I was just about to feed my son."

Alicia expertly moved a nude doll, a teacup, and a coloring book before she plopped down on her couch. I realized too late that once I allowed her to focus on the TV, I would lose her attention and probably all hope of getting any new information from her.

"Hey, what happened with that catfight the other day between the blonde and the brunette?" I asked pleasantly, in order to break the ice. I hadn't really noticed much about the fight, except that Sherm had been seriously into it until we intruded.

"Ooh, girl." Alicia's eyes didn't budge from the TV. "It turned out that Burdetta, that's the blonde, and Natalie, that's the brunette, were actually college roommates who got a little too close back then. That's what Burdetta's holding over her head. She has pictures and Natalie wants them back, because that guy Brock, who she is going to marry, would never understand their 'special' friendship."

Riley stared at the TV, riveted. I gave her a slight nudge in lieu of asking what the hell she was doing. She had the nerve to look irritated. I jerked my head to the rear of the home in a pointed reminder of the plan we'd discussed. Her mouth circled into an *O* and she moved in front of the television.

"Ma'am, may I please use your phone?"

Alicia peered frantically around her. "You can't make no long distance. I only got basic." She pointed toward the kitchen.

"That's fine, thank you."

Once Riley had disappeared through the kitchen door, I got down to business. I figured I would sit down on the couch, you know—invade her space a little so that she would have to pay attention. "Alicia, could you..." I jumped up as my butt connected with something hard and unyielding. I reached back and pulled the naked doll from beneath me.

"Sorry about that. Fee Fee's always leaving her toys laying around." Alicia didn't bother to check on either me or the toy.

I set the doll upright next to me so that it too could enjoy some quality television. The clattering noise inside its body told me that old Betsy Wetsy probably hadn't fared too well after having her head sat on. I pretended to be enthralled by the soap for a few minutes before asking, "Alicia, are you aware that Michael Stratford also uses the name Michael Albert?"

"What?"

I had her full attention now. "Michael uses the name Michael Albert, too."

"I didn't know that."

"Well, that's interesting, because I checked your daughter's birth records and her last name is Albert," I lied. "You wanna tell me what's going on, or am I going to have to haul you down to the station?"

She reached a decision quickly. "Look, Michael is a good guy."

I arched my brow in disbelief. In our last meeting she had called him a motherfucker several times. Now, all of a sudden, he's a good guy? "Okay, so what's your point? Why the alias?"

"People don't want to hire no con. So he got hisself an ID using his middle name. I gave Fee Fee the fake last name since Michael

Stratford couldn't find a job, but Michael Albert worked plenty. Long as he was working, I could get my child support from the state if he stopped sending it."

A nicer person would have pointed out the errors in Alicia's logic, but I let it go. "When was the last time you saw him?"

Alicia looked uncomfortable. "Well, me and him, you know, sometimes we get together. No big deal, just a mutual sort of thing."

"I understand. So have you seen him recently?"

At that moment Alicia seemed eager to redeem herself, or protect the source of her erratic child support now that I knew the truth about his identity. Either that or she wanted me out of her place so she could get back to her show. "Look, I lied to those other four cops, but I'll tell you the truth. He was here a couple of months ago. He brought Fee Fee this new doll." She held up the doll with the inflexible face. It looked like it was about two years old, not two months.

"Our records show that Michael had just quit his job and started another one. Do you know where?"

"No, I told the truth about that there. I don't know where he worked. Anyway, he was stupid. He leaves that good job with Stereo World and ends up getting suckered into some racket."

"What kind of racket?"

"I don't know, and that's the God's honest truth. He wouldn't tell me, said he didn't want me involved."

"What did he do for Stereo World?"

"He was a driver. You know, delivering equipment and stuff." I could see her getting antsy, trying to follow her soap while we were talking.

"Did he ever tell you what he did for the new employer?"

"Nah, he said the guy he's working for is a crazy motherfucker, that's all. The funny thing is, he had to lie about being clean to even get that whack-ass job. That guy doesn't want cops sniffing around if he hires ex-cons." She looked at me as if she had swallowed something distasteful. "Y'all never let people get on with their lives. Just like how you're doggin' him now. Michael's a decent man."

"So decent that he's okay with his daughter having a fake last name?"

"He doesn't want Fee Fee to know she has an ex-con for a daddy."

But it's okay for her to have a crackhead for a mother?

Alicia must have sensed my disbelief, because she continued with her defense of Michael. "He even called in about that missing little white boy."

Should I tell her that she's white, too? "What missing little white boy?"

"The one on the Amber Alerts."

"Okay, you're going to have to help me a little bit here. There are a lot of little white boys on Amber Alerts. When was this?" I asked. But I already knew the answer. It had to be connected to the cold case Smitty and I were working the first time I came in contact with Alicia.

"I don't remember."

"What was the information he had?"

"He didn't say. It was some bad shit. That's all I know. He saw the kid on a DVD or something."

Now that she'd decided to get truthful, I tried again for a location. "Do you know where Michael is?"

"Well, his grandpa used to live down in Barstow before they put him in a home. Last I heard, they hadn't sold his house yet."

"Would you happen to have a current picture of Michael that I could keep?" I could tell Alicia was going to balk, so I decided to be honest with her. "Look, I'm not after him. You have my word that I won't arrest him if I find him. I just want to ask him a few questions. Besides, I think he could be in trouble."

Alicia dragged a photo album from under her coffee table, turned a few pages, and extracted a small wallet-sized picture of Michael and Fee Fee. It was obvious where the little girl got her almond-shaped brown eyes. Michael kept his hair closely clipped and neat. His skin looked unblemished and his smile looked wide and genuine. He appeared to be the decent guy Alicia claimed him to be.

"That's the only one I can spare. Fee Fee got the other one in her room, and I ain't bothering it."

I nodded, glad just to be able to put a face to a name. "Thank you, this should help. The two cops you talked to? Did you get their names or a card?" I already knew who the two cops were, but I just wanted to confirm my suspicions.

"First it was a woman and a man. And then it was two guys. They gave me their cards, but Fee Fee drew on them."

I asked what the two detectives looked like and she described Wilson and McClowski. "And what did they ask you?"

"They wanted to know where Michael was. I told them I didn't know."

"That's all?"

"Yeah, they didn't even ask me about his other name."

"Good. So you didn't mention it to them?"

"Now why would I do that? You guys haven't even told me what you want him for. Shit, I ain't took no oath."

"Look, if I were you, I wouldn't tell them anything different if they come back. My partner and I don't care, but those others are hardasses." Okay, so add obstruction of justice to the litany of crimes I'd committed since this all began.

"That's what I figured, too."

Riley came out of the kitchen and gave me a nod, as if her fictional phone call had been successful.

"One last thing and we'll leave you alone. Do you happen to know Michael's grandfather's address in Barstow?"

"Yeah, hold on." With a despairing glance at the TV, Alicia plunged off into her chaotic house to find what I hoped was the address to Michael Albert Stratford's hideout. Although I doubted he had all the answers, I sensed that he would be able to get me a whole lot closer.

❖

The ride to Barstow was a hot one. Riley and I talked a little, mostly about things we would like to do once this was all over. I had a feeling she was still a little upset about her dream, so I wanted to ease her fears.

"I would love to go to Disneyland one day," I admitted.

"You've never been to Disneyland?"

"No, never. Have you?"

She nodded her head vigorously, but the smile on her face was so sad it made my heart heavy. "My father took me when I was a kid."

"Would you like to go with me one day?"

"Of course," she said without hesitation.

I busied myself looking out the window. I felt like I was asking her to marry me, and in a way, maybe I was. "One day" was such an obscure thing, not like saying a week from Tuesday or something. It was acknowledgment that there was no need to set more than a vague plan because we would be together no matter what. I found the thought comforting.

We found Michael's grandfather's house with no problem. I stepped out of the car and onto an empty, sun-bleached Doritos bag. Its loud crackle made me jump. The area looked dry and desolate. I couldn't imagine staying out here for longer than a few days without going crazy.

Riley and I knocked on the door and received no answer. I peered in a window, but couldn't see anything. An air conditioner droned from somewhere near the back of the house.

"If he isn't here, he'll probably be back soon," I surmised aloud. "People don't leave the AC running if they're not occupying the house."

Riley and I circled around to the rear of the property. A heavy, old air conditioner filled a window just to the left of the back door. A rusty-looking substance leaked from it and dried in the heat of the scorching sun, leaving an orange stain on the ground.

I pulled one of the 9's from my holster. "Riley," I whispered, "if this guy is here, it's because he's hiding from something. He may be armed, and I don't want to get caught without protection."

Riley nodded, and I took an improvised handkerchief from my pocket—a piece I'd torn from a T-shirt—and tried the back door. To my surprise, the knob turned and the door swung open, almost as if its hinges had just been oiled. The lack of sound was more eerie than a loud, dramatic creak.

A blast of cold air hit me in the face. I peered inside. All the blinds had been pulled, so the room looked dim. My body quaked as I stepped from the oppressively stuffy heat outside into the icy frigidity of the house. The eerie feeling I'd had when I first opened the door didn't dissipate as we entered. If anything, it got worse. *Who in the hell would crank up their AC this high?* The one comfort I had was that no one could endure this kind of cold for longer than a few minutes, leaving me fairly sure we weren't walking into an ambush.

It was obvious that the house had been searched. The sofa cushions looked as if someone had removed them and made a half-assed attempt at putting them back. An overstuffed recliner was pushed up against a wall. I trained my penlight on the floor and found long indentations in the carpet, indicating that the furniture had been recently moved.

Since all the curtains were closed, I went ahead and started searching the place I opened the refrigerator and found a reasonable supply of hot dogs, dry salami, Wonder Bread, ketchup, and a case of beer. "I think he was planning to stay for a while." Shivering, I took Riley's hand and led her toward the hallway. "Come on, let's check the rest of the house and then get the hell out of here. It's freezing."

The first door we opened was a linen closet stuffed with threadbare towels and sheets as old as me. Further down the hall, the bedroom door stood open. Heavy curtains covered the windows, allowing only a small crack of light to filter through. The bed, though sloppily made, was empty. I peered behind the door, signaled for Riley to wait in the hall, conceivably out of harm's way, then stepped into the room, gun raised in front of me.

There was no sound or movement, and I felt my heart start to slow to its normal beat. I opened the closet. "Shit," I yelled, as a large, heavy object brushed past me and hit the floor with a hollow thump. I pointed my gun down at it and ordered, "Hands out at your sides. Now!"

"Foster...."

"Riley, stay back, God damn it." The room was flooded with light.

"The lights work," she said quietly.

My gun shook as I stared incredulously at the large roll of carpet. It never ceased to amaze me what people stored in their closets. I pushed the heavy carpet back inside and slid the door closed. "I want to check the bathroom, and then we can get out of here."

The only personal object in the bathroom was a yellow toothbrush that didn't appear to have been used recently. The toothbrush was a small clue, and one I didn't take lightly. Michael had either left of his own free will, or someone had taken him by force. I was leaning toward the latter. Even if he was careless enough to leave an energy-guzzling AC running, he wouldn't forget his toothbrush if he'd been conscientious enough to bring it in the first place.

The next thing I noticed was that the shower curtain in the bathroom was closed and on the outside of the tub. Most people who take showers leave the curtains inside the tub, and people who take baths leave them out and usually open. Either way, I didn't like the idea of that shower curtain being closed. I suppose I knew what I would find before I pushed it back, but I was shocked rigid when I saw him.

"Oh, God." The two footsteps Riley took were enough to break me from my trance. "Stay back, God damn it," I snapped. Later I would have to apologize for cursing at her, but I had plenty to deal with first. Like the thick, nauseating stench wafting freely up to my nose.

"Foster, what's going on. Please?" Worry made her voice thick and the "please" was almost a sob.

"Just don't come in here, okay?" I softened my tone. "He's dead."

"Okay," I heard her answer.

"Shit, shit, shit!" I whispered as I shined the light over the body and back up again. He was dressed in blue jeans and a white T-shirt, his hair closely clipped. Dried blood trailed from his mouth, and the small bullet hole on his forehead was so neat it looked as though it had been painted on. Small caliber, I thought. Maybe a .22. I stared at the spatter pattern for a minute. I had never seen anything like it. The front of his shirt looked like someone had blown red paint on it through a straw.

"He's been shot in the head," I said.

"How long ago?" I could hear the worry in Riley's voice.

Just hang on a few minutes longer, baby, and we can get out of here. "Hard to say with the AC being cranked up like that, but not too long. I think we may need to talk to Alicia again, this looks like an execution."

I took the toothbrush from the sink and used it to pry open his lips, no easy task because he was still in full rigor. Whoever killed him had hit him so hard that several of his teeth had been knocked out. I aimed the penlight into his mouth and muttered, "Son of a bitch."

"His tongue is missing," Riley said from somewhere right behind me.

I thought about chastising her for sneaking up like that, but I figured she was shaken up enough already. Releasing Michael's lip, I stood up and steered her back into the bedroom. "Whoever did this was very angry at him for something."

"Where is it?" Riley's voice was calm, so calm that it bothered me.

"Where's what?" I asked, frowning as I got a better look at Riley's ashen complexion.

"His tongue."

"A better question is probably, where's all the blood?"

I watched Riley sway slightly. I was shivering, but she wasn't. Not unusual, considering her body temperature was naturally warm.

But she looked like she was in the early stages of shock, and I hadn't even noticed.

"Aw, shit. Sweetie?" I quickly hustled her out of the room.

"I'm okay," she mumbled. I could see she was having trouble keeping her speech clear.

"Do you want to go wait in the car?" I asked.

She shook her head. "No, I want to stay with you."

I looked around the room. It was too cold, and the heat from the car might keep her from going into further shock. But if the person who had done that to Michael came back, I didn't want her out there alone. I grabbed an afghan from the floor and wrapped it around her, than sat her on the couch.

"Riley, listen to me. I'm afraid you might be going into shock. Just wait here for two minutes, okay? Then we'll leave. Can you do that, for me?"

At her nod, I pulled one of the 9 mm's out of the holster and laid it on the couch next to her. She started to shake her head, which was a good sign. If she was coherent enough to argue with me, she would be okay.

"It's just in case, sweetheart. You'll see someone coming through either of the doors before I will. You don't have to touch it…just leave it there."

I noted that some of the color was coming back to her skin and lips, and she had started to shiver a little.

"You scared me," I said softly, and leaned in and kissed her lips. They parted for me and I pressed harder, just for an instant, before stepping back. I needed to finish up and get Riley out of here.

I did my best to ignore the corpse behind me as I went through the cabinets and drawers, looking for something I would know was important when I saw it. I found the answer to Riley's question almost instantly.

"Nice." I stared down into the toilet. The bloody mass floating there begged to be flushed, but I lowered the lid with the penlight.

The tongue made me sick for two reasons. One, the sheer cruelty of the act; and the amount of blood present in the toilet told me that Michael was probably alive when his tongue was removed. The neat little hole in his head was no doubt the thing that finally killed him. And two, it confirmed what I already knew. Michael had been silenced because he knew something he shouldn't have. His tongue being removed was a warning to someone that they should keep their mouth shut. Was it for me?

After I was satisfied that I'd missed nothing in the bathroom, I worked my way through the bedroom. The only thing keeping me moving was the fact that I knew I needed to get Riley out of there soon or she could go into shock. Careful to use my penlight and "handkerchief," and not to touch anything that could leave a print, I searched the place and found the answer to my earlier half-formed question when I pulled back the covers of the queen-size bed. It looked like someone had dropped a side of raw beef in there and left it to bleed all over the otherwise clean sheets. I grimaced and tossed the blankets back over the mess. This was obviously where they had removed Michael's tongue. I wondered if he'd told them what they wanted to know before they cut it out.

I sank to my knees and checked under the bed. There was no car out front when Riley and I had arrived, and I couldn't find a bag or anything else belonging to Michael. If he'd come here to hide, he would have brought clothes, but aside from the toothbrush, there was nothing. So unless I was to believe that Michael had arrived on foot with nothing but his toothbrush, and had somehow gotten into the house without a key, it stood to reason that whoever killed him had taken all of his belongings in a effort to make sure there were no clues left behind. Whoever was responsible for this was good, almost too good. I was certain when the police finally did show up, there would be no helpful fingerprints or forensic evidence to lead them to the killer.

I had walked around the body long enough. I would need to check him, and I wasn't going to be able to do that with just the use of a penlight. I grimaced as I was forced to reach first into his T-shirt pocket and then the two front pockets of his jeans. I pushed the body over as far as I could and felt the back pockets. I tried to think of anything other than the fact that I was now literally groping the rigor-hardened ass cheek of a man I didn't know, looking for clues that I was sure had long since been removed.

I repeated the process on the other side before letting the body settle back into the tub. It was time to leave. I took a moment to wipe down the places I knew Riley had been, hoping like hell I wasn't covering for the asshole that had murdered Michael Stratford. Riley had leaned back on the couch and appeared to be sound asleep. That wasn't a good sign.

As I walked toward her, I caught a glimpse of several DVD cases that had either fallen or been thrown behind the TV cart. They were empty, but the minute I saw the name of the video store on the spine, my pulse started to race.

"Reel Family Entertainment? What the fuck?" Surely that store wasn't a chain.

Almost as soon as I considered that possibility, I knew the answer. It made perfect sense that the video store would somehow be related to all of this. Was someone trying to get revenge for Canniff's death? Had I been the target, this whole time? And what of Stein and the others on the list? I hadn't known any of them before, I was sure of it. The only connection was that Smitty had arrested Stein before I became his partner. And Michael had known something about a kidnapping case that Smitty and I had been working. Now Michael was dead, Stein had disappeared, and Smitty had committed suicide. These thoughts thundered through my mind in seconds, confirming the fact that I had to get Riley and myself out of there. I had to think, had to regain my composure, otherwise I could be putting us both in even more danger.

"Riley, sweetheart?"

Riley blinked at me as if I had just roused her from a deep sleep. Riley wasn't the type of person to fall asleep with a dead body in the next room regardless of how little sleep she got the night before. She was definitely going into shock.

I wrapped my arms around her waist and helped her to her feet. "We're going to get you home."

Alarming questions clamored around in my head. What had Marcus stumbled onto, and was it somehow the cause of Smitty's suicide? Did the person who killed Marcus also kill Michael? And what about the still missing Stein? Was he somehow responsible for this, or was he also dead somewhere?

I didn't want to risk an anonymous 911 call, I just wanted out of there. So I closed the gate behind us and half carried, half dragged Riley to the car. I would like to say that I left Barstow at a decent rate of speed, but it would be a lie. I drove like I was in a race with Death himself. In truth, perhaps I was.

Chapter Twenty-one

I had to practically force Riley to eat some warm soup before I tucked her into bed without a fight. I asked if she might consider seeing a doctor but she refused, claiming that her pulse was normal and she was fine. She said she just needed to rest. I thought it was more than that, but I didn't argue. Regular folks could go through a full lifetime without seeing what Riley saw dumped in that bathtub.

I sat at the table and stared blindly at three pieces of paper. On them I had drawn boxes linked by common elements. Michael Stratford aka Michael Albert was a driver. He had Reel Family Entertainment DVDs in the house he'd holed up in. He knew something about a kidnap case involving a small white boy.

Harrison Canniff worked in, or owned, Reel Family Entertainment. I couldn't be sure, because I'd done what Smitty wanted and let go of the case. Smitty had covered up the killing and paid off the uniformed cops who were at the scene with us. Someone had provided the money for that payment, and Smitty seemed to be afraid of that person. Smitty had then killed himself. Maybe.

Someone wanted to shut me up. Whoever it was had also hired a couple of street thugs to beat me up. Later, Wilson and McClowski had tried to arrest me for Canniff's killing before they procured a warrant. They cited phony evidence they'd obtained from who knows where—a plastic bag with my prints on it, supposedly found with the body but not mentioned in the coroner's report. It sounded desperate, almost amateur. They had nothing on me, so they created evidence to arrest me.

Pistol Pete had the DVDs that led us to Reel Family Entertainment. But he also had a video we didn't recover. Someone had taken it from his room by the time we got there. The motel owner said an African American cop had gotten there ahead of us.

How were the other names on the list, Nathan Stein and Eric Ann, connected to all of this? What had Marcus found that I was obviously missing? Whatever it was, he'd been killed over it. And what, if anything, had Smitty known that made him desperate enough to kill himself? Or had he been silenced, just like I was supposed to be?

I jotted down stray loose ends. Smitty had arrested Nathan Stein for a case that didn't stick, and he was still interested in the guy. Why? Nathan Stein's neighbors loathed him. Caroline Stein hadn't returned a family heirloom platter to Zelda, and she was possibly having an affair with her pool boy. Mr. Dooley had seen Nathan in a white commercial delivery van, driven by an African American man, coming and going from the Stein home.

Wilson and McClowski held the key to what was going on. They'd interviewed Alicia, they were assigned to the missing person inquiry for Nathan Stein, they'd replaced me and Smitty, and they'd tried to arrest me. Someone had to have put them up to that. Since when did two detectives appear in the division and decide to arrest another cop of their own volition? I thought about Captain Simmons. She hated me. Was she involved somehow? Had she given the orders? Whatever was going on, Wilson and McClowski were in on it.

I needed to talk to them, preferably with a gun to their heads.

I checked Riley once more, noting the even rise and fall of her chest and that the color had returned to her face. I'd been sitting here for hours, but I wasn't ready to go to bed. Pistol Pete had worked at Reel Family Entertainment, a fact I'd tended to overlook because I was focused on the DVDs. Maybe he could fill in some facts. I felt like an idiot. I could have had Chandra researching the company. Instead I'd been pushing the place out of my mind, unable to confront what I'd done. My own guilt had blindsided me.

I kissed Riley on the forehead, whispered to her that I loved her, and left the theater. As I drove, the unease that constantly stalked me caught up with a vengeance. I eased up on the gas. What was I doing? For the first time in my life I had someone who genuinely loved me, despite all my faults. Every time I left her behind or followed another lead, it felt like I was putting our future happiness at risk. Was the truth really worth that? Would Smitty or Marcus ask that of me? No, they wouldn't, but I couldn't live with myself if they'd died in vain. Besides,

I was getting too close to give up now. I would just have to be extra careful; I had a lot to lose now.

❖

I found Pete much as I had the previous afternoon, except he now had three empty wine bottles lying on their sides next to him. I hoped he'd gotten something to eat, too.

"Hey, Pete." I kicked at his foot and he woke instantly.

"Oh, it's you." He picked up one of the empty bottles and turned it up to his lips before dropping it in disappointment. "What do you want? Can't a man sleep?"

I hated myself for propping up his habit, but took out several twenties anyway. I waved them in the beam of my flashlight. His eyes gleamed. I had his attention. "I have a couple more questions for you, Pete."

"It's all you ever do. Ask questions." He reached for the cash, but I held it back.

"When you worked at the video store…the place where you found those DVDs, what kind of work did they have you doing?"

He scratched his body in the routine manner of a man who shared his sleeping quarters with parasites. "I moved boxes. Put them on the pallet. Bring them to the van. Load them. Unload them."

"The owner of the store paid you for this work? Harrison Canniff?"

He give me a blank stare. "Was that his name?"

I reached into my back pocket, took out the picture Alicia Alexander had given me, and handed it over to Pete. "This guy look familiar to you?"

Pete found his broken glasses and studied the photo, his lower lip slack. There was no sign of recognition. I hadn't really expected anything else, I was just running with a hunch. As I reached out to take the picture back, Pete's mouth closed and he moved the picture until it was almost on his nose.

"That's him, alrighty. That's the guy that paid me to move the boxes."

"Are you sure?" The money had probably been a mistake. Pete could be telling me what he thought I wanted to hear. "Did you say the owner of the store paid you to move the boxes?"

"He did."

I pointed to the picture. "But he's not the owner."

Pete shook his head like I was asking trick questions. "It's him," he insisted. "He had a big white van that had the name of the store printed on the side."

"A big white van, huh?" I imagined I heard a click as two pieces of the puzzle slid into place. I handed Pete the twenties and asked, "Do you have anywhere else you can stay? I'm not sure you're safe here anymore."

Pete looked around, too. "Why not?"

"Remember those cops I told you about? They're looking for you, and I think they're bad news. You got somewhere to go just until everything blows over?"

Pete counted the cash and tucked the bills away. "Yeah, I guess I got someplace. What do they want me for, anyway? I haven't done anything."

He began to sniff. I rolled my eyes. All I needed was an emotional drunk to make my day complete.

"I know, Pete. So do us both a favor and hide for a few days."

He gave a mournful nod and I left him gathering his possessions. An accountant...I couldn't get the thought out of my head. When Pete had first slurred out the information I had wondered how someone with an education and a respectable profession could fall so low. I understood how it could happen now. One bad turn, one bad decision, one risk too many, and you could find yourself looking for a way to anesthetize the pain.

❖

When you're wanted, you can't afford to speed. You can't afford to call attention to yourself for any reason. The drive back to the theater, to Riley, was pure torture. By the time I'd parked the Blazer and locked the doors, fear had settled over me. I wasn't sure what I was afraid of, but I nearly ran down the stairs and into the small apartment. Riley was as I had left her. Only the top of her head was visible beneath the comforter. I quickly shucked my clothes and boots, and climbed into bed with her.

"Are you warm enough?" she asked in a sleep-blurred voice.

"No," I lied and she pulled me close, just as I knew she would.

CHAPTER TWENTY-TWO

I left Riley asleep when I left early the next morning. I wanted to talk to Nathan Stein, and if I had to threaten his wife, I would. I had nothing to lose. All the way to their house, I planned my conversation.

The antique knocker slammed against the door with a satisfying thwack. I took great pleasure in the fact that Caroline Stein was probably in the house having a conniption fit. A quick detour to see Mr. Dooley had already confirmed my suspicions. Michael Albert Stratford was indeed the driver of the late-night delivery truck, but I was still no closer to figuring out who had killed him, or why. On the fifth release of the door knocker, I heard the dead bolt turn, and Terry the pool boy, or whatever, inched the door open.

"Good morning, may I help you?"

Oh, and he's polite, too. "I sure hope so." I stuck my foot inside the entryway and hoped like hell he didn't slam the door on it. "I need to speak with Mrs. Stein again. There are a few more questions I was hoping she could answer for me."

"Caroline isn't here…"

"Well, perhaps you and I could—"

"No, I was just about to leave."

"I see. Well that's too bad. Question. Does she often leave you in her house alone while she's out?" The panicked look on his face made me go in for the kill. "Or do you live here? I had assumed that you only came for Mrs. Stein's workouts."

"Caroline's afraid to be here alone after her husband's disappearance, so she asked me to stay."

"Interesting. I had no idea. As I was saying, I really would like to talk to you. It should only take a few minutes."

Terry must have gotten a backbone, because he narrowed his eyes and asked almost triumphantly, "Do you have a warrant?"

Now I had two options. I could either wallop this boy toy over the head with my 9, or I could sweet-talk my way into the Stein residence. I was already reaching for the gun when a voice from farther inside the house saved his ass.

"Let her in." Caroline Stein walked up behind Terry, swept me with a dismissive stare, and repeated more sharply, "Let her in, I said."

This time Terry jerked as if she'd slapped him. He moved aside and I followed Caroline across an expanse of Berber carpet to the living room. Everything looked pretty much as I remembered: large, expensive, and new.

Caroline wandered to the fireplace and rested her arm on the mantel as if she was posing for one of those home décor magazines. Her emerald green velour sweatsuit looked like it would disintegrate at the first sign of moisture. It did show off her breast job to perfection, though.

"Caroline, I don't think…" Terry started to speak as soon as he had shut the door behind me.

"You don't think what? You don't think I should have allowed Officer…I'm sorry, what was your name again?" Caroline shook her head in a superb imitation of me. I panicked, because for half a second I couldn't remember the fake name I had given her before.

"Jones," I said with a smile that, to my surprise, was returned.

"Ah, that's right. Officer Jones, what can I do for you?"

"Well, I have a few more questions about your husband."

"I see, and what exactly would those questions be?"

Normally, I would have launched right into it, but Caroline Stein was looking a bit too relaxed in my presence. I had expected cynicism, even outright anger, but not the amused self-assurance that seemed to pour from the woman.

Disconcerted, I watched her closely as I asked my first question. "You mentioned your husband's business interests. I understand those include Reel Family Entertainment. Is that so?"

"And if they do?"

"The business isn't registered in his name." I was bluffing. I didn't know if it was or not.

"So perhaps he was a silent partner. Many of my husband's parishioners don't believe in attending movies or even renting them. They feel that it's giving money to the devil, so to speak."

"But even as a silent partner, his name would be on the paperwork. If he was making money on this store, or even losing money, the IRS would have to know."

Caroline Stein smiled again, and this time I really felt nervous. "I'm afraid you're going to have to ask him about that. Oh, but for that, I suppose you'd have to find him first."

"That's exactly what I'm trying to do, ma'am."

"Are you now? Well, that's odd, because it seems to me that about the only thing you've been doing is wasting my time."

This woman was really starting to get on my nerves, and it was time to play a bit of hardball. "Your neighbors claim that on several different occasions, a white van from Reel Family Entertainment came to your home during the night, loaded some boxes, and left. Do you have information about what it was carrying?"

The condescending smile froze on Caroline's lips. Terry's doleful blue eyes begged me to stop pushing her buttons. "Why don't you answer a question for me, Officer Jones?" she said through the tight lips that I would forever associate with her name.

"Detective," I corrected from long-standing habit, and then could have kicked myself. The triumph on her face was enough to tell me that the jig was up.

"I made some phone calls, one of which was to the two detectives that you seemed so interested in the last time you were here. They informed me that there was no Officer Jones working my husband's case. So I figure you're either out of your jurisdiction, or you're impersonating a cop. Which is it?

"Did you tell them I was here?"

"Why should I?"

"If I thought someone at my front door was impersonating a cop, I would call the real thing in a heartbeat."

"Well, maybe I'll do just that if you ever come around here again. Terry. The officer, or whoever she is, was just leaving."

I relaxed instantly. She was hiding something, and for once that was a good thing. I decided to push her buttons for a change. "Tell me, Terry, you were the personal trainer two days ago and before that the pool boy. Now you're the butler?"

We both turned to Caroline, who wisely chose to ignore the question.

"You knew it was me banging on the door," I taunted Caroline. "Why didn't you call the cops right then? In fact, let's call them now. Ask for Captain Gail Simmons."

Terry made a grab for my arm as if to escort me to the door. I swatted his hand away.

"I didn't call the police because I was curious about what you wanted," Caroline said.

"If I was curious, I would ask a lot more questions than you have."

Terry took another step, and Caroline held out her hand as if signaling to a dog. He stopped, obedient and well-trained pet that he was.

"All right, fine, I want to know who you are and why you want to speak to my husband."

"Who I am isn't important," I said. "I'm investigating the murder of a close friend. I think your husband may have information that could help."

Caroline pondered that and seemed to relax, as if deciding she would believe me. "Is that what this is about? You think my husband had something to do with your friend's death?"

It didn't escape my notice that she'd changed the context of what I'd said. Having information and having "something to do" with a murder were two different things. I followed the usual interview formula, turning the question back to her. "What do you think?"

"You know, up until recently I would have laughed in your face."

"What changed that?"

"That would be between my husband and me."

"Look, I don't really care what goes on between you and your husband. I really just want some information, and then I'll get out of your hair. Someone killed my friend. Your husband's name was on a list found among his private things. I just want to know why."

"I'm afraid I can't help you. I don't involve myself in my husband's other ventures. I'm too busy dealing with the needs of our congregation."

"I thought you said the church was destroyed after the abuse allegations."

"As long as one person wants ministering, there will always be a church."

I didn't miss the ring of piety in her words, nor could I keep myself from glancing dubiously at her boob job, expensive workout gear, and her hair. "You said you help with the church? What does that entail?"

"I'm his wife," she said as if that should explain everything. "I take it you're not a religious woman?"

"I was raised Catholic, but it's been a long time since I've been to church." I could tell she was mentally adding my name to the list of people that would be "left behind." She was probably right. I hadn't seen the inside of a confessional in years.

"I was born and raised Southern Baptist." A small accent snuck in when she said Southern, and I had to stifle a snicker that threatened to escape. "My parents were always poor, and when my mother got sick it just got worse."

Why was she telling me this?

"But you know what? The preacher's wife always made sure that we had something to eat, that our clothes were clean and mended. She organized shifts of the other wives so that me and my older sister could go to school and not have to worry about my momma."

"So you're saying these early experiences inspired you to stay active in the church?"

Caroline smiled. "Yes, I decided what I wanted to be when I grew up was a preacher's wife. The preacher of our church had two boys. Every young girl in that church wanted to be chosen to wed one of them. I knew that with my buckteeth and my hand-me-down clothes, they wouldn't show any interest in me. And I was right. They both ended up marrying little rich girls with pretty clothes and white teeth."

I tried to imagine what Chandra would say to such a disclosure. "Men are such asses."

She smoothed a hand over her svelte hip, no longer the ugly duckling. "It didn't make any difference that I knew my Bible inside out and never missed a day at church. The only thing that mattered was that I wasn't pretty enough or a part of the right social groups."

"So when did you meet Mr. Stein?"

"My daddy always drank too much, but things started getting worse once Momma got better. He even stopped going to church." She said this with the breathless dismay of a believer who thought not going to church was the true sign of being possessed by the devil.

Hoping this story was leading somewhere, I said, "It must have been hard for your family."

She sighed. "One day, he just never came home. Momma moved all us kids to Mississippi to stay with relatives. They were already members of a church, so naturally we joined, too. Nathan was the preacher, and it was love at first sight. He was so charismatic, so intent on saving us all that he would sometimes give himself migraines and have to be carried off."

A small frown appeared on her face as if she was considering something for the first time. "Anyway, I was surprised when he asked my momma if he could marry me. And when he told me he was coming out west to start his own church, I was delighted. I was going to be what those pretty little girls had a chance to be. I was going to be serving the Lord at my husband's side."

"But things changed when you got to California, right? Your husband was accused of assaulting a minor?"

"Of course it didn't change." Not one iota of mirth reached her eyes as she laughed derisively. "My husband was a religious man, the leader of our church. He would never do something as distasteful as beating or molesting a child. At least that's what I thought back then."

Finally, the confession. This was how lots of people worked up to the truth. They wanted you to sympathize and be on their side. Caroline had something to hide and she was ashamed. I could see it the tightness of her shoulders and the defensive angle of her chin.

"You know, I hated that girl for going to the police," she said. "I know she didn't pull the trigger, but I really did believe it was a ploy for attention or a prank that went horribly wrong." She lifted the picture from the mantel. "My son was killed in the raid on the barn where we had most of our services. We weren't even having a service then. Only the childcare center was open."

"The raid?" I guessed she was talking about Nathan's arrest.

"I never blamed Nathan," she said softly. "I never believed he was responsible. I blamed that girl. I blamed her and the police for my son's death."

"I hate to tell you this, but she probably wasn't to blame. I think she was telling the truth."

"I know. Terry found the DVDs." The smile on her lips died a slow death and I felt my stomach churn. Something was going on here that I couldn't put my finger on. The woman who always looked so calm and collected seemed to be coming apart at the seams.

I shifted my attention to Terry. "You found DVDs? Where?"

"I was trying to get the net to clean out the pool. Reverend Stein wasn't home and Caroline told me to break the lock. Inside, there were all these DVDs and recording equipment. It was like someone had a little mini recording studio inside."

"And you never noticed this stuff in there before?"

"Only Reverend Stein had a key to the pool house. Whenever I came to clean the pool, everything was already sitting at the door."

"Did you happen to see a videotape among everything? An old VHS?"

"No, I don't think so. But most of them were already boxed up."

"So did you watch any of these DVDs?"

Terry nodded. "I wish I hadn't."

"What was on them?"

"You know what was on them." Caroline Stein's voice dripped venom and disgust. "That girl was telling the truth. And if it wasn't the truth, it was a lie based on truth. Because of him, because of my husband, the police raided our land. They raided our land, shots were fired, and my child was killed. Do you understand me? He was responsible for killing my child, and he lay down with me every night. He lay down with me, and he never said a goddamn word." The last two words cut through the air like shards of glass.

I watched as Terry tried to console Caroline. This was real, not a show put on for my benefit. The composed woman I had talked to before was gone, and in her place was a mother, distraught over the senseless death of her child.

"When I found out what he was doing, what he was storing in our home, on our property, I told him to get it out of here or I would go to the police myself. That's why that van was here. They were moving every remnant of that filth from my home."

"Where is your husband now, Caroline?"

"In hell, where he belongs."

Terry shushed Caroline and settled her on the couch. "I think you should leave now."

"Answer one more question for me. All of that happened years ago, and it's between Caroline and her husband. Why are you involved? If it were me, I wouldn't want any part of it."

"I've always been a part of it. I lost my mother in that raid."

I looked him hard in the eye. "Do you know where Nathan Stein is, Terry?"

"Yes," he said without hesitation. "He's in hell, just like Caroline said."

As I left the Stein home, I took the tape from my recorder and thought about dropping it in the garden trash bin. Caroline and Terry had all but said Stein was dead, and there was only one way they could both be so sure of that. I opened the car door, took a Ziploc bag from the dash, and labeled my evidence.

If Nathan was dead, who killed Michael Stratford? I thought I finally knew why he was killed. Michael Stratford was the "cop" who'd visited Motel 6 before Smitty and I got there. He'd taken the missing videotape, and someone wanted it back very badly.

❖

I slammed to a halt next to Riley's Land Cruiser, glass protesting under the Blazer's tires. I couldn't wait to tell Riley what I'd discovered. "Shit," I grumbled as the sun tried to burn through the hair on top of my head. I stood back and looked around the building. I could hammer all I wanted, there was no way that Riley would hear me even if she was awake. I could have kicked myself in the ass for not taking Riley's keys.

"Use the lock picks, stupid," I said out loud after staring at the door angrily for a few seconds. I dropped to my knee and went to work. It took me a bit, but finally I was in the cool theater. I needed a shower.

Pulling my damp T-shirt over my head, I stumbled into the apartment. "Hey, baby, it's just me. How are you feeling? You're not going to believe this, but I think Caro..."

Chills swept across the fine sheen of sweat on my back and stomach, leaving gooseflesh in their wake. I stared at the rumpled bed and overturned chair. I stood frozen, my T-shirt imprisoning my wrists, my breath echoing in the emptiness.

Somewhere in the background, a faucet dripped.

"Baby?" I called out, though I knew she wouldn't answer. Riley would never leave a chair turned over; it wasn't in her nature to be untidy. She also would never leave a faucet dripping. I dropped the shirt back down over my head. My eyes would not allow me to turn away from the bed.

"Riley? Sweetheart, please, if you're here, please answer me."

I stumbled to the room that used to hold her weights. It was completely empty. Even though I knew she had left her weights at the cabin, the bareness of the room almost doubled me over. I ran through the rest of the theater, calling her name and losing hope with each step.

Maybe she's out front. Maybe she got tired of being inside and went for a walk. I burst through the door, sending it crashing back against the wall. The parking lot was as deserted as what I could see of the street beyond. I looked around frantically. The only movement I saw was the glint from the broken glass that littered the asphalt. *Maybe she needed some air. Maybe she needed to walk, or she saw something.* My heart started a low, deep thumping. *She's not gone. She's not gone.*

I approached the Land Cruiser. The window was still down from the last time we were in it, the water bottle she'd been drinking from still lay on the seat. I curled my fingers around the partially raised window for support. I backed away and started to run. I opened my mouth to call out her name, but there was nothing.

My first thought was to bang on doors. But there were no doors to pound on, no neighbors to question, no one who could help me find her. Riley had said that her place was quiet, and she was right. There was nothing for a half mile in any direction, just the theater. Someone could have taken her in broad daylight, and no one would have seen a thing.

I stopped in the middle of the lot and stared hard at Riley's Cruiser. If I stared long enough, maybe I would see something. Some clue, something, because I couldn't seem to think straight.

"Riley?" I yelled, turning in a slow circle. "Riley?" Nothing moved. Not a single bird chirped, no breeze to soothe my frazzled nerves.

My heart contorted painfully in my chest. I squatted down next to the passenger side door, unable to keep myself upright. The burning heat of the metal seared through my T-shirt and clawed at my back. I put my hands over my head and shivered violently in the ninety-nine degree heat. Suddenly I was seven years old, crouching in the corner of the bathroom, my hands over my head, as my father tried to tell me through the door that it wasn't my fault my mother left.

I did that to you too, didn't I, baby? Every time things got tough or I got scared, I hid in the bathroom. It's been over twenty years and I'm still hiding in the bathroom, making promises to God that if I could just have her back, I would be a good girl.

I started to rock as more chills passed through my body despite the merciless sun.

You ever wonder if, before you die, you get an early warning sign?

CHAPTER TWENTY-THREE

I walked back into the theater and down to the apartment, a part of me still expecting to find her sitting at the table, drinking her water or eating a fucking celery stick. Another sob left my throat when I found the place exactly as it was before. I righted the chair and turned off the water faucet. *Should I call her family? Dani?* I'd seen the numbers on her cell phone countless times when I called Chandra.

"Okay. Okay, you have to get it together." Though the first words were a sob, the last few sounded stronger. I owed Riley so much. The thought that I might never be able to tell her how I felt, how much I wanted to be with her, was making it hard for me to breathe. "Okay, just sit down and figure this out, Foster. You can do this; this is what you do. Remember? Just figure it out."

I pulled the 9 mm's from their holsters, laid them on the table, and sat down with my head cradled in my hands. I felt rage. Rage so hot and dangerous it burned through my heart and came out my mouth in the form of a sob that probably sounded more like a scream. And then there was hatred. I hated whoever had taken her. I hated them with a passion I had never felt before. I hated them for taking her, and I hated myself for letting it happen. Tears streaked down my face, and as I reached up to brush them away, I smelled her scent on my hand. The faintest trace from when I stroked her cheek as I kissed her good-bye just a couple of hours ago.

Should I go to the police? No, they won't look for her until tomorrow, and by then it may be too late. There was also the very real possibility that I would be arrested and no one would listen to me.

"Please, God, please." I tried to calm myself. I had no idea where I needed to go, or what I needed to do. I was scared, and I was without the one person in the world I could admit that to. And somewhere out there, someone might be hurting her. I wanted to kill them.

I weighed the guns, one in each hand. Michael Stratford's killer had removed his tongue. Not a subtle warning. The question was, who were they trying to warn? He had worked for Stein, who was now missing. I couldn't prove it, but I was sure his wife and her boyfriend had something to do with his disappearance. Did they have something to do with Michael's death as well? My gut told me no. Whoever had killed Michael had been cold-blooded and calculated. It didn't seem like a crime of passion.

I flipped open my file and flipped through paperwork, telling myself that if I could just solve this case I would find Riley. Panic would get me nowhere.

I stared at the sheets of paper that held the info on Harrison Canniff. I had avoided looking at them for the obvious reasons. I didn't realize until now that everything was connected somehow. The case file was a painful reminder of how I had almost ruined my life and possibly why Smitty killed himself. Had Smitty figured out what was going on? Had Marcus? Maybe I was going at this the wrong way.

I shuffled through the reports until I came to the paperwork on Smitty. This, too, I'd avoided. I traced the picture of him with my finger. It had been taken years before, when he was promoted to detective. He was thinner then; he hadn't yet acquired the beer belly he had when I became his partner, and he didn't smile like the Smitty I knew. He looked older than he had when he'd died. I turned the page and continued to read. Smitty and his partner had received many commendations when he was in San Diego, something I knew but that Smitty rarely talked about. Smitty's partner took early retirement at about the time Smitty moved back to Los Angeles. The dates coincided with the time I became his partner.

I fumbled with the cell phone. Riley's cell phone. I couldn't seem to remember if I'd told her that I loved her.

"Whoever this is, you better talk or hang up the damn phone."

"Chandra...Chandra, it's Foster."

"Damn, take it down a notch. I can hear you. What's wrong?"

"I can't explain right now. I need you to look up something. I need you to go on the Internet and see if you can find anything on Joseph Smith in the San Diego papers. Cross-reference Monica's name, too.

I'm looking for something that would have happened about five years ago. Hell, check Chief James, too, while you're—"

"I'm going to have to get back to you. I do have a job, you know." Her voice had that bitter sharpness that people get when they're busy.

"God damn it, would you stop being a bitch for two minutes. They've taken Riley. Please, can you help me? I need your help, okay?"

"Who took Riley? What are you saying, girl?"

"Please, just hurry."

"Okay. I'm pulling it up now."

I heard fingers hitting the keys viciously. *Please,* I begged any power that was listening, *she's a good person. Don't let anything happen to her.*

"Okay, the first article just quotes Smitty in reference to a case about some church. I don't think this is what you're looking for."

"No, tell me what it says."

"It's called the Church of the North Star. Says here the police thought the church was set up as a scam. They would entice these women to join them in phony prayer meetings and the like, then they would either use them or their kids in porn. They had themselves a regular casting couch. Let me scan this…Okay, anyway, its founder was…Holy shit."

Into the fuzzy phone silence, I yelled, "What? Holy shit…what?"

"Holy shit, it was a man named Nathan Stein," she said slowly and succinctly. "He was never indicted because the police entered the place illegally."

"Anything else?"

"The police had been watching them since an accusation of abuse, but they didn't have anything." She paused, and I could sense her confusion through the phone. "For some reason, one morning they opened fire on the place. Some of the women and children were killed."

The cell phone felt like it was burning into the side of my head. "Can you do a search on Harrison Canniff?"

"The autopsy report was inconclusive due to the fact that his body was burned and all of his teeth were missing. His ex-wife made the ID."

"No, I know about that part…do you have anything else on him?"

Her breathing got loud and deep. "Holy shit. You're not going to believe this. Canniff was there. He was arrested as well, but they couldn't make the charges stick because the bust wasn't legal."

Now my mind started searching. I felt like I already had my answer, but I needed to follow it to its logical conclusion. It didn't make sense, it was crazy, but it had to be true. "Can you find anything on the officers involved in the bust? They had to have been disciplined or something."

"It was Smitty and his partner. They were there."

If I had been in any other condition, I would have been as shocked as she was. But as it was, I felt like I was spent—no emotion, no anger, nothing. Just totally drained. "Do you have a name, an address, or something on Smitty's old partner?"

"Shit, I can probably get it, Foster, but I don't know. That's not something I have access to. They were down in San Diego. The only reason I can pull this stuff is because someone entered it into the database. I might be able to pull in a few favors, but you know how hard it is to get into an officer's records unnoticed."

Okay, think, Foster. Think. Smitty and his partner were involved. I couldn't very well waltz up to his old partner. I could try Monica, but I don't know if she would tell her father.

"Do you get any hits on Monica or Chief James?"

"There's close to five hundred on Chief James."

"No time. What about Monica? Take out the ones that look like they have anything to do with Chief James or the fact that she's his daughter." With my teeth gritted, I waited.

"Everything is about that charity she runs, burying those kids."

"Okay." I rubbed hard at my aching forehead and closed my burning eyes tightly. A pulse began to pound in my temple. "Go back to the oldest one and read it to me."

I listened intently as she read the article. I was certain it was the same one Riley and I had found back in Albion. I opened my mouth to tell her to go to the next one when something she said made me pause.

"Citing a near-fatal accident with her own son, she has made it her life's work—"

"Wait. Back up. Read that again." I pressed the phone hard into my ear, concentrating on what I was hearing. Smitty had never mentioned an accident with Eric. "Did Marcus ever talk to you about Smitty?"

"No, I told you, they didn't really know each other." Something in her tone didn't seem right.

"Listen to me, I need you to think long and hard about this. Did he ever mention anything having to do with Smitty at all? I need to know what he may have known that I don't."

When Chandra spoke, she was unusually hesitant. There was something she didn't want to tell me. "Like what?"

"Why is this so hard for you to understand?" Desperation crept into my voice. "Did Marcus ever say anything about him? Did Smitty's name come up, or Monica's, or hell, anything at all to do with either of them?"

"I can remember us talking about it a little when the article first came out."

"What article?"

"The one I'm reading to you. About Smitty's wife's charity. Marcus and I were talking, and I told him I thought it was sort of creepy."

I swallowed. "What…what did you think was creepy?"

"I mean, I understand about civic duties and I think she's doing a great service, but in her own van? And then how she would bury them and, I don't know, give them names. Marcus went over to the cemetery. He said all of them had her last name. I know Smith is common, but I mean, she had her own son in the same van she carried those dead babies in."

"Can you print the articles out? I need to see them."

"I'm not sure I can get away."

"Please, you have to. They might…I have to find her."

I felt like I was imploding. Nothing seemed to be adding up, but in the back of my mind something was. It was sick and it was dirty, and I had let Riley fall into that tide pool of filth. I had to get her back.

"It's okay, Foster." Her voice was calm, almost as if she was talking me down off a ledge. "I'll get away, okay? I'll bring it to you."

❖

Chandra agreed to meet me in the parking lot of a KFC about two miles from the theater. She got into the Blazer and handed me the articles.

"You okay?" she asked.

"No." I tried not to notice how dead my own voice sounded as I scanned the printed pages. There wasn't much more to them than what I already knew, but something was telling me that these articles could have been what Marcus keyed in on.

"Listen, I'm going to follow up on a few things. If you don't hear from me in four hours, go to one of the detectives in my division. Anyone except Wilson or McClowski. Tell him everything you know. Give him this address and tell him I'm in trouble. Do you understand?"

"Maybe you should go to him now."

"No, I can't run the risk that they might haul me in before I find her."

"What are you going to do?"

"I'm going to find Riley."

I watched Chandra drive off, and then got back on the freeway heading toward Monica's. I pulled a small card out of my back pocket, reached for Riley's cell, and dialed the number with one hand.

"Hello?"

"Sherm?"

"Who the fuck is this?"

"Foster Everett."

"I thought you were going to call me…"

"Sherm, don't. I need help, okay? They took Riley."

"Who took her? Where are you?"

"I don't know who took her. Probably the same people who killed Marcus."

"Tell me what you need."

"I need her back, Sherm. I need her back, no matter what."

"I know," he said. It was no comfort to me that he did know; Marcus was dead.

"I'm on my way to see my partner's widow. I think she may know something, but I'm not sure." To my horror, a sob escaped my throat. I gave Sherm directions to the theater and got him to write down Chandra's cell phone number. "I'm going to talk to Monica first. I'll meet you at the theater in about two hours."

I didn't know what I expected Sherm to do, but it helped knowing I wasn't in this alone.

I pulled up in front of my partner's old house and noted with dismay that Monica's van wasn't there and that a "For Sale" sign had been placed in the yard. I left the Blazer running as I sprinted to the side of the house and peered through a window. Eric's room was now empty; even the border of multicolored balloons had been pulled down. I ran to another window that illuminated the hall of the house. The pictures of Monica's mother were gone, and in their place was a wall of pristine white. There wasn't even a lighter patch of paint to prove that the pictures had ever been there.

It took me an unusually long time to get into the house. I couldn't seem to keep my breathing or my hands steady as I worked at the locks. Once inside, the acrid smell of fresh paint assaulted my nose as I walked from room to room. In the family room I got to my knees, searching for indentations in the carpet where a pool table had sat for all the years I had known Smitty. There were none. It was as if someone had gone through and wiped away every piece of evidence that this house had ever been lived in. I explored Eric's room, thinking that small children leave prints, dirt evidence of their existence. There was nothing; even the light switches were spotless. This felt so wrong, off kilter somehow, like watching a glass of water that was tipped on its edge but never fell.

Perhaps it was that very feeling of disorder that made me so alert, because I felt it the instant someone else walked into the house. You know the feeling. You can tell someone is there because the air moves, even though you don't actually hear anything. My first thought was to pull my gun, open a window, and scurry out. My second thought was that whoever was out there might know where Riley was. I pulled the .38 from my ankle holster and placed it in the deep pocket of my cargo pants. No brute force and no threats. I had to let myself get caught.

"Well, hello there. I hoped you would stop by."

I turned around, already reaching for the guns at my back.

"Go on, go on and pull the gun," Dan McClowski said. "I want to have to kill you."

Gritting my teeth, I brought my hands up in front of me. I stared down the barrel of the .45 pointed at my head. "Where is she?"

"Oh, you mean your big friend? Tell me the truth, she helped you in your apartment, didn't she? We figured it must have been her."

When I didn't answer, McClowski chuckled. His ponytail caught the light, making me vow to pull it straight out of his head after I found Riley.

"Come on." He gestured with his gun, indicating I should walk before him.

I stopped when he told me to, and he quickly removed both 9 mm's and, just as I'd hoped, didn't bother to pat me down.

"Tell me where she is," I demanded.

McClowski pushed his gun into the small of my back to edge me forward. "Well, let's see. I figure right about now she's getting the shit kicked out of her, but I can't be sure."

We had just reached the living room, and with a final shove to my back, he sent me stumbling forward. My body tensed as a searing pain started at the back of my head, jabbed down my neck, and sent me to my knees.

"God damn it, man, don't kill her." Alvin Wilson slouched into view. "He said bring her ass in alive. He needs that tape."

"I've earned some payback. This bitch tried to kill me last time."

"Yeah, whatever. Just get her up."

I heard McClowski holster his weapon. Cursing under his breath, he bent to help me up. As I was dragged to my feet, my hand went to my pocket, but at some point after I had been hit, the .38 had been removed from my pocket. I couldn't seem to keep my head from hanging down as I tried to catch my breath. I felt the prickly sensation of blood as it rolled over my cheek and then seeped into my mouth—warm, coppery, and somehow comforting. "W...where is she?" I said to give myself time to regroup.

"Don't worry, we're going to take you right to her. But first we want the tape."

"I don't have any tape."

"Look, we know that drunk stole it. Smitty said you and he were the only ones that had access to the tapes."

"I didn't take anything. I turned in everything we had."

"We know how Michael Albert got hold of the tape. We talked to him." The curl of Wilson's lip was meant to be a smile. Instead, it just seemed cruel, almost as cruel as the damage done to Michael's body. "He swore he didn't have it anymore. We're starting to think he gave it to you."

"You're crazy. I don't even know him."

"Then how did you know about the house in Barstow?"

"How did you know about it?" I fired back.

Wilson smirked. "His girlfriend told us."

Damn you, Alicia. "So what makes you think she didn't tell me the same thing?"

"Their apartment's been watched ever since the van was towed."

"What van, and what did Michael's girlfriend tell you?" I'm sure my face gave nothing away, but mentally I winced.

I realized McClowski knew nothing about Alicia. He was talking about the woman Michael was living with at the time of his disappearance. They must have questioned her about Michael.

McClowski really laughed this time. "You don't think we're going to tell you everything, do you?"

"You know what I think? I think you're just guessing. I don't think you know your ass from a hole in the ground."

The next blow barely even bothered me, but I pitched forward anyway and lay as still as I could. I was starting to understand something, but the pain in the back of my head was making it harder for me to connect the dots. I felt a tight hand on my arm.

"Man, she doesn't look so good." The note of worry in McClowski's voice gave me a small sense of pleasure. Never mind the fact that my life was seeping out of the back of my head.

"Yeah, well maybe you shouldn't have hit her so hard."

"Tell me where Riley is, and I'll get you the tape," I said as Wilson roughly hauled me to my feet.

"The boss has her, and that's all you need to know."

"Who's your boss?" I already knew the answer. There was only one person powerful enough to have two dirty cops on his payroll. The question was, why all of this? What could be so bad that he'd been having people killed?

"You'll find out soon enough," McClowski spat. "Now tell us —"

I jammed my fingers into his washed-out gray eyes and clawed for all I was worth. The scream that rent the air would have been satisfying if I hadn't been so worried about getting shot. I pushed the floundering McClowski hard into Wilson, hoping to make him drop the gun when he hit the wall. He didn't. He managed to get off a shot that I felt zip past my ear before my fist made contact with his chin. I put both hands around the hot barrel of the gun and pushed it up and away from me. I heard McClowski cursing behind us and knew that if I didn't get control of the situation immediately, it would be two against one.

I'd never liked those odds. So I released the gun just long enough to smash my right fist into Wilson's throat. Heat seared my left hand as he either reflexively, or in an effort to shoot me, pulled the trigger. My eardrums protested as the sound of the second shot echoed through the empty house until there was nothing left but the steady hum of the refrigerator.

Wilson stared at me blankly as his body slid down the wall, leaving a trail of vivid crimson. The floor stopped him and I watched as the life left his body, his knees up and together like a demure schoolgirl's. I turned the gun on McClowski.

"Oh God. Oh God," he screamed hoarsely. "You killed him."

"He killed himself," I said. "Get up."

Four long scratches ran down both of McClowski's cheeks like demented red sunbeams in a child's crayon drawing. Snot dribbled from his nose as he stared fixedly at his partner like he'd never seen a dead body before. I pulled the phone out of my back pocket and, without moving my eyes from McClowski, demanded his boss's phone number. He bit out the number and I dialed it, but before I pushed Send I met his eyes. Something about his reaction bothered me. He didn't seem like someone who could cut out someone's tongue, not to mention what they had done to Marcus.

"Who killed Marcus Vansant?"

"Wilson did," he said without hesitation.

"And Michael Albert?"

"Him, too."

"Why?"

"The boss just said they had to go."

"And what did you do while he was killing them?" I asked.

"What? Nothing!"

"You didn't do anything?"

"No, I didn't. I didn't want any part of it. I just kept quiet. He's crazy. He enjoyed it."

McClowski stopped talking then. Maybe he saw something in my eyes that he recognized, because in that moment I felt like I would have enjoyed killing him. I think I would have enjoyed it a lot.

I held out the phone. "Tell your boss you got me," I said. "Tell him to meet you back at the theater with Riley and that I won't tell you where the tape is without seeing her alive first. If you try anything, you die."

McClowski carefully took the phone from my hand as if he was afraid to touch me. I watched calmly for any sign, any reason, any excuse to kill him. He gave me none.

CHAPTER TWENTY-FOUR

In the police academy, they tell rookies that killing will never come easy, no matter how often you have to pull the trigger. They're lying. I put the gun against McClowski's ribs and kept my eyes on the rearview mirror to make sure no one was following us.

"Pull into that grocery store lot and park."

"All right. All right," he said, as if placating a crazy person.

"No." I pressed the gun more firmly into his side as he pulled into a parking space. "Go to the back." I tensed, waiting for him to protest. I was out of luck.

He slowly eased out of the parking space and drove toward the back of the store and parked.

"Good. Now get out."

"What are you going to do?" he whined.

"I said, get out." I kept the gun pointed at him as he scrambled out of the car.

"Please, I got a kid and a wife. That's why I did all this. You know how hard it can be."

I ignored his amateur attempt at negotiation. "Give me your cuffs," I said and he reached in his pocket and handed them to me. "Turn around."

He did so and started to cry as I opened the rear of the car. "You're not going to shoot me, are you?"

I stared at the back of his head, tempted. "No." I slammed the butt of my gun into his skull, then grabbed the collar of his white shirt and tried to guide his limp form into the backseat. I checked his pulse before pushing his legs in behind him and closing the door. "Paybacks are a bitch, aren't they, fuckhead?"

I got in the driver's seat and picked up the police radio that now felt foreign to me. Rolling the dice that this woman was too uptight to get involved in corruption, I said, "Patch me in to Captain Gail Simmons."

"Please repeat your unit number."

"Just patch me in to Captain Simmons, damn it. This is an emergency. Tell her it's Foster Everett."

I waited for a response but got none, so I closed my eyes and leaned my aching head against the headrest. Pain ripped through my scalp, reminding me that I'd had better ideas. I gently dabbed at the swelling with my fingers, trying to assess the damage.

"Everett!" Captain Simmons barked, and I jumped like I always did when she called my name.

"Captain, I—"

"You're in big trouble. Where are you?"

"I won't tell you until you listen. They have my friend, and they're going to kill her over some videotape that I don't have."

"Who are they? You're not making sense."

I closed my eyes. She was right, I wasn't making sense. This thing was a lot bigger than I was, and I was going to need more help than a small-time hood and a data clerk if I was going to have a chance.

"Captain, remember you said that I was going to need your help one day?" I felt my eyes blur. "I'm nothing but trouble. I'm not worth risking your ass for, but Riley is. And they're going to hurt her, and I don't know why. Please, I'm begging you to help me."

"Tell me where you are."

After I gave her the address to the theater, there was silence on the other end. Finally she took a deep breath. "Okay, I don't know what the hell is going on, but I know there's more to it than you killing a child molester. You stay put until you hear from me. Understand? Everett, you there?"

I turned off the radio. I had already wasted too much time.

❖

Evening used to be my favorite time of the day, but at that moment I could feel the darkness closing in on me as I pulled into the theater parking lot. A black Expedition and a tan Cadillac were the only other cars in the lot. The Expedition sat in a darkened corner with its lights and engine off, while the Cadillac was parked in front of the theater door as if it had every right to be there. I leaned forward, trying to see who was behind the tinted glass of the SUV. About two minutes passed before one of the windows rolled down and a man, a boy really, with a black do-rag around his head and dark brown skin glared out at me. I immediately got out of the car and walked over to the Expedition. The door swung open and I slid in, to find Sherm alone in the back. Two Uzi subs sat on the floor, along with three semiautomatics.

"Damn, girl, who clocked you?"

The wound realized that it now had my full attention and began to throb. Sherm handed me a handkerchief and I wiped the blood from my neck, then held it to the back of my head.

"Sherm, you've got to get out of here," I said finally. "I don't want to drag you into this."

"They got your girl inside, and you don't want my help?"

"No, I do want your help. But I don't want any more innocent people getting hurt. This is something big. I'm afraid they're going to try to pin some shit on me."

"So you just going in there alone?" Sherm looked dismayed.

"Yeah, I have to. I'm afraid they might kill Riley if I don't show up soon." I looked around the cab of the vehicle. "Do you have a pen and paper?"

Sherm reached up front and was immediately given a pen and a Taco Bell napkin. He handed it to me and I scribbled Smitty's address.

"The Blazer is in front of this house. I want you to go and get it before it gets impounded. There are some papers under the passenger seat. Make copies and send the originals to Captain Gail Simmons. Her address is on here, too." I handed him the napkin.

"You sure you can trust her?"

"No. I'm pretty sure she had a warrant taken out for my arrest, but I don't have a choice. I need someone high enough up that, if I get out of this, people will listen to me. She's my only option. But if she doesn't follow through, I want you to send those articles and my notes to every reporter in this city."

"You sure about this? I got some firepower here."

"I know, Sherm, but you're the only one I can trust. I need to know that these people will get caught, no matter what. Please."

"All right, but here, take these." He handed me two extra gun clips. I was now prepared for a mini-war, and although I was pretty sure I wouldn't have time to fire this much ammo, it did give me some comfort.

I got out of the Expedition and shut the door without looking back. I heard the engine start and the tires crunching on pavement as Sherm pulled off. With both guns securely in their holsters, I jogged toward the door of the theater, my head pounding like someone had taken a jackhammer to it.

❖

I used the lock picks and let myself into the building. As I crept down the hall, my heart pounded in tune with the pain in the back of my head.

"God damn it! Where is it?" A man's frantic voice echoed throughout the theater. I stopped breathing. The air seemed to thicken with tension. "Tell us where it is, and we'll leave you alone."

I rolled onto the stage and, in a crouch, started searching for an opening in the heavy curtains.

"Why can't we just go?" The question was a sob, almost indistinguishable, but the familiarity robbed me of my anger, and once again fear began to grab hold. It wasn't Riley. Riley didn't cry like that. *Calm the fuck down. You'll never hold her again if you get yourself killed.*

I took a deep breath and eased the curtain back. The light from a solitary bulb illuminated a man in a pristine white dress shirt. I recognized Chief James's silvery hair before anything else registered. Sleeves rolled up to his elbows, he hovered over a form slumped in a chair.

"Shut up, damn it." He turned toward a figure in the darkened corner to his left. "This is all your fault."

Monica. I had to blink against the pain in my chest.

"She doesn't know. Damn it, Daddy, don't you think if she knew she'd have told you by now?"

That was all I needed to hear. I trained my gun on Chief James and walked out into the open just as he raised his hand to strike again. With shock, I realized that his white shirt was open down to his T-shirt and there were small splatters of blood on it.

"I don't need a good reason, you know." I said it so calmly, I thought I was going crazy.

His eyes narrowed under his bushy white brows. He slowly lowered his hand and waited in rigid silence, the corners of his mouth turned up. "I'm really glad to see you. Thank you for coming. I'm sure your friend here is glad to see you as well."

My brain froze then; something told me not to look at her. My eyes clung to his like a drowning victim's. My body warred with my heart. I couldn't stop myself. I slowly broke contact and sought her out.

The front of her shirt was covered in blood. For a second that seemed eternal, I thought she was dead, and then I saw the rise and fall of her chest.

"Riley," I choked out.

She flinched but didn't look at me. Her lip was split in two places, blood trailed from her mouth, one eye was swollen shut, and there was a large knot on her forehead.

"Baby," I called her again. "It's me, Foster. I'm going to get you out of here. We're going to go home." She didn't answer me.

While I reassured her, I kept watch on Chief James, daring him to try something. "Please, make me kill you," I told him through clenched teeth. At a stifled sob from Monica, I nosed the gun a few degrees toward her and demanded, "What have you done?"

She just shook her head and continued to weep. "Oh God, Foster. Oh God, I'm so sorry. I didn't know. I didn't know."

Chief James eyed his daughter contemptuously. "How could you not know? You were his mother!"

"Get over there with her," I ordered him. "One foot wrong, and I'll blow your head off."

Without a word, he backed up until he was standing nearly in front of Monica. He trained his eyes on me as I moved the gun to my left hand and felt for Riley's pulse with my right. She flinched away from me and I knew I couldn't look at her anymore. If I did, I would break down. Instead, I coaxed her head to rest against my hip. When I felt her sigh, I had to will myself not to cry out.

In that moment, I wanted someone, anyone, to make me understand why someone as sweet and wonderful as Riley had to be hurt. Why Marcus was killed, and why my partner had committed suicide and I now had his widow and father in-law looking down the barrel of my gun.

The gun shook as anger flooded my body. I knew Chief James could feel my finger trembling on the trigger. "Why, God damn it?"

"For my family, of course." He looked entirely too calm, almost as if he were giving a speech in front of a delegation of important people. "You see, I was already slated to become chief back then. Not that my career was the only consideration. I couldn't have my grandson being raised in the wrong environment. That was the issue."

Monica heaved a shuddering sob. I'd never heard her so bitter. "You love being right. That's all that ever mattered."

"Anyone care to explain how your family shit got my partner beaten to a pulp?"

"Monica intended to leave Joseph. She was getting involved with some religious nut. You can understand how upset I was." Chief James paused as if he expected me to agree with him.

I continued to stare, wondering where the hell the captain was and how long I could keep myself from shooting this bastard. I needed to get Riley to the hospital, but I was keeping him talking till backup could arrive. If I wanted my life back, I couldn't let my temper take control now.

"I did everything in my power to get her back," the chief said, with an accusatory glare at his daughter. "But would she listen to me?"

Monica's sobbing seemed to have tapered off to a watery sniffle. I tried to see her, but she was obscured by her father's larger frame. He kept talking.

"You sure you don't want to tell this part, Monica? How you find out the love of your life was no better than the fucking pedophiles he catered to?"

I felt Riley's body tense. I soothed her with my free hand and murmured, "Soon, baby."

"They used my daughter to try to keep me away from their operation," the chief continued. "And it worked until Joseph decided he wanted his wife and child back. By the way, he never had any idea she was having an affair with Stein. My innocent daughter kept that from him. Didn't you, sweetheart?"

The shadows hid too much. I wanted a resolution, not a therapy session. "Get down on the floor, both of you."

Chief James didn't budge. "Don't you see, Everett? Everything I did was for Monica and Joseph. I was trying to protect them."

"You didn't give a shit about Smitty," I said, with so much venom it threatened to choke me. "All you cared about was your career. You didn't want it to get out about your daughter's affair, so you tried to cover it up. Smitty didn't need your help."

"Oh, he needed my help all right. He begged for it, in fact."

"Look, save your breath. I don't want to hear any more. The police will be here any minute, and you can tell them your story."

"Fine. But who do you think they'll believe? You destroyed your credibility when you killed Harrison Canniff. Let me explain how this is going to be written up." He had the audacity to bestow a benevolent smile on me. "You're a murderer, Everett. And instead of taking responsibility for your own actions, you blamed me, the chief of police. You kidnapped Monica and me, and when your friend tried to persuade you to let us go, you killed her."

"Nobody is going to believe that."

"No? Monica and I are heroes. She's the wife of a slain officer. Oh, by the way, you admitted to us before you died that you killed Joseph before you sent him off that cliff."

I lowered my arm slightly. "You killed Smitty?"

"Of course not. Oh, I see." He laughed. "You hadn't put that part together. I wish I had killed him, but I didn't. He took himself out. That made me look bad. And after all I'd done for him…"

"You're a liar," I said.

"And you're not listening. Smitty caused all this. He was supposed to wait until Monica was out of the compound with the baby, but he didn't. He went in and shots were fired." For the first time, Chief James's voice broke. "My grandson…my grandson was killed. So were two other kids and a few women."

"Smitty was cleared of charges arising from the raid," I said tightly.

"Of course he was. I pulled his ass out of the fire, just like I did with Canniff. How did he explain that to you? Did he tell you there's a group that helps cops when they're in trouble?"

Chief James's voice hung in the air like a solid entity. I felt as though a predator was watching me, waiting for me to make that fatal mistake. Apparently my expression gave me away. He chuckled.

"There is no conspiracy here, Everett, only a bunch of greedy people who are waiting for me to grease their palms or give them appointments and promotions. Joseph was either too dumb or too blind to care."

"Smitty—"

"Smitty should have gotten rid of you like I told him to, but he didn't. Instead, he started acting like this was all my fault, as if I caused Eric's death."

"What are you saying? I saw Eric a few months ago."

Chief James smiled. "Oh, wonderful. So you didn't watch the tape?"

"Watch the tape? I saw one DVD, it was enough."

"Yes, rather sordid business, that."

Monica's soft sobs had quieted and my focus was purely on Chief James. "What's on this tape?"

"Nathan Stein didn't trust anyone. He had cameras set up so that he could watch the members of his church constantly. The barn was being utilized as childcare in the daytime and sleeping quarters at night, so the cameras were on twenty-four hours a day."

"The raid was taped?"

"Yes, and a few copies got out there."

"What?"

"Harrison Canniff saw it and recognized Joseph. He said that if Joseph didn't let him go, he would tell what he knew for a free ride. Joseph had to kill him."

Smitty had to kill him. I shook my head in denial.

"Oh yes, your precious Smitty wasn't as innocent as you like to believe. He wasn't a hero. He was a man trying to protect his family, just like me."

"He was nothing like you," I muttered before nausea forced me to close my mouth.

"Oh no? He was willing to let you believe that you had killed someone, someone he'd actually killed."

Shocked, I said, "But why? If it was all an accident, the tape would have shown that."

"Oh no, you have it all wrong." The triumphant smile on his face made my stomach heave again. "The bullets that killed them weren't from Joseph's gun. No, a high-powered rifle killed those people. Joseph only had a .38."

I was starting to feel dizzy from the blow to the back of my head and from the weight of what he was telling me. I realized too late that Chief James had backed up so that I could no longer see Monica.

"You can put that down now," he said, as if he was telling me to put down a bag of groceries. For the second time that day, I was staring down the barrel of a gun.

"No," I said grimly. "You put it down."

How much of his story was a lie? How much of it was just intended to get me off guard? Well, it worked. And because of my own stupidity, Riley and I were about to die.

"I'm sorry, Foster," Monica blurted. "I had to give it to him. You don't understand; they'll take my boy away from me if this comes out."

"What the fuck are you talking about?"

"Joseph told me about Canniff soon after it happened," the chief replied. "I gave him the hush money, and those he couldn't shut up—"

"Wilson and McClowski. You had them kill Marcus. Why?"

"Monica caught him sniffing around the graveyard one day, so we bugged his computer. He was getting too close, so I had him eliminated. And now I'll have to do the same with your accomplice in the file room. What's her name? Mrs. Kennedy, isn't it?"

I felt my face go slack. "Please don't. She doesn't know anything."

"I suppose I owe her a debt of gratitude. I would have never known you were back in town, if not for her."

"She used Marcus's computer. You never removed the bug."

"You're starting to catch on. Now put the gun down."

"Why should I? You're going to kill me anyway." I stalled, sending out a prayer for Captain Simmons.

"Because if you don't, I'm pretty sure I can hit your friend there before you kill me. I also know where her family lives. The brother in the wheelchair. The self-sacrificing foster mother who saved her from her drunken mother. Quite the sordid tale. I'll make sure they don't make it through another week."

The gun felt heavy. My palm was damp around the grip. I wasn't even sure if I had the strength left to pull the trigger. I wouldn't put it down, though; the chief couldn't let us live if he expected to get away.

"Why did you have to hurt her? Why not just find me?"

"Because I needed the tape, and I figured you'd cough it up to save your friend. Those two idiots were supposed to rough you up and get the information. What happened, did you kill both of them?"

I didn't answer. "All of this was over a tape that showed people getting killed in a bust? Why didn't Smitty just admit that he fucked up? That his wife and kid were there, and he lost it? The most that would have happened is that he would have lost his job, especially if he didn't pull the trigger."

"It wasn't about the fuckup. It was what he did afterward."

Again the hairs on my arms stood up and the ones on the back of my neck followed suit, a subtle change in atmosphere that usually meant someone was behind me. A small flicker of hope passed through me. I wanted to look at Riley, but I couldn't. The chief must have sensed the change too, because his eyes searched behind me. A snarl transformed his features as he pointed the gun at Riley.

"Everybody drop the guns! Drop the guns!"

In slow motion, I heard a loud roar and saw a look of anger and then sorrow pass over Chief James's face as he went rigid. I felt like I knew what was going to happen even before he did. His gun went up, and he aimed it at Riley and me. I pulled my second 9 and backed into Riley hard, sending her and the chair crashing to the floor as I began to fire. It could have been my imagination, it could have been real, but I saw my bullets hit him. I watched them as they went toward his chest, and for some reason, I thought he saw them, too, because he smiled before he fired his gun.

The bullet slammed into me, spinning me around and knocking the gun from my left hand. The 9 fell to the wooden stage floor and slid to a stop at the edge of the curtain. I landed on Riley.

The chief's body seemed to pause in midair, then topple forward. His head crashed into the edge of a table before he slumped to the floor. Someone was screaming. I thought it might be me, but my throat felt too tight to emit a sound.

I looked down at Riley. Her eyes were open, but unseeing. I could feel her trembling beneath me. *She's alive*, I thought weakly as my hands went up to the sides of her face. Her hair was barely contained in its braid, and for some reason I wanted to help her braid it again, because I knew how neat she liked to keep it. A tear slipped down my cheek and fell onto hers.

I heard people yelling and running around us, but it didn't matter. I had found her. She looked so hurt, so bruised. I started to shake as I tried to make her look at me. But her gaze was blank. She didn't recognize me. She didn't recognize anything.

"No," I said as I felt someone touch me.

"You've been shot. Hurt pretty bad."

I continued to stare at Riley. "He should have taken me. I would have told him anything he wanted to know as long as he didn't hurt you. He was wrong. You're the strong one, aren't you? You wouldn't have told him. Even if you knew, you wouldn't have made a sound." I was babbling, and she wasn't moving. My tears mixed with her blood and rolled down her cheek.

Suddenly everything made sense. And there was something so fucked up about it that I wanted to scream. I was lifted from her body, and my shirt was ripped open. I felt a sharp pain and sucked in a breath. But it wasn't enough, and I could hear myself gasp and moan for air. I was moving fast, so fast.

"Riley." Her name clung to my lips. *Please help her. I need to tell her...I need...*

"She's going into arrest. We're losing her. We're losing her..."

"Foster..."

"God damn it, Everett. Breathe, breathe."

"No...Foster..."

"She's gone."

CHAPTER TWENTY-FIVE

Heaven…Want to know what it feels like? It's like being held close and protected by the most beautiful light in the world. It's knowing you will never be beaten, hurt, tired, or hungry again. And no matter what, you will be cared for. That's what heaven feels like…at first. But then you remember. You remember that there are people who love you back there in that hell called Earth. People who are hurting because they will miss you. And if you're lucky, like me, there's someone whose heart is breaking every time yours stops beating. And knowing all that, knowing what kind of pain you've left behind, what kind of heaven would heaven be, anyway?

So I simply decided not to stay. And when I opened my eyes, Riley was there, asleep in a chair across from me. For a moment I felt peace. The only thing that mattered was that we were both alive.

Dawn filtered through the partially open blinds, segregating light and shadow on Riley's sleeping face. Her lip was almost healed, making me wonder how long I had been out. Wisps of dark hair had escaped the restraints of her braid. She looked so disheveled that it broke my heart. White plaster encircled her arm from knuckles to elbow. Another cast? *Damn, I'm sorry, baby.*

Even in sleep she frowned, her fist balled up in her lap as if ready for combat. I winced, because I somehow knew that if she wasn't in that chair she would be curled into a fetal position.

I watched her every breath and waited for those beautiful eyes to open. When they did, it was like drinking lemonade on a sunny day, just the best feeling in the world.

She sat up in the chair, her good hand gripping the armrest so hard I was sure it would crumble from the pressure. Neither of us said anything. She just stared at me until I was forced to blink from the heat of her eyes. And then she smiled so widely that if I didn't know her better, I would have thought she was going to laugh out loud. Almost as quickly, her smile crumbled away like the foundation underneath an eroding building, and she shook so hard it scared me.

"I thought I had lost you," she said in my ear.

"No," I said. My throat felt like someone had scraped it raw.

"Thank you."

I didn't answer her. How do you answer something like that? You don't.

❖

I'd been shot in the chest. The bullet had passed cleanly through my lung and nicked my heart. They were able to repair the damage, but when I didn't wake up, they hadn't held out much hope for me. I'd slipped into a coma for three weeks.

Riley hovered near the bed, unconsciously checking my monitor as she pulled a blanket around me. At first, I was so relieved she was okay that I didn't notice the dark circles under her eyes, how pale her face looked, or how her hand lingered against my heart while she adjusted my bedding one too many times. For three days she sat and pretended not to watch me breathe. And for three days I let her, without complaint, because I knew how she felt. I was glad she was alive, too.

"Everett, can I speak with you for a moment?" Captain Simmons stood in the doorway.

I'm sure my expression hardened, but it wasn't aimed at her. I was angry with the people responsible for putting me in the hospital, the ones who had killed Marcus and were to blame for the fragility that hovered just below the surface of Riley. I hated that the most, because it was a constant reminder to me that I'd failed to keep her safe.

Riley stood up.

"No, stay," I rasped, and she glanced toward the captain.

"I don't mind if you stay, Riley." Gail Simmons seemed to soften her voice when she spoke to Riley. I wondered if she sensed the damage, too. "You have just as much right to hear this as she does."

"No, if it's okay, I'll go ahead and get cleaned up."

"It's all right sweetheart, go," I said.

She paused at the door as if she was going to speak. But instead, she left us alone.

"How are you?" the captain asked.

She's nervous. I wonder why. I shrugged slightly and raised an eyebrow.

"Look, Everett, you're a good cop. I never believed you had anything to do with this mess. I asked them to bring you in to talk to me, and when you ran, it just looked so bad that I had to get the warrant so that we could haul you in. I had no idea that those two were in with the chief. They came highly recommended." Her mouth twisted. "By the chief, so—"

"I understand."

She shifted uncomfortably, probably wishing she could take back some of the shit she'd said and thought about me in the past. I felt exactly the same way, maybe more so since I knew my thoughts had been even less flattering than hers. All of it seemed trivial now, at least for me it did.

I stopped, frustrated that the pain and breathlessness left from having a ventilator shoved down my throat kept me from voicing my thoughts. I looked over at the chair that Riley, aside from restroom visits and a trip to the cafeteria, had sat in since I woke up. I had also learned that she had basically lived there for the three weeks I was in a coma, too. The captain had made that possible, and I was grateful to her for that. Not for my own sake, but for Riley's.

"Thank you."

"For what?"

"For being here when we needed you," I said.

"You should thank Big Sherm and Chandra. Without them telling me what was going on, the outcome could have been different. I wish you had come to me earlier."

"I didn't know who I could trust, other than Riley."

"She cares about you a lot. I thought she was going to rip us apart when we first tried to give her medical attention." The captain's expression made me smile. "I wanted to tell you how sorry I am that, you know, we never got along."

I shook my head. "I was an asshole."

She smiled. "So was I."

I raised my eyebrow. "Was?"

She looked startled for a moment. The animosity that I used to feel for this woman seemed like it belonged to someone else. Like rumor and innuendo that had proved incorrect. Whatever she had done to me, whatever perceived misunderstandings we'd had, were gone.

"Okay, now that we have the warm fuzzies out of the way, maybe we can get down to business." She pulled out her pad. "I thought you could tell me what you pieced together. I've already talked to Riley, and she told me what little she knew. We also found your notes, but I couldn't make heads or tails of some of it. Monica lawyered up. The chief is dead, and we can't find this mythical tape, so it's kind of up to us."

After she finished talking, I pointed to my throat and grimaced.

"Oh, sorry. We can do this another time." She hesitated. "It's just that you've been out of commission for three weeks and this has turned into a media circus, so I was hoping to have something to throw them."

I hadn't thought about the blow it would be to the department. I mouthed, "Sorry."

"Not your fault."

We stared at each other for a minute, then I pointed to her pen and paper. Smiling, she tore off a few sheets for herself and passed me the notepad and a spare pen. I spent the next ten minutes writing until my penmanship degenerated to the point where I was blinking at every word. I then invited her to read.

"We should use this system more often," she said with deadpan humor. "You completely silent and me doing the talking."

I couldn't laugh, but I think my grunting noises worked for her. She concentrated on my notes for a few minutes before concluding, "So you think this Michael Stratford went in and stole the tape from Pete's room?"

I nodded.

"But why? Did Canniff put him up to it?" She handed the pad back and leaned in close so that she could read what I was writing.

"Michael is the one who paid Pete to move the boxes. When the tape turned up missing, Stein must have sent him to look for it and he saw an opportunity."

"But why take it in the first place?" she asked after reading my scribbles.

"Security blanket."

"He was going for blackmail?"

I shook my head. "He knew he was working for a jerk and he wanted a lever so he could get out. They let him go with no strings attached, he gives the tape back. They go after him, he goes to the police and makes a deal."

"Instead they kill him? Makes no sense. They still didn't have the tape, otherwise why would they have gone after you and Riley?"

I shook my head and whispered, "Wilson and McClowski."

The captain groaned. "I didn't even clue in to them until I found out about the bag."

I cocked my brow, and she explained. "I didn't buy the 'Oh yeah, and we forgot to mention we found a plastic bag with her fingerprints on it' story. So I had the damn thing tested. I found out the day before you were shot that the plastic bag came from the same batch that we use in our office. I would bet a month's salary that they used the bag from your own garbage can to try to frame you."

I grimaced as I remembered emptying a trash can over Alvin Wilson during our fight in the office. The prints would have been fresh and ripe for a framing. It was yet another occasion where my own temper and lack of control had almost cost me more than I cared to think about.

The captain's voice broke into my morose thoughts. "I can't believe two of my detectives killed that man."

"Marcus, too."

"I'm sorry, Everett."

I wrote, "I don't know where the tape is. All I know is that Chief James said Smitty didn't fire the gun. Smitty wasn't the one who killed those kids. Something happened afterward. If I'm wrong about Stein, and he's still alive, maybe he can fill in some of the blanks."

The captain shook her head. "Stein's body showed up in the morgue a few days ago. We got a positive ID yesterday. A blow to the head is what killed him, but his body was mutilated postmortem. We found your notes on Mrs. Stein and her boyfriend, and turned them over to Homicide. They're trying to gather enough evidence to take to the DA, but so far it doesn't look good."

I nodded, not really caring how their investigation was going. My eyelids drooped and I wondered where Riley was. I wanted to see her before I fell asleep.

"Oh, one thing we did find out from Monica. She claims that Smitty admitted to killing Canniff in his suicide note. He said he was sorry he let you go through all of that for so long. She says her father forced her to forge a new note, omitting that information. She seems to think Smitty purposely made his death look suspicious, hoping someone would investigate."

I blinked rapidly. I hadn't even thought about Smitty. I hadn't thought about anyone but Riley. But now pain coursed through my chest as I realized that my partner, the man I'd thought of as my best friend, had let me go through hell. He had let me believe I was a murderer to suit his personal agenda.

I think I retreated into myself for a moment, and when I came back, the captain was holding my hand and patting it awkwardly. I was touched that she would even try, but I was growing weary of this question-and-answer session. All I really wanted was to be left alone so I could grieve. I pulled my hand away and picked up the pen.

"Thank you. I'm sure that at some point it will mean something that he left a note. Right now..." I stopped because I didn't want to think about how many lives Smitty and Monica had ruined.

The captain sighed. "Well, I should go." She placed the pad in her briefcase and stood. "It's our niece's birthday, and I promised I would get her a new doll. I'll stop back by in a few days if I have any more questions."

"You have family?" I asked, before I realized it might have sounded rude.

She grinned. "My partner has two sisters, two brothers, three nieces, and one nephew, with one on the way. I guess you wouldn't have known that." She sounded almost regretful. "Well, I'd better go get that damn doll before the stores close. Give me a call if you need anything."

I frowned. Something was bugging me. "Captain." My taxed throat finally gave out completely. I shook my head and mouthed, "Doll?"

"What about it?" She was looking at me as if she thought I was nuts. I pointed at her briefcase. With a frown and a glance at the wall clock, she reluctantly handed me the pen and pad.

"What you said about the doll, it reminded me of something," I scribbled. "Michael Stratford bought his daughter a doll right before he went into hiding. I remember because it was a mess. You know, for it to be fairly new. When I picked it up, it sort of felt like something was moving around inside."

"You think the tape's in there?"

"Could be." I thought the doll was probably just big enough to hold a VHS tape.

"I know it's got to be hard for you to just sit back and let me take care of everything, but I want you to concentrate on getting out of this place." She looked around distastefully.

I nodded.

"I'll give you a call if I need anything else," was the last thing I heard her say before I fell asleep.

❖

Riley and I sat in Captain Simmons's office, both of us looking like several miles of bad asphalt. Whatever glow I had managed to get in my weeks with Riley at the cabin was gone, and in its place were hospital pallor and a case of the jitters that seemed to attack at the most inopportune moments. I didn't really trust myself to walk alone yet, so I made sure Riley was close at hand to help if my body decided to take a dive on me.

I was still worried about Riley. She didn't look quite right to me. She had lost her peace, and I felt responsible for that. She was still sleeping with her hands balled up and her eyes closed too tightly. I wanted to go somewhere where we could nurse each other back to the way it had been before. Only this time, there was no reason for me to hold anything back. I was looking forward to that.

"Are you sure you're okay with this?" I whispered. "You don't need to be here, Riley. You've been through so much already." My eyes wandered to her fingers, which were already picking at her plaster cast. I squeezed her good hand and we both gave our attention to the tape that had caused so many deaths.

A black-and-white picture came into view. The barn was actually a converted, wide-open space with beds lined up from one wall to the other. With cradles lining each side and people walking in and out of view, it looked more like a summer camp for adults than a church daycare.

"Is there sound?" I asked.

"No, doesn't seem like it. But we can have some specialists look at it later. You don't need sound to figure out what happens."

All of a sudden, chaos seemed to erupt. Smoke billowed around the room as people ran out of the camera's view. If there had been sound, I'm sure I would have heard terrified screams that would have left me sick to my stomach.

"Pay close attention here," Gail Simmons said.

For about two minutes there was nothing, then what could only be a younger version of Smitty came into frame. I could see now how much this whole affair had aged him. Even though the film was only about five years old, Smitty looked a lot younger than thirty-five on the tape. I saw him bend over a bassinet, his face contorted in rage and grief. Surprisingly, my heart ached at the sight. I didn't know if I would ever be a mother, never thought I wanted to be, but I hoped like hell I never knew the pain that Smitty must have felt in that moment. He reached into the bassinet and picked up a small, bloody bundle and held it close.

I saw his mouth move. "What did he say? Is he talking to someone?"

The captain rewound the tape and played again. Both Riley and I leaned forward as Smitty said something, probably to the dead baby in his arms, then placed it back in the crib.

"He said, 'I'm sorry I didn't get here in time, Eric.'" Riley's voice was sad as she read Smitty's lips.

Smitty turned in a slow circle and then paused, his face slack and blank looking, his .38 hanging limply at his side. He moved out of camera range, then came back into view a few seconds later, carrying a baby. He returned to the bassinet that held the body of his dead son, removed a blanket and wrapped it around the baby, then walked out of the frame again.

"What just happened?" It came to me then, in a burst of realization so clear, it was as if I had been there in that barn years before. "His son died, so he just took another baby."

The captain shut off the video. "That's what it looks like."

"But wouldn't someone miss their baby?" Riley asked.

"Not if they thought he was dead, or if the mother was one of the women killed in the raid," she explained. "Most of the people were either runaways or transients before they joined the church. Stein made sure that ties to interfering family members were cut. One of the ways he kept control. Several of the bodies were never claimed. In fact, most of them had to be buried by a charity."

"I think Eric might be Stein's child." I didn't realize I had spoken aloud until I saw the shocked look on Riley's face.

"What? How's that possible? Wouldn't Caroline know her own son?" she asked.

"The baby Caroline Stein buried died from extensive gunshot wounds," Captain Simmons said. "There wasn't much that was identifiable."

"So you've already considered that possibility?" I shouldn't have been surprised that the captain had put one and one together and come up with the same thing I did, but I was.

"We can't prove anything yet. The footprints from the hospital where Monica and Smitty's baby was born were too damn smudged to get an accurate match." I recognized the sneer as one that had been directed at me on many occasions. "I wish they would get those people better trained. Anyway, we're going to have to wait on the DNA test. What I don't understand is why they would leave the original tape just lying around."

"I think I stumbled on the answer to that when I was talking to Caroline Stein." The captain gave me her full attention. "When Terry found the tapes, Stein probably got scared and was forced to move everything over to the video store just in case Caroline decided to poke around. That tape would be the last thing he would want her to see. Unfortunately, when his driver, Michael Stratford, hired Pete and the original video vanished, all hell broke loose. You gotta figure Michael knew Stein was going to blame him, so he had no choice but to run. He probably tracked down Pete, stole the tape back, and hid it where he knew no one would look."

"In his daughter's doll," the captain said with disgust.

"But how did Marcus get the name Michael Albert?" Riley asked.

"Now that one, I know the answer to." The captain slid a folder across her desk and I opened it to the first page.

"Michael Albert, witness testimony. Where did this come from?"

"San Diego. Apparently Marcus called down complaining that one of the detectives had torn some documentation out of a file. He asked them to send copies, but as you know, we've been shorthanded, so these documents didn't get opened until a couple of weeks ago. I called down and spoke to the manager in San Diego. He said that he and Marcus had a really lengthy conversation about the missing document. He can't swear to it, but there is a distinct possibility that he mentioned Michael Albert's name."

As the captain spoke to Riley, I scanned the documents, only half listening to what she was saying. "Michael was a member of Stein's church, in fact, he was there during the raid. I'm pretty sure the only reason Smitty pulled these pages was to remove any mention of Monica from the witness testimony."

I closed the file in exasperation. "But Marcus couldn't have known all of this."

"No, he wouldn't have known everything, but there was probably enough there to make him suspicious."

"I know where he got Nathan Stein and Michael Albert, but who the hell is Eric Ann?"

The captain pulled out several pictures and slid them across the desk. I picked up one, and Riley picked up another. "You never went to the funerals, did you, Everett?"

"No."

"Me, either," she admitted. "I wonder if that would have made a difference."

I was looking at row after row of tombstones, most of them marking the grave of children less then two years of age, and all of them with the last name of Smith.

"Foster?" Riley's voice sounded odd. She handed me a picture of a tombstone that read, HERE LIES ERIC SMITH.

"They buried him?" I glanced at the captain for confirmation.

She nodded and Riley handed me another picture. A single tombstone that was right next to the one marked Eric Smith.

"We read an article that said Monica named one of the babies Ann, after her mother. That's what must have tipped Marcus off. He went to the funerals. I never did. He saw them all and…"

"He probably never knew what he had, Foster. He just knew something wasn't right. I think all of us thought it." The captain shifted and looked down at her notes. "I always thought there was something odd about it, but I was just so happy that someone was taking care of them and giving them a good burial, I didn't think to ask why. Bottom line is, Monica wanted to bury her son, so she started a charity for unclaimed babies."

"But if he was the first, didn't anyone think it was odd?" I slid the photo, face down, across the desk toward the captain.

"She didn't start naming them until she had about fifteen already buried along with Eric. Guess it made sense that she would name them. You can't have forty Johnnie and Janie Does." Even though she had had time to deal with everything, the captain looked momentarily overwhelmed, but quickly regained her composure. "I guess I'll see you two back here in a few weeks for the inquest. Make sure you get some rest, I have a feeling we all are going to need a vacation by the time this is over." Riley nodded and I prepared to stand up. "What about after you get better?" A small smile lit the captain's face as she asked the question that had been tormenting me. "You planning on coming back to work?"

I could feel Riley tense. "If you want to, I could find something here or go back to work at the university," she said.

I directed my answer to her, even though the captain had asked the question. "I'm confused about everything right now." To my embarrassment, my throat started closing up. "But I do know that I really need to spend some time with you."

I think the captain was starting to get a little bit green around the gills at our display, because she cleared her throat.

"Everett? Please refrain from slamming the door on your way out."

"All right, Captain." I grinned, and Riley and I headed out the door.

"If you need anything, let me know, okay?"

I was stopped few times as I walked through the office. It felt good to be vindicated, but as we finally stepped into the elevator, I couldn't help but glance in the direction of the desks that Smitty and I had occupied for three years. I figured I hadn't really dealt with my pain yet; I hadn't really dealt with any of it. I knew that at some point, it was going to hit, and it was going to hurt. But at that moment it just felt good to be alive. Alive and loved.

I reached for Riley's hand; she drew me into her arms and whispered into my hair, "What's wrong, are you hurting?"

"No, I'm fine. I've just been..." I took a deep breath, mustering up every ounce of courage I could summon. "Ever since I woke up, ever since they took you, really, I've been promising myself that I would tell you how I feel about you. And now I can't seem to find the right words."

Riley eased me away from her as the elevator slowed its descent.

"I just don't know what I would do without you." I said it so softly that I knew she hadn't heard me.

I took a deep breath and looked up into her face. Her eyes were watery, but there was that huge smile on her face that told me that she understood. It wasn't all that I wanted to say to her, not by a long shot. But her smile told me that she would wait for the rest, and I vowed to myself that she wouldn't have to wait long.

We got off the elevator to the sound of snapping gum and laughter. I walked up to the window to see Chandra sitting at her desk. I smiled at her and she smiled back, holding her finger up as she got off the phone. She yelled to two heads that were almost hidden behind a stack of files that she would be back. The door swung open and she walked out, still popping that damn gum.

"So you guys are out of here, then?" she asked.

"Yeah, I guess so."

Chandra brushed a tear from her cheek.

"Well, damn, Chandra. I don't know what to say," I joked.

"You're a good person, Foster Everett."

I elbowed Riley, hoping she would help me out, but I only got a smile and a shrug. "Thanks, Chandra, so are you," I said weakly.

"Y'all better get going before traffic gets too bad. Call me when you get there." She sniffed and grabbed me in a bone-crushing hug. "I'm going to miss your trifling ass." She released me and pushed me toward Riley.

We stared at the closing file-room door. "What does trifling mean, anyway?"

"I think it means you've got yourself a new friend." Riley grinned, and her body started shaking.

"A new friend, huh? Cool." I was quite proud of myself.

I had myself a new friend, a family, and best of all—a woman who loved me more than I could ever hope to deserve. I felt really good, like I'd just found something I'd been missing all my life. Like I was whole. Complete and wanted. And to think I'd been running away from belonging for years. But shit, who knew?

I heard Chandra tell someone to "Get off the phone and get to work," then a barrage of annoyed popping that I found both comforting and sad. I would miss her, too.

We waited for the elevator doors to close. Riley's bright blue eyes silently asked me if I had changed my mind. I shook my head and kissed her hand. "Do you think she would've taught me how to pop my gum like that?"

We held each other and laughed. Then we lost ourselves in a kiss, the steady pop, pop, pop of Chandra's gum serenading us as the doors slid soundlessly closed on my old life.

About the Author

Gabrielle Goldsby grew up in Oakland, California, where a childhood illness left her confined to bed for weeks when she was nine years old. It was then, thanks to her mother's efforts to save her own sanity, that she discovered a love of reading. After receiving a bachelor's degree in criminal justice administration, she spent time as a gang and drugs prevention counselor, a flooring specialist for a large home-improvement store, a facilities manager inside some of San Francisco's largest law firms, and an administrative assistant in the semiconductor industry. These varied occupations have become the basis for many past and future writing projects.

She resides in Portland, Oregon, with her partner of eight years.

Her next novel, *Remember Tomorrow*, is due from Bold Strokes Books, Inc. in 2008.

Books Available From Bold Strokes Books

Wall of Silence, 2nd ed. by Gabrielle Goldsby. Life takes a dangerous turn when jaded police detective Foster Everett meets Riley Medeiros, a woman who isn't afraid to discover the truth no matter the cost. (978-1-933110-90-5)

Mistress of the Runes by Andrews & Austin. Passion ignites between two women with ties to ancient secrets, contemporary mysteries, and a shared quest for the meaning of life. (978-1-933110-89-9)

Sheridan's Fate by Gun Brooke. A dynamic, erotic romance between physiotherapist Lark Mitchell and businesswoman Sheridan Ward set in the scorching hot days and humid, steamy nights of San Antonio. (978-1-933110-88-2)

Vulture's Kiss by Justine Saracen. Archeologist Valerie Foret, heir to a terrifying task, returns in a powerful desert adventure set in Egypt and Jerusalem. (978-1-933110-87-5)

Rising Storm by JLee Meyer. The sequel to *First Instinct* takes our heroines on a dangerous journey instead of the honeymoon they'd planned. (978-1-933110-86-8)

Not Single Enough by Grace Lennox. A funny, sexy modern romance about two lonely women who bond over the unexpected and fall in love along the way. (978-1-933110-85-1)

Such a Pretty Face by Gabrielle Goldsby. A sexy, sometimes humorous, sometimes biting contemporary romance that gently exposes the damage to heart and soul when we fail to look beneath the surface for what truly matters. (978-1-933110-84-4)

Second Season by Ali Vali. A romance set in New Orleans amidst betrayal, Hurricane Katrina, and the new beginnings hardship and heartbreak sometimes make possible. (978-1-933110-83-7)

Hearts Aflame by Ronica Black. A poignant, erotic romance between a hard-driving businesswoman and a solitary vet. Packed with adventure and set in the harsh beauty of the Arizona countryside. (978-1-933110-82-0)

Red Light by JD Glass. Tori forges her path as an EMT in the New York City 911 system while discovering what matters most to herself and the woman she loves. (978-1-933110-81-3)

Honor Under Siege by Radclyffe. Secret Service agent Cameron Roberts struggles to protect her lover while searching for a traitor who just may be another woman with a claim on her heart. (978-1-933110-80-6)

Dark Valentine by Jennifer Fulton. Danger and desire fuel a high-stakes cat-and-mouse game when an attorney and an endangered witness team up to thwart a killer. (978-1-933110-79-0)

Sequestered Hearts by Erin Dutton. A popular artist suddenly goes into seclusion, a reluctant reporter wants to know why, and a heart locked away yearns to be set free. (978-1-933110-78-3)

Erotic Interludes 5: Road Games, ed. by Radclyffe and Stacia Seaman. Adventure, "sport," and sex on the road—hot stories of travel adventures and games of seduction. (978-1-933110-77-6)

The Spanish Pearl by Catherine Friend. On a trip to Spain, Kate Vincent is accidentally transported back in time—an epic saga spiced with humor, lust, and danger. (978-1-933110-76-9)

Lady Knight by L-J Baker. Loyalty and honor clash with love and ambition in a medieval world of magic when female knight Riannon meets Lady Eleanor. (978-1-933110-75-2)

Dark Dreamer by Jennifer Fulton. Best-selling horror author Rowe Devlin falls under the spell of psychic Phoebe Temple. A Dark Vista romance. (978-1-933110-74-5)

Come and Get Me by Julie Cannon. Elliott Foster isn't used to pursuing women, but alluring attorney Lauren Collier makes her change her mind. (978-1-933110-73-8)

Blind Curves by Diane and Jacob Anderson-Minshall. Private eye Yoshi Yakamota comes to the aid of her ex-lover Velvet Erickson in the first Blind Eye mystery. (978-1-933110-72-1)

The Devil Unleashed by Ali Vali. As the heat of violence rises, so does the passion. A Casey Clan crime saga. (1-933110-61-9)

Dynasty of Rogues by Jane Fletcher. It's hate at first sight for Ranger Riki Sadiq and her new patrol corporal, Tanya Coppelli—except for their undeniable attraction. (978-1-933110-71-4)

Running With the Wind by Nell Stark. Sailing instructor Corrie Marsten has signed off on love until she meets Quinn Davies—one woman she can't ignore. (978-1-933110-70-7)

More Than Paradise by Jennifer Fulton. Two women battle danger, risk all, and find in each other an unexpected ally and an unforgettable love. (978-1-933110-69-1)

Flight Risk by Kim Baldwin. For Blayne Keller, being in the wrong place at the wrong time just might turn out to be the best thing that ever happened to her. (978-1-933110-68-4)

Rebel's Quest: Supreme Constellations Book Two by Gun Brooke. On a world torn by war, two women discover a love that defies all boundaries. (978-1-933110-67-7)

Punk and Zen by JD Glass. Angst, sex, love, rock. Trace, Candace, Francesca…Samantha. Losing control—and finding the truth within. BSB Victory Editions. (1-933110-66-X)

When Dreams Tremble by Radclyffe. Two women whose lives turned out far differently than they'd once imagined discover that sometimes the shape of the future can only be found in the past. (1-933110-64-3)

Stellium in Scorpio by Andrews & Austin. The passionate reunion of two powerful women on the glitzy Las Vegas Strip, where everything is an illusion and love is a gamble. (1-933110-65-1)

Burning Dreams by Susan Smith. The chronicle of the challenges faced by a young drag king and an older woman who share a love "outside the bounds." (1-933110-62-7)

Fresh Tracks by Georgia Beers. Seven women, seven days. A lot can happen when old friends, lovers, and a new girl in town get together in the mountains. (1-933110-63-5)

Tristaine Rises by Cate Culpepper. Brenna, Jesstin, and the Amazons of Tristaine face their greatest challenge for survival. (1-933110-50-3)

Too Close to Touch by Georgia Beers. Kylie O'Brien believes in true love and is willing to wait for it. It doesn't matter one damn bit that Gretchen, her new and off-limits boss, has a voice as rich and smooth as melted chocolate. It absolutely doesn't... (1-933110-47-3)

The Empress and the Acolyte by Jane Fletcher. Jemeryl and Tevi fight to protect the very fabric of their world...time. Lyremouth Chronicles Book Three. (1-933110-60-0)

First Instinct by JLee Meyer. When high-stakes security fraud leads to murder, one woman flees for her life while another risks her heart to protect her. (1-933110-59-7)

Erotic Interludes 4: Extreme Passions, ed. by Radclyffe and Stacia Seaman. Thirty of today's hottest erotica writers set the pages aflame with love, lust, and steamy liaisons. (1-933110-58-9)

Unexpected Ties by Gina L. Dartt. With death before dessert, Kate Shannon and Nikki Harris are swept up in another tale of danger and romance. (1-933110-56-2)

Passion's Bright Fury by Radclyffe. When a trauma surgeon and a filmmaker become reluctant allies on the battleground between life and death, passion strikes without warning. (1-933110-54-6)

Sleep of Reason by Rose Beecham. Nothing is as it seems when Detective Jude Devine finds herself caught up in a small-town soap opera. And her rocky relationship with forensic pathologist Dr. Mercy Westmoreland just got a lot harder. (1-933110-53-8)

Carly's Sound by Ali Vali. Poppy Valente and Julia Johnson form a bond of friendship that lays the foundation for something more, until Poppy's past comes back to haunt her—literally. A poignant romance about love and renewal. (1-933110-45-7)

Sweet Creek by Lee Lynch. A celebration of the enduring nature of love, friendship, and community in the quirky, heart-warming lesbian community of Waterfall Falls. (1-933110-29-5)

Sword of the Guardian by Merry Shannon. Princess Shasta's bold new bodyguard has a secret that could change both of their lives. *He* is actually a *she*. A passionate romance filled with courtly intrigue, chivalry, and devotion. (1-933110-36-8)

Turn Back Time by Radclyffe. Pearce Rifkin and Wynter Thompson have nothing in common but a shared passion for surgery. They clash at every opportunity, especially when matters of the heart are suddenly at stake. (1-933110-34-1)

Promising Hearts by Radclyffe. Dr. Vance Phelps lost everything in the War Between the States and arrives in New Hope, Montana, with no hope of happiness and no desire for anything except forgetting—until she meets Mae, a frontier madam. (1-933110-44-9)

Innocent Hearts by Radclyffe. In a wild and unforgiving land, two women learn about love, passion, and the wonders of the heart. (1-933110-21-X)

Justice Served by Radclyffe. Lieutenant Rebecca Frye and her lover, Dr. Catherine Rawlings, embark on a deadly game of hide-and-seek with an underworld kingpin who traffics in human souls. (1-933110-15-5)

Justice in the Shadows by Radclyffe. In a shadow world of secrets and lies, Detective Sergeant Rebecca Frye and her lover, Dr. Catherine Rawlings, join forces in the elusive search for justice. (1-933110-03-1)

A Matter of Trust by Radclyffe. JT Sloan is a cybersleuth who doesn't like attachments. Michael Lassiter is leaving her husband, and she needs Sloan's expertise to safeguard her company. It should just be business—but it turns into much more. (1-933110-33-3)

Storms of Change by Radclyffe. In the continuing saga of the Provincetown Tales, duty and love are at odds as Reese and Tory face their greatest challenge. (1-933110-57-0)

Distant Shores, Silent Thunder by Radclyffe. Dr. Tory King—along with the women who love her—is forced to examine the boundaries of love, friendship, and the ties that transcend time. (1-933110-08-2)

Beyond the Breakwater by Radclyffe. One Provincetown summer, three women learn the true meaning of love, friendship, and family. (1-933110-06-6)

Safe Harbor by Radclyffe. A mysterious newcomer, a reclusive doctor, and a troubled gay teenager learn about love, friendship, and trust during one tumultuous summer in Provincetown. (1-933110-13-9)

shadowland by Radclyffe. In a world on the far edge of desire, two women are drawn together by power, passion, and dark pleasures. An erotic romance. (1-933110-11-2)

Love's Masquerade by Radclyffe. Plunged into the indistinguishable realms of fiction, fantasy, and hidden desires, Auden Frost is forced to question all she believes about the nature of love. (1-933110-14-7)

Honor Reclaimed by Radclyffe. In the aftermath of 9/11, Secret Service Agent Cameron Roberts and Blair Powell close ranks with a trusted few to find the would-be assassins who nearly claimed Blair's life. (1-933110-18-X)

Honor Guards by Radclyffe. In a wild flight for their lives, the president's daughter and those who are sworn to protect her wage a desperate struggle for survival. (1-933110-01-5)

Love & Honor by Radclyffe. The president's daughter and her lover are faced with difficult choices as they battle a tangled web of Washington intrigue for…love and honor. (1-933110-10-4)

Honor Bound by Radclyffe. Secret Service Agent Cameron Roberts and Blair Powell face political intrigue, a clandestine threat to Blair's safety, and the seemingly irreconcilable personal differences that force them ever farther apart. (1-933110-20-1)

Above All, Honor by Radclyffe. Secret Service Agent Cameron Roberts fights her desire for the one woman she can't have—Blair Powell, the daughter of the president of the United States. (1-933110-04-X)